Wha
ADD WATE.
FOR BEST

Hetta Coffey's hilarious string of misadventures after being suddenly plunged into the "yachtie world" is a great page-turner for the quarter berth!— Capt. Pat Rains

A romp of a read, with snappy dialogue and memorable secondary characters, but it is Hetta's story. It's easy to sympathize when she takes her yacht out alone into San Francisco Bay, to nurse her broken heart and start A LIST OF THINGS TO DO AS AN INFINITELY UNATTACHED PERSON. Then, of course, all heck breaks loose. —Pat Browning, Author of Absinthe of Malice

Can't get a man? Just add water.
Hang on tight for a rollicking adventure with Hetta Coffey, a globetrotting civil engineer with an attitude. After a lifelong swath of failed romances, Hetta prefers living with her dog and commiserating her single status with best friend, Jan. But old habits die-hard and one morning while brunching with Jan at the waterfront, Hetta's attention is snagged by a parade of passing yachts and their hunky male skippers. She decides that if she had a boat, she could get a man.

Despite her naiveté of all things nautical, Hetta buys her dream boat and sets about learning to sail. A series of events, including a shadowy stalker and an inconvenient body threatens to imperil her new lifestyle. As her past comes back to haunt her, Hetta must use all of her gritty resources to foil an attempt on her life to figure out who is determined to kill her and why. —B, Bramblett, for Fiction Addiction

Author Jinx Schwartz will need to change her name to Lucky when readers discover *Just Add Water*. Schwartz has not only hit a home run; her first book is out of the ballpark. Schwartz is a twinkling, bright star on the mystery genre horizon with her witty and sometimes irreverent heroine, Hetta Coffey. Book One of the Hetta Coffey series, *Just Add Water*, is a refreshing antidote to the seriousness of the mystery genre without sacrificing a well-constructed plot, enjoyable story, and colorful characters. Readers will fly through the pages in anticipation of what Hetta will do, and say next. Schwartz ties up all the loose ends at the conclusion of the book, leaving this reader eagerly anticipating Book Two of the Hetta Coffey series.—BookwormBriefing

JUST ADD WATER
BY
JINX SCHWARTZ

Just Add Water

BOOKS BY JINX SCHWARTZ

The Hetta Coffey Series

Just Add Water (Book1)
Just Add Salt　　(Book 2)
Just Add Trouble (Book 3)
Just Deserts (Book 4)
Just the Pits (Book 4)

Other Books

The Texicans
Troubled Sea
Land of Mountains

Acknowledgements

Heartfelt thanks to the following folks:

The red pencil gang: Anne Kelty, Holly Whitman, Rebecca Dahlke, Lurah Magee, Marilyn Oliveras, Monica Brooks, Monika Madden, Sheran Vaughn, Geary Ritchie, and Katherine Baccaro.

Medical advice: Dr. Betty Carlisle who, via e-mail from her post in Antarctica, gave invaluable medical info.

Moral Support: Ed and Nicole Gribble, Maggie and Van Pomeroy, and Paula and Dennis Lepak

As always, My best friend and husband, Robert (Mad Dog) Schwartz, offered patience and input.

And they know why! Jane Stris, Martha Farrington, Marian Morse, Jane Portis Sheffield, Carmen Austin, Kristin Henry Erikson, and Rae Presley.

DEDICATION

To my sister, Arleigh.

And Jane Stris, who has been like a
sister all these years.

Prologue
Tokyo

Hudson's master plan was unraveling.

His cleverly orchestrated year-long juggling act was crashing in on him. If he didn't make that flight this afternoon, his life wouldn't be worth two red yen.

Hudson Williams thought he was well-prepared for this day, but when a team of auditors from corporate showed up unannounced at his office this morning, his blood ran cold and his mind went into overdrive. *Friggin' sea gulls. They fly in, crap all over everything, and fly out.*

Of course, bean counters were the least of his problems. All they could do was get him fired, maybe prosecuted for embezzlement. Once his house of cards began to tumble, one thing would lead to another and very quickly the guys he *really* had to sweat would get clued in. The ones who could get him dead. He really hadn't planned on double-crossing *them*, at least this soon, but now he had no choice. *All's fair in love and crime.*

During that interminable morning, he produced files for his unwelcome visitors, all the while keeping up a seemingly easy banter. His practiced charm, which usually worked for him, began to flag. Minute after stressful minute ticked by, until he pasted a smile on his face and walked into the conference room they'd commandeered.

"How's it going, guys?" The auditors' heads snapped up from some documents they were poring over, discussing in hushed voices. Thinly veiled suspicion permeated the air. Or was Hudson's imagination working overtime? He shook off his paranoia. They couldn't have found anything so soon. Certainly not with the files *he'd* given them. "So, got everything you need?" *Or what I think you need.*

The head auditor, Garth Jones, stood up and stretched. "We could use a break, but we have a few questions for you. How about we discuss them over some lunch?"

Crap. "Uh, sorry, dude, but no can do. Got a doctor's appointment that won't keep. But we'll make dinner an occasion." He gave them a meaningful leer. "This town can show a guy one good time, if you know what I mean."

Jones didn't rise to the bait. "Not my cup of tea, Williams. And I'd strongly advise you to break that appointment. Boston is standing by for some answers, and we need you here to help get them."

"Like I said, no can do, buckaroo." Hudson turned abruptly, left the conference room and shut the door behind him, but not before registering, with some satisfaction, the look of helpless dismay on Jones's face. *What are a couple of bureaucratic number crunchers gonna do, tackle me? Take away my birthday?*

Picking up the briefcase he'd been slipping small packages into all morning, Hudson headed straight for the elevator. As he passed his secretary's desk, he growled, "Doctor's appointment."

"Williams-san, I—" but the elevator doors slammed shut behind him, leaving her confused by his abrupt departure. Her boss, if a little secretive, was, unlike most foreigners, always polite and friendly. Now he'd left her at the mercy of the rude men who invaded the office this morning. Tinny, loud music suddenly filled the room, and she automatically stood up to do her mid-morning stretches. When the five minute exercise routine was over, she made tea for herself, leaving the auditors to fend for themselves. *Not that the coffee-swigging Barbarians would even appreciate a decent cup of tea.*

Hudson didn't look back. Sweating profusely, even though a chilly November breeze whistled through Tokyo's financial district, he walked—wanted to run—to the nearest subway entrance. As always, the terminal bustled with commuters, but blending in was out of the question; at only five-eight, he still towered above most Japanese.

One stop later, he hopped off the train at the last second before the doors closed. *Just like the movies.* He made a show of checking his watch as he scanned the crowd for foreigners. *Not a* gaijin *in sight. Of course, my "associates" could have a gook keeping tabs on me, but I doubt it. After all, up until now they haven't had a reason* not *to trust me.* He'd held up his end of the deal, shipping their goods all over the Pacific Rim concealed inside Comtec's hardware. He'd followed the equipment and, before installing it for his customers, remove the stuff and hand it off. *Smooth as glass.* He hustled up the steps and hailed a cab

This morning, however, everything had changed. He'd made a big show of opening boxes in the warehouse, purportedly taking an inventory for the auditors, actually slipping small packages into his pockets and briefcase. Thousands of dollars belonging to Comtec, deposits from customers for equipment he never intended to deliver, had already disappeared into his Cayman account. He was set for a long, long while. And what the hell, his escape plans had only been moved up a few days.

Exactly one hour remained before he had to catch the "limo"—actually a bus—to the airport, barely enough time to get to the apartment, pick up the suitcase he kept packed with his new passports and enough clothes to last for days of changing planes and identities.

As he passed through the lobby of the apartment building, he smiled at the concierge, who bowed in return.

His so-called fiancée was probably in her office, but just to be sure, he called. Her secretary put him straight through, as always. "Hey, how're things at Tanuki Engineering today?"

"Same ole, same ole. Putting out a fire started by some jerk in San Francisco. What're you up to? I called your office, and they said you'd gone to the doctor. You okay?"

Damn, were there no secrets in Japan? "Actually, I lied. Had a bunch of guys in town from corporate, didn't feel like eating lunch with them."

"What do you want for dinner tonight?"

I want to be the hell out of this country. "Oh, whatever. What time will you be home?"

"Probably by six. No meetings planned this afternoon."

"Great, see you then. Love you."

"Love you, too. Bye."

Hudson hung up and had a slightly guilty moment. Wedding presents, still wrapped, filled one corner of the living room. RSVP's were piled next to the phone. The caterer's proposed menu hung on the refrigerator door. *How did I let this friggin' charade go this far?* There was no way any wedding was going to take place, even if those auditors hadn't shown up today. They just accelerated his plans by a few days. *A guy's gotta do what a guy's gotta do.* The kitchen clock chimed, catching his attention. *Time to saddle up, buckaroos.*

Retrieving his suitcase from the back of a closet, he added a few toiletries and was about to leave when he spotted his betrothed's ATM card on the bedside table. For all her smarts, that gal was way too trusting; he had the PIN. *Every little bit counts, ya know.*

Now all he had to do was—*Crap! The key!* His wannabe bride wore the damned thing around her neck and he had neither the time nor a reasonable plan for getting it. *Why didn't I get the damn thing back before now? And what was I thinking when I gave it to her, along with some bullshit line about it being the key to my heart. Must have been the Crown Royal talking.*

Too late now. But he could get that key back later when the heat was off, when he needed money again. He ran back into the living room and snatched up an address book from under the phone. They'd discussed selling her house in California after they married, but he'd be willing to bet that once she got through boohooing and realized he was gone for good, she'd return there when her stint was up in Japan. Checking to make sure the book held her Oakland address, and that of her parents in Texas, he stuffed it into his briefcase.

Waving a friendly bye-bye to the concierge, Hudson Williams jumped into the waiting taxi and ceased to exist.

1
FIVE YEARS LATER

From our window table at a trendy
waterfront eatery in the People's Republic of
Berkeley, Jan and I commanded a postcard vista of
where Tony Bennett left his heart. Piped music
spared us Mr. Bennett's signature song, but not
Dock of the Bay. San Francisco Bay sparkled
despite washy late summer sunshine. A fog bank
glowered on the horizon, held in abeyance by the
famous red steel guardian at her gate.

Settling into velvety, overstuffed armchairs
under a canopy of Boston ferns, and surrounded by
enough stained glass to compete with a European
cathedral, we projected a studied *image.* Our
makeup was meticulously applied to look as
though we weren't wearing any. Chic, sleek, blunt-
cut coifs, hers long and naturally ash blonde, mine

a short "naturally enhanced" red, were designed to look oh, so casual. After all, we were on a mission.

Jan's Brooks Brothers jacket draped gracefully on her tall frame while my Armani tested its button's tensile strength across my unfashionable boobs. We both wore *de rigueur* Gap khakis. Chunky gold bracelets, rings, Rolexes, and loop earrings—no *démodé* dangles or diamonds—along with Fendi bags and Ralph Lauren turtlenecks completed our ensembles. I sported my favorite red Converse hightops for a touch of whimsy.

Jan's tall, slim, blondness contrasted with my short, chunky, perkiness, saving us from Tweedledee and Tweedledum-dom. Cute enough to draw looks, but not so done up as to telegraph "gals on prowl." Even though we were. If, that is, one could call two aging broads out trolling for triceps *cute*. And since I seem to operate on an ecologically correct catch-and-release system, one might wonder why I even bother baiting up.

As we sipped cheap complimentary champagne between forays to an overpriced buffet, a boat peeled off from the winged flotilla plying the bay, sailed toward the guest dock, executed a smart turn, dropped its sails, and coasted gently alongside the restaurant's courtesy dock. Two windbreaker-clad men bounded from her decks, tied the boat, and strode up the ramp towards us.

"Well lookee here," I drawled, "fleet's in." I hummed a couple of bars of "It's Raining Men."

"Hetta Coffey, you are not," Jan whispered as the mariners neared, "going to use your 'Hi there, sailor, new in town? Wanna buy me a drink?' line, are you?"

"Why not? It worked fine in that Greek dive on the Houston ship channel."

"Don't remind me. It's a freakin' miracle we haven't spent the last ten years rolling grape leaves into dolmas in some leaky cargo ship's galley."

"*Au contraire*, y'all. You would be. I, at least, had the good sense to pick up the captain instead of the cook. You are, at times, far too plebeian. Hush, here they come."

Seemingly studying my newspaper and ignoring the newcomers, my legendary crawdad vision raked the men as they chose a table next to us and ordered coffee. They turned down the free champagne.

It was too much to bear. Looking over my rumpled *San Francisco Examiner,* I said, "Hi there, sailors. New in town? Wanna give *us* that champagne?"

"Sure," the tall one said, dazzling me with a show of perfect teeth set in a fashionably tanned face. Ruffled, grayish blonde, razor-cut hair and Ralph Lauren shirt bespoke "man with a job." *Hmmmm.*

His shorter, nerdier looking companion called the waitress back and waved his hand in our direction. "Please give our champagne to the ladies."

Tres charmant. Double hmmmm. "Y'all are too kind," I cooed, letting my on again, off again Texas drawl transform the word *too* into two syllables. Jan gave me a sour look and buried her head in the Business Section. Or Bidness Section, as we say back home.

The men went to the sumptuous spread and returned with heaping plates of salmon pâté, quiche Lorraine, croissants and tiny red potatoes stuffed with caviar and sour cream. Jan stared at their plates. "Shit," she mouthed, "gay."

I always say if one can't have love, then settle for knowledge. While my new friends, Joe and John, munched on brunch, they graciously answered my barrage of questions about boats and sailing. Finally feeling I had garnered all the men had to offer, I left them to their quiche and turned my attention on two women who had taken a table on the other side of us. I like to think of myself as a keen observer of humankind.

"Will you *puhleeze* quit ogling and pestering people?" Jan hissed, mistaking my sentience for snoopiness.

I forgave her her misconceptions and continued to snoo...observe.

Sheathed in spandex that left no doubt as to their cellulite free status, the aerobically buffed women passed on the buffet and champagne, opting for dry English muffins and decaffeinated coffee. The chef was obviously out of tofu. Why bother going to brunch? But I knew the answer. Brunch lures singles like chum entices piranhas, Berkeley is prime fishing ground and these two had all the proper tackle. That superior specimens such as these were reduced to using my own angling tactics was a lit-tle disheartening.

Joe and John finished brunch, said good-bye, left arm-in-arm and raised their sails.

Buffed Buns next to me sighed as she watched them flutter away. "I'm seriously thinking of moving back to Arizona," she told Titanium Thighs. "I mean, I love the Bay Area and my job, but my bio-timer? At least there are real men in Tucson."

Her friend nodded, took a dainty nibble of naked muffin while managing to flex a bicep. "There are men here, too, but they're all gay or married."

"Or both," I interjected. The women eyed Jan and me with distrust and lowered their voices, obviously wishing to continue their conversation in private. I grabbed the paper and sulked. People are so touchy these days.

The spandex twins departed, prompting our waitress to look hopefully in our direction, sigh, and uncork another bottle. As she filled my glass, I was on the very verge of asking for the check when, in a tidal wave of white water, a large powerboat entered the channel and bore down upon us.

"I hope that sucker has brakes," I said, striving for nonchalance while mentally judging the distance to the nearest emergency exit.

Jan looked up and eeked in alarm, but sat her ground.

The waitress grumbled, "Idiots at the helm," and hustled off to safety behind the bar.

Although tempted to follow her, we were held in thrall, gaping as the boat suddenly turned and was washed against the dock by her own wake, a tsunami that sent several tons of water crashing against the building's pilings. The restaurant swayed slightly, or maybe it was the effects of free champers catching up with me.

"Cradle robbers," Jan pronounced as we watched three men—one stout, one tall and lanky, one medium—and three very attractive women a couple of decades their juniors reel towards us on the wave-pitched landing. They took the table recently abandoned by the treadmill twins.

The tallest man, a Nordic type with that big boned, square shouldered look I love, had his arm slung casually around a stunning brunette who couldn't have been a day over twenty-five. The other two men, my piercing peripheral vision confirmed, were also fortyish. They, too, sported twenty types. And all six wore red windbreakers embroidered with the name of the boat: *Sea Cock.*

"Oh, my ears and whiskers, Miz Alice," I whispered, twitching my nose as I pictured White Rabbit would, "do you suppose there's truth in advertising? And there, my dear girl, is why you and I are eating brunch with each other. The men we should be with want twenty-year-olds. Maybe we should start looking for a couple of seventy-year-olds."

"Hush, they'll hear you," Jan whispered. Then she added, "Besides, the septuagenarians want duagenarians, too."

"I don't think there's such a word as duagen—hey, the chubby, windburned guy in the middle is staring at you. Don't look."

She never listens. Her cherry cheeked admirer gave Jan a wide smile and bid us good morning. We nodded and lifted our glasses. I bestowed the sextet with a recently bleached smile of my own, hoping I didn't have spinach quiche or caviar stuck to my dazzling dentistry. Evidently not, for after a few pleasantries were exchanged, we were invited to join their table. A couple of the women didn't seem all that pleased, but Jan swears I could talk myself past a White House marine.

The waitress returned to take their orders, noted our change of locale, sighed, and with her flair for the obvious, asked if, by some *wild* chance Jan and I would care for another glass of champagne.

Lars Jenkins, Jan's hefty admirer, made introductions. I quickly dismissed the women and concentrated on Lars's brother, Tall Nordic Bob, and Garrison, the owner of *Sea Cock*.

Bob, after complaining about the prices, rudely ignored my witty badinage, preferring to converse quietly with his nestling. Too quietly, even though my acute auditory antennae were aimed in their direction. He had pulled off his *Sea Cock* jacket to reveal a truly ugly, polyester print shirt. For shame: poly-ugly on a guy who could wear almost anything and look good. I could forgive the shirt, but not his blatant disregard for my precious self. But so what? Who needed the badly clad Viking cheapskate? And who dressed this guy? The Salvation Army?

I turned my attention to the more receptive and nattily attired Garrison, who at least had a boat and supported the cotton industry.

An hour later, when our newfound friends made a splashy departure, I proffered my American Express Platinum to our long-suffering waitress. She grabbed it, rushing away to tabulate before we changed our minds.

"My stars, Miz Jan, that was purely depressing. Here we have three perfectly good men who are chronologically, geographically and heterosexually suitable for us thirty-somethings, glommed up by Campfire Girls."

"I never saw any Campfire Girls who looked like that. Let's face it, we ain't spring chickens any more," Jan said, "and you are swiftly taking leave of thirty*anything*." This from a thirty-five-year-old. The young can be so cruel.

The waitress returned with my charge slip, I signed my name and then, as she hovered, I started to write in the tip, stopped, and squinted at her nametag. "Nicole," I asked, "how old do you think I am?"

Nicole looked at the ballpoint pen poised above the tip line, then at me. "For . . . uh, . thirty, uh, one?"

I shot Jan a self-satisfied grin and wrote a gratuity generous enough to win a smile and a topped off champagne glass.

"Shameless bribery," Jan huffed.

I sat back, watched *Sea Cock* power out of sight, and took the sip of champagne that tipped me into stage two inebriation: Socratic.

"Dog years," I slurred.

Jan sighed. After over fifteen years of friendship, she knew whatever fell out of my mouth next could range from abjectly stupid to moderately brilliant. I could tell from the look on her face she was not going to encourage either. But, of course, that didn't stop me.

"Men 'n' dawgs. Dogs ain't worth a diddlydamn until they're five, and men 'til they're fifty. Canine maturity must have something to do with getting their pockets picked at an early age. And they skip the infernal midlife crisis stuff. Must be why dogs don't buy corvettes and yachts."

Jan giggled at my convoluted conjecture, we clinked glasses, and another profundity effervesced as I squinted in the direction of the departed *Sea Cock*. "Buy it and they will come," I whispered.

"What?"

"Remember that movie? Where Kevin "the hunk" Costner builds a baseball diamond in a cornfield? Buy it and they will come," I repeated. "If we had a boat, Miz Jan, we could get men."

2

Our morning, before my champagne inspired and somewhat specious pronouncement about using a boat as a mantrap, started out crappy.

"Men 'n' dawgs," I told Jan as we sat in my living room earlier that day.

My friend dabbed a tear and snuffled, "They sure are, Hetta."

"Jan, I didn't say men *are* dogs. I said men *and* dogs. In my opinion, men aren't worth a damn until they're fifty. And dogs until they're five."

Jan bobbed her head and said with a pout, "Nice dogs are easy to find. Not like men."

"So true," I agreed. "Of course, some say that men and buses come along every fifteen minutes, but I say most aren't headed in the right direction. That Richard of yours? He sure ain't no first class ride, so to speak, but never fear, because," I cranked up the CD player and sang along with Martha Wash as she belted out, "It's raining men, hallelujah!"

For effect, I added a few Holy Roller moves to my routine and finished by tossing a chenille throw over my shoulders à la James Brown. It was a spectacularly uplifting performance, should you ask me.

Jan, however, gave me a dolefully and decidedly *un*lifted and sodden gaze while blowing her nose into her equally sodden Hermes kerchief. Critics abound. "Buh . . . but, what should I *do*?"

"Dump him. BD... " I caught myself before using my nickname for her boyfriend: BDR. Big Dick Richard. I didn't think this the suitable moment to remind Jan of, in my opinion, Richard's sole asset. "The man is a *roué*. A common *boulevardier*. A gigolo, if you will."

An unwelcome image of Richard Farnsworth III—he pronounced it *Ree*shárd, the phony—popped into my mind. Tall, honey hued, honey tongued, and handsome. Charming in a smarmy sort of way. I slapped my mind from his crotch and concentrated on his *bad* points.

"Richard Fartsworth has no job, unless you count those brief stints modeling briefs, and no prospects. He's been mooching off you for over a year, all the while screwing some fat twenty-year-old across town. And goodness knows who else. Dump him," I repeated, using my best "off with his head" pose and sloshing a drop or two of vodka and V8 Picante onto my peach-toned carpet.

This she found amusing. Jan smiled crookedly at my antics and wiped salty rivulets from her laugh lines. Then, unfolding to a full five eleven, she focused her baby blues down on me and announced, "You know, you're right. I should and will dump the sorry SOB." Then her face fell as she plopped back down on the couch. "But then I'll be all alone. Like you."

I flumped down beside her. "I'm not alone. I have RJ."

"Humph," she grunted.

"Humph, yourself. RJ has many desirable attributes. Beautiful red hair, big brown eyes with lashes to die for, keen intelligence. And he's totally devoted to me. I can quite overlook his house rattling snores and noxious farts."

"RJ is a dawg," Jan declared unkindly.

"Yeah, well, so is BDR. At least RJ has a pedigree. Reechard's a cur."

"I suspect RJ's papers are forged," Jan challenged. "How come a yellow Labrador has red hair?"

"How come I do?" I asked, handing her a huge opening in an attempt to get her mind off BDR. The things you do for your friends.

It worked. She chortled. "In your case it's Preference by L'Oreal when you're feeling cheap and René l'Exorbitant when you're flush."

RJ, who had been following our repartee with the concentration of an avid tennis fan, thumped his tail in agreement.

"Tattle tail," I growled.

Jan suddenly recalled her crisis *du jour* and sniffed, "Okay, so you're not all alone. You have a dog. But you don't have a boyfriend."

My hand automatically flew to the small key hanging from a chain around my neck, a reflex Jan didn't miss. "Sorry, Hetta."

"No big deal." And I meant it. I only wore the key, I told myself, as a reminder to be more careful. I also had myself convinced that I was fully recovered from my disastrous affair with Hudson "the jilter" Williams, in Tokyo five years before. Shoot, it's not like I'd been *totally* devoid of male companionship for eighteen hundred and forty two days. Just sex. And that didn't count, did it?

Mulling over my manless state, I took another sip of Saturday morning heart starter. "You know," I mused, "we both need a change. New horizons. First things first, though. Brunch."

* * *

Our Zairian taxi driver, after politely putting up with my chatty Kathy self all the way from Berkeley, just as politely passed on my invitation to stay for a drink. He pocketed his tariff and fat tip and chugged away from my Oakland hills home in a yellow and rust clatter.

RJ, who had been whining and snuffling through the mail slot, pounced when I opened the front door to my house. He circled, his ecstatic tail walloping the air as he sniffed for doggy bags. I scratched his ears with one hand while punching numbers on a blinking alarm pad with the other. Once the security system was disarmed, Jan began to pace and wail.

"Are you out of your mind, Hetta Coffey? It's a jungle out there. You can't invite strange men into your house anymore," she railed. "Don't you watch the news?"

"Oh, pshaw, Miss Kitty, I reckon I only *know* strange men. Besides, that hombre weren't no danger to the likes of us." I broke with my *Gunsmoke* routine and added, "Jesus, what's the world coming to? Our mothers only had to worry about getting knocked up, then the seventies came and no one cared. Along came the eighties with herpes horror and killer sex. And I don't mean that kindly. What happened to the good ole days when our motto was, 'A shot of penicillin in the ass ain't much fun, but neither is sleeping alone?' Now you tell me I can't *talk* to people?"

Jan gave me that look, the one that says, *imbecile.* "Gee, Hetta, I can't even imagine it. You'll talk to a fence post. I mean you need to be more careful. A little more discerning, perhaps?"

"Jean-Luc is an exchange student and taxi driver, not a mass murderer. And he isn't from the jungle, as you would know if you'd learn to speak French."

"Oh, get off your high horse. Not all of us were lucky enough to learn French as a child like you did. Or go to college in France."

"Hey, Daddy built dams all over the world, and I was a camp follower. What can I say? I like speaking French and rarely get to, what with consorting with the unlettered and all." Jan launched a throw pillow at me. Touchy, these *bourgeoisie.*

"Jan, that's not why they're called throw pillows," I said, tossing back the cushion. "And to get back to the subject of Jean-Luc, it's taxi drivers like him who're getting mugged. He probably figured we were gonna mug him and—*zut, alor!* RJ, put a brake on that tail," I scolded, righting a potted palm that fell victim to his derriere of doom. I headed for the couch, an unrepentant and still-wriggling RJ in close pursuit.

"You know, Hetta, he probably thought you were coming on to him."

"Who?"

"The cab driver. Not *everyone* understands your, uh, friendliness. Especially men. You come off as sort of forward."

"Forward, fooey," I said with a wave of dismissal while sinking into down-filled cushions. "I don't know why everyone takes themselves so damned seriously. I like meeting new people. I can't believe...." My hand settled onto the middle of a cushion. "Ah-hah! What do we have here? A warm spot? Bejeweled with goldy red hairs? On my chamois leather Roche-Bobois settee?"

RJ averted his eyes and raised a paw, the one attached to the leg he'd broken in a dustup with a truck several years before. He'd led with his left.

I fought a smile and asked, "Auntie Jan, do you think such a *really bad dog* deserves a dollop of pâté?"

RJ's ears moved with each dreaded word. REALLY, twitch. BAD, half-mast. DOG, flat out. He gave me his best hangdog look and inched forward.

"How warm is the spot?" Jan asked.

"Medium warm."

"Give him a medium dollop."

Slowly, teasingly, I dug a soggy napkin from my pocket while RJ trembled with anticipation. His patience pushed to the limit, he raided my hand and gulped down the napkin and contents, belching liver breath in appreciation.

"Would you care for a Tums chaser with your *papier-mâché* treat?" I asked. He nosed my hand for more.

"You should buy him his own couch, Hetta. Hell, you bought him his own car."

"I paid more for this couch than I did RJ's Volkswagen, and I'll thank him to keep his furry rump off my overpriced Roche."

"You heard her, RJ, come sit here on the floor with your favorite auntie while we watch a little tube."

3

I woke to a very young, slightly fuzzy, Bette Davis wiping down the countertop in a shabby diner. Jan and RJ slept on the carpet, their heads sharing a throw pillow. The clock read eight. I screamed, "Get up! You're late for work."

Jan sat up in a confused daze, then glared at me. "Hetta, you moron, it's Saturday night."

The sour aftertaste of our champagne brunch verified that fact. As I made a dash for the Mentadent, I grumbled, "Then, we're late for terrorizing some skuzzy bar."

"I've got a unique idea. Let's stay home," Jan said with a yawn. RJ opened one eye and moved his head into her lap. "We can build a fire, maybe pop some Orville. Caramel coated."

"Listen, Girl Scout, just because you have no date tonight doesn't mean *my* social life has to stop."

"What social life?"

She had a point.

We made a double batch of macaroni and cheese laced with canned Rotel tomatoes and chiles, added extra Velveeta Pasteurized Processed Cheese Spread, opened a package of Fritos and uncorked a fiasco of rotgut red. To hell with that pestiferous food pyramid.

While we ate on the floor in front of a roaring fire, Jan rummaged through a box of DVDs and came up with *Imitation of Life*.

"Good choice, Jan, but one which calls for a roll of toilet paper. Much too intense for mere Kleenex. Better get some for RJ, too, he's a sucker for tearjerkers. Which reminds me, can you dog-sit Wednesday night? I gotta go to Seattle and kick some subcontractor ass."

"No can do. I gotta go to La Tuesday and probably won't be back until Friday." Jan always called Los Angeles "La," as in do-re-me-fa-so-*la*.

"What's going on down there?"

"Long-winded waiters and weirdoes. Smog and traffic jams. The usual. I'm being sent on a training mission. They installed a new security system at LAX and kindly used our software. I gotta go whip some aeronerds into shape."

"Whip 'em well, we can't have too much security these days. Well rats, RJ, looks like you gotta spend a night with Dr. Craigosaurus while your aunt and mommy go out to fight for equality in this man's world."

Jan gave RJ a sympathetic pat and her plate to lick. "Too bad. He loves Craig, but ain't too keen on his kennel."

"What can I do? Besides this hound is overdue for a tooth cleaning, nail clipping, and debugging. And he's been favoring his leg again."

"Gonna have his oil changed and the air in his tires checked while you're at it?"

"Why not?" I asked, ignoring the ringing of my phone.

After three rings Jan cocked her head and glared at me. "You gonna get that, or are you waiting for RJ to answer."

"Let RJ take it. He speaks dawg."

"Answer the friggin' phone."

"Oh, all *right*." I snatched up the phone, growled, "She's not here," and hung up.

"Real nice, Hetta Coffey. How do you know it wasn't some kind of family emergency in Texas? Or your sister in Denver? Or Mary?"

"For one thing, all of our relatives and friends in the whole wide world know we're never home on Saturday night. Mary is draped over some Austin kicker bar by this time of night. Besides, it was for you."

"How do you know? You didn't even listen...." The phone rang again. This time I picked up after the first ring and listened.

"I told you she wasn't here, *Ree*-shard. Where are you? If I see her I'll have her give you a call, but please don't call back here tonight. I'm going to bed early." I hung up before the jerk could make a snide comment or Jan could grab the phone.

"Where is he?"

"At your apartment."

"Maybe I should talk to him. I mean, if he's worried?"

"You're worried that BDR's worried? After last night? Does the term, self-esteem, mean anything at all to you? RJ, you shit, quit drinking my wine. You're dribbling on the carpet."

Jan pouted for a few minutes while I concentrated on the movie. Lana Turner was making cookies. I muted the sound and tried to make up. "Wanna bake cookies?"

"With extra chocolate chips?"

"Why not? Let's put both Lana and BDR on PAUSE. Let the SOB stew, *then* dump him. But first, tomorrow, when we're sure he's not at your apartment, let's change the locks. Then you can stay here until you leave for La. Oooh, don't you wish we knew where the fat broad lives? We could dump all his clothes in front of her place," I said, warming to a plan, "after we let RJ chew them into little pieces."

Jan looked a little uncertain and I pounced. "You *are* going to dump him, aren't you? Please tell me you're not gonna let him get away with it this time. You saw him with your own eyes. And after he told you he was going to Tahoe with his brother."

"Maybe it wasn't him we saw."

"Pitiful," I said, scorn dripping from my wine-reddened tongue. "Of course it wasn't him. That was surely some other guy wearing the Armani jacket you gave him for Christmas, and driving BDR's car. Maybe we were mistaken and it wasn't his head buried in the fat broad's décolletage."

"You have a mean streak, Hetta," Jan whimpered, tears gathering in her periwinkle eyes.

"I'm sorry, I don't mean to be mean. I hate to see that man use you the way he does. You have everything going for you. You're smart, have a good job, and you're not *too* ugly. You deserve better. Enough lecture. Let's make cookies, eat some and then, if you've still *got* to call him, I won't say a word. I promise."

The phone rang. We both stared at it, then Jan grinned and commanded, "Hetta, kill!" giving my basal bitchiness the green light.

I grabbed the phone and growled, "What part of 'don't call here again tonight' don't you understand, you inconsiderate Lothario?"

"Uh, is this Jan? This is Lars Jenkins. We met this morning in Berkeley?"

Oops. "Oh, dear, I'm sorry, Lars. I thought you were, uh, well, never mind. This is Hetta. Her friend? Anyway, here she is." I gave Jan a thumbs-up and the phone. I simply had to either get caller ID or a better phone presence. Or both.

After a brief conversation she hung up and asked, "I wonder how Lars got this number?"

"I slipped him your card, and this number, under the table this morning."

"What!"

"Well, it was obvious he was interested and since you are untrained in the art of prestidigitation..."

"Spell that."

"P-r, oh, never mind. Sleight of hand. In this case, sleight of card, which I took into my own hands."

She opened her mouth to yell at me, but changed her mind and smiled. "Thanks. I needed that call."

"I know. Glad I didn't scare him off. I'm gonna sign up for caller ID. Monday morning."

"How come? I thought you hated those things."

"Yeah, well, I've been getting some annoying hang-ups lately, and I'd like to know from whence they come so I can call 'em back and hang up. Anyhow, what did you and Lars talk about?" As if I hadn't heard every word on her end.

"It's so cool. He and his brother work in the security business and know all about my company's software. And he wants to meet us for lunch one day."

"Us?"

"He thought maybe he'd bring his brother."

"His brother, Bob, the fashion plate? If he's paying we'll be eating at Burger King. *If* the ninety-nine cent Whopper deal is still on."

"I thought you kinda liked him. You *did* flirt, Hetta."

"And was soundly ignored. No loss, he isn't my type."

"And that would be? Criminally insane? Internationally sought after by major law enforcement agencies? Or maybe married?"

I laughed. "You know me all too well, Tonto. But count me out on the lunch."

"What can a little lunch with a couple of nice guys hurt?"

"I have an appointment that day."

"You don't even know what day. Suit yourself, Hetta, but one of these days you need to do a little soul-searching, decide if you want to end up a lonely little old lady with thirty cats."

"Cats! We hate cats," I yelled, covering RJ's ears. "Besides, that Bob person completely ignored me. The girl he was with wasn't a day over twenty-five. And stunning. Why on earth would I think he'd be interested in me? Now, let's do cookies, then, like I said, I won't even bitch if you call BDR."

She didn't.

We finished off the wine, ate those cookies RJ didn't get to first, watched another movie, and went to bed early.

RJ, ever on the alert for an opportunity to break my house rules, slept in Jan's room. During the night when I peeked in to check on them he was under the covers, his head on her pillow. They looked so peaceful I only whispered gruffly, "RJ, remind me to kick your doggie ass in the morning for getting on the bed."

He feigned sleep, but I swear I saw him smile.

4

"Hand me the Phillips head, *si'l vous plait.*" I held out one hand while gripping a deadbolt lockset in place with the other. The door was original to Jan's 1910 building and had probably been painted at least once a year without benefit of removing the old coats. Lead poisoning came to mind as I wiped away dust and fitted up the lock.

"Gee, this looks easy," Jan said, handing me the screwdriver.

"Not rocket science. We could have had it re-keyed, but getting a locksmith out in San Francisco on a Sunday would cost a fortune. Especially here in the Marina District. Lucky for us I had this extra deadbolt at home."

"How come you had an extra?"

"Took it out of my front door last year when I decided Wade wasn't a keeper." This was my way of saying I had decided not to sleep with him.

"Wait a minute, does this mean that lunatic might still have a key? To *my* apartment?"

"Not to worry, I'm sure they took it from him. And he's going to be away for at least five years. You never live in the same place for five years. Besides, he's found Jesus and wants to be my friend."

"How do you know?"

"He called last week."

"He gets to make calls?"

"Evidently."

"Holy shit, what did you say to him?"

"I was very polite, then told him the truth."

"That being?"

"That I'm getting married and moving to Mexico. I figure even with time off for good behavior I've got ample time to find a husband and move," I reasoned.

"How do you figure that? You've had many, many, *many* years to find somebody."

"One more 'many' and I'll brain you with this screwdriver."

Jan grinned. "Okay, I take back a 'many.' Anyway, do you think that was a good idea? I mean, the reason you told Wade you were ending your whatever-you-called-it, was you had decided to remain celibate. Now you tell him you're getting married?"

"Shoot, everyone knows marriage and celibacy go hand in hand. I know this must be true, for all the married men who hit on me tell me they don't sleep with their wives."

We locked eyes and yelled in unison, "And married men never lie!"

After a high-five, I went back to fiddling with the lock and Jan asked, "About Wade. I thought he was in for a million years. Do the criminally insane really get time off for good behavior?"

"Damned if I know."

I concentrated on the task at hand, but made a mental note to find out more about the California penal system. I didn't think I had anything to worry about. Wade "the perp" and I had ended our friendship long before he took his brief, but ruinous, walk on the felonious side of life. Up until that fateful foray, Wade had been a much decorated hero during a fifteen year firefighting career. Jan and I had followed Wade's trial in the newspapers, fascinated that we knew someone who could be so incredibly stupid.

Somewhere in the saga of a convoluted crime spree involving a drug deal gone wrong and kidnapping, one of Wade's coked-up cohorts put out a cigarette out on his then girlfriend, now the State's star witness/victim, thereby earning a mayhem conviction for all concerned. In California, that drew a quick one-way ticket to a facility catering to the criminally insane. I pictured him playing Ping-Pong with Charlie Manson.

That wasn't the first time I'd been involved with someone strolling the shady side of Justice Street. The way I choose men, it's no wonder I prefer living with a *real* dog.

"There. Done," I said, clicking the deadbolt back and forth.

"You're pretty good at this handyperson thing."

"Hey, when you've lived alone as long as I have and renovated a ninety-year-old house, changing out a lock is kid's play. Let's try the key. Just in case, you'd better go inside."

She did, and as I bent to unlock the door, the small key I wore around my neck swung forward and clinked against the door handle. I wondered, as I unlocked Jan's door, if I would ever know what *my* key unlocked. Actually, not *my* key, but Hudson the jilter's key.

I threw open the door with a little "Ta-dah," a shuffle ball change step, and a bow. "That'll be one-hundred dollah. American. Does *madame* wish to put this on one of her overextended credit cards?"

"*Mademoiselle*, thank you. And she wishes to put it on her tab. Now, let's get to work, for we have important labors ere this day ends."

Exorcising Jan's one room Victorian apartment was made simple by virtue of its small size and BDR's lack thereof—virtue, that is. The sleaze kept only enough of his stuff at her place to keep Jan from entertaining thoughts of entertaining other men there. God only knew if hers was a *pied-à-femme* amongst many.

I found the slimeball's Armani jacket draped over a chair. Plucking a long black hair from the shoulder, I held it aloft as if it had cooties. "Fat broad hair, my dear Watson," I announced, then proceeded to go through the pockets.

"What are you looking for, Hetta?"

"Nothing. It has been my experience that only faithful and honest men leave stuff in their pockets for women to find. Show me a cheater and I'll show you clean pockets every time." I pulled out the empty pocket linings with a smug, "*Voila!*"

We piled BDR's crap, with the exception of the Armani, in the stairwell as a "Dear Reechard, you're screwed" greeting on his next visit and trudged down two flights to where RJ waited patiently in his VW. Luckily for us, no one else had thought to park in the NO PARKING zone in front of Jan's building.

"Where to now?" Jan asked. "I'm famished."

"Me, too. But first, a quick search for a deserving soul, then, how about Mexican? I feel a strong urge for a refried *frijole*," I said.

We headed downtown, where we found a gaunt and hairy man of indeterminate age leaning against his Safeway cart of worldly possessions. I left him wearing an Armani jacket and a toothless smile.

"How much did you put in the pocket, Hetta?"

"What are you talking about?"

"Het-ta."

"Fifty bucks. That Armani fairly screams for a silk cravat."

"You're a phony, you know it? How come he knew your name?"

I gave her the disdainful look she deserved, sniffed, "Very funny. Let us retrieve my car," and drove to the Berkeley restaurant where we'd spent the previous morning slurping champagne. My candy apple red Beemer convertible sat unmolested except for a polite note on the windshield from the Night Owl Security Company reminding me that this was not a public parking lot. We parked RJ's Volkswagen and piled into the BMW.

"RJ, just because I'm feeling a bit guilty about leaving you in Craigosaurus's critter clink next week, you may ride in my car. There will be, however, no scratching, farting or throwing up on my white leather upholstery."

I put down the top, hit the CD's PLAY button, and half of Berkeley learned that Jeremiah was a bullfrog. As we sped toward a fresh tortilla, RJ's ears flapped in the breeze and an occasional rope of doggie drool spattered cars' windshields behind us.

At Jack London Square I parked in the loading zone in front of a Mexican restaurant where the friendly staff tolerated RJ's presence on their patio so long as he didn't steal too much food from other tables. I ordered cheese enchiladas with refried beans and extra sour cream for me and a beef burrito, no beans, for RJ.

"Champagne?" the waiter asked, a knowing smirk on his face.

"No *gracias*, Carlos, I'll stick with ice water."

Carlos reeled back in shock, then refilled my water glass while Jan grinned from behind her newspaper.

"I love doing that to 'em once in awhile. Keeps 'em on their toes," I said. "Besides, now we've got two cars to get home, so no taxicabs today. You can use RJ's car while I'm gone this week if you want. It'll save you the indignity of public transportation. It's so...public."

"Snob. I will, thanks. Did you call the V-E-T yet?" For some reason Jan thought it necessary to spell in front of my dog. RJ looked suspicious.

"Remind me to call him later. Hey, gimme the Entertainment section when you get through with it. There's something good on the back."

Jan flipped over the paper. "Boat show? I thought you were drunk yesterday. I hoped you were drunk."

"I was, but some of life's major decisions are made while imbibing stars," I said loftily.

"Yeah, some of your major worst ones."

"True. But this is different, there's no man involved. Besides," I said, sweeping an arm towards the packed marina at Jack London Square, "how much can a boat cost?"

* * *

"Fifty-nine will get your name on her stern," the blue blazered salesmen told us, pinching a pleat to hitch up his white polyester pants. Inside his open shirt collar, curly black hair almost obscured at least five heavy gold chains. As I was opening my mouth to comment upon his fashionable ensemble, I received a preemptive jab in the ribs from Jan.

"Fifty-nine hundred?" I said, moving my attention from his white patent leather boat shoes— no socks, of course—to the thirty-two foot sailboat in front of us. "That's dooable."

The salesman lost a little of his toothy smile. "Good one," he said, smoothing his gelled poof with a heavily ringed hand. He looked like a skinny Italian Elvis.

Jan gave me a look, then turned to Captain Elvis. "You meant fifty-nine thousand, didn't you?"

The salesman's head bobbed. His hair didn't.

"What?" I yelped. "You people been smoking funny cigarettes?"

The smile faltered completely and, with the resignation of one who knows he's wasting his time, he handed me a specifications sheet on the boat. "You'll find it's a bargain. Of course, that price doesn't include any add-ons."

"Add-ons?"

"Accessories."
"Like what?"
"Sails."

* * *

"Who in the hell would consider sails an accessory on a sailboat?" I groused four hours later as we sat in a waterfront dive munching on double cheeseburgers with avocado sauce. I sipped sugarless iced tea while looking through a stack of brochures, magazines, and other freebies given out at the boat show. "I cannot friggin' believe it."

"Pricey little buggers, eh? And don't forget, you have to put it somewhere. God knows what a parking place costs," said Jan, the practical one.

"Slip. You put it in a slip. According to these," I waved a pile of flyers, "they can run over three hundred a month. And that's cheap. In La you can double that. 'Course in La you can double everything. They do lean toward excess, you know."

"Like you don't? I hope this plethora of information puts an end to our little sailing adventure, Hetta?"

"Certainly not. Look here," I said, showing her a handout. "We can take sailing lessons."

"*You* can take sailing lessons. There's no way in hell you're getting me out there."

Dismissing her objections I countered, "You said that about skiing."

"I think you'd best pick a better example. I was in that leg cast for weeks."

"Oh, come on now. As long as you can swim, how could you possibly get hurt on a boat?"

"You can't."

"Get hurt?"

"No, Hetta. Swim. You can't swim."

"I can learn?"

5

Sunday night we recovered from our weekend of drinking, exorcizing, and boat hunting and got down to preparing for the workweek ahead. I hate Sunday nights.

While Jan made a tuna salad, I checked for faxes and e-mail in my upstairs office. There were four hang-ups on my answering machine, so I made a note to myself to call the phone company the next day and order caller ID. I then joined Jan in the kitchen for our one and only allowed glass of Sunday night wine.

RJ halfheartedly nosed the dry dog food plaguing his bowl, then gave me a dirty look. I was reminded of Sunday nights when I was a kid. After all the fun on the weekend, we had to get back to the dull routine preceding Blue Monday. And here I was, dooming us to repetition. Certainly no way to embark upon a major life change, especially if I wanted to do it before my change of life.

I dumped out RJ's dish, gave him two scoops of Ben and Jerry's, poured myself an extra wine, and heated garlic bread to go with our salads. Take that, Sunday Night Blues!

After dinner, Jan and I exfoliated, masked, waxed, and steamed. All those things "they" tell us lead to younger looking skin. Yeah, as soon as it grows back.

Jan touched up her acrylic tipped nails while I sorted my wardrobe for the week. Selecting a blue pinstriped suit from my "meeting and work" closet, I added a cream blouse, pinned my grandmother's cameo to the high Victorian collar, and laid the entire ensemble out on my ashes of roses duvet cover for inspection. A rummage through an antique *tansu* chest produced taupe hose. Navy and ecru spectator pumps completed the getup. After a quick inspection for dog slobber and wine stains, I pronounced the outfit, "Wednesday."

Jan gave an approving nod. "Very nice. Chick, even. But is it suitable subcontractor, butt-kicking attire, Miz Hetta? Looks more like IBMer duds. Well, except for that slit up the side of the skirt."

"I keep it buttoned, except for emergencies."

"What kind of emergency, pray tell? Them buttons go mighty high on the thigh."

"This week's emergency might entail distracting the client's in-house buffoon who thinks he's God's gift to the computer world. Lucky for me, the house nerd also thinks he's God's gift to women. A button or two might divert the little pervert's attention while I convince his boss of what they *really* need in their new system. If I can't persuade the big dogs to pay for good tech support up front instead of relying on their house jerk, they'll pay through the teeth later. So, I slip a couple of buttons, the nerd spends the day covering up a boner, and I save the client a fortune. That's why they pay me the big bucks."

"Hetta, they have a name for women like you."

"Yep, they most certainly do. Chief Executive Officer."

"Gee, the great and glorious Gloria Steinem was right. You are becoming the man you once wanted to marry. Very scarily, I might add."

"I prefer to be compared to Hunter S. Thompson, thank you. I like being scary. Inspiring fear and loathing has its place in business." I surveyed my outfit once more and hung it up. "Now, what have I forgotten?"

"Other than woman's humanity to man? Your D-O-G." She cocked her head at RJ and handed me the phone.

I hit the speed dial and heard, "Noah's Bark."

"This is Philinda Blank of the Oakland Chapter of the You'd Better Be Kind to Animals or We'll Shoot You Organization. We've had a complaint, doctor, that you have been dallying with some strange pussy."

"How you doin', Hetta."

"Begging, Craig. I need a favor. I gotta go to Seattle and I'd like to park RJ with you. He needs some clipping and dipping, and he's favoring that leg he stuck under a speeding truck a while back."

"No problem. I'll pick him up. What day and when's your plane?"

"Oh-dark-thirty Wednesday. I'll leave him here at the house. Use your key. I'll retrieve him from that dog prison of yours Thursday night, okay?"

"No need. I'll drop him off at your house and say howdy. And RJ won't suffer dog prison because I'll take him home with me. He loves my house."

And no wonder, the place smelled and looked like an animal lair. I vowed to schedule my semi-annual den cleaning assault on Craigosaurus's cave soon. Dr. Craig Washington, RJ's huge, but gentle, giant of a vet, was a hundred pounds overweight, black, shy, and one of my best friends. I never called him Craigosaurus to his face, although everyone else did. I *know* about weight jokes.

"You are a prince among vets, Craig darlin'. Thanks." We went on to chat about his week, his love life, and his latest veterinary venture. He was all excited about a new thing he'd picked up at a conference in Las Vegas: dog balls. And not the ones you throw for Fido. Seems some folks down Argentina way are so hung up, so to speak, on appearances they have silicon testicles implanted in their neutered pets. I vetoed Craig's offer to make RJ Oakland's first cosmetically enhanced canine, then said good-bye.

"RJ's all set. I should marry Craig," I sighed.

"What would his boyfriend say?"

"Minor detail. Think what I'd save in vet bills." I told her about Craig's new venture into pet plastic surgery.

"You're shittin' me. Well, gee, maybe Craigosaurus can do something for the poor dude in Seattle. Sounds like you ain't gonna leave him with any."

"Really cute, Miz Jan. Well, yawn, I'm gonna hit the hay as soon as I pack my gym gear."

"You know, if you'd lay off all the junk food on weekends you wouldn't have to work out for two hours and then go to bed hungry Monday through Thursday."

"Where's the fun in that?"

* * *

Dale Stevens was my VOD. Victim of the Day. He pulled his chair close to mine and aimed his color-enhanced contacts at my front. What he found fascinating about my grandmother's cameo, I have no idea.

Under the table, I slipped open five buttons up the side of my skirt, shifted slightly to face him, crossed my legs, and was rewarded with a sharp intake of jerk breath. He couldn't take his eyes off my exposed, albeit pantyhose clad, expanse of thigh. Some things are way too easy.

"So," I said, giving each person at the conference table my most sincere look, "let's get started by going around the table, each of you defining your job description as it applies to our project. As a guideline, I've prepared a sample organizational chart." I held up a magenta bordered piece of paper, giving everyone time to shuffle through their folders and find their own color coded sheet.

"You will, of course, create your own chart, but I've found that the better each department understands its relationship to others, and to the project, the more efficiently they interface."

The in-house imbecile forced his eyes from my leg slit long enough to check out my proposed org chart. His position on the chart and suggested title, Systems Manager, seemed to please him, especially since I had purposely elevated him to a direct-line of command right below the Project Manager. The yahoo gave me a wink and a 'so you *do* think I'm hot shit' look. He didn't notice his little box of glory had no lineage to the rest of the project. Anyone with a modicum of sense wouldn't like seeing himself dangling off the pyramid of command, so to speak. I winked back.

"Let's start with you, Mr. Ritchie," I said, making eye contact with the head dude. "As Project Manager, you have overall control. Of course, with that responsibility you will be the first to take it in the shorts when things go south." Ritchie looked a little surprised, then laughed with the rest of us.

"Gee, Hetta" he said, "don't feel you have to beat around the bush."

"Not to worry. You guys hired me to try to avoid cost overruns—that's French for pissing off the client by spending too much of his money—and by golly, that's what I'm here to do. By doing so, Mr. Ritchie, I am also trying to keep you from ending up a sacrificial goat to the client's displeasure."

Ritchie nodded. He'd been around long enough to know that project managers, like professional coaches, have a potentially short shelf life.

I then encouraged each member of the team to describe how they fit into the picture and what, specifically, their particular talent brought to the project. I left Dale for last. When it was his turn, the smug bastard spouted credentials, as I knew he would, but little substance. An ally on my client's staff asked key questions, supplied, of course, by *moi* before the meeting. By the time my mark quit blathering, he had bragged himself right off the project. God, I love the smell of burned jerky in the morning.

6

The next afternoon, still harboring a satisfactory glow akin to post-coital smolder—as near as I remembered, that is—I drove into the hills from the Oakland Airport. A huge leopard-spotted van with paw, claw, and Tyrannosaurus rex footprints painted all over it was parked in my driveway. When I hit the garage door opener, the ever so large and gay veterinarian opened his slider.

I wasn't quite out of the car when sixty-five pounds of happy Lab knocked me back into the front seat. I nuzzled my dog and asked, "You two have a good time? And a bath? Oh RJ, you smell so good."

"Smell his breath," Craig prompted.

"I'd rather have a root canal."

"Come on, Hetta, just do it."

I held RJ's big red head still and took a cautious sniff. "Have you two been into the York mints again?"

"Nope. Something I invented, peppermint dog biscuits. What do you think?"

"I'll take ten cases. Now can you do something about his farts?"

"I'm only human," Craig joked, but his tone fell a little flat. I wondered if he and his sig-other, Raoul, had suffered a tiff. Guy problems. Something I can certainly relate to.

"Want something to drink? You can give me an RJ report along with your inflated bill."

Craig nodded, but didn't smile at my jibe. We went to the kitchen where he accepted a glass of Chardonnay, the second alcoholic beverage I'd seen him take in ten years. The last one was when his father died. Something was definitely amiss.

"Well?" I said, as we settled onto the couch. Craig's uncharacteristically solemn behavior put an edge to my voice.

He sighed. "There's a problem."

"With you and Raoul?"

"No, with RJ."

"Well heck, Craig, I didn't even know you two were dating."

Craig finally smiled, but didn't laugh. Not a good sign. Neither was the deep sigh. Nor his large gulp of wine. "I'm almost certain RJ's got bone cancer."

My heart threatened arrest. The mouth of the South, the gal with the glib comebacks, the queen of repartee, could only manage, "No."

"I'm sorry, Hetta, but I'm ninety-nine percent sure. We'll get a second opinion, though. I hope it proves me wrong."

I chugged my wine. Got another. Craig waited. I morphed into All Business Bitch.

"Where do we get the second opinion? And if you're right, what are our options?" I caught myself before asking for the bottom line.

Craig sighed again. "For the other medical input we go to the University of California at Davis. My alma mater. If they agree with my diagnosis, we have to make a decision. We can amputate his leg and try radiation treatments, or we could let the disease run its course and keep him comfortable."

"Not acceptable." *And if you sigh again, you leviathan, I'll cut your heart out with this wine glass.*

"Hetta, we aren't in a board meeting here," Craig said gently as he took me in his arms.

I dissolved into tears, and Craig held me until RJ, not liking the looks of a dogless huddle, poked his nose between us. I kissed his hairy face—RJ's, not Craig's—and blubbered, "Amputate? Radiation? That's it?"

"Maybe not. That's why I'd like to take him up to U.C. Davis. Maybe they can offer some better ideas."

"Jesus, it wouldn't be hard. When do we leave?"

"Tomorrow morning. I've already set up an appointment for ten."

* * *

During the somber ride back to Oakland late Friday night, even RJ seemed to sense the doom and gloom pervading his humans. He'd had a trying day of strangers taking blood, x-rays, and being generally intrusive. The jury was in, the verdict read, and a death sentence passed. RJ had maybe nine months on death row if I agreed to amputation of the leg. Less than six if we did nothing.

An hour into the drive, I reached a decision. "I can't see subjecting him to surgery unless it'll save his life."

"I think that's a wise decision," Craig said, keeping his eyes glued to the road.

"You mean I finally, for once in my entire life, make a wise personal decision and it dooms my dog to a painful death?"

"Hetta, this isn't your fault. It's not all that unusual for a dog to develop cancer in a bone break, especially one as severe as his was. Most people would have put him down right after that truck hit him, but you spent a fortune on orthopedic surgery."

For years I'd referred to RJ as the three thousand dollar dog, my bionic bow-wow. Now it wasn't the least bit funny.

"Craig, I want my money back."

* * *

Jan, whom we'd called en route, waited in my-oh-so chic, oval living room. A fire roared in the turn of the century, hand sculpted, granite fireplace. The lights of several Bay Area cities glittered through plant framed casement windows. Years of renovation, poring over *House Beautiful* and *Architectural Digest,* and hounding salvage yards and estate sales had paid off. Chez RJ was as pleasant to the eye as it was to live in.

It normally gave me a moment's pride and pleasure when I walked through the front door, but tonight all I could think of was one day coming home to find it empty. No wagging tail, no joyful barks.

Craig joined us for fettuccini Alfredo à la Jan and the Nieman Marcus takeout deli, then yawned and said he was going to turn in early, but I knew better. He would work at his office into the wee hours to make up for his lost day at U.C. Davis. Jan and I took our wine to the hot tub deck off my third floor bedroom.

"Thanks for making dinner," I told Jan, not even giving her a hard time for buying exorbitantly priced pasta at Needless Markup.

"You are very welcome. Hetta, that Craig is a saint," Jan said. Steam rose from her shoulders as she pushed herself up from the one hundred three degree water into the cool evening air. We had turned off the jets and were adrift in the hot, still water while taking in the view. The lights of the Golden Gate, Bay, and San Mateo bridges glittered like necklaces spanning the throat, waist and ankle of the Bay. A full moon bathed us in its own pearly light.

RJ was stretched out on a redwood seat surrounding the tub, his front paws dangling in the water. He extended one leg, testing the waters in more ways than one.

"Don't even think about it," I told him. He looked guilty.

"How can you read that dog's mind?" Jan asked, pulling a bottle of chilled wine from its ice bucket.

"Great minds and all that. One of these days I'm gonna let him come in," I said. An overwhelming feeling of loss stung my eyes. One of these days, and soon, RJ would be gone.

"Oh, what the hell. Come on in, boy."

RJ's tail thumped uncertainly once, twice, then he stared at me with the same twitchy anticipation as when he smelled a hidden treasure in my pocket. There was enough light so he could study my face. "Does she mean it?" his eyes seemed to ask.

Jan slapped the water. "Come on in RJ," she cooed.

RJ, not a dog to be asked thrice, launched himself forward in a full body belly flop that sent a tidal wave of hot water into my wine glass.

7

A persistent thump on my pillow heralded an *après* Chardonnay kind of day. The logjam of dog hair in my hot tub dictated my morning's main activity.

Jan wisely decided to abandon my place and snitty attitude for her own BDR-less abode.

RJ watched, with the irksome smugness of a teetotaler, from a safe, splash free distance while I drained, washed, polished, and refilled the tub.

Adding insult to self-induced injury was my discovery of several loose deck planks, a leaky water pipe under the tub, a suspiciously slow drain in the basement sink, and two hanger-uppers before

I could figure out how to use my new caller ID. An epic headache, hairy hot tub, disintegrating house, nuisance caller, and dying dog pushed me to the tottering edge of a severe pity party. After a morning of hard work laced with liberal doses of self-loathing, I gratefully set the tub controls to HEAT, turned on some Pavarotti, and collapsed on the couch with a half liter glass of cold wine. It didn't taste as good as it had the night before. And I don't really like opera all that much, but I have a deep affection for anything of value featuring fat people. Sumo wrestling is my all time favorite.

It was time to whine.

"Mama," I blubbered into the phone, "why me?"

"Hetta Honey, are you intoxicated?" Mother drawled.

"I'm not drunk, but I've been drinking. My ship has not sunk, but it is sinking," I singsonged, quoting a poem a friend composed one tipsy night at the beach.

I could picture Mother giving my father her "Hetta's on the phone and it isn't good news" look. Although it was midafternoon in Texas, I also knew she was perfectly coifed, she had her "face" on, and her petite form was adorned with something linen by Liz Claiborne. Pressed. I've long suspected I was adopted.

"And I plan to drink more," I sniveled. "My life is the pits." I would have said my life was shit, but one does not use the word "shit" when addressing my mother. "Pits" was even pushing it, as it could be construed as referring to a body part.

62

"Oh? May-un problems?" Mama asked, trying to sound sympathetic even though she and my father had to be sick of my historically histrionic love life.

"No, no man this time" I wailed. "I wish it was only that. RJ's got cancer and he's gonna die."

"Oh, dear. I'm putting your father on." Mother, like me, doesn't do well with bad news. That's Daddy's job.

My second sip of wine tasted better. I blew my nose and waited. RJ, upon hearing his name, had put his head in my lap so I could scratch his ears. Mother covered the phone's mouthpiece with her palm, but I could catch muffled snatches of conversation.

"Hetta . . . upset."

"What . . . another . . . hope . . . real job," I made out before Daddy took the phone. "Hetta, are you all right?"

"I am, but RJ's dying."

"What of?"

"Bone cancer."

"Too bad. Can't they do anything?"

I explained the options. Daddy was silent for a few moments, then said, "Best dawg I ever had was an ole Red Bone hound with three legs. Lost one to a bobcat when he was just a pup. He got around mighty fine. 'Course he fell on his nose when he tried to point, but he was still a fine fella."

I smiled. A little homegrown homily goes a long way to boost the spirits of a displaced Texan.

"What did you call him? And don't give me that old 'Lucky' joke."

"Tripod."

I laughed aloud, then sighed. "Daddy, I wouldn't mind having a three-legged dog, but taking his leg off won't buy us anything. And he'd have to go through all the pain. I mean, he's bound to suffer anyhow, from the cancer, but it doesn't make sense to cut off his leg and still have him die in six months. I wish I didn't have a choice. Like with people."

"I'm not so sure about that. There's a few folks woulda put down Grandmaw Stockman if they'da had a chance."

I snorted into my wine. My great grandmother had died at one hundred and one, some say of disappointment. After claiming to be fading away from every known disease for fifty years, she finally succumbed to old age. Very mean old age.

"I guess it's true, only the good die young. In our family we live long and get meaner with each year. There's a depressing thought. I'm doomed to feel like this for another fifty someodd years?"

"Beats the alternative. Wish there was something I could do to help you and RJ."

"You already have."

"Hell, I didn't do nothin'."

"You were there. I needed to whine and you listened. Thanks. Let me say good-bye to Mama, then I'll talk to you next week, okay?"

"Okay. Love you."

"Love you, too," I said, then waited while my mother took the phone.

"The thing to do is keep busy," she advised. "It'll take your mind off RJ's problems and let you enjoy him while you can."

"I will, Mama. Actually, I was thinking of taking sailing lessons."

There was a long pause. "Mama?"

"Use sunblock, Hetta. Boating is very bad for your ski-yun."

I hung up and decided to take her advice about keeping busy. And the sunblock. Sitting around, moping all afternoon or getting drunk, wasn't going to get me anywhere except mopey drunk. I fired up RJ's car and we went for a drive. Three hours later, I called Jan.

"How's you?" I asked.

"More importantly, how are you? I called twice and when you didn't answer I thought maybe you'd decided to end it all after I left."

"I felt like it when I saw that hot tub. But I'm too much of a coward to kill myself. Death hurts, I'm sure of it. Besides, if I didn't commit *harakiri* in Japan when Hudson jilted me, I never will. Stupid, ain't it, how you think something is so damned tragic you can't possibly live another day. Now, years later, I'm facing a real loss and the thing with Hudson doesn't amount to a hill of beans. Although," I said, fingering the key hanging around my neck, "I would like to know what happened to the dirty rat bastard."

"We'll probably never know. When was the last time you heard from Interpol?"

"At least a year. Anyhow, enough of that. RJ and I just got back from the library. You should see all the books I've got on sailing. Oh, and I've signed us up for a U.S. Coast Guard boating safety class."

Jan groaned. "Why can't you have a hangover, like I do?"

"Well, I do, but I decided to take RJ to the park and the library was right there and one thing led to another. We start in two weeks."

"Start what?"

"The Coast Guard class."

"Hetta, I'm not going. No way. No how. Not a chance. And that's that."

"We can buy real cool sailing gear."

"No."

"There'll be men there."

"What kind of cool gear?"

8

A snowy-bearded man in smart whites waved us to school desks at the front of the room and wrote his name, Russ Madden, on the blackboard. Well, the board was actually green, but I'm a traditionalist.

The classroom, decorated in a blend of high school rah-rah and "don't do drugs" signs, flags of the world, maps of the rapidly changing global scene and a wide screen TV, brought back memories of days long past at Richland Springs High, Richland Springs, Texas. Home of the fighting Coyotes. Well, scratch the wide screen. Our one-horse town didn't even have decent television reception.

I had a sudden urge to pass a note or throw a spitball. Or buy a pair of straight legged jeans, soak them in a number ten galvanized tub of hot water and starch and then let them dry to a life-threatening fit on my sixteen-year-old body. But I wasn't sixteen. I was, uh, something more than that. I was making mooneyes at a gray-haired man, for crying out loud. When did I develop this Kenny

Rogers syndrome? At what point did I lose my attraction for hardbody cowboys in skintight jeans, and start gawking at old men?

Kenny, uh, Lieutenant Madden, burst into my thoughts by throwing a stack of booklets on my desk. "Since you're early, maybe you'd help me by passing these out? Put one on each desk, please."

"Will it affect our final grade point?" I vamped. I love a man in uniform.

He grinned. "You don't get a grade. You either pass the test or you don't. If you pay attention, you'll pass."

Jan and I went about our assigned task, then perused the pamphlets while other would-be mariners filtered in. Most of them, my crabwise vision recorded with satisfaction, were men. In fact, by the time the class began, the only other women in the packed room were a Coast Guard Auxiliary volunteer and a sour-faced matron who huffed down into the desk next to me. Her ample derriere had no more than touched the seat when she told me this boat thing wasn't her idea and if her husband thought this silly toy wasn't going to cost him big time, he had another think coming. Why, just this morning she'd called her decorator, Dion, for an estimate to get the entire house redone....

I was spared her plot for spousal punishment by means of the dreaded Dion, when Lt. Madden cleared his throat, welcomed the class, and turned out the lights.

For the next fifteen minutes we were subjected to a video tape reminiscent of a chainsaw flick featuring bigger than life photos of what appeared to be boat and body parts. Nautical disaster leftovers of those whose horsepower exceeded their IQ's by a factor of four.

Jan breathed, "Oh, Lord, Hetta, I told you boats were dangerous."

Lt. Madden heard her. "Boating can be dangerous, but not to the informed and cautious. Now, let's get down to learning how you can avoid being a star in my horror movie. It isn't all that hard if you know the rules of the road, use common sense, operate a well-maintained vessel and keep in mind one important thing. Boats don't got no brakes."

They don't? This was a worrisome piece of information, but it faded to fast second when we got to the part about navigation. After an hour of hand to hand combat with a protractor, a pair of dividers and a map—nix that, a *chart* —of the California coast, we tackled the art of dead reckoning. I dead reckoned that, with my skills, we'd end up as flotsam. Or was it jetsam? Whatever, we'd end up beached.

"Jesus," Jan grumbled as we left the classroom, "I guess this crap is easy for you. You're an engineer. And what's with this 'north' thing? How can there be a *true north* and a *magnetic north*? Why not a true north and *un*-true north? Oh, I knew this was going to be a disaster. First time on a boat we're gonna hit the rocks."

"No, we're not."

"Oh, and what is going to prevent it? Your exceptional navigational know-how?"

"GPS, my dear. A global positioning satellite receiver, that's what. Clever little buggers bounce a signal right onto a chart or map, telling you within a few feet exactly where you are. We use them to survey these days."

"Like the ones in cars? They work on boats, too?"

"*Ab-so-lu-ta-mente.*"

"Cool. Then why are they teaching us to navigate the hard way?"

"Well, for one thing, just because you know where you are doesn't mean zip if your don't know how to read a chart. I suppose there's also a remote possibility the satellite could fall from the sky when you're half way to Tahiti. We ain't going to Tahiti in anything smaller than the QEII, but we gotta learn this *merde* anyhow so we don't come off as complete idiots when we take our sailing lessons."

"Hetta, I'm not taking sailing lessons. And I don't want a boat."

"Did you see the blonde hunk in the green turtleneck sitting in our row?" I said, directing the conversation toward more positive ground. "Don't look now, but he's coming our way. Dammit, I wish we weren't in RJ's crappy old car."

"Let RJ out. It's dark and the guy could be a masher."

"Masher? Where do you get words like that? Hush, here he comes," I said as I coaxed a reluctant RJ from his nice warm car. He had a sleepy dog smell that reminded me of freshly baked bread.

"Nice dog," the hunk said, patting my vicious guard dog's head and receiving a grateful lick. He pulled keys from the pocket of his snug Dockers and opened the Mercedes next to us. "Yellow Lab?"

"Yeah. His name is RJ. Mine's Hetta. This is Jan. How did you like the class?"

"It's okay, but I already know all that stuff. I need a certificate of completion to get a discount on my boat insurance."

Jan perked visibly. "You have a boat?"

"Still shopping. You?"

"Oh, we're still looking, too. But we hope to find the right vessel soon," says Jan, the flexible.

"Yeah," I said, suppressing a guffaw, "we're still looking."

With a gleam of white teeth, the man quipped, "I'm thinking a nice fifty-foot gaff rigger that's spent its life in a little old lady's garage."

"How can you get—" I elbowed Jan before she made her own gaffe.

"Good one." I tittered like a teenybopper, trying to think of something clever. From the puzzled look on Jan's face, I knew I was on my own. "One with sails?" How clever was that?

Evidently clever enough, for the hunk laughed. "Good one, yourself. Well, see you next week. When I do get something, you guys wanna crew for me one day?" As we nodded like those goofy dogs in the back windows of old ladies' cars, he drove away, giving us a good gander at his designer license plate: *Wetdrems*.

We dissolved into giggles.

"Oh, we're still looking," I mimicked. "What were you thinking?"

"I wasn't. I guess we'd better do some more boat shopping this weekend so we have a clue," Jan said, wiping laugh tears from her cheeks. "I still don't want to take those damned sailing lessons, but if I want to be good crew, I guess I'd better."

"Now see, isn't this more fun than sitting around waiting for some a-hole to call? Speaking of which, anything heard from BDR?"

"Nope. Well once, but I told him to take a hike. I didn't even tell him I'd seen him with the fat broad. I said I wanted someone on my own intellectual level."

"You did? Fantastic. What'd he say?"

"He wanted to know if he could have the Armani jacket."

"You're shittin' me? Please tell me you're joking. Even *he* couldn't be so shallow. What'd you tell him?"

"That you gave it to a wino," she told me with a shrug.

"What! Are you nuts? Richard is, you know. Jesus, I hope he doesn't do anything to even the score."

"He won't, Hetta. He's scared of you. He told me so."

"He's scared of me? I like it. Why?"

"Maybe you don't want to hear this."

"Hey, I'll consider the source."

"Well, okay. What he said was, 'Hetta's unbalanced and it's only a matter of time before she goes off the deep end.' "

"He said that, did he? Well good, I'm glad he thinks so. A fearsome reputation is a good thing to have when it works to your benefit. Unbalanced, huh? I should have rubbed the inside of that Armani with poison ivy and let you give it back to him."

Jan eyed me warily. Okay, maybe I am slightly demented.

She dropped us off and took the VW home with her since she was returning the next day to stay with RJ while I went *true* north, to Seattle. See what a fast study I am?

9

Seattle was heating up, business-wise, and I had scheduled meetings for three days running. RJ was pouting when I left the following morning, but I called him from the airport so he could hear the message I'd recorded for him on my non-business answering machine. The phone rang three times, then I heard my voice and knew RJ could, as well.

"RJ, my man, what are you doing? Are you being a good doggy? Yes, I miss you, too. Mommy will be home before you know it. Get off the couch." I hoped I didn't get any important personal calls. Who was I kidding? The only person who called me was Jan.

I called her that evening and heard RJ barking and growling in the background. "How's Seattle?" Jan asked over the din.

"Rainy and dull. Popular movie aside, seems like all they do here is sleep. What's RJ's prob?"

"Mailman."

"At this hour?"

"Actually, it was a postal inspector. He just left and he ain't real happy."

"Churlish, those postal employees. What now? I always worry they're gonna show up with an automatic weapon in lieu of my mail."

"Oh, that's not going to be a problem for you, Hetta. Your mail service has been cut off. From now on, you have to pick it up at the post office."

"*Zut alors!* Why?"

"For one thing, RJ went walk about. He terrorized the mailman, wouldn't let him out of his Jeep. Bit his tires. Amongst other things."

"We can get to those 'other things' later. How in hell did RJ get out?"

"I don't know. You want to ask him?"

"Very funny, Miz Jan."

"All I know is dog jail was still padlocked and the garage door was closed. Only thing I can figure is he's found a new escape hatch under the house. I looked everywhere, but I can't find it."

"*Merde*. So, let's get to those 'other' things. What do I have to do to get mail service restored?"

"It depends on the hearing."

"Hearing? RJ bit tires, not people. I hope."

"True, but that's not the charge."

"Jan, why do I get the feeling you're enjoying this? Quit screwing around and give me the bottom line."

She giggled. "Your dog, RJ Coffey, is charged with carjacking. Of a federal vehicle. There was also mention of mail tampering and the FBI."

"Stand by," I said. I put down the phone, crossed to the minibar in my room, grabbed a minute bottle of Jack Black and swallowed it in one non-mini gulp. Then I went back to the phone. "Let's have it."

"One of the neighbors, Bunnie Adams? Well, she heard the mailman hollering bloody murder. When she went out, she found him sitting in his Jeep, threatening RJ with a can of mace while your dawg munched his tires. Bunnie scolded the vicious cur, grabbed him by the collar, and put him into your backyard."

I couldn't help myself, I laughed. "So, how did the postman *like* my backyard?"

"Very damned funny. You know what I mean."

"Yeah, yeah. Look, if barking at the postman was a federal offense, every dog in the whole wide world would be a felon."

"Oh, that's not all."

I eyed the minibar, but resisted its call. "What *is* all?"

"Well, the postman delivered the mail just fine, but when he got back, RJ had his furry rump firmly entrenched in the Jeep's driver's seat. A tussle ensued, the mailman got maced, and the Jeep somehow got put into neutral and rolled two blocks before crashing into Mr. Fujitsu's hedge."

"Oh, hell. Is RJ all right?"

"He's fine. But," I heard her take a sip of wine to stifle a laugh, "he may lose his license." Great guffaws. "Sorry, Hetta. Anyhow, the only damage is to Mr. Fujitsu's hedge, the postal department's Jeep and the mailman's disposition. Which, by the way, I hear wasn't so sunny to start with."

I started laughing and couldn't stop. Finally I gasped that I couldn't talk anymore or I'd wet my pants. I hung up and laughed until I started crying. Was there life after RJ?

When I called the next night, there was no answer. I hung up before the machine could take over, then did some work, and called back. I was hearing my own message, the business version, when Jan grabbed the phone. "I'm here."

"You sound out of breath. Postal employee after you?"

"Nope, ran up the front steps. Heard the phone ringing from outside. I got home early, so I took RJ for a walk. Did you call before?"

"Yep, but I hung up on the third ring."

"Oh."

"Oh?"

"Well, yeah, I thought maybe...never mind."

"Never mind what?"

"Someone breathed."

"Excuse me?"

"Someone breathed into your machine, Hetta."

"Did you check caller ID?"

"It said something like 'unidentified.' "

"Well fooey, Jan. I didn't sign up for caller *un*-identification. What the hell did I get if for if it doesn't work? Oh, never mind, it's probably some kid. Or mailman."

"Well, RJ didn't like it. He growled."

"At my answering machine?"

"Yep."

"Maybe it was a cat burglar. RJ hates cats. Oh, well, I'll be home *mañana*. So, other than the breather, what kind of day have you and my perp pup been having?"

"Grand. By the way, you're getting low on steaks and Hershey Bars."

"Why don't you two try eating some veggies. I'll shop this weekend."

"You're busy this weekend."

"I am?"

"I found us cheap sailing lessons. It's a group called Nineties something or other Sailing Club, and we can pay by the day. One thing though—it's all women."

"I don't find that a problem. One of those books we got said it's easier to learn without some guy yelling at you. And you don't have to worry what your hair looks like. Gotta run. See you tomorrow. Kiss RJ for me."

I hung up, ran a brush through my hair and smeared color on my lips and cheeks. My client had decided on a dinner meeting to wrap up the week so I could take an early flight out the next day. I arrived at the restaurant humming a Jimmy Buffet number, all aglow with the promise of salty adventures to come.

"Okay, you guys," I told the group of electrical engineers gathered around the table, "let's get this show on the road. I wanna go sailin'. "

One of them looked out the window into drizzling fog and shrugged. "Whatever floats your boat, Hetta."

10

I knew in my heart that, well-hidden above a shroud of spooky fog, a Saturday sun lurked, but there was room for some serious doubt.

"Are we there yet?" Jan yawned.

"We probably would be if you'd sit up and help me look for a street number in this soup. Where the hell *is* this sailing club of yours?"

Jan flipped up the seat back and squinted at barely visible warehouses and docks lining the brick paved road. A foghorn echoed through the deserted streets. I half expected to get a glimpse of Vampire Lestat folding his wings for the night. I hit the door LOCK button.

"When I called yesterday, they said we'd see a sign. There," she said, pointing to a faded blue and white sign on a dilapidated wooden structure. Even with the car windows up I detected a fishy odor.

"What kind of sailing club is this?" I demanded. "Where are the colorful banners? The sport cars? Hell, where are the *boats*?"

I parked in the loading zone in front, under the modest sign reading:

GAY NINETIES SAILING CLUB
MEMBERS AND GUESTS ONLY
RING BELL

"Oh, well, Miz Jan, you said it was cheap. The object here is to learn to sail, right?"

Jan cast a cynical eye in my direction. "Don't give me any stiff upper lip crap. You're gonna mouth off about the place having a certain air about it. Probably get us kicked out before we begin."

"You know me all too well, sailor. Okay, I'll stow the sarcasm for the sake of my shipmates."

As their sign instructed, we rang. After a small delay, during which I suspected we were being checked out through the peephole, a willowy blonde in white ducks, Docksiders, and a pink windbreaker swung the door open and greeted us. "You must be Hetta and Jan," she said. "I'm Doris. Come on in. We're getting organized for today's sail. We need you to fill out a form or two before we shove off. Did you bring your Coast Guard certificates? Gotta be careful these days. Lawyers and all."

We gave Doris copies of our certificates and followed her into a pennant-festooned room with round, dark wooden tables surrounded by captain's chairs. A steaming coffee pot sat on a counter lined with cups, and marine charts littered a large conference table. Several women glanced up from poring over the charts, waved, and went back to planning our day. Jan and I were given questionnaires and pens.

"Sailing experience?" Jan said, studying the form.

I shook my head. "Nada."

"If we say that, they might not let us go."

"Jan, three weeks ago you said there was no way in hell you were going to take these lessons. What brought on your sudden dire need to be accepted?"

"You did. You said if we sailed, we'd meet men. I'm willing to put in the time."

"Good girl." I waved the form at her. "Let's be honest."

Picking up my ballpoint, I filled in under SAILING EXPERIENCE, *Caribbean, Mediterranean, and trans-Pacific.* I left out the fact that all of this cognitive content was gained on cruise ships the size of small cities.

The next question was easy. WHY DO YOU WANT TO LEARN TO SAIL? It is against my nature to answer this type of question with any honesty, but I thought, *what the hey?* and wrote: *Meet new people. Learn a skill. Find a mate.*

"You two about ready?" Doris said. "We'll be out around four hours. Hope you had breakfast."

Jan and I looked at each other. "Uh," I said, "not exactly. I thought maybe we'd stop for brunch at some waterfront establishment."

Doris grinned, shaking her head. "Sorry, girls. We're out to sail, not bar hop. I suggest you grab some crackers from the coffee counter. Sailing on an empty stomach is a real bad idea."

Jan and I stuffed our pockets with packages of Premium Saltines, she grumbling something about no peanut butter. We trailed Doris to a rickety dock where others waited. "Shipmates," she yelled, "newbies."

Twenty women were quickly divided into four teams and assigned a boat. Mine was a thirty-two foot Catalina under the command of Dilly, a sturdy looking woman with silvery crew cut hair and yellow, crooked teeth. Dressed in shiny, dark gray, foul weather gear, she resembled an overweight shark. After perusing my flimsy sailing curriculum vitae, she glared at my French manicured silk wraps, ruby ring, and Rolex watch. An unrefined snort of derision preceded her command to take off the jewelry. "It's dangerous," she spat.

I quickly began shoving everything, including my neck chain, into a zippered pocket. "Anyone else dressed for cocktails?" she snarled. Head shakes all around. "No? Then let's go sailing. If, that is, Princess here is finished stashing her jewels."

Feeling like a six-year-old who'd farted at a family funeral, I slunk onto the boat and gazed longingly towards Jan, who was being welcomed aboard another vessel by her teammates. She waved, smiled, and gave me a thumbs-up. I pouted.

Two hours later, I was cold, tired, hungry, humiliated, and livid. Dilly gave me no quarter, screaming orders I barely understood and then dressing me down when I didn't react properly or promptly. So much for the friendly female atmosphere.

Winch handles reduced my seventy dollar manicure to bloody stumps, a diabolical boom repeatedly attacked my head, and I ached from unaccustomed physical labor. Cowering before the mast, I was grateful for the pitying looks of the others. I'd seen many a pirate movie so, fearing a keelhaul in my near future, I tried sweet talk.

"So, Dilly," I wheedled, "how did you get the cute nickname? Because you're a dilly of a sailor?"

"Nope," she said, then unaccountably stuck out her tongue. My look of total incomprehension, one I had worn most of the day, prompted a huff of exasperation. "Because, you fluff ball, I don't need no stinking dildo."

Hooting arose while I tried to close my mouth. Hetta Coffey—world-traveler, bon vivant, sophisticate—blurted, "You're a dyke?"

Hostile silence fell upon the good vessel *Sappho*. I belatedly remembered who Sappho was. *Zut Alors!* I was in the middle of San Francisco Bay, surrounded by now antagonistic shipmates and sharks, on a boat named for the poetess of Lesbos.

"No, girly," Dilly snarled, "I'm a lesbian. Are you telling me you don't know this is a lesbian sailing group?"

"Well, of course I...uh, no."

* * *

"Jan, I'm going to kill you."

"How was I supposed to know?"

"Gee, I don't know. Why don't we start with the name of the damned club? *Gay* Nineties, Jan, not Nineties *something*."

Jan raised a weak defense. "I learned a lot today. The women on my boat were very nice and they taught me a lot of neat stuff."

"I'll tell you what I learned. To stay away from dykes on docks, the Sisters of Sappho, and women named Dilly. And to make my own sailing reservations."

Jan grinned and despite my chagrin, so did I. By the time we climbed onto barstools at my tennis club and downed a beer, we were giddy with laughter and fatigue.

"I guess we're even," Jan chortled into her drink.

"For what?"

"Oh, let me count the ways. How about when you made me take belly dancing lessons because you heard it turned men on. All we attracted was an alcoholic Arab. Then there were the skiing lessons so you could schuss after some Swedish instructor. I ended up in a cast. And how about the—"

"Okay. Enough. We're even. More than even, because today was way up there in one of my worst day experiences. Maybe you were right in the first place. Maybe this sailing thing wasn't such a great idea."

"I disagree. I enjoyed myself. Oh, and I lined you up for a couple of dates. Two can play your sleight of card game."

"Cute. Okay, so to your own amazement, you like to sail. What next?"

Ester, the bartender, had been eavesdropping. A woman after my own heart. "Hard day on the Bay?" she asked.

I rolled my eyes. "Let's put it this way, Ester. If I ever do buy a boat, I'll name it the *Hetta Row*, so there's no confusion." I told her of my delightful morning with Dilly.

"Oh, boy, you did have some day on the Bay. I got a story for you. Two of my more desperate friends found out about a group of lesbians planning a trip to a Club Med in Mexico, so they signed up, thinking with all those Lizzies there, the man-field would be wide open. Turns out, though, the gals arranging the trip had dictated that all other guests, and any male staff, be banned during the entire week. My friends spent the whole week holding hands to fend off unwanted attention."

The bar was empty, so Ester came around and sat down with us. "You know, there's a yacht club in Oakland with a sailing group called Women on the Estuary. I'm a member."

I narrowed my eyes with mock suspicion and Ester laughed. "And no, Hetta, it's not gay. Maybe a couple of them, but who cares?"

"Not me. I just don't want Dilly the Destroyer at the helm."

"Our sailmasters are men," Ester explained, "because they own the boats." I saw Jan's eyes light up, but I wasn't overly eager for another flogging before the mast real soon.

"Where does one purchase a cat-o'-nine-tails these days?" I asked. "The Haight?"

"No Captain Bligh crap, Hetta. These guys don't yell or anything, and they're super instructors. I'm getting off in an hour, why don't you guys meet me at the yacht club and check it out for yourselves?"

11

The Jack London Yacht Club, appropriately located on Jack London Square, was in an old two story building overlooking the Oakland Estuary. A sailmaker's loft at one time, now the interior was all polished mahogany and funky atmosphere. Jack London would have considered it a suitable hangout for trashing his liver had it been there when the great writer was penning and ginning.

Posters depicting Jack London's boats, dog, and book jacket covers were scattered around the room, but my favorite was a snapshot of the man himself. He was wearing what appeared to be a leather aviator's jacket. His hair was windblown around his handsome face, and he sported a roguish grin that personified his roguish reputation. Beneath the photo was a poem he wrote summing up his take on life:

I would rather be ashes than dust!
I would rather that my spark should burn out in a brilliant blaze
than it should be stifled by dryrot.

I would rather be a superb meteor

every atom of me in magnificent glow,
than a sleepy and permanent planet.
The proper function of a man is to live,
not to exist.
I shall not waste my days in trying to
prolong them.
I shall use my time.

As I read the great adventurer's self-fulfilling words, I couldn't help but think I would have liked the bounder. With my penchant for bounders, maybe even loved him.

Jan evidently had similar thoughts. "Gee, Hetta, his philosophic attitude on life reminds me of yours."

I wasn't all so sure I cared for the comparison. After all, old Jack, for all his brilliance and wanderlust was, like his prophetic ode indicated, a literary flash fire who flamed out before his excesses extinguished his talent. A victim of his own immoderation, he died at forty and didn't even leave a beautiful corpse.

"Not really. I mean, I do admire his give a damn attitude, but don't you wonder what he could have accomplished if he'd lived longer and taken better care of himself?"

Jan gave me a meaningful look and said, "Food for thought, Hetta, food for thought."

We shook off our moment of thought and proceeded to the bar, hoping for food. The jukebox played a Jimmy Buffet number and a man was performing some kind of jig on top of the long, mostly empty, bar. Ester didn't seem to notice him.

Jan and I took barstools as far away from the skinny sailor's gyrations as possible while Ester went to the office for a copy of the rules and sailing schedule for Women on the Estuary.

"What can I get you ladies?" asked the Filipino bartender. Paul, according to his nametag.

"Draft beer for me, unless you have something to eat besides peanuts," I said, warily eyeing the dancer grind his way towards us.

Paul glanced over his shoulder. "Don't mind him. He's drunk. Kitchen's closed, but Ester can raid the fridge for you. Should be something left in there from last night's buffet. Also, in case you're interested, we have splits of champagne on ice. Cheap."

I liked this club already. "Great. Champers for me, then. Uh, does he do this bar dance thing often, Paul?"

"Oh, yes."

Ester returned, waving papers. "Good news. WOE has a sail next Sunday. If you want some fun in the meantime, the yacht club is sponsoring a beer can race Wednesday night. Wanna come?"

"What do we have to do?"

"Drink beer."

"We qualify. Uh, don't look now, but Popeye is jigging our way."

Ester's eyes followed my head nod and she yelled, "Hey, Jacky, show 'em your twin screws!"

Jacky smiled, turned, dropped his pants and gyrated the twin propellers tattooed on his bony butt.

"I'm thinking we'll like it here," I breathed. "Do you allow dogs?"

"They're mandatory."

* * *

RJ looked mighty nautical in his new red, white, and blue doggy life jacket and rum-keg collar. I had tried a black patch over one eye, but he kept shaking it off. When we were introduced to Frank, the owner of the boat I was to crew on for the evening's beer can races, he scratched RJ's ears and fondled the rum keg. "Welcome aboard, mates. Can this pooch handle a winch? It looks a might blustery out there, and we'll need all paws at the ready."

"I can leave him in the car if you want me to. If you think he might get in the way." After the Dilly thing, I was all too willing to please.

"Naw. I have a nice bunk that'll fit this salt just fine if he gets bored with the race. Although it should be exciting with a breeze like the one we've got tonight. I'm surprised they haven't canceled. Now, what position do you feel comfortable handling?"

Remembering attack winches, flailing booms, billowing sails that threatened to put one over the side, and heaving decks, I said, "Bartender?"

* * *

"Wasn't that a blast? My boat won!" a breathless, pink-cheeked Jan asked when we met at the yacht club bar after the race.

"Jan, *my* boat T-boned another one and we were disqualified." My cheeks were red, too. With mortification.

"Oh, dear me. How did it happen?"

"Don't ask."

"Cheer up, sailor, there's men about," she whispered, nodding down the bar. "Oh, look, there's Lars and Bob. The ones we met in Berkeley? Remember? You gave Lars my card and he called me. We never did get together for lunch."

"Who? Oh, them. What? No girl children with them?"

"Be nice. And no, they seem to be alone. They see us. Smile."

Lars beckoned us to the other end of the bar where the slap of leather cups on mahogany announced a round of Liar's Dice. More interested in Jan than dice, Lars bowed out, leaving his brother, Bob, and eight others to the game.

"So, did you two enjoy the race?" Lars asked. Tall and portly, dressed in a white anorak and white pants, he resembled a friendly, handsome, polar bear.

"I did," Jan breathed. "Hetta's boat porterhoused another."

"T-Boned," Bob interjected, taking his eyes from his dice long enough to glare at me. "And it was my boat. Wasn't that you driving? You and the hairy guy with the red, white and blue jacket?"

"Uh, yes. We've got to quit meeting this way."

Bob continued to look at me for a few seconds while my cheeks flamed redder. A hint of a grin passed his lips before he turned back to his game.

Lars shrugged. "My brother hates getting hit. Let's go get a table."

I glared at the back of Bob's graying, blonde head and his leather bomber jacket. I had noticed, when he'd turned to glower at me, a patch over his heart that read, Robert "Jenks" Jenkins, USN Ret.

"You two go ahead," I said, signaling Paul for a split of courage. I sipped stars while studying my prey.

Now, don't get me wrong, I know I'm no great beauty, but I have been known to attract a man or two in my day. And I certainly wasn't used to being snubbed by them. The challenge was set.

Painting a sincere look onto my face I sidled up to Robert "Jenks" Jenkins, United States Navy, Ret. "I'm really sorry about hitting your boat. I couldn't see because of all those sails."

Bob nodded, looking straight ahead, not at me. "Ten fives," he said. He was called up by his neighbor and threw out a die with a snort of disgust.

I tried again. "Jan and I recently joined the club. Don't you find it ironic we should meet again so soon?"

"I guess." Bob pounded the bar with his leather cup and peeked under it at his dice. "Eight sixes."

"Well, it was real nice seeing you again," I said sweetly. "Oh, by the way, does the 'Ret' on your jacket stand for 'ree-tard'?"

"Fifteen fives."

* * *

Due to the late hour, we decided it was better for Jan to spend the night on my side of the Bay rather than drive home in RJ's VW, or brave BART and then a city bus. Like many city dwellers, Jan did not own a car.

"What do you think of Lars?" she asked as we drove into the hills.

"I think his brother's a prick."

"Lars says Bob's not all that bad. Maybe a little...distant."

"Distant? Mount Kilimanjaro's distant. This guy's on Mars. Son of a bitch *invented* aloof. So what's his story? Married? Gay? Child molester?"

"None of the above. No serious significant other, either. And Lars just broke up with someone. They invited us to go sailing one day."

"They? Us?"

"Lars figures he could drag Bob along."

"Oh, he does, does he? What am I, a charity case? I think not. I'd rather go out with Dilly."

"I've already arranged it. Dilly's delighted."

12

My doggy desperado's hearing, for which many neighbors, including a few Oakland Raiders, Warriors, and A's, turned out in case he needed character references from some of our city's finest athletes, went in our favor. We played the paw card.

Craigosaurus, veterinary witness *extraordinaire*, testified that RJ, now on Prozac and painkillers due to his debilitating and terminal illness, was neither a future threat to the United States Government nor society in general. In fact, he said, were the alleged pup, er, *perp*, to again escape house arrest, his medical condition and medication would render him incapable of terrorist activities. Like Jeepjacking.

The accused fixed the judge with a dewy-eyed look, raised his paw and licked the large knot on his foreleg. The only dry eyes in the joint belonged to the alleged victim. His were mean and beady.

Mr. Fujitsu, my neighbor and other star witness, said his hedge was undamaged, and at any rate, he liked my dog better than he did the postman, a Korean whom he suspected had a prejudice against those of Japanese heritage. Not that anyone except me and his wife, Mariko, could understand a word Mr. F. said. Despite years in California and an extensive English vocabulary, his accent was atrocious. He was getting up a fair head of steam when the judge got a word in edgewise and politely, but firmly, cut Fujitsu-san's tirade short.

We were let off with a severe warning and fined two hundred dollars, the cost of fixing a cracked headlight on the Jeep. I was to regain mail service the next day even though as we left the room, Mr. Kim—obviously a sore loser—shook his fist and shouted some very nasty things at us. I think.

As it happened, RJ's triumphant romp through the halls of justice coincided with our Fifth Annual Raymond Johnson Coffey Adoption Bash and Weenie Roast. Friends, neighbors, and their pets attended the yearly fete. Cats were excluded due to RJ's propensity to eat them.

The do, as most "dos" do, had its origins as a small gathering of friends to celebrate RJ's good sense in adopting me. He must have known I needed a friend.

Not long before RJ made this wise decision, Japan Airlines had dumped me onto the tarmac at SFO in a psychological body bag. Two years in Tokyo as a resident project engineer had taken their toll. The disastrous Hudson affair, coupled with an unusually heavy work and party load—

seven days a week, twelve hours a day at work, and drinking four of the other twelve—sent me to the brink of a breakdown. The final blow was delivered by a back stabbing, corporate climbing, home office desk jockey who managed to become my boss. The work problem devolved into an ego murdering *coup de grâce* that sapped any remaining vitality I had left. I was plumb burnt out. And had developed an unreasonable hatred of soy sauce.

Already at an all time low-water mark, I returned to the United States to find my house trashed. The renters had fried every appliance, including the hot tub pump and heater. They'd left the place so filthy I had to live with Jan for three weeks while I cleaned two years of scum, grease and, in the master bathroom, some very strange gunk better left unidentified. I ripped out the carpets. Painted inside and out. Fumigated. Mr. Clean and I became intimate. Then, and only then, did I call the movers to deliver my furniture.

I knew I'd feel better when I was back in my home, surrounded by my own stuff. What I didn't know was the renters had also failed to notify my rental *mis*management firm of a nasty roof leak. All of this led to what I call—organ fugue here, please—The Day of the Rat!

It was raining buckets as the movers carted in a vanload of both stored and shipped-from-Tokyo belongings. Water poured through my kitchen roof into hastily purchased galvanized tubs. Although the moving guys had covered my new carpet with butcher paper, I suspected tracked-in mud was leaking through. My spirits were soggier than the weather.

After seeing the indoor waterfall, the moving company boys mumbled something about their minimum wage salaries not covering electrocution. They hastily dumped crates and boxes all over the place and skedaddled. Even if they had been willing to risk death by roof leak, my now ex-employer, a multigazillion dollar corporation, was too cheap to pay for unpacking. Especially since, shortly after reentering the United States, I found myself exiting their badly decorated offices under a cloud of suspicion.

In between bailing out my kitchen and mopping mud, I had managed to find a set of dry sheets and a pillow, but my bed was still chunks of brass scattered hither and thither. Way too tired to contemplate its reassembly, I planned to crash on the couch.

"Tomorrow will be brighter. This too shall pass. Every cloud and all that crap." I chanted. The clichés and mantras were to prevent me from standing under the cascade in the kitchen and sticking my finger in a socket.

Right before dark I found candles, a wine glass, and a bottle of Pouilly-Fumé, the perfect complement for my box of *poulet frit à la Colonel Sanders*. Extra Crispy only hours ago, but no longer so. I finished off the last doughy drumstick and called Jan.

"Man the pumps," I wailed, "I'm sinking."

"Everyone's sinking. The worst Pacific Storm in decades, they say. It quit raining here. How're things over there?"

"I'm looking for my snorkel and fins." I told her about the roof leak. "My TV's not hooked up yet. What's the forecast?"

"No more rain tonight. Probably no more, period, until the next—" My scream cut her off.

"What is it, Hetta? What happened?"

"Rat!"

"Mouse?"

"No, Jan, R-A-T! And he's looking at me. He's fuckin' huge."

"Calm down, Hetta. Where is he?"

"Between me and the front door."

"Throw something at him."

I looked around for something to launch, then thought better of it. "Jan, if I scare him and he hides there's no way in hell I can sleep here tonight. I want to know exactly where he is. I want him . . . hang on."

Behind the couch was a storage box labeled, "Family stuff." I reached over and ripped off the tape, making a noise which sounded to me like an oncoming freight train. But the rodent did not budge. I removed several handfuls of plastic peanuts, rummaged through more,, and pulled an antique wooden box into my lap. Slipping the latch on the case, I removed my .38 caliber Smith and Wesson revolver from her—in my family, guns are "her"—padded felt bed.

The police special's cartridge belt and holster were also coiled in the box, smelling, even after two years in storage, of saddle soap and gun oil. I opened the loading gate on the .38, slid six bullets into the cartridge holder, and eased the cylinder shut. Pushing off the safety, I whispered a little prayer that two years in storage didn't cause the gun to detonate in my hand. Shakily, I stood up, took a straight-armed, two-handed aim, and slowly pulled the trigger.

The rat's head disappeared in a halo of red, as did a large chunk of plaster in the wall behind him. And my new paint job. My ears rang, but I could hear Jan screaming into the phone. I picked up the receiver.

"I got the dirty rat bastard," I said, pleased I hadn't lost my touch. All those years of murdering beer bottles on fence posts had finally paid off.

"You shot him? Hetta, you shot a rat inside your house? Are you insane? Haven't you ever heard of rat poison? You can't shoot things anymore. There are laws. I'm sure of it."

"Oh, fooey. For crying out loud, I have a right to...oops, I do believe sirens approacheth."

* * *

The police were less than pleased, even though I had registered the gun several years before and my carry permit was still up to date. They gave me a warning about discharging a weapon within the city limits, to which I said, "You have *got* to be kidding me. We're talking *Oakland* here." They didn't find me at all humorous and called Animal Control to pick up the rat carcass. Had to be checked out for rabies, they said.

"Biggest friggin' wharf rat I've ever seen," said the Animal Control officer as he bagged the rodent's remains. "Must 'a hitched a ride in one of them Jap cargo crates."

I was cleaning up rodent blood when one of Oakland's finest said, "Nice head shot, ma'am. You know, though, what with you living alone and all, you might consider getting a dog."

So I did. Or rather, he got me.

And today marked the Fifth Annual Raymond Johnson Coffey Adoption Bash and Weenie Roast. Most likely our last.

Mr. Fujitsu's hairless Chihuahua, Pancho-san, took the "Homely Hound" award, as always. His prize, a scoop of liver and cheese ice cream from Doggie Delights in the People's Republic of Berkeley, almost cost Bunnie Adams's sweet, but dumb as dirt golden retriever her "Best Behaved" trophy when she tried to nose in on Pancho-san's treat. At the last minute Miss Goldie Manners remembered hers and backed off, but RJ streaked in for the steal. Pandemonium was narrowly avoided when Dr. Craig launched a scattershot of minty biscuits.

Mr. Fujitsu and Dr. Craig's sig other, Raoul, discovered a common interest when they spotted my ancient Japanese *tansu* chests. Raoul, an antiques dealer who in a former life was a farm boy from Marfa, Texas, speculated perhaps my underwear resided in Mr. F's Samurai ancestors' furniture. It wasn't an interest in my underwear they had in common, though, but rather a passion for things Japanese.

They inspected the *shoji* blinds in the dining room, checked the quality of the rice paper, and made some suggestions for repairing those doggy nose holes with paper butterflies. Then Mr. Fujitsu zeroed in, you should excuse the expression, on my Pachinko machine, a cross between pinball and slots.

Lights flashed, bells rang, and curses and whoops filled my office as the elderly man showed off skills indicating a misspent youth in Tokyo's Pachinko parlors. He emptied the machine of tokens in record time. As I was reloading, the key hanging from my neck swung forward and clinked against Mr. F.'s glasses. He was squatting on his haunches, giving me instructions at the time, and almost tumbled onto his butt. Pushing himself up, he grabbed the key, taking little consideration that it was still attached by a chain around my neck.

Inspecting the only physical evidence I had left to prove Hudson Williams, the jilting scoundrel, ever existed, Mr. Fujitsu sucked his teeth. "You big drink," he said with a grin.

"Pardon?"

"Whiz key?"

I was at a total loss. After living in Tokyo and working with an all Japanese staff for two years, I thought I could figure anything out, but Mr. Fujitsu could still throw me on occasion. This was one of them. We looked to his wife, Mariko, for help. She fingered the key, trying to read the inscription.

"Ah. Loyal Clown," she explained. Her husband nodded and smiled in agreement.

"Loyal Clown?" I asked.

"*Hai*. Clown whiz key."

Call me stupid, but I didn't get it. It must have been obvious, for Mariko took me by the hand and led me to the bar. She rummaged among the bottles and came up with a purple bag. "Whiz key."

"Crown Royal, Hetta," Jan said impatiently. "And I thought you were a linguist."

"Mariko, are you saying this key is a bar key?"

"*Hai*, Hetta-san," she said. I took off the key, and she squinted closely at the tiny Kanji lettering. "Key Noturu Crub, Loppongi."

The Key Note Club in Tokyo's Roppongi section. One of the few jazz bars I'd missed. But Hudson, it seemed, had kept a bottle of Crown Royal there. In most key clubs in Tokyo you bought a bottle of overpriced liquor, they gave it a number, and you received a card identifying you as the owner. When you returned, they'd give you a bucket of ice, your mixer and the bottle. As long as there was liquor in the bottle, you only paid for set ups. Evidently, the Key Note Club gave out an actual, engraved, key. At last, I knew what the key was for.

13

"Get rid of it, Hetta," Jan said later that day as we drove to her flat in the city after the adoption/birthday bash ended in a brawl. Even some of the dogs got involved.

"What?"

"You know what. The damned key. As long as you hang on to it, you won't be able to get over what happened."

"I am over it. I keep the key to remind me not to be so stupid again. Ever."

She shrugged. "Could have happened to anyone. Hudson Williams had all the credentials. Good job, good education, great promise. Good looking, too, from the sounds of it. You never showed me any pictures. Think about it, girl, you were screened up one side and down the other before you were allowed to work in Japan. As an American working there, so was he. Even his company's president said Hudson hoodwinked them, too."

"True. You'd think the SOB would have been satisfied stealing Comptec blind. But nooooo, he had to clean out my bank account, as well. How could I have been so damned dumb? I'd only known him six months, and he had PIN. Duh! Thank heavens I didn't keep a big yen account. I should have a tee shirt printed up that reads, 'Hudson Williams took a powder out of Tokyo, and all he left me was this damned key.' "

But the Fujitsu's new information about the key set me to thinking. Did I still know anyone in Tokyo who could check out the Key Note Club for me? Probably not. At least, no *Gaijin*.

I soon found after moving to Tokyo that *Gaijin* did not mean *foreigner,* but really means Not Japanese. The Not Japanese distinction lumped all foreigners into the Barbarian category. The Japanese engineers I'd worked with probably wouldn't, or couldn't, bluff their way past the tight security of these key clubs. I needed a sneaky *Gaijin*, but my fellow Barbarian friends, perfect for the job, were probably all gone by now. They were, after all, getting a little long in the tooth to still hold down their jobs as high-class hookers.

Hookers?

Well, maybe not officially. Officially they were *hostesses.* Dad's generation would have called them B-girls: bar girls. These gals were all stunningly beautiful, mostly foreign, and were paid barely enough by their Japanese employers to afford rent on very small apartments and keep themselves in sequined gowns.

Monday through Friday the hostesses worked at ritzy nightclubs, hired to entertain Japanese businessmen and their clients. Mix their drinks, smile a lot, and carry on polite conversations in English. Sort of Berlitz meets burlesque on the company tab. Whether the after hours goings-on went on the company's very liberal expense reports or not, I never really found out, but the going rate for such high-toned harlotry was a grand. A thousand big ones, U.S. dollars, per night. I was definitely in the wrong bidness. But then again, I am neither tall, blonde, nor willing to suffer the attentions of short drunken men, so I guess I'd better stick to engineering if the rent is to be paid.

Anyhow, after the Hudson calamity, I found myself stuck in Tokyo without any non-business related acquaintances. It was to that end that one Saturday night I wandered back into the bar where I had met the jilting bastard: Red's Revenge, Home of the Fightin' Roo. The gin joint was, as I knew it would be, frequented mostly by foreigners who liked to get together, drink, and bitch about their host country. My kind of place.

Red, a diminutive, feisty, titian-haired Aussie, ran a great bar and a tight ship. She was also an ex B-girl who had made some good—read, Japanese mafia—connections and ended up with a successful bar. Her place was a gathering spot on Saturday and Sunday nights for foreign hostesses whose Japanese clients went home to wife and family for the weekend.

My newfound friends, including Aussie Red, ended up spending most Sundays at my apartment. The Baxter Brothers Corporation had generously set me up in an American-sized two bedroom apartment capable of housing at least six Japanese families. Not only did I have lots of space, I had cable TV. In English.

After drinking ourselves silly at Red's on Saturday nights, we'd end up eating a Korean Barbecue breakfast at four or five in the morning. Reeking of *kimchi*, we staggered back to my place. Sunday mornings found a litter of somewhat bedraggled beauties sleeping all over my apartment. The day was spent cooking, watching movies, and educating Hetta as to the subtleties of soliciting mink coats and the like from ever horny Japanese men. I never had the opportunity to put my lessons to work, but by golly if I ever need a mink, I know how to get one. "The same way minks do," vamped a stunning blonde from Washington, DC. I heard she later entered politics, working as a PR officer for Bill Clinton.

But those Tokyo beauties were long gone by now, replaced by a new set of younger women willing to make special dates after working hours for a thousand bucks a pop.

So, who could I ...? Jan's voice interrupted my thoughts. "Hetta, you missed our turnoff. Are you all right?"

I shook off my musing and turned at the next block. "Sorry, I was thinking about the key and what could be in the Tokyo hooch box besides Clown Loyal. Maybe Hudson left something there I could sell. The jerk still owes me fifteen-hundred bucks."

Jan shook her head and glared at me. "Now you listen to me. There's nothing in the box. All that's yen under the bridge. End of story. Forget the whole thing. Throw the key in the garbage, and get on with your life. And cheer up. How are we supposed to terrorize a street fair in our usual style today if you aren't your usual self?"

"And which usual self would that be?" I grumped. "Pushy? Demented? Terminally manless? Jobless? Bordering on dogless?"

Jan wisely did not answer, leaving me to contemplate losing RJ. His birthday/adoption party had painfully reminded me of the day he got me.

The day after the day of the rat.

* * *

The Oakland dog pound was noisy, smelly and heartbreaking, but I knew that's where I'd find my dream doggy.

She would be small, but not too fancy. Mannerly, of course, perhaps even well-bred, but also fiercely protective. Cute. Cuddly. Maybe she'd look like Benji. She'd be smart, like Lassie. But smaller, without all that hair.

Escorted by a gentle, weary Hispanic volunteer in his seventies, I walked past cage after cage of barking, howling, cringing, or jumping canines of every make and color. I stuck my fingers through the wire to pet those that would let me. My heart hurt for each one. I wanted to take them all home, protect them from the cruel world that put them behind bars for the crime of being born.

My escort, Juan, pulled on my elbow, guiding me away from one cell and the low, menacing growl from deep within. "Stay away from him, *señorita*," he warned. "Don't put your fingers in there."

I heard the dog rumble again, but as I hurried to get past, something held me back. Doggy ESP?

"What's wrong with him?" I asked, keeping my distance as told.

"He don' like people, so they gonna put him down tomorrow."

"Really?" I stepped closer to the cage.

"Careful now, he's...." But I didn't hear the rest. Soulful black-rimmed dog eyes locked me in a visual embrace, then pulled me forward towards the forbidden cage. A foot away, I stopped.

"Hi, baby," I said.

Hesitant tail wag.

"Come over here," I cooed, sticking my finger through the cage. I ignored the attendant's fearful intake of air and continued talking in soft tones to the dog. "I won't hurt you, honey, I promise." I squatted down to the dog's level and focused my gaze right above his head so I wasn't looking him in the eye.

Tentative steps forward on four stiff legs brought him within biting distance of my finger.

"You wanta go bye-bye with—" I didn't get the "me" out before the dog charged the wire in what can only be called an ecstasy of wiggles, wags, and grins. He whined his plea, "Get me out of here, and I'll follow you to the ends of the earth."

I scratched his ears through the wire and said, "Wrap him up, Señor Juan, I'm takin' him home."

Juan shook his head and shrugged. "Your funeral."

"And Juan, you're wrong. He likes people, he just don' like men."

But I was wrong. My dog was a racist.

14

"RJ's losing weight, isn't he?" Jan asked after we arrived at her apartment with only one more wrong turn. The birthday bash, plus Mr. Fujitsu's revelation about the key, had left me unable to concentrate on driving, but we finally got to Jan's place.

We both looked at my dog. He was still wearing his red velvet bow tie and was lounging in the bay window of Jan's Victorian flat, his red coat glistening in the late afternoon sun. He was alertly watching passersby on the street below. Someone who didn't know better would see a happy, healthy dog. Only his swollen leg and slightly protruding ribs told the real story.

I nodded. "Two pounds in the last three weeks, even though we've upped his Ben and

Jerry's allotment. He eats well, though, and doesn't seem to be in much pain. Craigosaurus keeps a close eye on him."

"What was that about you being jobless?" she asked, referring back to what I'd said in the car while we were crossing the bridge.

"Oh, nothing. Feeling sorry for myself. My Seattle gig only has nine or so months to go, and you know how I am. If I don't have something new lined up, I start getting antsy. My malaise will pass. As soon as I get a new project, marry a handyman to save my decaying home, and a dog angel descends to heal RJ. Oh, and porkers go airborne."

Jan wasn't buying my "poor me" act.

"Hetta, get off my bed and comb your hair. We're hitting the street fair. Move it!"

I went to check myself in the mirror while Jan straightened her comforter.

"And when," I demanded, "did *that* happen?"

"What?" she asked in mid pillow fluff.

"When did we get neat? Tidy? My dorm room resembled a garbage dump. Your first apartment was practically condemned by the Department of Sanitation. We both had cockroaches with NASCAR numbers on 'em," I raved. "When did we start *cleaning?*"

"What in the world are you talking about?" Jan looked as though she were alone with Norman Bates. She moved between me and the kitchen cutlery.

I sat down next to RJ and buried my head in his fur.

"Hetta?"

"Sorry, Jan. It's just, well, the other day, when we were in the Coast Guard class, I suddenly wondered when I started finding men with gray hair attractive. At what point did I begin to clean house and pay bills on time? I even voted Republican, for pity's sake!"

Jan planted her hands on her hips and smiled. "Midlife crisis. Buy a red convertible."

"I have a red convertible."

"Then buy something else. Let's go to the fair and shop."

"Good thinking."

We cruised Union Street, trying on earrings and embroidered vests, grazing on Polish sausages, pizza, gelato, and Belgian waffles, ending up in our favorite bar, Perry's. Using RJ as a shill, we conned two tourists out of their choice table so we could keep an eye on him through an open window, and tied him to a parking meter six feet away. His chagrin at not being allowed inside was soon soothed by strangers' ear scratches and coos of "cute dog."

"Isn't that your dog?" a cop asked me, pointing at RJ.

"Uh, maybe. What's wrong, officer, his meter run out?" I quipped. Jan's face lit with approval and the cop burst out laughing.

"No, I was wondering if I'd have to arrest him again this year."

Uh-oh. "Ah," I said. "Officer Jones, I presume."

"The one."

"Entrapment, sir, pure and simple. I should like to point out that you *did* leave your car windows down, and cookies on the seat, thereby enticing my mutt into a life of crime. He's a minor, you know. You will notice, however, the alleged criminal is fettered this year to protect him from your obvious ploy to entrap."

"Tell it to the judge. What's wrong with his leg?"

"Bone cancer."

"No shit? Damn." He scratched RJ's ears and fondled the baggage tag, a miniature American Express Card, hanging on my dog's neck. "Maybe he can buy me a hot dog later. Then, if he wants to get in my car again, it's all right. Long as he doesn't fart."

Jan and I giggled, then, as the cop left, she grabbed my arm and pointed down the street. "Gee, Hetta, look who's coming."

Lars and his brother, Robert "Jenks" Jenkins—USN Ret—were sauntering down the street towards us.

"Oh, great," I growled. "Can't we act like we don't see them?"

Jan looked guilty.

"Fess up. You invited them, didn't you? You told them we'd be here," I accused.

"Busted. Guilty as charged. I like Lars. As a matter of fact, I'm going out to dinner with him next week."

"Goody gumballs for you. I'm in no mood for that Bob. He hates me."

"Hate is a strong word, Hetta. Lars says it's more like, uh …" She stopped, wishing back her words. But it was too late.

"Like what?" I pounced. "What did that Bob person say about me?"

Jan looked uncertain. "You know, calling him 'that Bob person' is very hostile."

"Okay, okay. Tell me what *Bob* said. I promise not to have my feelings hurt. What'd he say?"

She sighed. "Just that you were flighty."

"Flighty?" I barked. "Flighty?" I repeated, not believing my ears. "I have been called unbalanced, bossy, loud, overbearing, driven, caustic, funny, chubby, short, and an old maid, but never flighty. What does that mean? And where does he get off making judgments about me? We only met twice. Okay, so one of those times I hit his boat and called him a retard. Flighty," I scoffed, took a large gulp of wine, and glared at the approaching men.

"Oh, Lord, what have I done? Please, please, Hetta, don't say anything. I really like Lars and if he knows I told you what he said, he might....Oh, hi there, Lars, Jenks."

"Got room for us?" Lars asked, leaning through the window.

Jan looked nervously in my direction.

Taking another swig of wine I nodded. "Sure. Welcome to my nest." Jan widened her eyes in warning. I shrugged and said, "What?"

Lars and that brother of his went through the front entrance, then worked their way through the standing room only crowd to our table.

And I *was* good. I minded my P's and Q's, listening to the brothers tell sailing tales and stories of their childhood in Brooklyn. I didn't even call them Yankees.

They worked together, designing and installing security and fire protection systems. Neither, it seemed, maintained a real office. Or worked very hard.

Somehow, it was closing time and RJ, Jan, Bob and I packed ourselves into Lars's Porsche and headed across the Bay Bridge. Why, I do not know; my car was parked in front of Jan's apartment. Perhaps I thought I was too drunk to drive. Maybe Lars figured the only way to get rid of me, thereby getting Jan alone, was to take me home. Whatever, I was far too wasted to notice Lars was drunker than any of us.

Jenks sat in the passenger seat, Jan gingerly straddled the gearshift console, and RJ and I were crammed into a tiny space behind the seat.

"Nice car," I said.

It was a mistake.

"Yeah, she's a beauty. Want to see what she can do?" Lars slurred.

Suddenly sober, I yelled, "Noooo!"

But it was too late.

Lars downshifted.

Jan giggled.

Lars hit the accelerator.

15

At a little after three in the morning—an hour and several lifetimes after I had, in a moment of unbridled moronity, jumped into a Porsche with a lunatic—I was back home.

I paid the cab driver the fortune he'd demanded to allow RJ into his crappy old heap, unlocked my front door, turned off the security alarm, checked the mirror to see if my hair had turned white, and gratefully sank onto the couch.

Had I the strength, I would have kissed the tile in my foyer.

My eyes burned from worn off booze, fatigue, and no small amount of residual anger. I forced my eyelids closed, hoping for relief, but instead got an instant replay of my rocky ride into Hell. And that was *before* I got into the taxi.

When Lars floored that Porsche, we rocketed into a guardrail and continued scraping alongside for a least a quarter of a mile. Metal tortured metal, sparking a meteor trail in our wake. When we at long last bounced off the rail, the car began a hair-raising, reverse loop waltz.

A series of explosions—blowouts—were instantly followed by even more sparks as tire rims sliced through shredded rubber, then struck the pavement. Our pyrotechnic spectacular, well worthy of a Frances Scott Key composition, thankfully brought traffic to a halt. I say thankfully, for when we ultimately skidded to a stop, we were nose to nose with the grinning grill of a humongous eighteen wheeler. The truck's driver was not amused.

There was a moment of eerie silence before horns began blaring, headlights flashed, and the truck driver threw open his cab door and climbed out carrying what looked suspiciously like an automatic weapon.

"Lars," Jan screeched, "*do* something!"

So what does her lard assed Lothario do? He jams the accelerator to the floorboard, spins the car one-eighty and takes us on a four rim, sixty mile per hour bronco ride across the bridge. I know I smelled brimstone.

Now safely back in my living room, I opened my scorched eyes and shook my head to clear the lingering screeches—metal, mine, and Jan's. I wondered if she was all right. When RJ and I bailed at the toll plaza to flag down a cab, she chose to remain with that maniac Lars and his machine of doom. I reasoned that because Lars was insane didn't mean he was a serial killer. Just your everyday psycho with a death wish. And as for that brother of his! I was building up a good head of steam, moving from very pissed off to furious, when RJ's frantic barks sat me bolt upright.

"What is it, boy?" I asked. His nose was glued to a closed door leading from the living room to a downstairs bedroom, bath, laundry room, and garage that were his quarters when I was gone.

Behind the door lay a set of stairs leading down to what had, at one time in my house's life, been a mother-in-law set up. Because my home was built on a slope, the basement level bedroom window, with its lockable dog door flap, was directly under the hot tub. When we were both away from the house, RJ's private passageway to his outdoor pen remained locked, as did the door into the main part of the house. The very door my dog was now threatening to eat.

Although badly frightened by the frantic snarls and yelps, I forced myself to the door and sighed with relief when I saw the deadbolt engaged. The downstairs area was sealed off. We were safe as long as that door was secure. But RJ was still raising holy hell, and I trusted his instincts. Then, in a heart stopping moment, it dawned on me that I had forgotten to reset the alarm before collapsing on the couch ten minutes earlier.

Cold dropped into my stomach faster than thermometer mercury at the onset of a Texas blue norther. My arms went numb, as did my feet. If I didn't move fast, I'd probably faint. I made it to the closet housing the alarm system panel in ten molasses-slow steps. Every window and door in the house was wired and each of the three zones had its own bank of lights. Since the system was off, they were all yellow. Nothing obvious was amiss. I was beginning to think that RJ's night had caught up with him, right up to the second I punched in the code to reset the system. ZONE ONE—downstairs—blinked a furious red. Something, either a window or door down there, was open.

A quick look at the diagram told me it was the dog door. And since I couldn't have set the system before leaving the house if any door or window was ajar, someone must have opened it in the last few minutes. My shaking finger hit the PANIC button as I cursed the day I had agreed to a thirty second delay to avoid false alarms.

Even though I knew the alarm on the roof would go off and wake the entire neighborhood in a few seconds, I ran to the kitchen and dialed 911. Not waiting for an answer, because I knew the police would trace the call, I left the phone off the hook, ran back to the foyer closet where the alarm panel was housed, and grabbed the only thing my great grandmother Stockman had left me.

No, not a family Bible. Nor a quilt. Certainly no blue chip stock certificates or the deed to downtown Austin. Nope. Grandmaw Stockman, ever practical, bequeathed me her most precious possession, her shotgun. Said with a smart mouth like mine I'd probably need it.

I hauled RJ into the closet with me just as the roof horn, all jillion decibels of it, shattered the early morning calm. I could picture lights blinking on all over the neighborhood, and many Winchesters, Smith and Wessons, Remingtons, and their automatic cousins coming out of their closets. The rising price of ammo was a major concern in my community.

Although I could barely hear anything above the siren's din, I felt RJ's low rumble—the one reserved for garbage men, postal employees and cops—and figured the police had arrived. I *hoped* the police had arrived.

Flipping off the wailing horn, I recognized the unmistakable growl of souped-up patrol car engines. With salvation at hand, I grabbed RJ by the collar, left the closet, opened the front door, and stepped out under the porch light. Several million candlepower worth of spotlights blinded us. James Cagney in *The Public Enemy* came to mind. I wanted my mommy.

"Freeze and drop your weapon!" a voice bellowed from the dark. RJ went bonkers, and it was all I could do to hold him. In my fatigue and fright, I had forgotten I was packing a shotgun.

With a howling hound in one hand and a double-barreled over and under in the other, I probably looked, to the OPD, like a redneck survivalist.

"It's not loaded, officer," I wheedled. "Almost not loaded. I'm afraid to throw it down. It might go off. What do you want me to do?"

"Put on the safety, sit on the ground, then lay the gun down and scoot away from it. And hold on to that dog."

Easier said than done, but somehow I managed with only minor skin loss. Once the gun was out of reach, I was allowed to stand. Sort of. They told me to put my hands on my head, but if I did, I would have to let go of RJ. We had a momentary standoff until a neighbor intervened.

"It's okay, officer," I heard my neighbor, Bunnie Adams, yell, "she's the homeowner."

A baby-faced cop, gun at the ready, advanced cautiously into the blaze of light. Picking up the shotgun, he handed it off to his partner, who broke open the breech. Homemade shotgun shells fell onto the ground.

"Not loaded, huh?" the cop said.

"Only rock salt and bacon rind."

"No shit? Jesus, lady, where did you get the crazy idea to load your shotgun shells with stuff like that?"

"My great grandmother."

* * *

"I think I might have found your problem," a cop hollered from downstairs. There were now six of them and three patrol cars. I was in the living room being grilled by the boy cop, who seemed pissed because he couldn't find anything to charge me or my dog with. He waved his hand in disgusted dismissal, indicating I could go down and see what his crony had found.

RJ, who had lost interest in barking and menacing men in blue, docilely followed me down the stairs to where a grinning officer stood in three inches of water.

"Looks like you need the water police," he quipped. All the cops in the city and I gotta get one who thinks he's Jerry Seinfeld, only black. He pointed to a busted pipe. Water shot up onto the wiring around a door. "System shorted," was his brilliant verdict.

I turned off the water main and tromped upstairs to call a plumber who lived down the street in a home that rivaled those of the professional athletes on the same block. I could hardly wait to get *his* bill.

Oakland's finest, laughing and shaking their heads, began filing out to their cars. "Hey, you guys, why don't you each take a damned bucket of water?" I called out to what I thought was an empty house. I was startled to hear a reply.

"You want us to mop the floor as well?"

Crap, leftovers. At least that's what I hoped. I followed the voice to find a man in a rumpled suit sitting on my couch, scratching RJ's ears. RJ's obvious approval notwithstanding, I was judging the distance to my shotgun when the man flashed a badge. I relaxed.

"Martinez," he said as an introduction. "I got here a little late. Looks like things are wrapped up, so guess I'll be going. Here's my card if you think you have any more problems."

I took the card, read it, and nodded. "Thanks, Detective Martinez. I guess it was a false alarm. Anyway, that's what your guys think."

"And you don't?"

"I'm not sure. Could be. One thing for sure, I got a mess on my hands. How did I rate a dick?"

Martinez did a double take and grunted. "You have some fairly important neighbors who don't like being woken up in the wee hours."

"Ah, yes. The plumber."

He smirked. "Nope, the NBA. Nearing the playoffs, you know."

"Aha, so all those decibels on my roof *did* wake the dead? Or is it my imagination that Oakland died on the court weeks ago and refuses to lie down?"

His lips twitched. "They do have a big game tomorrow, so let's don't bury them quite yet."

"Such loyalty. Well, you can tell the NBA..." the doorbell rang. "Oh, never mind. With any luck at all, that'll be my plumber. You might stick around and arrest him when he's done. He's sure to commit highway robbery."

16

My bedside alarm clock went off at eight, exactly two hours after Mr. Handy Pipe departed with the following warning: "I've left a sump pump working on that downstairs flooding. Check it after two hours, cuz if the pump runs dry and burns up my motor, I'll have to charge you for a new one." What happened to the good neighbor policy?

I needed sleep, but I needed the three hundred bucks I'd have to pay for a burned out pump more, so I dutifully set my alarm clock.

Stumbling down the stairs, I found that most of the standing water was gone. I turned off the sump, dug out my Shop-Vac, and sucked what I could from the soggy rug. The house alarm people were due later, and I was anxious to hear what they had to say, because I remained unconvinced that moisture alone was the culprit for all the havoc. After all, the police confirmed that the dog door flap was indeed unfastened, and I distinctly remembered securing it after my brunch guests left the day before. Which by now seemed like an eternity ago.

Maybe the alarm company guy would have an explanation. One of the reasons I had them zone the house when they installed the system was so I could leave the downstairs system off when I was gone for more than a few hours. That way, RJ could go in and out of a window fitted with a lockable pet flap, and into dog jail, as I called the fenced area under my hot tub.

When we were both gone, the gate from the backyard into dog jail was padlocked, and the dog flap into RJ's bedroom was fastened shut and was wired into the main alarm system. Unless an intruder smashed out another window, the only way they could get into the main part of the house from downstairs was to jimmy the lock, open and squeeze through RJ's doggie door, go up the stairs, and then break down, or through, a bolted door into the living room. Up until now, I had been enjoying what may have been a false sense of security.

I was positive I had hit the "whole house" setting when Jan and I left. The alarm won't set unless all lights are green. Had the system malfunctioned, or had we a mystery visitor capable of squeezing through the four inch slats of the padlocked dog jail, then opening the pet flap? Raccoon? Maybe, there were a few around.

I had the kennel designated as dog jail specially built for a dog that could easily jump my six-foot yard fence in a single bound. RJ could go outside, into a twenty-by-twenty foot area, and not be cooped up in the house all day. If it was cold or raining, he would retreat to his bedroom inside where he had food, water, and a basket. Most of the third world population would kill for such a set up.

RJ was less grateful. He much preferred to be either in the main house, lounging on my leather furniture, or even better, free to roam and terrorize. But, being the pampered, registered, licensed, and therefore, restricted, American pet he was, my dog had to settle for what the City of Oakland required. So, dog jail it was.

I crawled wearily back into bed and reset my Big Ben for another hour's sleep before the alarm guys showed up. Ten minutes later the phone rang.

"Where are you?" Jan demanded. Aha! She was alive. But not for long, if I had anything to do with it. "I mean, I know *where* you are, Hetta, I want to know *why*. As you may recall, we're taking our first real sail with Women On the Estuary this morning and if you hurry, we can catch some breakfast before we leave."

Shit. I had my own woes, I didn't need WOE. "I can't," I moaned. "My house is under water."

"That's the worst excuse you've ever come up with. It's not raining, and you live on top of a mountain."

"It's a long story, Jan. Go on without me."

"Nope. Get up and get down here. Now!"

"What time are you leaving?"

"We, Hetta. *We* are leaving at ten."

"Oh, what the hell, I'll try. If I'm late, go on ahead. I'll see you at the club later."

I hung up and tried to think of something, anything, positive about the past twenty-four hours. The only thing I could come up with was I'd been too cheap to re-carpet RJ's abode after the renters trashed it.

By the time the alarm guy arrived, RJ's bedroom was all relatively dry, so I loaded up RJ and left Mr. Home Security to work his magic. I arrived at Jack London Yacht Club just in time to see the transom of Frank's boat, *Elegant Lady*, motoring away, Jan at the helm.

"You having brunch?" Paul asked. I wondered when the bartender slept, since it seemed no matter what time of day or night I was at the club, so was he.

I yawned and slipped my sunglasses onto my head. "I might as well, since my ship saileth without me." Just like my life these days.

"Then the mimosas are free."

"In that case, I'm buying," a deep voice said from behind me.

I turned to meet watery gray eyes. Garrison, of *Sea Cock* renown. His longish, steely hair was wind tossed, his clothes yachtish. Tanned boyish features and an easy grin almost masked telltale dissipation. Almost. I *knows* a rascal when I sees one, matey.

"Remember me?" he asked, slipping onto the barstool next to me.

"Yep. Berkeley. Almost didn't recognize you without your boat."

"You're Hetta, right?"

I nodded and sipped my drink. Paul hovered. I declared it the best mimosa I'd ever tasted. He beamed and said he'd give me the recipe.

"Hetta's strange in this day and age," Garrison said.

"Beg your pardon?" How in the hell did he know I was strange? He'd only just met me.

"Is it a family name?" His smile was friendly, his tone conversational. Nothing in his manner bespoke come-on, but I smelled one.

"Oh. Yep, my great grandmother. She left me her shotgun, too."

"I consider myself warned." He laughed. A nice laugh, but a lit-tle practiced. "Are you a new WOEie?"

For a moment I wasn't sure. Was I?

"I guess I am. Sort of. They want you to take two sails before you officially sign up. I have a temporary club card, but unfortunately missed my boat because I had a few problems at home and ran late. Are you a member here, Garrison?"

"Yep," he pointed to a picture of himself, sporting dark brown hair, on the wall above the bar. "I was Commodore a while back. Tell you what. If you'll agree to join me for brunch now and then later for a drink, I'll ferry you out to catch your boatload of women. I can overtake them with one engine tied behind my back."

He wasn't jist awolfin', as we say back home. In a little under two hours, I was being transferred from *Sea Cock* to *Elegant Lady*. There had to be something Freudian there, but I couldn't put my finger on it.

Jan was impressed I'd finally made it and I was impressed that she, unlike me, seemed none the worse for our evening careen across the Bay Bridge with a mad man. I looked up at that very bridge and pictured a Porsche dropping onto us.

"Welcome aboard," Frank said with a smile. We waved good-bye to Garrison as *Sea Cock* belched diesel fumes and roared off.

"Stinkpot," one of the WOEies grumbled.

"Is Garrison that bad?" I asked.

She grinned. "Not Garrison. His boat. *Real* boaters don't need no stinkin' engines. We sailors call powerboats stinkpots. And as for Garrison, he's kinda the club Don Juan, but basically harmless. Let me guess. If he brought you out to catch us, you probably agreed to have a drink with him when we get back to the club?"

"Yep."

Another woman chuckled. "Has he gotten to the cocktail cruise part?"

I barked a laugh. "There was mention."

The women traded knowing looks. There was more information to be garnered here, but I didn't have time to delve, for we were told to ready ourselves. *Elegant Lady* was about to round Treasure Island and enter the "slot."

For years, and from the safety of a waterfront table at our favorite Berkeley grazing ground, Jan and I had stared down the "slot" while brunching. Afforded an unobstructed view straight out the Golden Gate Bridge to the Pacific Ocean, we had especially relished those days when waves pounded against the breakwater below the plate glass windows, rocking the building and salting the windows. We had not known that alleyway of water in front of us even had a name. Now I was told it was called the "slot." Slot, schmot. So what?

"Get ready," Frank warned as the boat left the protection of Treasure Island.

Forewarned is not necessarily forearmed. At least not in my case. *Elegant Lady,* Frank's thirty-eight foot sailboat "manned" by a six-woman, relatively inexperienced crew, cleared the protection of the island and fell over. I later learned the nautical term for what we did, but as far as I was concerned, the damned boat fell over. Quite *in*elegantly. Back at the clubhouse later I was told we almost broached.

Broach: To incline suddenly windward, so as to lay the sails aback and expose the vessel to the danger of oversetting.

Ain't that the truth? I also learned that brunching is far superior to broaching.

When we broached, water poured over the rails and into the cockpit, chilling my feet and soul. Then, when I was certain we were going over, the boat righted slightly and began to lurch—probably not a nautical term, either—from one wave top to another. Lucky for me, my stomach didn't lurch with it. I don't get air, car, or seasick easily, but my fellow sailorettes weren't so fortunate. I made sure I stayed upwind.

I'd seen the Americas Cup on television. Even admired those hardy souls who braved stinging salt spray and bodily injury to compete for the coveted trophy. But it never occurred to me that that was *sailing*. Sailing was sitting in the cockpit sipping martinis, like the boat brochures showed. I planned to sue for broach of promise.

And even though I am an engineer and I know, on an intellectual level, that the keel of a sailboat is weighted with thousands of pounds of lead to keep it from turning turtle, I was absolutely certain we were going to go tits up. I huddled and cursed.

Frank, who seemed to be having a grand old time dodging sea and lady spit, finally noticed I wasn't tossing my cookies like the others and bribed me into reluctant service with the promise of a cold beer.

"Keep the sails full," he said, turning the wheel over to me and going below for beer. Jan was down to dry heaves, but when she saw me take the helm, she found something more in her stomach.

Three beers, four broken nails, one minor head wound, and several boat bites later, I hauled my sleep deprived, salt encrusted body off the boat, said something ungracious, and stomped to the yacht club bar. Garrison, as promised, waited.

"Have a good sail?" he asked.

"Is there such a thing?" I growled.

"Not as far as I'm concerned. Tell you what, why don't I take you for a nice quiet dinner on the estuary later?"

"Thanks, but I've had about all the saltwater I can take for one day. Besides, I've got to take Jan home, then get back to my home because...never mind, it's a long story."

"Where does Jan live?"

"The City."

"Why don't I take you for a nice quiet dinner in the City? We can drop Jan off."

"The logistics and my mood are all wrong for tonight, Garrison. Can I get a rain check?"

"Sure," he said, barely covering his chagrin. "As long as it's for tomorrow evening."

Too tired to protest, I capitulated. Besides, I like a man with persistence.

As I drove Jan home, she caught me up on what happened with Lars and his Porsche after I threw my full-blown, Texas hissy fit and demanded to be let out of the trashed car at the Bay Bridge toll plaza. Jan had refused to leave with me, but insisted they stand by until RJ and I were entrenched in the relative safety of a Yellow Cab. And was Jan at all put off by her late-night ride with Dr. Death? Nope, she was smitten with the lunatic.

"Lars is so much *fun*, Hetta," she gushed. "You know, he drove his poor ole car all the way across Alameda, right into his driveway and he wasn't even upset. I mean, it's a really expensive car and he laughed it off. Most guys would have been beside themselves."

"Most guys have at least a modicum, a tiny *soupçon,* of common sense. Not that Lars isn't common. And that brother! He acted as though we were out for a Sunday stroll in the park. Did he ever say anything at all?"

"Jenks said Lars was nuts and, even though his brother was goaded into doing something so dumb, he'd probably never ride with him again."

"So, at least one of them has some...wait a minute. Goaded?"

"Hetta, you *did* say it was a nice car," Jan said primly.

"Listen to me, Miss Prissy Britches, only a psychopath would construe a compliment for his car as an invitation to commit vehicular suicide. Homicide. Whatever. It was *my* fault a demonic drunk stomped the accelerator on a curve and trashed his car, almost killing us all? There's some kind of genetic defect in that family."

"Jenks didn't exactly say it was *all* your fault. He said to tell you not to egg Lars on."

"Why are we suddenly so buddy-buddy with Bob, and since when are we calling him Jenks?" I demanded, using the royal *we.*

"Jenks is Bob's nickname. You can call him that."

"I don't plan to call him anything. I have absolutely no intention of ever seeing or speaking to Lars, or his brother, old whatchamacallit, again as long as I live. Which, I figure, will be longer the further away I stay from your bilge brothers."

17

I was looking forward to dinner with Garrison, even though it smacked of being a date. I don't date. I hate real dates. I rationalized that since I was driving my own car to his boat, not waiting at home for my escort while nervously primping in the mirror like a teenybopper on prom night, it wasn't a real date. Not that I ever *had* a prom night date. Boys, made apprehensive by my viperous tongue, preferred palling around with me and going steady with others. Even if someone had asked me to the prom, I'm sure I would have hated it.

Throughout singledom, anything resembling a date had seldom worked out. Actually, never worked out. Date hate was deeply ingrained in me, but I figured a quiet little dinner for two would be harmless enough, so long as Garrison didn't expect *me* as his just dessert.

Sea Cock rocked gently alongside the yacht club dock, the velvety croon of Sinatra wafting from her deck speakers. I stood alongside—I was quickly picking up nautical speak—looking for the doorbell. Okay, so I'm not *that* quick a study. Anyhow, I heard my name called from above.

"Hetta," Garrison yelled from a yacht club window, "go on aboard. Get a beer or some wine, whatever. I'll be right there." The club was officially closed on Monday nights, but I could hear the slap of Liar's Dice cups through the open window. Every member had a key and the bar was open on a members only, write down your drinks and pay later policy, an honor system which more or less worked. Mostly less.

Settling into a deck chair on the aft cockpit, I watched tourists in Jack London Square watching me. It felt good, sitting there on the back deck of a large yacht, wondering what the poor people of the world were doing this beautiful evening. Then I remembered I was aboard a boat named *Sea Cock* and my smugness dissolved.

Through the open yacht club windows above, I could make out and hear shadowy figures slamming dice cups on the bar. Garrison, the only person I could actually see, waved between rounds to let me know he was almost finished playing.

He was, I thought for the second time in two days, handsome in a yachtie kind of way. Yachtsmen always get enough sun to make them look healthier than your run of the gin mill drunks, whose neon pallor is evidence of too much time spent basking in the glow of beer signs.

Garrison was a libertine, I knew, but it didn't bother me. Knowing what he was gave me one up on him. Through vast experience, I knew exactly what to expect. He didn't know it yet, but I had no intention of becoming another notch in Garrison-poo's transom. I fiddled with Hudson's key hanging around my neck as a reminder, and wondered, for the millionth time, what it would unlock. I had half a mind to jump a plane, spend money I could ill afford, to find out.

A creaking ramp and loud laughs and voices preceded Garrison's arrival at the boat. I turned to greet him and saw Lars and that Bob person trailing behind him. So much for my vow never to lay eyes on the Jenkins brothers ever again.

"Hetta, I think you've met Lars and Jenks," Garrison said.

"Oh, yes indeedy I have. We recently spent a horrible night together," I told him. Garrison looked puzzled, so I guess his best buds hadn't told him of the night of the Porsche. I nodded in greeting and added, "Good evening, gentlemen. You too, Lars."

Garrison, not knowing what else to do, shrugged. "Oh, yeah, right. Anyhow, I know I said we were going to have a quiet dinner, but we were playing dice, and I invited them to join us. You don't mind do you?"

"It depends. Who's driving?" I asked in a waspish tone.

Lars scowled at me under his bushy eyebrows, but Jenks grinned. And in spite of my former resolve to eschew the company of the brothers Jenkins, the evening turned into a pleasant outing. We cruised over to Pier 39, picked up Jan and then voyaged on to Sausalito for dinner.

Garrison, very attentive and charming, monopolized my time. He left the operation of the boat to Jenks so he and Lars could drink and flirt with me and Jan. Only at the dinner table was our little *ménage à cinq* all thrown together. After Jenks finished grousing about the upscale prices, the conversation leaned towards car repairs, the rising cost of car insurance—go figure— and then meandered on to yacht club gossip. While I enjoyed both the gossip and the dinner, most of all I was delighted by the fact that we smoothly crossed San Francisco Bay and I didn't lose a single nail. Or sustain a head injury.

When we docked back at the yacht club, Jenks departed immediately, then Jan and Lars said they were leaving as well, which was my cue to vamoose lest I be left alone with the increasingly amorous Garrison.

Faking an overly dramatic yawn, I asked Jan and Lars to wait up and walk me to my car, as it was dark in the parking lot. And it was Oakland. Then, to be polite, I added, "Unless you're ready to leave now, too, Garrison."

Garrison didn't look pleased, but couldn't figure a way to gracefully turn the situation to his advantage. "I'm not going anywhere, Hetta. I live here."

"Here?"

"On the boat."

"You can *live* on a boat? You don't have a house or anything?"

"Nope. It's home sweet boat for me."

"Wow," was all I could say. All the way home I thought about this revelation. Wow. Living on a boat, full time, on the water. Water that didn't smell like sewage, which is what my house still smelled like when I got home.

The GITROOT folks had removed a blameful tree root from my sewage pipes for a mere six hundred dollars, the plumber returned for his sump pump and finished repairing the house pipes to the tune of five hundred. Because I had left the garage door open all day and run fans to dry out the ground floor, the stench was diminishing. Of course, I would have to repaint and partially drywall and plaster the downstairs bedroom walls, definitely put in new carpet or refinish the wood floor, and—God, would it never end?

RJ charged into the living room as soon as I unbolted the door to downstairs. Being relegated to guard duty for the past few hours, even though it was his job, had put him in a snit. He whined and growled his displeasure, even refusing a chunk of prime rib I pulled from a doggie bag as a peace offering. An all-time first. He was doggone mad, I tell you.

By the time I crawled into my bed, RJ had quit bitching and was snoring softly in his. It worried me a little that he was so tired after an evening of confinement. And that he had turned down prime rib. Maybe he was pouting. I didn't ponder his surliness long, for I was lulled to sleep by the aftereffects of my evening cruise.

The bed gently swayed, as though riding on bay swells, rocking me like I'm sure my mother did so many years ago. It was better than Valium. I slept sounder than I had in years and woke up with a fairly decent outlook on life for the first time in weeks.

18

I woke really refreshed the morning after my uneventful cruise across the bay on *Sea Cock*. I stretched happily, sprang from my bed, and let RJ out through the deck door. While he went to whiz, I made mental notes for what I would accomplish that day as I made my bed, gathered dirty clothes for the hamper, and picked up my rings and bracelet from the bedside table. Walking over to the *tansu* chest, I opened my jewelry box and was stashing my bracelet when I stopped and stared. Palming the bracelet, I was still looking dumbly into the box when the phone rang.

"Hey! It's me. Wasn't that a nice date last night?" Jan asked.

"It wasn't a date."

"Oooh, someone got up on the wrong side of her perpetually empty bed this morning. Now come on, admit it, you had a good time."

"Yeah, okay, so I did. Got me to thinking about a few things. But I gotta ask, Jan, and you're probably going to think I've finally gone over the edge, but did you rearrange my jewelry?"

"Rearrange? Is that your sneaky way of asking if I borrowed something you've misplaced?"

"No. Nothing's missing. And you know I don't care what you borrow or wear. I was wondering if you'd moved things around? Kinda straightened things up or something?"

"Not me. Maybe RJ's taken up cross dressing. He's always been partial to bows and beads, you know."

"Yeah, mayhap he's been hanging out with Raoul's Catamite too much. Oh, hell, I guess I'm having a brain cramp. Another indication that I need to *do* something with my life. Like a major, major, change."

"Let me guess. You're gonna get botoxed."

"Naw, I hate needles worse than I do wrinkles. But I might consider getting detoxed."

"I ain't going to no stinkin' meetings, Miz Hetta."

"Some friend you are. Listen, my house is falling apart, the piece of shit engineer I, uh, relocated in Seattle."

"You mean screwed over, don't you? Depth charged? Sold down the tubes?" Jan interjected. She never lets me slide.

"Okay, yeah, him. His name is Dale, and the bastard's trying to get even with me by sabotaging both me and my project. On top of that, someone is still breathing into my phone, my house has haints, and now my jewelry is rearranging itself. Something's got to give. I'm going to sell the house and buy a boat to live on."

"O-kay, I might consider one lit-tle meeting."

"I'm serious."

"You hate sailing."

"I'm thinking powerboat."

Silence hung heavy on the line, then she sighed. "Hetta, do the words '*major* mid-life crisis' mean anything at all to you?"

* * *

RJ ate his prime rib for breakfast, but still kept giving me nasty looks while I munched a bowl of Total and sliced bananas. I ignored RJ's sulky attitude and leafed through local boating magazines. Scanning yacht brokerage listings, I jotted down a list of desirable features I wanted on my boat. Yacht. Whatever. Unfortunately, not one of the ads listed the interior color scheme. I made a couple of calls. They went something like this, with me just imagining what they were thinking..

"Good morning, Old Tub Yachts."

"Good morning. I see you have a fifty-seven foot Dream Machine for sale."

"Sure do. Give me a minute and I'll pull up the details on her Missus, ah?"

"Ms. Coffey. Hetta."

"My name is Ralph, *Ms.* Coffey, and I appreciate your call." *Shit, I finally get a hit on that garbage scow and it turns out to be a single broad. Single broads never buy anything.* "Let's just see...yep, here she is. *Windsong.* Beautiful boat.

What would you like to know?" *This should be good.*

"What are the colors?"

This is worse than I thought. "White, with blue canvas."

"No, I mean inside. What's the color scheme?"

Is this a joke? I bet some of those guys over at Pristine Marine put her up to this. Well, two can play this game. "Lime green and hot pink."

"What? Do you have anything in peach? Or at least neutrals?"

"Listen, *Ms.* Coffey, you tell those guys over at Pristine to stick it where the sun don't shine."

I hung up, slightly confused but undaunted. I tore pages from magazines, got out a map, and planned my yacht *ne plus ultra.* Hey, not a bad name for a boat: *Perfection.* Using the organizational skills I'd developed during my career, I put together a plan, a search for perfection. The future looked rosier, despite the fact that my dog wouldn't speak to me.

I cheerfully put in a few hours in my office, then decided to give myself a reward in the form of a nice, midafternoon, hot water soak. Dropping clothes as I went, I grabbed a towel and, since I was alone, decided to go in *au naturel.* My deck was not visible from any of the neighbor's houses, and except for the occasional helicopter, I had total privacy. I stepped onto the sun warmed redwood, and holding the towel in one hand, flipped back the tub cover and stepped in. And screamed. The water was ice cold. This house was definitely *histoire*.

* * *

The unseasonably warm weekend was ideal for the Big Boat Hunt.

Armed with a list of questions and boat data, Jan and I began in Alameda, worked our way back to Oakland, then on to Berkeley and Emeryville. The boats I liked were too expensive. The ones I could afford were too small. And badly decorated.

Exhausted from a day of repeatedly removing our Birkenstocks to board yachts, we stopped at Macys, bought deck shoes, then headed home to meet my hot tub repairman.

Jim "Dr. Hot Water" Evans had his own key to the dog jail gate so he could service the pumps and plumbing housed therein. And since we had RJ with us, Jim could get to the equipment without losing any limbs. When we got home, Dr. Hot was on the deck, fiddling with control knobs.

"Hiya, Jim. What's the verdict?"

"Don't know. Can't get in."

"Forget your key?"

"Nope. Fuggin' key don't work."

"Whaddyamean 'fuggin' key don't work'?"

"Don't work." Jim is a man of few words.

I tromped down the redwood steps to the padlocked gate, dug out my own key, and tried the lock. I tried again. Jim was right, fuggin' key don't work. It slid into the keyhole smoothly, but wouldn't turn.

"Did you try WD40?"

"Yep."

I looked a little closer at the Master Lock. Something about it wasn't quite right. It was the same model, same make, but shinier. I hadn't opened the lock in ages, and Jim hadn't been over to service the tub for at least a month. Since then, someone had changed the lock!

I left Jim cussing and hacksawing into hardened steel while I drove to my local Ace Hardware for a new lock. During the short trip, my mind raced, bouncing from one question to another. Who changed that lock? And when? And why? It was time to call the *gendarmes*.

19

"How about them Warriors?" I said when I met Detective Martinez at the door.

He gave me a grimace that passed for a smile. Judging from his gray crew cut, soft middle, and permanently pained expression, Martinez looked to be on the ragged edge of a long career. He thumbed a Tums from a frayed roll and popped it into his mouth. Between chews he mumbled, "Yeah. Amazing what a good night's sleep will do for a guy's game. You been outta town?"

"To paraphrase that other great comedic genius, Fred Flintstone, 'Droll. Ve-ry droll, Detective.' "

We moved to the living room and got down to business. Martinez asked a few questions, took notes and made a comment or two that only slightly indicated he thought I was a total simpleton.

Okay, so it hadn't occurred to me to leave the lock alone until the police had a chance to dust for prints. Who am I? Kinsey Millhone? So now, between Dr. Hot's hacksaw, our communal handling of the lock, and a few licks from RJ, chances were slim for lifting any useful fingerprint evidence. And evidence of what?

"So," I said as Martinez carefully bagged the mangled lock, "is it against the law to change a lock?"

Martinez contemplated my question for a moment before answering. Either that or he was waiting for his antacid to kick in. "Not exactly."

"Then what, exactly?"

"Well, it appears someone did trespass. If we can find that someone, you can press charges. Can't say, though, I ever charged anyone with breaking and locking before." His little joke amused him greatly, but his laugh deteriorated into a hacking cough. I waited while he had his fun and caught his breath.

"Now," he said, clearing his throat and getting back to crime scene concerns, "is there anyone you can think of who might want to do you harm?"

"Gee, can't you cops come up with a new line? That one's been used for decades of movies and TV shows."

"And the answer is?"

I laughed. Gotta get up early to stay ahead of this legal fireball. "I can't think of anyone off hand."

He shrugged. "Just a thought. This is the second time I've been here and I don't believe in coincidence. Looks to me like someone took the time to make sure they could get in and out of your house, so maybe they want to get to you. Can you think of anyone who might fit that bill?"

"Certainly not," I said, crossing my arms across my chest.

Jan, who up until now sat quietly, groaned and rolled her eyes towards Heaven. The cop caught it and stared me down until I admitted, "There might have been a couple of, uh, contretemps."

"Contretemps? Can't say as I've heard that one in awhile. Ever. Tell me about them." Martinez flipped to a new page in his ubiquitous little notebook and waited, pen poised.

"Let's see. I gave Big Dick Reechard's Armani jacket to a wino."

"Does Big Dick have a last name?" Martinez said without a hint of a smile. He wrote down Richard's real name and a phone number supplied by Jan, and then urged me to continue.

I listed people I might *possibly* have pissed off. Besides BDR, there was Dale, the yahoo I had torpedoed on the Seattle project and who was turning out to be a real pain in the ass, and Mr. Kim of the postal Jeepjacking. Then there was Wade, who, although I didn't really consider him an enemy, *was* incarcerated with hundreds of his new best friends at an institute for the criminally insane.

"Medical facility," Martinez said.

"Huh?"

"Not called institutes for the criminally insane anymore. They're State Medical Facilities. PC."

"I like loony bin, myself," I countered. I hate PC.

Martinez almost smiled. He wrote something on his pad, then looked up. "Anyone else?"

"Nope."

Jan gave me a look. "What?" I asked her.

"Hudson," she mouthed.

Martinez, it seems, lipreads. "Hudson who?"

"Williams. But I really don't think he...I mean...Interpol told me a year ago that I probably had nothing to worry about. They said he might be dead, even."

Mr. Cool Cop almost dropped his pen. "Interpol?" When I nodded, he said, "I think you'd better tell me all about Williams. Dead or alive."

So I did. Seven or so years before, while on a business trip to Tokyo, I slipped away from my business associates for a little solo foray on the town. Since I was moving to Tokyo for a two-year stint, I told them I was going to look for an apartment and not to expect me for dinner. I headed straight for Rappongi, the district where I'd heard many foreigners lived and partied. Especially partied.

After actually checking out a couple of preposterously priced apartments, I began my evening of checking out drinking establishments. Although a disapproving Jan had given me my very own copy of *Looking for Mr. Goodbar*—both the book and the movie—I steadfastly refused to consider my international, nocturnal wanderings hazardous.

Truth is, I instinctively knew in which type of bar I would find the people with whom I'd be chummy for however long I'd be in any one place. In Brussels I homed in on an English Pub, in Mexico City it was a hotel bar. You show me any large city anywhere in the world and I'll show you a ginmill where foreigners meet, drink, tell lies, and grouse about how nothing in the stinkin' country works right. I was looking for just such a place and the men who frequented them.

Hudson Williams was draped over the bar at Red's Revenge, Home of the Fightin' Roo.

At seven a.m. the next morning, I was making my way back to my room when I ran into my Baxter Brothers cohorts. I was still a little drunk and probably reeked of the *kimchi* Hudson and I had consumed at an all night Korean BBQ, but my colleagues thought I'd been out for an early morning walk. I let them keep those thoughts. I didn't think it wise to apprise my fellow employees, and thereby my employer, that they had a barfly of international renown on their hands.

Two months later, when I did relocate to Tokyo, Hudson and I began a hot and heavy affair that lasted for six months. Until the day he disappeared, along with funds belonging to his company, several of his clients, and me.

I had fully cooperated with Interpol, giving them copies of my phone bills since Hudson had moved in with me right after I arrived, saying his place was too far out of town. I gave them the names of any of his associates I'd met, addresses he'd given me for relatives in the States, and everything else I could come up with. As far as I knew, no one ever found him. Dead *or* alive.

"Dead would be good," I told Detective Martinez, "but even if he is alive, I don't think Hudson, wherever the dirty rat bastard may be, would be looking to harm me," I said. "As a matter of fact, if I ever see him again, he's the one who's gonna get harmed. Some folks, like old granny used to say, 'just need killin''."

Martinez raised his eyebrows at my threat. "Do you happen to have a photo of the alleged dirty rat bastard?" He was enjoying this. I think.

"Nope."

"Tore them up, huh?"

Feeling really, really, stupid I reluctantly admitted, "He never let me take one of him. Said it was bad karma to be photographed."

I glared at Jan before she could say anything like "So, what was your *second* clue?"

Martinez made a little humming sound, closed his notepad and struggled to his feet.

Jan cleared her throat. "Breathers," she said.

The cop sighed and sat.

Jan was becoming a pain in the ass. I scowled a warning at her, then told Martinez, "Someone keeps calling. Hanging up, or breathing. My caller ID can't ID the number. Could you? I wouldn't object to a phone tap or something like that."

"Maybe," he said slowly. He looked at me in what I can only call a quizzical manner. Either that or his Tums totally failed. "Ms. Coffey, for a well educated, successful professional, you appear to walk on the shadowy side of life's little lane. Brinkmanship, as I call it, is a fine art. Be careful you don't take one step too many and topple over the edge."

My ears burned and white heat rushed all the way to my toes. It took every ounce of self-control, something I'm light on anyway, to keep from letting him have a piece, the murderous piece, of my mind. I bit my tongue. Hard.

Martinez rose, handed me his card, walked to the front door, then turned back and said, "I'll get back to you on the phone thing. Have a good evening, girls."

"OhBesides submitting proposals, please, call me Hetta," I said, "I mean since we're becoming so close and all."

If Martinez caught my hateful tone, he ignored it. When the door shut behind him, I shot off the couch. Both Jan and RJ watched warily as I paced and fumed. "*Girls*? *Girls*? And where," I spat, "does that sumbitch get off lecturing me? He's probably never been out of the friggin' state.

He's probably a high school grad-u-ate. He's probably...." I ran out of venom.

"Right?" Jan finished my sentence. "You know Hetta, we do have a history of hanging out with guys who aren't, well, exactly good for us."

Now there's an understatement.

She was right. Martinez was right. I plopped down on the couch and RJ, who had retreated from my anger, returned to put his head in my lap.

"Dog," I said, scratching his velvety ears, "how would you feel about living on a boat? We're blowing this Popsicle stand. It's jinxed." RJ's tail thumped. After all, he had vowed, back at the pound, to follow me to the ends of the earth.

Jan went to the kitchen and returned with a bottle of wine and two glasses. "Hetta, I know things are a little squirrelly around here right now, but are you sure about selling this house? I mean, you don't know diddley-squat about boats."

"I didn't know anything about renovating houses when I bought this place, either. But after years of turning this place from a sow's ear to a silk purse, I'm bailing before it reverts. I've been hearing distinctive oinks. I'm sick and tired of maintaining this money pit. It's either sell or we start cruising the parking lots of San Leandro bars looking for pickup trucks sporting tool boxes and logos like 'Mr. Big Tool.' I've had it."

Jan sniggered. "Sounds okay by me. You can have Mr. Handy Hand, I want Big Tool for myself. But seriously Hetta, maybe you need some advice on this boat thing."

"I called my dad."

"What did he say?"

"Keep the tanks topped off."

"See what I mean? We don't even know what's *in* those tanks or how much it costs to keep them topped off. Lars says—"

"Lars is a menace to society."

"Not so. He happens to be a kind and generous person. I like him a lot. And despite being a little wild, he's the kind of guy we should both be looking for. So is his brother."

"He's not my type."

"Hetta, your type isn't good for you. You're so stuck on wasting your time on the likes of that *Sea Rooster* person, you....Oh, never mind. You never listen to anyone, anyhow."

"*Cock*. The boat is *Sea Cock*. Garrison is a friend, only a friend, and I plan to keep it that way. In fact, he's agreed to help me boat hunt during the week while you're at work."

"I don't like him. He's not...good."

"A rat? I know, but it's not like I'm having an affair with him or anything."

"Everyone thinks you are."

"Who is everyone? And since when do I give a big bull's rump what people think? Garrison is useful to me right now."

"So, if you are *using* a rat, does that make you a ratess?" Jan snarled.

I was wounded. "Let me summarize all the labels your ex-boyfriend, a psychotic lesbian, your present boyfriend, his dorky brother, an aging flatfoot, and now *you* have anointed me with recently. Unbalanced. Fluffball. Weird. Flighty. Brinky. And now I'm a ratess. Gee, is there anything else? Why don't y'all tell me what you truly think."

"Brinky? Anyhow, what I, or they, think isn't worth a hoot. It's what you think of yourself that counts."

I waved my hands in the air. "Psycho-babble. I hate that crap and all of those *I'm Okay but You're Shit* books. I know what I am. I'm opinionated, judgmental, and bossy. I like that in myself."

"No one else does," she said. Seeing the look on my face, she put her arm around me. "Oh, Hetta, I'm so sorry. I didn't mean to hurt your feelings. And hey, since when am I able to do that, anyway? We always talk like this."

Embarrassed by my uncharacteristic dip in the self-pity pool, I replaced my pout with a grin and poured more wine. "I'll be all right. I have the distinct feeling my life is not under my own control lately and you know how I love control. I'll get everything back on track. I always do, don't I? Anyhow, what time is it? Don't you have a date with Lars?"

Jan shook her head. "I broke it. I called him while you were at the hardware store. He said if I changed my mind he'd be at the yacht club, but I can stick around. I don't want to leave you all upset."

"I'm fine. Honest. The lock thing rattled me a little, but I'm sure there's a perfectly logical explanation. You know, extraterrestrials or something like that. If I get lonely tonight, I'll come down to the club. You take RJ's car and go on. I'm gonna read up some more on boats. Then at least I'll have a better grip as to what questions to ask tomorrow. Even if I don't know what they mean."

"Okay, then. If you're sure. I guess I'd better get dressed. Uh, Hetta, I probably won't be back tonight, so meet me tomorrow at the yacht club for brunch and then we'll resume the hunt for your luxury liner, okay?"

"I don't mind braving yacht salespersons on my own. You're sure you don't want to go sailing with WOE instead?"

"Naw, sailing's no fun unless you're there to get hit in the head and cuss a lot. I'd rather watch you make a fool of yourself with yacht brokers."

That's what friends are for.

20

After Jan left for her date with Lars, I carefully locked all my doors and set the alarm, something I rarely did until ready to go to bed. I wanted a soak in my reheated hot tub, but for the first time since I owned the house, I was reluctant to go out on my own deck by myself. This really, really, pissed me off.

With grim resolve, I picked up a stack of yachting magazines and brokerage listings. Somewhere in the pile lay my ship of dreams. I dozed off on the couch and was preparing to board my own *Dream Mary* when the phone rang. Martinez. Did this man never sleep?

"We got a hit on a partial print from the padlock, Hetta."

Oh, so it's "Hetta" now? Didn't this cop *get* sarcasm?

I sat up. "So soon? Gee, you guys are fast."

"New equipment. Everything's computerized and I had a hunch, thanks to you. Actually, we got real lucky."

"Anyone I know?"

"Oh, yes."

"Are you going to tell me, or is this going be multiple choice, Martinez?" I can get real cranky when people wake me up. And then play games. Besides, I was still smarting from his little brinkmanship lecture.

"Touchy, Ms. Coffey, very touchy."

"Mar-tin-ez," I growled in warning.

"Okay. Are you sitting down?" He sounded downright gleeful. Well, for him. "The prints belong to your long lost Tokyo guy, Hudson Williams. He sure as hell isn't deceased, and thanks to your telling me about him, I went straight to Interpol, and whammo! Modern technology, ain't it grand?"

My hand flew to the gold chain and bar key hanging around my neck. My stomach turned cold. I guess I gasped, because I could hear Detective Martinez saying, "Hetta? Are you all right, Take a deep breath."

I did, finally, but I was sure it was my last. My heart and eardrums would surely explode any second. I choked out, "We need to meet. Soon. Can you come over? Tonight? I think I know what Hudson wants."

* * *

What do men really want?

If I knew that, I probably wouldn't be in this mess. I was pretty sure, though, what Hudson was after: The Key Note Club bar key or, more accurately, whatever was in the box at the bar. The question here was, should I give the key to Martinez? And if I did, would it be the end of Hudson? I think not.

By the time Detective Martinez arrived, I'd decided to stall. I was working up a story when he rang the bell.

After accepting a cup of coffee, he dug into a pocket and handed me a piece of paper folded in quarters. The black and white image was grainy, obviously faxed to Martinez. Grainy or no, the man I was looking at was Hudson Williams.

I stared at the eyes I knew to be blue and marveled I never before noticed their beadiness. Shiftiness. How could I have ever considered Hudson's smug face handsome? The world would be a much safer place if foreplay and hindsight could be reversed. But boring.

"Oh, yes. That's Hudson Williams all right."

"Read the details, see if they agree with what you know."

I read the Interpol description below the photo, adding my own mental comments as I went:

Williams, Hudson O. *Dirty Rat Bastard*
Sex: Male. *Not if I get my hands on him.*
Date of birth: 1959. *More like spawned.*

Place of birth: New York, USA *Under what rock?*

Language spoken: English *And not a word of it true.*

Nationality: USA. *I couldn't think of a comment here.*

Height: 1.78 meters (70 inches) *Bullcrap!*

Weight: 72.5 kilos (160 lbs) *Of evil.*

Color of hair: Blonde *Dirty dishwater.*

Profession: Computer sales. *Computer THEFT.*

After reading the Interpol data, I nodded. "Yep, looks right, but he's shorter. More like five-six and a half. He was real sensitive about his height and probably lied on his passport application. I've disliked short men ever since he disappeared.

"Anything else?"

"His occupation. It should be professional jerk." My eyes fell on a handwritten note next to the photo of Hudson. "*Merde*, Martinez, That's my old address in Tokyo."

"Don't worry, you aren't considered an accomplice. Read on."

I did. Hudson was wanted for misuse of company property, fraud, larceny, and murder. Murder?"

"Murder? I thought he just stole stuff and jilted women."

"Oh, there's even more. The guy I talked to at Interpol thought your old buddy was also mixed up in drugs and gem smuggling. Quite versatile, your Mr. Williams."

I gave him a dirty look. "He ain't *my* mister, mister."

"A figure of speech. So Hetta, what was it you wanted to tell me about Williams? You said you think you know what he wants from you?"

I'm a really good liar—accomplished, some of my detractors might say—but for all my apparent bravado and disdain for rules, some authoritative types can bully me pretty good. Preachers, cops and the IRS, in that order. Having been raised by an eclectic mixture of hard-shell Baptists, Baha'is, and redneck backsliders, I harbor a host of divinely inspired phobias. You see, I have it on good authority, and believe in my soul, that liars burn in Hell. Ask any one of my great aunts or grandmothers. So I don't lie, I fib. I prevaricate. I equivocate.

"I guess I said it wrong when we were talking on the phone a few minutes ago," I prevaricated. "What I meant was, maybe I can tell you more about what he *might* be looking for. Maybe he thinks I have some of his stuff. But I don't, I threw it all away." Jesus, that sounded lame.

Martinez thought so, as well. "Cut the crap, Hetta. What stuff?"

Decision time. "Nothing. Maybe he *thinks* I do, though. He left a television, some furniture, things like that, but I sold it all in Tokyo. That's all."

Martinez arched a brow and wrote a couple of jots in his ever-present little book. From my upside down vantage point, it looked like the last words were "pants on fire."

He agreed to a cup of tea, then pursed his lips when I added a smidgen of Slivovitz to mine.

"What?" I asked. "Never heard of *thé Slav?*"

It was after ten when he rose to leave, and I wondered again about his hours. He wore a wedding ring, and it occurred to me I'd been remiss in inquiring after his personal life, what with us becoming such bosom buddies and all.

"Detective, are you married?" I asked.

He gave me a sly grin. "Why? You interested?"

"Gee, I dunno. Do you have a lot of money?"

"Nope."

"Then nope."

Martinez left and I went back to my stack of yachting magazines. I tried concentrating, but the idea that Hudson Williams was alive and stalking me kept creeping into my thoughts.

For the first time since I owned the house, I closed all of the drapes and blinds. I tried shaking off this chagrin with promises of a new life through yacht listings, but soon threw them on the floor. RJ, who had obviously been whacked with a newspaper or two when he was a pup, looked up in alarm.

"Sorry, baby," I said, soothing his fear with a pat. "It's all right."

RJ settled back down with a sigh, and I retrieved the listings. Damn Hudson Williams's eyes. He was not going to have us to terrorize much longer. I intended to find safe refuge for me and my dog. Sanctuary on our ship of dreams.

21

My dream ship, which I now perceived as a seaborne panacea and an escape from all my pyramiding problems and slumping spirits, continued to elude me. But I hung in there, climbing in, out, and over every available vessel in the Bay Area.

Over time, I refined my list of minimum requirements. No less than forty feet, with a double or queen bed in the master cabin, office space, and a comfortable main saloon. That's boatspeak for living room, and is pronounced salon, as in beauty salon, not saloon, as in cowboy drinking establishment. Oh, and a fully equipped kitchen. Uh, galley.

What I was finding in my price range and size had few of those redeeming factors. Not only that, many were wooden. I was strongly advised, ad nauseam, by *everyone* at the yacht club that I had to have a fiberglass hull for easy maintenance, both upper and lower steering stations for navigating in bad weather, and twin engines for ease of handling.

Navigating in bad weather? Ease of handling? Who was I kidding? This tub was probably never going to leave the dock. I most likely didn't even *need* an engine, much less two.

I had all but given up hope of finding something both affordable and habitable when manna from heaven showered down on my yacht club barstool.

"I hear you're on the lookout for a good liveaboard boat," said a distinguished looking gentleman in his late sixties or early seventies. While others were dressed in windbreakers, T-shirts and khakis, he wore a blue blazer, turtleneck and linen pants. Just under six feet, he wore his age as confidently as he did his clothes. He also sported a timeworn wedding band. Not that I notice that sort of thing.

"Yeah, and I'm about looked out," I grumbled. Great, that's what I needed, another barstool sailor giving me *more* friggin' advice on boats.

He tapped the bar in front of me, signaling Paul to serve us both another split of champagne, and then he introduced himself.

"I'm Morris Terry. We haven't been formally introduced. I used to be Commodore," he told me, motioning toward his photo hanging next to Garrison's in the Past Commodore rogue's gallery. Morris was actually better looking now than he'd been when younger.

"Hetta Coffey. I think I met your wife last week. Betty?"

"She told me. She likes you."

"I like her, too. Do you guys have a boat for sale?"

"Might. Do you like *Sea Cock*?"

"I love her. Well, everything but the name."

"I know. Betty's been on my ass to change it for the past two years."

I had to cut down on the champagne. It was affecting my hearing.

"Past two years?" I echoed dumbly.

"Lazy, I guess." He shrugged, misunderstanding my misunderstanding.

Mystified, I shook my head. "I don't get it. Why would your wife want you to change the name of Garrison's boat?"

"Because we own it. I meant to change the name as soon as we acquired her, but never got around to doing the paperwork. Garrison was supposed to be doing some work on *Sea Cock* in exchange for a place to live. You know, taking her out once in a while to keep her running.

"Betty and I have been on a world tour, now we're back and nothing's been done to the boat except hours added to the engines. If you're interested in buying, I'm interested in selling, but I'd appreciate it if we can keep this our little secret for now. I'll take care of Garrison when the time comes."

Sea Cock! My mind reeled. Forty-five feet of perfect boat. *Almost* perfect boat; the interior décor was predominantly blue. "Can I afford it, Morris?"

"That's up to you and the bank, but if you can get the financing, I'll cut you a deal you can't refuse."

"Ballpark?"

"Two."

I was stunned. I had looked at comparables in the beginning of my quest, but soon narrowed my search to those boats of a size and vintage to match my budget. Forty-five foot Californians were beyond my reach. Certainly beyond my reach at three hundred thousand, but not at two.

I wanted to kiss the man sitting next to me, but kept my cool and said, in what I hoped was a businesslike tone, "Morris, I think we can deal, but my house is on the market, so I'd have to make the purchase contingent on the house selling."

"I'm in no hurry. Here's my card. Like I said, let's keep this between us for now."

"No problem at all. My lips are sealed. But, uh, Morris, I have to ask. Why would you sell me a boat at a hundred thousand under market value?" So much for my cool business act. It's a good thing I stay away from poker.

"I got her cheap. Guy owed me money and I took the boat. I don't feel like going though a bunch of crap with brokers and all to unload her. Besides, Betty told me to make you the offer and what Betty wants, Betty gets. See what you can do and call me. I won't do anything with the boat until I give you first dibs."

After he left, I walked to a window and looked down on *Sea Cock,* doing a mental tour, not as a guest, but as her owner. Okay, so there was a lot of blue and white, but I could work in peach and ashes of roses. *Sea Cock* was carpeted throughout in a rich marine blue, the furniture—real furniture, not built-ins like I'd seen on so many boats—was ivory. She had a large aft master's suite with a queen-sized bed, tons of closet space, a separate office area in the main cabin, and a drop dead stainless steel galley. She even sported a verandah. Oops, sundeck. *Sea Cock,* sans the name, was everything I wanted in a boat.

But could I really afford her, even at two hundred grand? Then I remembered that, when considering a change of locale a few years back, I'd qualified for a big enough loan to buy a two hundred and fifty thousand dollar condo. Finally, something was going my way!

Ecstatic, I jumped up on the bar and did a tap dance. Or as much of my *Downtown Strutter's Ball* routine as I remembered from Miss Rita's School of Dance, circa 1968. After several decades, I was a little sloppy, and my tennis shoes kept sticking, but the bar patrons evidently found my act a nice change from Jackie's twin screws, for they applauded. Or maybe they were relieved that I, unlike Jackie, didn't drop my drawers.

I concluded my impromptu shuffle-ball-change, took a bow, and was climbing off the bar when I spotted that Bob Jenkins person watching from the doorway. Gawking, is more like it.

Jenks waist-steered a tall curvy blonde to my end of the bar, gave me a nod, and ordered two drinks. I was in such good spirits, I opened my mouth to say something clever, but the fading blonde—who, I noticed with glee, was older than I—picked up on his nod and practically crawled into his lap to divert his attention. And he called *me* flighty?

While his date clung to him and spouted inanities, I finished off my champagne and decided to leave before Jenks and Beldame Barbie clouded up my parade. *Screw him and the ship* he *rode in on, so to speak. My ship just came in and I ain't gonna let his chronic standoffishness spoil it for me.*

I overcame my desire to tell him he ought to do something about that static cling, slid from my stool, threw my sweater over my shoulder, and sashayed away in my best Bette Davis bumpy ride imitation. It was one of my finer moments for, in the foyer mirror, I saw Mr. Jenkins looking past the blonde, watching me leave. He was actually smiling. Hey, maybe we did have something in common after all. I consorted with the criminally insane and he dated the criminally inane.

22

The next day I made a beeline for the bank, and my new future.

Aline Watson, my good friend, was a loan officer at Wells Fargo. She listened to what I wanted, raised a finely tweezed, decidedly *un*-bankerly brow, fixed me with skeptical green eyes, and shook her curly platinum locks.

"Let me see if I understand this, Hetta. You want to sell your three thousand square foot home, buy a forty-five foot boat, and then *live* on it." It wasn't a question, but a statement delivered in a monotone that sounded as if she had said, "So, you recently stepped off a space ship and you want me to give you money?"

"Yep, you've got it, Aline. I've made out a financial statement." I shoved a folder across her desk. "My house is on the market, and I've entered the asking price, which my real estate lady says I'm sure to get, and the price of the boat. There's also a copy of my last three IRS tax returns. What else will I need?"

She did a quick perusal of my paperwork, leaned across her desk and whispered, "A fuckin' miracle."

"What? You prequalified me for a two hundred and fifty thousand dollar condo a couple of years ago."

"That was before you lost your mind," she said, then remembered we weren't sitting in my hot tub and put on her professional face. "Hetta, I don't want to rain on your parade, but let's go over this point by point. A boat is not a house. Nor is it a condo. The rules are different."

"How different?"

"First and foremost, boats, unlike houses, can sink."

"Ha! You haven't been to *my* house lately, have you?"

She ignored me and continued. "Boats are considered a bigger financial risk. Also, the maximum period I can finance one for you would probably be fifteen years. They don't appreciate like real estate, you know."

I whipped out the handy payment spread sheet furnished by my handy realtor. "Okay, so if I want to finance a hundred grand at eight percent for twenty years, that's nine fifty six a month. That's two hundred bucks less than my present house payment."

"Not exactly. You can't get a boat loan for eight percent. More like ten. And you have to rent or buy a dock."

"Okay, at the yacht club I can get a deal, two hundred a month," I said smugly. "We're still up to only a little over twelve hundred. And there's no property tax."

"True, but you have to pay *personal* property tax, insurance, and then you have to pay for the water you displace."

"Excuse me?"

"In the Bay Area some brain-challenged bureaucrat at the BCDC—that's the Bay Conservation and Development Commission— came up with the idea that a boat is landfill and you have to pay accordingly. Now," she punched numbers into her computer at the speed of light, "with insurance, we're already up around thirteen hundred a month."

"Which is, with my house insurance and all, about the same as I'm paying now," I said stubbornly and a bit defensively. "Jesus, this reminds me of what it was like years ago when I bought my first house as a single woman. The bankers went bonkers, but I finally got my loan."

"Hetta, there's no discrimination here. Trust me, you're being treated like any man who came in here with the same problem."

"A few minutes ago it was a request for a loan and now it's a problem?"

"You *are* self-employed. That could be a problem, but let's sit here and work through it. If we're even close, I'll go to bat for you, but we really need to talk about these credit cards."

* * *

Steam rising from the hot tub almost obscured Jan's round-eyed reaction. "You are shittin' me," she said. "Charge cards are a liability? What are these folks? Communists?"

"Worse. Bankers. And they obviously don't understand the basic principles of capitalism."

"Yeah, and we're certainly superficially shallow and overextended enough to qualify as bona fide capitalists. What's wrong with those people?" She took a sip of wine and lifted her glass. "Here's to us, us, us."

"Hear, hear," I said, clinking her Waterford with my Waterford. "Anyhow, they say I have to pay off all the plastic, then cancel most of them because the max limit on each card you own is considered a liability."

"How many do you have?"

"Only twenty."

Jan almost choked on her wine. "Twenty credit cards? You're kidding. You owe on all of them?"

"No silly, only on half. You know, two hundred to Macy's, same to Sears. A grand on a couple on Visas, five hundred to Neiman Mar ..."

"Neiman's? You tell me Neiman's is overpriced. You call them Needless Markup. What did you buy there?"

174

"Escargot Helper? Hell, I don't know. What a wake up call. Aline tried her best, but she told me I should be looking for a cheaper boat. Actually, she said I should be looking for a shrink, but she's sooo conservative. She finally admitted she could probably push the loan through, mainly because the boat is being purchased way under market value and I actually do have a great credit rating despite the credit cards—*if* I were not self-employed. I'll have to fax her a copy of my latest contract with the Seattle folks, then she'll see what she can do. So, I wait. With any luck, *Sea Cock* will be mine."

"That name definitely has to go."

"First thing I'll do, trust me. But I'm a long way from changing boat names. I gotta lotta creative financial stuff to pull off and debts to dump. I think I'll sell the Beemer. It won't do it any good to sit in a waterfront parking lot, and besides, I can use RJ's car. It's paid for."

RJ's ears perked at hearing his name. He wagged his tail and tried to stand up, but yelped when he put weight on his bad leg. My heart sank as both Jan and I moved quickly to hold and soothe him while he whined in pain.

"It's okay, boy. Stay still and Mommy will get you a pain pill," I whimpered.

"You stay with him, Hetta. I'll get it. What's he taking?"

"Vicodin," I said, nuzzling the soft fur behind his ear with my nose. "Shit, bring me one, too."

23

Other than the bank loan debacle and RJ's failing health, things settled back to normal. I checked the new padlock on the dog jail daily, making sure my key still worked. Naturally the breather, whom I was sure was Hudson, had stopped calling just as the cops began monitoring the phone. And the fool in Seattle seemed to let up on his barrage of memos accusing me of everything from price-fixing to cronyism.

I threw myself into putting together bid proposals, attempting to snag a new project before this one ran out, all the while dodging lookyloo would-be buyers my real estate agent ran through my house on what seemed to be an hourly basis.

In my spare time, I tried to figure out a way to finance *Sea Cock.* It wasn't going to be easy. I called Morris Terry one day when I had to admit to myself that my abilities at financial wizardry were severely lacking. "Morris, this is Hetta Coffey, and I'm afraid I have some bad news. As much as I want her, I'm having a problem getting financing for the other hundred thou on *Sea Cock*."

"Credit problems?"

"I didn't think so. I have a triple A credit rating and could qualify for a comparable condo, but not a boat. At least not your boat. I guess I'll have to be realistic and start looking at condos."

"Any bites on your house?"

"Lots. According to my real estate lady, it's only a matter of days until I receive an offer. I'm about to join the residentially challenged. That's Sanfran-speak for homeless. I can't even rent a decent apartment 'cause I've got a dog." I don't know why I was telling this poor man my problems. All he wanted to do was sell his damned boat.

"Hey," Morris said, "don't give up your dreams. I'm a patient man and you are a clever gal. You'll get what you want. Meanwhile, don't worry too much. Things have a way of changing."

Boy, he wasn't kidding.

Ten minutes later I lost my job.

* * *

According to the tersely worded, one page fax I found in my office, the services of Hetta Coffey, *S.I.*, were no longer required. I had to laugh in spite of the devastating news. Didn't *anyone* pick up on my little joke? I tacked the *S.I.* title on my card for *Civil Engineer,* and not one soul had ever asked me what it stood for.

Anyway, I was off the Seattle project. I could expect, via courier service this very day, a check covering any expenses incurred to date, a prorated percentage of my total contract, and an extra ten grand to offset any inconvenience caused by early termination of the contract. Damn! The bastards followed the terms of the contract exactly as I'd written them.

Some quick numbers crunching told me I was okay for three months if really careful. Because I was self-employed, I always kept "screw you" money in reserve for house payments and bills, but my financial future was looking downright grisly. And it didn't take a Mensa member to figure out that any *Sea Cock* deal had to be put on the back burner. No wonder the banks hated me. It was people like me who gave me a bad name.

I called Seattle and got stonewalled. I left messages, but no one returned my calls. I sent faxes. I sent e-mails. Nada. The promised courier arrived with a check and a sheaf of legalese stipulating when I endorsed and cashed the check I was, in effect, agreeing to the terms of my dismissal. Don't call us, we'll call you. No further explanation as to why, but I smelled a rat named Dale.

"Well shit, RJ, we've been fired!" I'd never been fired, not even when I got in hot *misu* with

Baxter Brothers, my former employers who-em I'd royally pissed off in Japan.

It was time to call in the Trob.

Fidel Wontrobski—his dad was a Polish communist, thus the name—still worked for Baxter Brothers Engineering and remained my friend despite my lousy track record there. A few years my junior, Fidel was skinny and topped six-five if he'd unfold his horrible posture. With a hooked nose, a black scruffy topknot of frizzy hair, and an entire wardrobe of baggy black clothing, he looks like a buzzard. A buzzard savant.

The Trob, engineering genius, headed up a think tank from the exclusive top floor of the Baxter Building. Only the elite, such as the brothers Baxter and a couple of former high-ranking politicos, shared his lofty location. Which was amazing, in light of the fact that Fidel possessed not a single social or political skill. But corporate heads, former Secretaries of State, and their minions all deferred to Fidel Wontrobski's brilliance.

Of course they rarely encouraged the Trob to interact with other employees and certainly never let him talk to clients. Fidel was a prisoner of his own intelligence. A thirty-three-year-old wunderkind. Lunch was delivered to his office and, most nights, dinner. He lived in a nearby hotel, slept only four hours a night—midnight to four— and was the first one in the Baxter employees' cafeteria for breakfast each morning. I was usually second.

For weeks after I first joined the firm, the Trob and I sat at opposite ends of the mostly empty cafeteria, studiously ignoring one another. Then one morning as I was passing his table, we experienced a power failure. Hearing a frightened whimper, I reached in my purse, pulled out a flashlight, and sat with him until an emergency generator kicked in and the lights came back on. We ate breakfast together that day and every workday until I was shipped out to Japan.

We also fell into the habit of, after breakfast, taking a very private elevator car to his tower of wisdom, where we'd play dominoes until I had to join the lesser grunts at eight. I never won a single game.

After I left for Tokyo, we called each other regularly on the company's dime and if I had a work problem, he'd help me out. And when I had my *big* problem, Wontrobski saved my ass. Maybe he could do it again. Or at least find out what the hell was going on.

"Yo, Trob," I said when he picked up the phone, "wanna play some dominoes?"

"Right now?"

"No, dear, I'm in Oakland and you're in San Francisco right now. I was thinking of meeting you for breakfast tomorrow morning and we could play then."

"Oh."

"Do you want to or not?" Talking to the Trob was often times like conversing with a four-year-old."

"Okay."

"Fidel, you need to leave a pass with the front desk guard so I can get into the cafeteria. Okay?"

"Oh."

"Are you gonna do it?"

"Okay."

"Bye now."

"Bye."

I hung up and screamed. You can see why the Trob doesn't get invited out much. Monosyllabic to the point of appearing simple, yes, but give him a keyboard and a modem and the man can communicate like a Dale Carnegie. Dale Carnegie with unlimited cyber-contacts in the engineering world and computer equipment nonpareil.

The next morning we had breakfast, played dominoes, and then I laid out my problem, writing down the names of all the players. When I left, Fidel was already absorbed by his monitor screen, performing electronic magic. By the time I got home, he had sent me a three page e-mail. Even by Trob standards, this was fast. And, as I suspected, Dale Stevens, the guy I'd burned in Seattle, was the culprit. The son of a bitch was playing by my rules. What a dirt bag.

One of the things I've learned over the years is that buttering up chief execs and the like is a waste of time, but their secretaries—most of them called "executive assistants" now—are another matter. A rose here, a little sincere sympathy for their difficult, thankless, underpaid jobs there usually greased the skids when needed. This time was no exception.

After Audrey, the Seattle project manager's right hand gal, had told me, officially, for the fourth time in so many hours that her boss was in a meeting, she called me, unofficially, from a pay phone during her break.

"Hetta," she whispered, "he's really not in a meeting."

"Surprise, surprise."

"You've got a problem, Hetta Honey. Check your e-mail. Gotta go." Deep Throat in Laura Ashley florals hung up.

Her e-mail had three attachments, all bad. I was being accused of bid package tampering and pandering to favored bidders. Two memos, written by GUESS WHO, said I had unnecessarily complicated the bid request packages, thereby jacking the price and insuring my own handpicked bidder won the contract. Dale the Dork had stopped just short of accusing me of receiving kickbacks, but the implications were clear.

Attachment number three was a copy of an old letter on Baxter Brothers corporate letterhead stationery summarizing their never-proven suspicions that I was disloyal to Baxter in my dealings with Superior Oil, the client in Japan. Presumably this little tidbit was presented to my Seattle client as further proof of my nefarious nature.

I forwarded the blasphemous documents to the Trob, then called Jan.

"I've already heard," she said. "Bad news travels fast. My boss is talking to lawyers as we speak."

"And?"

"Nothing yet, but other than being a big pain in the ass, he thinks we're dealing with a nuisance thing. The fact that you and I are friends is beside the point. We bid it fair and square, we got the purchase order and shipped the goods. It's the goods that are being questioned by your now-ex-client; you know, whether all the equipment you spec'd out was necessary. The boss is writing a rebuttal letter as we speak. Defending your honor, I might add."

"Tell him thanks, but I'm a big girl. I'll handle it."

"What are you gonna do, Hetta?"

"I'm going to Seattle and whup up on Dale."

Jan giggled. "Now that's mature and businesslike."

"Okay, maybe not, but it sure would make *me* feel better. I don't know yet what to do, but I'll be damned if I'll take this besmirchment lying down."

"Atta girl. You going to get a lawyer?"

"I'm going to call Allison. She's meaner'n a rattlesnake with a tummy ache."

"You go, girl. See you tonight?"

"Yep. Hot tub huddle, comin' up."

24

Allison Cuthbert, all five feet one of her, dangled dainty feet in the tub while her almond-shaped eyes scanned steaming copies of documents. A product of Houston's fifth ward and the daughter of a black, second generation welfare mom, Ms. Cuthbert came up hard, as we say back home. A prosecutor with political ambitions, she possesses the body of a gymnast, the beauty of a model, the professional scrappiness of an alley cat, and a politician's savvy. My kind of lawyer.

Zeroing in on the Baxter Brothers missive hinting I was not what they'd call a "team player," she asked what that was all about.

I sighed and told her. "It's about change orders, Allison. Used to be, when the engineering and construction industry was in its heyday, contracts were let on a cost-plus basis. In other words, whatever it cost to complete, plus a set percentage over that. The Alaska Pipeline killed cost-plus forever. Murdered the goose *and* the egg. After the pipeline thing, the industry had to start bidding hard money. Actually estimating what a job was going to cost and, in theory, sticking to it. What a concept."

"Sounds reasonable to me," Allison said. "Like getting an estimate for car repairs."

"Right. If a mechanic finds an additional problem with your car, he calls you for authorization to do the extra work. In our business we have something similar. It's called a change order. I call it a ticket to ride. I've been on projects where the change orders numbered in the thousands. The client expects change orders, budgets for them, and usually approves reasonable charges without much comment. It was those old dreaded change orders, however, that got me in trouble with the Baxter boys."

"Hetta, I've never heard the whole story," Jan said. "I don't understand. How could *you* get in trouble? The change orders all originated in Baxter's home office in San Francisco, right?"

"Right. But over in Tokyo I discovered some of the specification changes precipitating massive change orders were unnecessary, and I naively tipped off Nippon Oil, the client's client. Needless to say, I was about as popular as dandruff back home. If it hadn't been for the Trob, they'd'a boiled me in oil. He stepped in, pulled off some miracle, and I didn't even get fired. Put on the back burner, for sure, but not fired."

Allison took a sip of wine. "The Trob? What, or who, in the hell is that?"

I told her about Fidel Wontrobski, then spent a better part of an hour telling Trob tales.

"Sounds like a great guy," Allison said. "Refreshing, to say the least."

"Oh, he's different all right. And like I said, he really saved my ass after the Tokyo debacle."

Allison slid back into the tub. "Boy, those two years in Tokyo weren't exactly a pinnacle of happiness for you, were they? Not only the work thing, but Hudson, the jilter. No wonder you were so stressed out when you got back."

I almost told Allison and Jan about Hudson's fingerprints the OPD had ID'd, but decided against it. No use getting Jan all het up. She hets good. I glugged wine, and then quipped, "Oh, it wasn't so bad," I flashed my finger, "I ended up with a ruby."

My friends laughed, for they both knew I'd bought the ruby for myself. One of Hudson's twenty-four karat lies was he was going to buy me a two carat ruby engagement ring. He'd hinted he had friends in low places who could get rare, perfect Burmese stones with murky provenances. After Hudson took a powder, I was feeling sorry for myself one day and, on a whim, bought my own ruby ring.

"Back to our present problem, Hetta," Allison said, "I wonder how that Dale guy in Seattle got a copy of this letter from the Baxter files? Not that it matters, I guess." She took a sip of wine, smiled sweetly, and added, "Oh, what the hell. Let's sue the bastards."

"I don't really want to, but I *do* want my good name restored," I said in all sincerity, which prompted raucous hoots. "My *professional* good name," I corrected.

"Of course you do," Allison said, all lawyerly and properly indignant on my part. "And I was joking, sort of. Litigation will take time, be messy and probably do you more harm than good. But," she added, and in the dim light I swear I detected a ghostly fin sprout between her shoulders, "perhaps if I were—on my letterhead, of course—to request a copy of the alleged," she shook the papers, "documents, it might get someone's attention. They don't have to know that I'm not in private practice."

She was just warming up. "I'll also let them know I'm holding that insulting recompense check they want you to endorse and cash. That way they'll know they ain't playing with kids, here. Their legal counsel will call and I'll suggest a *very* discreet investigation of the entire affair before they make any decisions that might prompt legal action. Trust me, they'll be pissin' their pants to return those calls of yours. Which, of course, you will refuse to take until I say so. Tell them to talk to their lawyer."

"You, my friend, are a genius."

"No, but I am a respectable lawyer and ... "

She was cut off as both Jan and I shrieked, "Oxymoron."

25

While the slow wheels of injustice rolled along with Allison at the helm, I suddenly had a great deal of time on my hands.

I busied myself by submitting proposals for new projects. Allison let me take an occasional call from Seattle, answer a few questions, and fax requested documents. Mostly, however, I waited. I hate waiting.

Normally, time on my hands precipitates a windfall profit for sleazy bars, ice cream parlors, Elizabeth Arden's Red Door, and RJ, but in my newly impoverished mode, RJ was the sole benefactor. And the timing was ironically good, for my best buddy was failing. Fast.

As he deteriorated, our daily routine revolved around twenty-four hour drug doses of painkillers, mood elevators, and tranquilizers. And then there were *RJ's* pills.

The only thing RJ would eat was Ben and Jerry's and Craigosaurus's mint biscuits. He even turned up his nose at prime rib. I buried megavitamins in his ice cream and hoped he wouldn't spit them out. He could flat ferret out a vitamin pill.

For a dog who required constant attention, RJ had drawn a bum paw. He had a nurse who abhorred sickness.

The stairs became too tricky for him, so after he took a couple of heart wrenching tumbles, I carried him both ways. And it was getting easier to lift him, for as he dwindled on an ice cream diet, I ballooned.

With a little help, he could still go outside to do his business, but it was becoming a trial for both of us. More often than not, RJ would lift his back leg and fall over on his nose. Had it not been so tragic, it would have been comical.

Unless Jan could fill in for me, I rarely left the house, afraid to leave RJ alone unless he was in a drugged slumber. Even then, in case he got up and lost his bearings, I locked him in the kitchen—oh, the guilt!—where I'd moved his daybed into a sunny corner.

When I was home, RJ wanted to be where I was. All the time. If I left the living room to get a drink of water, he tried to follow and would end up hurting his leg. So I carried him, from room to room, all day long. I got to the point where I waited until the last possible minute, or until his drugs kicked in, to go to the bathroom. We were both exhausted, both hurting.

But I was the human. I knew what was going on. RJ would sometimes gaze at me in pain and question, his big brown eyes asking, "Why do I hurt? Why can't you make it stop?"

And I could.

But the decision was beyond me.

Dr. Craig, bless his heart, made it for me.

* * *

I carefully carried RJ down the stairs that last morning, placed him gently on his warmed electric blanket on the couch and covered him with a throw. His tail thumped weakly as I kissed him on the nose. The knockout pill I'd given him earlier had kicked in and he soon drifted into a drugged doggy dream world where, judging from his movements and noises, he was still a pup chasing an elusive postal employee. I made a note to get some of those pills for myself.

Jan brought in coffee and we sat quietly, each lost in our own grief, until Dr. Craig let himself in the front door.

"Is he asleep?" Craig asked.

I started to say yes, but the sound of Craig's voice roused RJ enough for a tail thump. Craig sat down on the couch with RJ between us, gave him an ear scratch, and my dog went back to sleep.

"Rough night?" Craig asked.

"No, he slept real good for a change."

"I meant you, Hetta."

I nodded numbly. "Pretty bad."

Jan burst into tears and headed out the back door.

"Are you ready, Hetta?" Craig asked. At the sound of his voice, RJ stirred again and licked his vet's hand. Tears sprang into Craig's eyes. "Do you want to leave?"

"No."

"Okay." He quickly tied off RJ's back leg with a length of surgical tubing, slipped a preloaded syringe from his pocket, removed the casing, and inserted the needle into a large vein in RJ's leg.

RJ sighed, and it was over for him. His humans, however, were left with a big empty space he had filled in our lives.

26

"Hetta, go home," Jan demanded. "But first take a shower, wash your hair, and put on something besides that crappy old kimono. You look like hell."

I poured myself another glass of wine.

"I mean it, Hetta Coffey. You can't stay here anymore. I'm evicting you. You've got to clean up your raggedy assed act and put it on the road. What have you been doing all day, watching TV?"

"Naw. Too many dog food commercials. What Madison Avenue genius thought up using dogs to sell cars, I ask you? Or toilet paper? Do you have *any* idea how many ads have dogs in them these days?"

"No. I don't. I do not sit around counting canine commercials. I have a life. You need to get one, too. And frankly my dear, your roots are showing."

"I have no roots," I whined. "No dog, no job, no money, and my house is being sold out from under me in three weeks. I'll be homeless. Living out of a shopping cart. And double frankly, my dear, I don't give a damn. I don't want to see my house ever again. It's too empty and lonely."

Jan planted her hands on her hips and glared at me with disgust. "Well, you have to," she spat. "I've endured almost a month of your . . . despair. I miss RJ, too. I grieve for him. But he's dead and you're not. Although right now I'm tempted to kill you myself. I've had all I can stands, I can't stands no more. One of us has to move, and it's you."

"Gee, what did I do? Why are you so mad at me?"

"Don't play dumb and pitiful with me, Hetta Coffey. Today was a nightmare, a nightmare I tell you."

I gave her a two thumbs down. Not since the '40's British flicks has anyone successfully employed a line like, "A nightmare, a nightmare I tell you."

Unfazed by my unsolicited critique, she continued to rail. "I couldn't get a damned thing done at the office today. Would you like to venture a guess as to why?"

I shook my head and took a gulp of wine.

"Because, Sorrypants, I was fielding *your* crap. I understand why you had *your* phone calls forwarded from your house to my apartment, but why, in God's name, did you then call forward everything to *my* office today? All I've done all day is take messages for you, and I couldn't even call you because I got myself!"

"Ain't modern technology a wonderful thing? I didn't want to talk to anyone," I whimpered.

"Dammit, you are going to."

Jan reached into her briefcase and waved a handful of pink WHILE YOU WERE OUT SCREWING AROUND sheets. "The neighbors called. You didn't pay your gardener, he quit, and the yard looks like hell." She threw the message in my lap.

Crushing it into a ball, I launched it across the room, through a basketball hoop hanging on the bathroom door. Nothing but air. "Let the new owners worry about it."

"I think *not*. Your real estate agent called. If you don't get over there and make the place presentable, the new owners are going to send in some professionals and charge it to your escrow account."

"Let them eat weeds."

"Your mother called. She wants you to come home."

"I don't have the energy."

"We'll go together."

"I'm busy."

"She said she'd fry okra."

"When do we leave?"

Jan smiled. "That's more like it. Now, for cryin' out loud, take a shower and pull yourself together." She snatched the wine bottle from me and threw a clean towel in my face. I reluctantly climbed out of bed and started for the bathroom. Then I remembered something.

"Oh, Jan, you got flowers today. They're in the kitchen."

"Who're they from?"

"I didn't look at the card."

"Boy, now you're really scaring me. *You*, Miss Nosy Britches, didn't look at the card?"

I shrugged. I have to admit, I'm slipping. I've been known to steam open "Occupant" mail. And the demise of the telephone party line? I considered that a great tragedy.

Jan tromped to the kitchen to check out her flowers. I heard tissue paper rattling, then water running. When I stepped out of the bathroom all scrubbed up, she handed me a vase of daisies and roses. "Actually, these are for you."

"Really? Flowers for me? Maybe someone thinks I died."

Jan handed me the card. I was nonplussed, for the flowers were from Bob "Jenks" Jenkins.

"Did you put him up to sending me flowers? Posies for the pitiful, something like that?"

"No, I did not."

"Fancy that," was all I could say. Maybe, just maybe, that Bob person wasn't so bad after all. Gosh, since he sent me flowers, maybe I'd even call him Jenks. I'd call tomorrow, thank him. Suddenly I felt better. I was clean, I had the possibility of a new friend *and* a trip to Texas. My horizon lightened, slightly lifting a month of heavy sorrow from my heart.

I put down the flowers, picked up Jan's hair dryer and tried to fluff up an overdue clip. Examining my roots, I saw that Jan was right and that my spirits weren't all that needed lightening. A call to René le Exorbitant was definitely in order. Then I'd go back to the house and get things in order there. As I dialed my overpriced hair guru, I caught Jan smiling.

"What?" I asked.

"Nothing."

"Bullcrap. What's so humorous?"

"Nothing. I'm glad to see you *doing* something."

"Yeah, well don't count your chickens before they pack. I ain't gone yet."

Jan picked up a suitcase and began throwing my stuff in it. "Oh, yes you are."

Ain't friends fab?

* * *

I turned the front door key, took a really deep breath and stepped into the foyer's dead air.

Although sun bled through the living room mini blinds, gloom pervaded the atmosphere. The only thing missing were black dust covers, bunting, and perhaps a dirge. No, something more was missing. I didn't hear the high whine of my alarm's warning signal.

Throwing open the closet door, I found the alarm turned off. Had I been so upset after RJ died that I had forgotten to set it when Jan and I left for her apartment? Or had the real estate people been here and neglected to reset the alarm? My heart skipped a beat. Had the house been sitting here for weeks, unprotected?

I checked out the living room, barely able to look at the sofa where RJ died. Fighting back tears, I walked from room to room. Everything was as I'd left it, only dustier. My wilting plants seem to glare at me.

Upstairs was fusty, so I opened all the windows and doors and went out on the hot tub deck for some fresh air. I half expected RJ to come bounding from behind the orange tree, up the stairs and into my arms.

I inspected the hot tub water, saw the filtration system had worked perfectly, then turned the controls to HEAT so Jan and I could have a soak after dinner. But before she arrived, I had stuff to do, so I channeled my energy away from grief, into action.

Mama says I have what she calls "bounce-ability," and I put it in full gear. In no time I had arranged for storage space for those items I didn't want to sell or give away when I returned from

Texas, touched base with my lawyer, Allison, on the Seattle thing, bribed my gardener to return, had the alarm people change my code, and called my real estate agent to share it with her. All this activity enlivened me. Except for the odd sad moment when I ran across a squeaky toy or a can of dog food, I was getting back to being Hetta.

I'd worked myself into a fairly good mood by the time I got to the item on my TO DO, AND I MEAN IT list reminding me to call Jenks Jenkins and thank him for the flowers. After four rings I heard, "Hunhnm."

"Uh, Jenks?"

"Yes."

"This is Hetta Coffey. I called to thank you for the flowers. They were beautiful and really helped to cheer me up."

"Oh, yeah. Good." Silence.

"Did I wake you?" It was one o'clock in the afternoon.

"Kind of. I was in the middle of a nooner."

What? "Oh, well, then," I stammered, "sorry to disturb you. Bye."

"No problem. Bye."

I hung up and stared at the phone. A *nooner*? What kind of kook tells a woman he's in bed with another? Miffed, I stomped upstairs, determined to throw off my chagrin with some power packing. But my anger died in a hurry, replaced by a tingle on the back of my neck. When I opened my closet door to get a suitcase, I saw my clothes, all of them, on the floor.

Backing away in surprise, I fell against the bed, and like I had when I was a little girl, jerked my feet up so the boogieman couldn't grab them from underneath. While trying to catch my breath I reached for the phone and called Jan.

"What's up?" she asked.

"My clothes. They're all on the floor."

"What do you want *me* to do? Come over and pick 'em up?"

"No, Jan. I wanted to know if you knocked them down."

"Hetta, I told you to lay off the wine. Now cut the crap and get packed so we can leave for Texas tomorrow."

"You don't understand. All of the clothes in my closet are on the floor. Like someone threw them there."

"Oh, shit. Anything else?"

"Not that . . . my jewelry box! It's not on the *tansu* chest. And the house alarm, it was off."

"Hetta, call the cops. I'll be there right after work. Before, if you need me. Call them right now and get out of the house until they arrive."

I called 911, but didn't leave. All I could think about was my grandmother's cameo, the one piece of jewelry I treasured. I went back to the closet, rummaged through the pile of clothes with shaking hands and found my silk Victorian blouse. The cameo was pinned to the high collar. Cradling the brooch, I fought the urge to run and stiff-kneed it down the stairs. All nerves aflutter, I flung open the front door and melted onto the porch steps to await the OPD.

27

Detective Martinez surveyed the closet and breathed his now familiar rattling sigh. "You haven't touched anything?"

"The clothes. I pulled out a blouse." I held up the cameo. "I was looking for this."

"And you can't remember whether you turned on the alarm or not when you left last month?"

"I was distracted. Distraught actually, when I left. RJ had just died and I wanted to get away from here as fast as possible. I truly don't remember about the alarm."

"Sorry about your dog. I liked him, and I don't like dogs much. You say you've been away about a month?"

"Yes, sir."

"Where were you?"

"Wallowing in self-pity at Jan's apartment in San Francisco."

Martinez allowed a small smile to spoil his dour visage. I wondered if he had ever heard of Metamucil. "I understand," he said. "I've lost a pet or two in my day. You never quite get over it."

I was surprised by the emotion in his voice. I guess I tend to think cops don't have any. He sighed again and said, "Let's go back downstairs. As soon as my guys get through dusting for prints, you can determine what, besides your jewelry box, is missing. Meanwhile, can you think of *anything* you have, or had, that someone, particularly your Mr. Tokyo, might want?"

"I think we can rule out my body, since he only comes when I'm not home," I quipped.

"I think," he said, "we can put that in the 'good things' column."

"Thanks, Martha," I said. Detective Dour didn't get it. Who knew he didn't watch Martha Stewart?

After the print guys finished up, Martinez and I went to work. Well, *I* went to work. He stood by while I methodically hung clothes and then began checking for missing items. Which was a problem. How do you know something's missing when it's not there? Was all my underwear accounted for? Martinez had actually asked. Had I left any money around? I couldn't remember. Jewelry I *always* remember, but for the rest I booted up my trusty computer, which was thankfully in place, and downloaded a home insurance inventory.

Using the printout we backtracked through the entire house. All there. In fact, as far as we could determine, the jewelry box was the only thing stolen. That and any remaining affection I harbored for my formerly happy home.

"Detective Martinez, if someone is trying to scare me, they're doing a right smart job of it. The padlock thing, those calls. And you know what? I thought I was going goofy before, but this time someone *really* rearranged my jewelry."

Martinez wanted to know what I meant, and I told him that several weeks before it looked like someone had moved things in my jewelry box.

He didn't say anything. The pensive look on his face led me to believe he was either ruminating over my problem or waiting for a gas bubble to pass. Whichever it was, he finally asked, "Was that jewelry thing before or after the lock was changed on your hot tub housing?".

I called Jan. She thought, as I did, the two were close in time. I hung up and asked Martinez, "Do you think someone, namely that rat bastard Hudson Williams, broke in here before and looked through my stuff?"

"I wouldn't rule the rat bastard out. His prints *were* on the padlock." He made a note on his little notepad and was preparing to leave when the phone rang. It was Jan.

"Hetta, you know what?" she said, "I think Hudson changed the lock before RJ hijacked the mail truck. Think about it. How else could RJ get out? The son of a bitch made friends with RJ, let him out, then came and went at will."

Now there was a thrilling thought.

"But Jan, how about the alarm?" She didn't have an answer, but I relayed her idea to Martinez who told me alarms were play toys in the hands of a professional. Professional? I guess Hudson qualified, according to his Interpol rap sheet.

"And I don't like the idea even a little bit, Ms. Coffey. I have a gut feeling that Williams, if that's who we're dealing with, has the determination and skill to get what he wants. I also think you might know what it is and are holding out on me. Not real smart on your part. Are you staying here tonight?"

"Yes, but Jan's coming over. And if you recall, I have a couple of guns and....Oh, hell." I went to the hall closet, threw it open, reached into a false compartment behind a shelf and smiled. "Still there. Both guns."

"Good. I guess. According to an old police report I found, you're a pretty good shot, too. Make sure any rat you vaporize around here in the future is already inside your house, if you know what I mean."

Did I know what he meant? What was I, an idiot? He meant I might really be in danger. But if so, why? The key around my neck? It made me all the more determined to keep the damned thing. But again, why?

Martinez walked to the door and asked, "Are you still leaving tomorrow?"

"Yep, Jan and I are headed for God's country."

There was a lengthy pause then, "Does God know this yet?"

"Was that humor, Martinez?"

"I'll let you know when I tell a joke. You two have a good trip. And Hetta, let's not have any Thelma and Louise stuff out there, okay?"

Martinez left, and I pondered the situation. First off, I pondered why I hadn't given the key, or at least knowledge of the key, to the detective.

I fixed myself a *thè Slav* with a lavish splash of Lacho slivovitz—Polish plum brandy—dumped into my Earl Grey. Then I had another, this one with a diminished percentage of Earl. The Polish moonshine was just the ticket to opening a gate into morbid introspection.

Was I holding on to the key in hopes of seeing Hudson again? Was I dangling a carrot? And if I did see him, would I shoot him or kiss him? Could it be that I, like those pitiful sob sisters with whom I had little sympathy or patience, longed for this man, one who had betrayed, jilted and robbed me, to declare his undying love, beg my forgiveness, rip off my bodice, loosen the one pin holding my tumult of heavy copper tresses from my swan-like neck, and ravage me with his throbbing, tumescent manhood?

Nah.

I oiled my guns.

28

I am the sovereign of shilly-shally. Always put off thinking today about something I can possibly forget by tomorrow, that's my motto.

So the minute we left for Texas, Hudson, padlocks, missing jewelry boxes, and the like ceased to exist. I also realize that my proclivity for living in the present is probably a defense mechanism triggered by my perilous past. And although my future was probably equally crappy, there's nothing like a road trip to make one hopeful.

"I've been thinking," I said, three days later as we rolled along I-10 through West Texas.

"It's about time. What were you thinking back in Laughlin when you started making fifty-dollar bets? You know you can't play poker worth a damn."

"Hey, Harrah's gave me free drinks. It was the least I could do. Anyway, I won, didn't I?"

"You broke even, which is a miracle. Might I remind you, Hetta, you are unemployed? Let's skip Nevada on the way back. Neither I nor your bank account can take the strain."

"That's what I've been thinking about. I might not come back."

"What?"

"My life in California isn't exactly coming up roses, so I was thinking I might look for a job in Texas. Then I'll rent me a y'all haul and move back to my native state."

"You hate Texas."

"Not so. It's my homeland. My roots. My people have been here for nine generations. We arrived when Spain still owned the territory, long before you *norteamericanos* invaded."

"Snob. But you left, all the same."

"Granted. I was tired of Houston, so when I got the job offer in California, I took it. Now that I think about it, Texas isn't all so bad. Look at our friend, Mary. She's never left and she's happy."

"True, but Mary's in Austin, where living in a crappy old apartment she pays a fortune in rent for and driving a junker is still seen as groovy. We left groovy behind long ago. You can't make good money in Austin unless you work for one of the new high-tech outfits. You hate working high-tech. All those techies and damn-comers have driven up the real estate prices and plumb *rurnt* Austin."

"Maybe I'll go back to Houston. Lord knows, real estate is cheap there."

"Not where you want to live. Hetta, we aren't twenty any more, and living dangerously on the cheap side of town isn't for us. In the neighborhood where we used to live, this Beemer wouldn't last two minutes. And besides, Houston has the same climate as Calcutta, India, or have you forgotten."

"Air conditioning, my dear, air conditioning."

"They need to air condition the whole damned state."

"Oh, lighten up and smell the bluebonnets, Miz Jan. And look at them!" Purple blanketed both sides of the road as far as the eye could see. "Let's blow this interminable interstate and cut through the Hill Country to Mom and Dad's."

We took the Iraan exit, named not for the Shah's former empire, but a couple named Ira and Ann Yates who cleverly traded a grocery store for a several acres of rock and cactus that began gushing oil. Now the hilltops also sprouted whirling wind machines.

The next three hours we traveled state roads while oohing and aahing at rolling hills awash in a sea of bluebonnets, black-eyed Susans, Indian paintbrush, and every other flower known to grow wild in the Lone Star State.

"You know, Jan, this is Lady Bird Johnson's doing. Remember, years ago when she initiated that program to bring back the wildflowers? We kids spent Saturday mornings spreading seeds along the roadsides like this one. Look at the payoff. I've never seen the flowers like this. I'd forgotten how beautiful the Texas 'sprang' can be. For the life of me, I can't remember why we left."

"I followed *you*," Jan said. "I came to visit and fell in love with San Francisco."

"You fell in love with Ronny. So you dumped old whosit back Houston and moved in with Ron. Do you know what they call women like you, Jan?"

"I'm afraid to ask."

"Serial monogamists."

"That's me all right. Faithful, true, and blue, right up to the minute I leave 'em. But at least I keep my men for a while, Hetta, which is more than I can say for you."

"Sad, but true."

We entered an area along the San Saba River where large cottonwoods lined both sides of the meandering water. "God, it's so beautiful here. Why did I ever leave?"

"The heat?"

"Naw, I was never outside anyway."

"Mosquitoes?"

"Ditto."

"Money?"

"Maybe that was it."

* * *

The Texas Hill Country was experiencing a spring that blindsides visiting Yankees who, entranced, buy a place, then damn near croak all summer. It was nothing short of glorious.

Catfish practically threw themselves onto Daddy's Lake Buchanan dock, and then rolled themselves in cornmeal and dove into his propane fryer. We water-skied daily and went tubing down the Comal River. To make sure we kept up our cholesterol levels, we chowed down on chicken fried steak, fried okra, Blue Bell peach ice cream and washed *cabrito* down with gallons of ice cold Shiner Bock. Although an animal lover, I steadfastly refuse to equate the savory, mesquite grilled *cabrito* with those cute little goat kid darlings I bottle-fed at my grandmother's ranch. One can get a lit-tle too hung up on such matters.

We visited with old friends and family, reveling in our home state with her best boot forward. Jan and I were entranced with the friendliness—after all Texas *means* friendly—of our home folk and the flower-blanketed, resplendence of the Hill Country in full regalia. It was hard to believe I'd been so all-fired eager to abandon such a paradise for old cold northern

California. Made me wonder if I harbored some Yankee blood. Nah.

"Jan," I said from my porch hammock one lazy afternoon following a hard morning of drinking beer and shooting the empties in the back pasture, "I've a hankerin' to hit a honky-tonk. What do you say?"

Jan dropped her *Texas Monthly* onto a sun-warmed flagstone and nodded. "Fine by me. But let's take your daddy's pickup, 'cause we'll stand out like a sore toe in the Beemer."

"Did you bring your drankin' tee?"

"Is there a cow in Texas? I have my T-shirt, but dang it, I seem to have misplaced my chaps and spurs."

* * *

When Saturday night rolled around, we loaded ourselves into Daddy's Ford F-350 (complete with gun rack) and did a dos-si-doed on down to the Lil' Bitta Tejas Beer Hall and Cantina.

Live Country Western twanged through the parking lot. When we opened the heavy mesquite door, a rush of ice-cold air, Lone Star Beer fumes, and mesquite smoke rushed out. About a jillion cowboys were bellied up to the bar.

The barn-like structure was packed to capacity with beer drinking two-steppers in Levis, Tony Lama boots, and Texas Hatter's *chapeaux*. We found a table and ordered nachos and beer.

When the band struck up *Cotton-Eyed Joe*, Jan jumped to her feet. "I'm gonna grab me a cowboy and dance," she announced as she headed for the bar.

I opted to sit this one out and made a bet with myself as to which guy she'd pick. I was right. Jan grabbed onto the one with the biggest hat, belt buckle, and beer gut. She and I had concluded long ago, after extensive empirical research, that the hefty ones are the smoothest dancers. Perhaps something to do with dense centers of gravity.

Jan's choice, at first taken aback by being asked to dance, was soon gliding and guiding her across the floor, entranced by this Melanie Griffith look-alike who had fallen into his arms.

After everyone stomped their boots and hollered "Awww shit" one last time, the band moved on to a waltz. I roped me a bronc buster by his belt loops, and for the next half hour we danced our little hillbilly hearts out. After a lively *Beer Barrel Polka*, we were plumb done and staggered back to the table for a beer or six.

By mid-evening, we'd attracted a herd of admiring Bubbas as well as the narrow-eyed scrutiny of several skinny Bubbettes wearing life-threateningly tight jeans. This bevy of hillbeauties, who all seemed to evolve from some special gene pool that breeds women whose thighs never touch, twirled loose strands on the fringes of their *bouffants extraordinaire* and scowled. They didn't take kindly to city gals poaching the local talent.

"Don't go to the little heifer's room alone," I warned Jan. "You might come back with claw marks."

The band took a break. During the lull, one of our fan club decided it was time to get chummy. "You say y'all are from San Francisco?"

We nodded. It was too much trouble to explain about Oakland.

"Well, hell," he said, "we hear you got queers on your po-lice force."

"We do have gays on the force," Jan said, sounding very prim and liberal. "They represent a certain percentage of the population."

"So," our new friend drawled, and I could tell the way he paused he was getting ready to entertain his buddies, "when a Frisco cop says he's gonna blow you away, it takes on a whole new connotation."

Guffaws exploded around the table, along with knee slaps and hoots. I was amazed. Not by the fact that the guy told the joke, but that he used a word like "connotation." Ah, the wonders of Texas.

One of his fellow revelers pointed his Lone Star long neck at the T-shirts Jan and I wore. "Whut kinda beer is that on them shirts? Jap?" Obviously we had attracted a man of the world.

"How very astute of you, Jim Bob," I said. "Yes, it's Sapporo Beer. I got these shirts in Tokyo."

"Whut was you doin' in Tok-yo?"

"I was there on business."

"Bidness? Whut kinda bidness?"

"I'm an engineering consultant."

He smirked for the benefit of his fellow Bubbas, took a gulp of beer, and turned a bleary eye towards Jan. "And, li'l lady, I reckin you to be a brain surgeon?"

"Nope," Jan said with a toss of her head. "You reckon wrong, cowboy. I'm a computer consultant."

Silence fell like stars over Alabama as Jim Bob filtered this information through the grits he had for brains. "Well shee-ut," he said, "jest how in the hey-all do *wimmin* git jobs like that?"

Jan and I looked at each other. "I just remembered why I don't live in Texas," I told her. "It's not the heat, it's the stupidity!"

29

"Hetta Honey, phone," Mother shouted. Actually, she didn't really shout, she never does. It just sounded that way.

I bear hugged several pillows over my head, trying to block out the noonday sun. Mom tugged them away, shoved the phone in my face, and clucked about the room picking up discarded clothing and a half empty beer bottle. A white ring marred the surface of the wooden bedside stand, but I knew from experience it wasn't permanent.

" 'Lo," I rasped.

"Hetta?"

"Uh-huh."

"This is Morris. From the yacht club? I guess you're call forwarding. Your mother sounds real nice. When are you coming home? You aren't thinking of running out on our deal, are you? I made you one hell of an offer on *Sea Cock.*"

"Oh, hi, Morris. I still haven't gotten anywhere with the financing. I can only come up with half and the damned banks think I'm the leper of the financial world."

"Bankers are idiots. You give me the half and I'll finance the rest myself."

I sat up, suddenly wide awake and feeling much, much better. "No, shit?" Mother frowned. "I mean, oh, really? Oh, Morris, I think I love you."

Jan and mother left the room. They hate it when I love someone.

Morris chuckled "Don't tell my wife. So far she likes you. I'll have the papers drawn up. Don't forget, this deal is kept between us. I'll see Garrison today, let him know what's happening."

"Tell him 'hi' for me. And the only other person who knows I'm buying *Sea Cock* is my best friend, Jan. I told her not even to tell her boyfriend, Lars."

"Lars Jenkins?"

"Yeah, they've been dating."

"Can she keep a secret? Lars is a friend of Garrison's, you know. I wouldn't want Garrison to find out from anyone but me that I've sold the boat to you."

"She can and will. Besides, she's here in Texas with me. We'll be back later this week. And thank you."

I hung up, threw off the covers and bounded into the kitchen where Jan and Mother sipped coffee. My mother had, of course, overheard some of the telephone conversation and was grilling Jan, who was filling her in on Lars.

"Oh, Miz Coffey, he's the nicest guy," Jan babbled, then went on to list Lars's attributes until she caught me sticking my finger down my throat.

"Now, Hetta," Mother chided. "You should be happy your friend has found such a nice young man. Does Lars have a brother?"

"Arrgghh!" I grabbed my neck, trying to choke myself. Mother ignored my antics and got back to more important matters. "What was that call about?" she asked. "And who is this Morris you love? Or do I want to know."

"Morris is a happily married man whom I simply adore," I chirped.

"Oh, no, Hetta," she said with a little sigh, "not another *married* one."

* * *

For the record, I've never knowingly dated a married man. It just turned out that way. But then, there was a great deal I didn't know about Hudson until after he disappeared. Little things. Like the wife and two kids he had back in Boston.

Oh, and years before there was that Trinidadian, but shoot, he got married *while* we were dating, so I don't think that should count.

Anyhow, mother need not worry about my love life anymore, since I didn't have one. Also, I hadn't deemed it necessary to bother my parents with some of the more recent and squirrelly events in my life. Like the fact that I was *not* gainfully employed and *was* being terrorized by a mad lock changer.

Nope, as far as *mère et père* Coffey knew, I was headed back to the Bay Area to start a new adventure as a boat person. A boat person with a whole case of SPF 700 sunscreen that Mom insisted I take with me. With a goodly slather of that goop, a vampire could go out in broad daylight.

In case there wasn't a single restaurant between Texas and California, Mother loaded us up with road essentials: a basket of fried chicken, potato salad, pecan pie, a cooler of soft drinks, and a dime for the phone. Evidently mom hadn't used a pay phone in several decades. Before she could check us for clean underwear, we drove west.

"The sun has riz, the sun has set, and here we are in Texas yet," I chanted as we entered the El Paso city limits. "Blimey, I thought we'd never get out of the Lone Star State."

"New Mexico coming up," Jan encouraged. "Maybe we should get a Tex-Mex fix before we cross the state line."

"We could, but I was thinking chicken fried steak with cream gravy."

"Yes, yes, yes."

Jan and I have so much in common.

We grazed through four western states and, per Jan's insistence, we didn't make the detour through Laughlin. As we rolled along I-10 for miles and miles of nothing but miles and miles, we whiled away the time thinking up boat names. I was kidding about *Hetta-row* .

"How about, "*Hi, Sailor?*""

"Hetta, get serious. This is a very important decision. As you well know. Think of what we thought of folks when we saw some of those boat names on the bay. Absolutely nothing with "sea" in it and certainly not *Seaducer* or anything like that. Crude and unimaginative."

"*Cirrhosis of the River?*"

"Apt, but gross. Maybe something dreamy, like *Wanderin' Star.*"

"Too . . . sailboaty. *No Forwarding Address?*"

"No, Hetta, it's not you. How about *Country Girl?* The problem there is figuring out which country."

I nixed it and munched on a chicken leg.

Jan contemplated for a while, finished off a thigh, gave me a wicked grin and said, "Hetta, I've got it. It's you. *Bullship.*"

I gave her the look she deserved. "Cute, Jan. Have you ever hitchhiked?"

Jan looked at the barren roadside stretching for miles into parched desert. "Maybe I can come up with something a more apropos. *Hydrotherapy?*"

"Gag. I'll think of something. But I wasn't kidding about the no forwarding address. I'm gonna change all my addresses. I'll get a post office box, change my e-mail address, and everything. That way, whoever is bugging me can't find me after I move onto the boat."

"Good thinking. Maybe you should get an answering service for your business, too."

"What business? But you're right. I do have a few proposals out, so I'd better keep the old phone number and put a service on it."

"Anything from Allison about when Seattle will reach a decision regarding your undeserved sacking?"

"Naw, not yet. But she hasn't let me cash their check, so there's still hope. Also, I'll call the Trob when we get back, see what he's heard. I need to talk to him anyhow, because I'm thinking of having a memorial service, kind of a delayed wake, for RJ. I want to invite Fidel. For RJ, the Trob might come out of his treetop. Allison went over to meet him not long ago to get info, and she said she actually had a conversation with him that lasted more than five minutes. I think the Trob might be coming around to understanding us lesser mortals."

"Good. He can't spend his whole life in the tower of Baxter. A wake for RJ, huh? No funeral?"

"Nope. Maybe a little get together at the house before the new owners take over, then I'll do something creative with RJ's ashes later. Maybe cast them upon the bay from my own boat. Save myself the grand demanded by Critter Cremains. Besides, I hate funerals and weddings for the same reason. I prefer to think of folks as they were when still alive."

30

We arrived in Oakland a day earlier than planned due to an overwhelming desire for a decent vinaigrette. Someone needs to tell America that salad should consist of more than chopped up iceberg lettuce topped with gooey substances and flanked with stale saltines.

My determination to never spend another night in the house went down the tubes, overridden by the deep fatigue of fifteen hours on the road. The good news was Jan had another day of vacation and we could sleep in. The other good news was I'd arranged to move aboard *Sea Cock* the very next day.

The bad news started when we got to the house. The alarm was off. Again. By now we were so used to it that, after a half-hearted search for lurking bad guys, we shrugged it off to equipment malfunction. After opening all the windows to air the house, I pushed the HEAT button on the hot tub and whipped up a red meal.

Sun-dried tomato fettuccini marinara, a salad of red leaf lettuce, radicchio, arugula, red bell peppers, and red onion topped with a red wine vinegar dressing, accompanied by, what else? Valpolicelli. Strawberries for dessert satisfied both our pallet and palates. A girl can take just so much road food.

We'd finished our *banquet rouge* when Martinez called. A passing patrol car had seen lights in the house.

"So, anything new on your jewelry?" Jan asked when I hung up.

I shrugged. "Martinez said it could have been some punk that took advantage of the situation and stole the jewelry box. I mean, the place did look a little deserted. And the alarm *was* off."

"You should have told him the alarm was off, again, Hetta. And this time I am absolutely sure we set it when we left. And last time, too. I distinctly remember, right after Craig took RJ's, uh, RJ away. We left and we set it on the way out."

"God, I'm glad this joint is sold. Let us retire to the hot tub for one final boiling, drink a lot of really good wine, and bid adieu to Chez RJ."

We iced down my last bottle of 1998 Chassagne Montrachet, grabbed towels, and went up the steps to the hot tub deck. I was gratified to see steam billowing out from under the cover of the tub. We stood at the deck rail and took in the panorama. The Bay Area sparkled below us as Oakland's city sounds rose on a light breeze: A siren's wail, a waft of music from the Coliseum, and the occasion report of a gunshot.

"I will miss this view," I said.

"Yeah, I remember the first time we sat up here. Before you left for Tokyo. I sure did miss you while you were gone."

"I should never have gone. I knew I would hate it. I mean, I'm single. All the women over there are short and cute and all the men short and ugly. What was my first clue? And then the unkindest cut of all: Hudson. To paraphrase W.C. Fields, the bastard drove me to drink and I forgot to thank him. It was a piss poor time, my worst. At least that's what I thought then. What with losing RJ, I now know things can get worse."

"It'll get better. I'm sure of it. Heck, it already has. Let's get wet."

We clinked glasses, toasted the night. I walked a few steps, grabbed the hot tub cover and threw it open as I smiled back over my shoulder at Jan. "You're right. Things are getting better. I mean, what else can go wrong?"

Evidently, from the horrified look on Jan's face, a great deal. I reluctantly turned my head and saw, floating in the steaming water, two things: my jewelry box and Hudson Williams.

I was really glad to see my jewelry box.

* * *

"Maybe you really should rent me a room," Detective Martinez grumped.

"You can have the whole damned house." I was sitting next to Jan in the living room. We'd sunk to tapping a boxed wine. No flowery, pear-y bouquet like the Montcharet, but by now our taste buds were as dead as Hudson Williams.

Cops crawled all over the place, a helicopter whomped the night air above, dogs howled, and neighbors lined up outside a yellow police tape in the yard. The new owners would probably get letters from the NFL, ABL, *and* the NBA.

"Oh, hell," I whined, "I wonder if the buyer will try to back out now? Do we have to tell them about the, uh, body?"

"I believe," Martinez said dryly, "there's some law about disclosure."

"Great. Just great. Hudson wasn't content to mess up my life once, he has to do it again. Inconsiderate bastard."

"Ms. Coffey, I need to ask you some questions," Martinez said, suddenly sounding all formal and officious. "Perhaps you'd prefer to have a lawyer present?"

"I don't need no stinkin' lawyer. Wait a minute. You don't think *I* killed Hudson, do you?"

"I am a detective, you know. And I detect a certain lack of remorse over the demise of your old boyfriend. Let me read something to you. *'Dead would be good. But as you can see, Detective Martinez, even if he is alive, I don't think Hudson, wherever the dirty rat bastard may be, would be*

*looking to harm me. As a matter of fact, if I ever
see him again, he's the one who's going to get
harmed. Some folks, like old granny used to say,
just need killing.'* Sound familiar?"

Oops.

"Just big talk. Besides, I was in Texas," I
protested, thanking my lucky lone star that Hudson
got himself done in when I had an alibi.

Martinez nodded, then said, "But, by your
own admission, you have friends in low places."

Jan said, "Uh, Hetta, maybe we should call
Allison?"

"Is she your lawyer?" Martinez asked.

"Sort of. Yes." I didn't think he needed to
know that Allison wasn't in private practice. Or
that she was actually a prosecutor for another
county. Who better than Allison to determine if he
had any kind of case?

"I can meet you downtown, unless you
want to call her and have her come over here right
now."

"Look Martinez, you know damned well I
didn't drown Hudson Williams in my hot tub. I
might'a shot him if I'd had a chance, but I damned
sure wouldn't pollute my own tub."

"I believe you. I just got to do my job."

"How do we even know he was murdered?"
Jan said hopefully.

"Oh, sure," I scoffed. "Maybe he was in for
a quick dip and fell asleep after closing the cover?"
Jan gave me her look.

Martinez rolled his eyes. "We don't know
anything yet. I should have the coroner's first take

in a few … " The front door swung open and a tiny Oriental man walked in. "Speak of the devil."

Martinez introduced the coroner, and they went upstairs. An hour later, we watched as Hudson's drippy, parboiled body was hauled out the front door and carted away. I'd have to have the rugs cleaned. Once again Hudson had rained on my parade.

After for*ever*, Martinez and the coroner came down the stairs talking quietly. My extrasensory hearing picked up only one word: icepick. Either we were gonna have a cocktail party, or it was going to be a very long night.

It was a very long night.

Allison came over within an hour, did her lawyerly magic, and got us cleared to go to Jan's for what was left of the night. Allison left, Martinez followed, and then the last of the Homicide squad. Yep, Homicide. They suspected Hudson was offed when someone shoved an icepick in his ear. Someone with great taste, I might add. A quick trip to the kitchen with the detective on my tail revealed that my Georg Jensen icepick was missing. *Zut, alors!* It was part of a set.

Only a rookie remained. His job, it seemed, was to make sure Jan and I didn't tamper with evidence. We left for the City, our flight fueled by a burning desire to be shut of my haunted house. It was a sad farewell to what had been a happy home for so many years.

Trying to cheer me up, Jan said, "Look on the bright side, Hetta. Hudson won't be messing with you anymore."

"All too true. One slight problem, Sherlock. Someone killed him at my house. Or at least left him in my tub. Doesn't that sound like someone's trying to scare me? Or threaten me? Or both?"

"Well, yes." She chewed her lip, a signal that she had more to say, but was reluctant to do so.

"Well, yes but *what*?"

"You won't get upset?"

"I'm too tired."

"Okay, then. How about this. Hudson came to your house, found you gone, decided to stay until you got back, went into the hot tub and someone, seeing him out there in the dark, thought it was you and killed him by mistake."

"Gosh, Jan, I feel sooo much better now. Thanks oodles."

31

"They say the two of the happiest days of your life are the day you buy a boat and the day you sell it. I guess that makes us a couple of very happy people, Hetta. Here're the keys to *Sea Cock*," Morris said, handing me two keys on a hopefully non-premonitory miniature life ring.

As I stared at the keys to my new life, he drew an iced bottle of Mumms from a silver bucket, fiddled with the foil and wire, and bellowed, "Betty, come on up here and join me and Hetta in a toast."

A waft of Joy, tinkling bracelets and the swish of silk preceded Betty's arrival. She fluttered, aglitter in gold and jewels, into an oversized chair. As always, she looked as though she just stepped out of a fashion magazine, albeit one for graciously preserved seventy-year-olds. Her eyes sparkled like the five carat stone on her finger. "So, the deal is done? How very nice for you, Hetta. Are you all ready to move aboard?"

"Getting there. My morning marathon of sorting, storing, throwing and tagging giveaways is done. I own much more stuff than any individual should. I feel like a great weight has been lifted from my shoulders." I didn't mention that a very drippy, dead weight had also been extracted from my hot tub, or that while I was packing up this morning, I had a cop looking over my shoulder. I knew for sure Betty wouldn't be able to keep a prime piece of info like that from her fellow yacht club members.

"Morris and Betty, I really appreciate your faith in my being able to pay for *Sea Cock*. I won't let you down." I raised my fluted crystal glass to them and hoped I wasn't telling a bald-faced lie.

Morris cocked his head towards his wife. "You had a little angel on your shoulder, Hetta."

"Let's say Morris saw the wisdom of my ways," Betty cooed, smiling affectionately in his direction. "I admire your spunk, Hetta. The yacht club needs more women who own and operate their own boats."

"I don't know about that 'operating' part. I still have to learn how to drive it. Her."

"My dear," Betty said, taking a dainty sip of Mumms, "how hard can it be? I mean, *men* do it."

Now if I'd said that I'd be called a castrating you-know-what, but Betty got a sweet smile from her husband. Maybe it's all in the delivery. Or maybe the man.

* * *

"Jan, I've got the keys. Can you meet me at the yacht club?"

"Oh, this is sooo exciting. I'll be there in an hour. Do you want me to stay on the boat with you tonight? Or would you rather enjoy it alone?"

"I know you've got plans with Lars. I'll be fine on the boat by myself for the night. But I wanted you to be the first aboard with me this afternoon. We can have a little champers. I didn't want...I just.... "

"I know, honey. It breaks my heart RJ can't be with us today, but you're starting a whole new life and you can't let missing him get you down on such a momentous occasion. If it'll help, I'll fart."

Friends. Ain't they the best?

* * *

Sea Cock, her fiberglass hull agleam in the spring sun, sat alongside the yacht club dock. Someone, probably Morris, had decked her out in full regalia with all dress flags aflutter.

Majestic? Nope, too dramatic.

I was preparing to step into the aft cockpit when Jan yelled, "Stop, Hetta! Let me take a picture."

"Why don't you carry me over the transom?"

"Do I look like Arnold Schwarzenegger? You know, you haven't been to aerobics lately and I've been meaning to mention the fact that you're getting a lit-tle tubby."

I sucked in my stomach and posed. "Take the picture and belay the back talk, matey, or you'll surely walk the plank."

"Aye, aye, Captain Coffey."

Captain Coffey. Now that had a nice ring to it. Or did it sound too much like an adult cereal?

I slid open the door to the main saloon and stepped in. The aroma and beauty of a huge fresh floral arrangement—Betty's doing, no doubt—greeted me. The bouquet of roses, daisies and irises sat on a high-low teak table in front of a nine foot L-shaped settee. *My* L-shaped settee.

Enthralled, touching things as I went, I walked through the main saloon and descended, via two wide teak steps, into a down-galley equipped with a full-sized refrigerator, three burner stove, oven, microwave, and built-in banquette for informal dining. All the comforts of home. My home.

From the looks of it, the entire boat had been professionally cleaned, so all I had to do was go get my own things. I made a mental note of what I had to do first. Like strip off the custom made bed cover and replace it with my own ashes-of-roses duvet and linens. Everything I needed for the boat was boxed and ready, waiting for me to pick them up at the house. And even though my peaches and pinks didn't exactly match the new blue décor, I planned to live with them until I could afford new stuff. Life is full of little compromises, *n'est-ce pas*?

The aft sundeck, furnished in slightly faded but freshly scrubbed Brown Jordan fake rattan with blue and white striped cushions, sported an ice maker filled with fresh ice, a rack of blue and white plastic stemware and a wet bar. Everything was showroom immaculate and in its place.

Everything.

"Uh, Hetta," Jan said, pointing to an open cabinet over the wet bar, "isn't that Garrison's stereo?"

"Uh-huh. And those are also his CDs." We went back inside, and a stem to stern inspection revealed Garrison's clothes in *my* closet, his toiletries in a cabinet in *my* bathroom. Head. Whatever.

Livid, I grabbed the telephone, the one that, as of ten that morning, was unlisted in my name. "Morris, this is Hetta. I'm on *Sea Cock*."

"Great. How's she look?"

"The boat looks great. It's the accessories I'm not crazy about."

"What accessories, Hetta?"

"Garrison's crap. It's all still on the boat."

Silence. Then, "Is this a problem?"

"Damn right it's a problem, Morris. I bought *Sea Cock*, not Garrison."

"Hetta, there's some kind of misunderstanding here. Garrison assured me you two, uh, were...." His voice dwindled off as my blood pressure skyrocketed. I opened my mouth to commence a tirade, but thought better of it. No sense in railing at poor Morris over a misunderstanding of some kind that surely could be easily sorted out.

I took a deep breath, battling to control my fury.

"Let me see if I have this straight, Morris. Garrison led you to believe he was remaining aboard? For the record there is no *you two,* and for everyone's information..." As my voice involuntarily rose, I heard Morris muffle the mouthpiece and say something unintelligible to someone in the background. Then, after a minute, Betty's soothing tones replaced Morris's confused ones.

"Hetta dear, poor Morris gave me the phone. Actually, he threw it at me as if it were radioactive. Leave it to men to screw things up, poor devils. They think communication means something like Morse code. But, in dear Morris's defense, I think you should know Garrison has given not only Morris, but everyone in the yacht club, the definite impression you and he are having a fling. I found it hard to believe, but Garrison as much as told Morris he expected to continue living, with you, on *Sea Cock*."

"That rat! Thanks for the info, Betty. Please tell Morris not to worry. Everything will be fine. Just as soon as I murder Garrison."

Jan shot me a look, one reminding me that, not twenty four hours ago, one of my idle threats had already come back to haunt me. "Kidding, of course. By the way, the boat looks wonderful and thanks for the flowers." I hung up and told Jan what Garrison, Morris and Betty said.

"You know, Hetta, I told you weeks ago Garrison was hinting around that you two were an item. So now what?".

My guns were still at the house, so I examined the door lock. Not your standard Master or dead bolt. Fooey, I'd have to hire a professional to change it. "Exorcism, Jan, pure and simple. We'll have the joint cleared of all things Garrison in no time."

* * *

I was carrying a load of Garrison's belongings from my cabin to the sundeck, when someone rapped on the hull.

"Permission to come aboard?" a voice bellowed. I looked out to find an entourage of about twenty yacht club members standing on the dock, Garrison at the forefront. He was holding a magnum of champagne and a large bouquet of flowers. I shrugged helplessly at Jan and invited them all on board.

32

Sea Cock, on Sunday morning, resembled Times Square on January one. There was hardly a square inch of boat not littered with empty glasses, beer bottles, confetti—white, thank God— shredded gift wrap, or soggy canapés. From the deck speakers, Jimmy Buffet lamented bad drinking habits and cheeseburgers in paradise. Jimmy was accompanied by loud snores emanating from somewhere in my boat. Tracing the sonorous trail, I found Garrison in my guest cabin.

"Garrison, wake up. We have to talk," I yelled, the shout echoing through my own throbbing head. Garrison snorted awake and sat up, dazed.

"Oh, Hetta. Hi."

"Garrison, I—"

"I know," he said, "you want me off the boat. No problem. I haven't had time to find a new place, and I thought you might like me to stick around and show you all the systems. Boats aren't like houses, you know. All sorts of complicated stuff."

I'd already noticed. Sometime during the night I'd flushed the toilet and an alarming red light marked HOLDING TANK FULL lit up. What did that mean?

"Yeah, okay, I guess it'll be okay for a day or two. Come on, help me clean this place up, then we'll go up to the club for brunch."

An hour later, Garrison's gear was moved into the forward guest cabin and *Sea Cock* was shipshape again. Except for that holding tank thing.

While I took note of the phone number and jargon, Garrison called Privy Patrol, Inc., You Dump It, We Pump It, for dockside pump out service. While we waited for them, we ate breakfast at the yacht club. We had just finished our eggs Benedict when a workboat chugged up alongside *Sea Cock*.

"Sewer rats are here, Hetta, we'd better go down. You got any cash? Unless you're a regular customer, they don't take checks."

"I've got some money. How much is it?"

"Well, being Sunday and all, probably a little pricey."

"Garrison, when was the last time you had the holding tank pumped out?"

"I don't recall. I mean, jeez, Hetta, who knew you were gonna have a party?"

Tempted to push him off the dock, I nonetheless bit my tongue and signed up for twice-weekly pump out service. I carefully noted the holding tank service's phone number and invoice amount in my new Boat Expenses book, a gift from a well-wisher. My first entry and it's a crapper zapper. Who knew? But what the hey, I'd had to pay a city sewer bill at the house. My first omen of things to come, however, should have been that someone even *made* a Boat Expenses book. And that it had lots and lots of pages.

Jenks Jenkins knocked on the hull as the sewer rodents were motoring away with their toxic cargo. Before I could say a word, Garrison invited Jenks aboard *my* boat and offered up a drink.

Mustering every ounce of grace I had left in my soul, I said "Hello, Jenks." After all, the man *had* sent me flowers. Gritting my teeth, I tromped below to gingerly strip my bed. Unwilling to sleep on Garrison's sheets, I had spent a chilly. but luckily mostly comatose, night rolled in the bedspread. And I wasn't too sure about *it*.

My sheets were still in my garage, packed with stuff I'd intended to bring to the boat the day before. Before I'd ended up with a houseful, uh, boatful, of uninvited, if well-intentioned guests.

Tonight I planned to sleep under my own silk comforter, swathed in 800 count Egyptian cotton. Tomorrow, Garrison could take his ratty old bedding to whatever lair he found to inhabit. I stuffed his pillows, sheets and even the bedspread that was custom-made for *Sea Cock,* into a plastic garbage bag and climbed to the main saloon.

Garrison and Jenks were playing cribbage, unaware I was royally pissed at their cavalier attitude towards *my* boat.

"Where do you want this, Garrison?" I asked between grinding molars. If I didn't get rid of him soon I'd have to have a whole new enamel job.

"Oh, leave it there. I'll stow it later."

I'll stow you *later.* "Fine. I'll be back soon. I'm going to get my things from the house."

"Need any help?" Jenks asked.

"No, thanks." *Yeah, you can help. You can get your ass off my boat and take Garrison with you.*

"Sorry I missed your welcome party last night. Everyone says it was great," Jenks said. "Anyhow, welcome to the wonderful world of boating."

I looked at my watch, thinking, gee, wasn't it about time for his *nooner*? But I said aloud, "Thanks." They teach us grace under fire in the South and, once in a great while, I even use it. Albeit reluctantly.

Already engrossed in their cribbage game, the men mumbled a "bye" in unison. Then Garrison looked up and added, "See you when you get back."

Lucky me.

Sigh. Oh, well, tomorrow was another day. Tomorrow I'd get control of this situation. Tomorrow I'd have my fresh water pump burn out, right after I tried flooding the bathroom. Head. Whatever. But, of course, I didn't know that yet.

I left the men to their card game and drove to my house. The police were gone, a mixed blessing. I spent a couple of very jumpy hours packing my things into RJ's car. I planned to leave the Beemer in the garage while I still had one, then sell the little yuppie toy. After all, I now owned forty-five feet of ultimate prop. Who needed a status car? And besides, I didn't think it a good idea to park my thirty-someodd-thousand dollar convertible in an uncovered, salty air parking lot in West Oakland. Chamber of Commerce glamorization and Gertrude Stein witticisms notwithstanding, I *know* where Jack London Square is, and it is there, in West Oakland.

I got back around six o'clock to find *Sea Cock* amazingly devoid of people. Maybe I'd gotten lucky and Jenks had adopted Garrison.

Chic, alors! I cranked up a little Mozart, shoved a frozen Stouffers into the oven, Beringer into an ice bucket, and my hungover head under a heavenly stream of hot water. I'd slathered a gooey gob of ten dollar a drop crème de platypus placenta or some such moisturizer on my hair when the shower quit. Which was just in time, for I noticed water threatening to slosh over the side of the stall.

I could hear the continual gallump of what sounded like the sump pump the plumber had left running at my house a few weeks before. The throb came from the bowels of my boat. My own bowels had set up a pretty good throb themselves. "Now what, Ollie?" I growled, grabbing a towel.

I turbaned my slimy hair, found some sweats, rummaged a pot from under the stove, trudged out to the very chilly dock, turned on the hose and filled the pot. All of this, of course, in full view of an amused contingent hanging over the yacht club bar.

Three chilly trips later, during which the club members were waving as well as laughing, I'd managed to remove enough conditioner from my hair to attempt a blow dry. Back in the head, I plugged in my Conair, then had second thoughts as a wake rocked a gallon of shower water onto the floor around my bare feet. "Woman Dies of Shock on Boat," BART commuters would read in their newspapers the next morning. They'd probably figure she got her monthly pump out service invoice.

In the main saloon, I finally found a plug near a mirrored wall and was all set to flip on the dryer when I remembered something: wattage.

What was it they told me about hair dryers and boats? I looked at the side of the Conair. 1600 watts. Being an engineer I can both add and convert. 1600 watts equals thirteen point three amps. Shoot, according to Garrison I had fifty amps of dock power, so that meant I had thirty-six point seven amps to spare, didn't I?

I was about to hit the dryer switch again when I smelled lasagna. Twenty minutes to go. How many amps did the oven draw? The hot water heater? Fridge? And wasn't there something about a battery charger? *Merde*.

After choking down a half cooked dinner, I crawled into bed, trying not to think about what my slimy, damp locks were doing to forty dollar pillowcases and hundred dollar feather pillows. I was droned to sleep by that faint gallumping sound. Tomorrow I'd figure out what it was.

Tomorrow came early. Three a.m., to be exact. That's when a smoke detector went off. Garrison and I almost collided as we both scrambled into the main saloon to see what was on fire. I'd never even heard him return to the boat, but as bad as I hated to admit it, I was glad he was there. Fire is one of my phobias, right up there with drowning. So here I was, on a burning boat.

"So, Hetta," Jan said when I called her the next day looking for sympathy, "it wasn't a real fire? Just smoke? And Garrison was the hero of the hour?"

"I guess he was," I admitted.

"How bad is the damage?"

"Burned out water pump. Cost me a hundred bucks for a new one, but Garrison saved me an installation charge."

"That's good, I guess. What happened? Did the stupid pump just decide to self-destruct?"

"Evidently. Garrison said something about the water tank, but said he'd make sure it didn't happen again. Also, I guess the drain in the shower was plugged, but he fixed that, too."

Jan was quiet for a moment or three, always a bad sign. "Sounds like Garrison's making himself right handy. You *are* still gonna make him leave, aren't you?"

" 'Course I am. Soon. But I figure it can't hurt to let him stay a little while. Only until I get used to all these systems."

"Or until the body returns to your hair, whichever comes first? You know, Hetta, maybe you should have the boat checked out by a professional."

"Like?"

"Like Jenks. Lars says he knows boats better than almost anyone."

"I'm sure Garrison can handle everything for me until he finds a place to live. After all, he's been living aboard *Sea Cock* for a long time, so he knows the boat. Okay, so Morris said Garrison didn't do much, but Morris wasn't here to check on him and I am. With Garrison taking care of my boat, I can get back to gainful employment. I've got a yacht to support, you know."

"Sounds like you may have more than a yacht to support."

"What do you mean? Garrison? Nah, he's history, and soon."

"It's your bank account, your life."

"Yeah, and I've got to get on with both. Speaking of, don't forget I've got fifty people coming to RJ's wake at the house Saturday night."

"Not a hot tub party, I trust?"

"Cute. No, the tub was drained by my service guy after the cops finished with it."

"Thank God for that. It'll be creepy, being back in your house, but I'll come over early to help if you need me."

"I need you for moral support, not work. The house is completely devoid of furniture now, so the caterer is bringing everything, including chairs and tables. It'll be a two hour wine and dog biscuit affair."

"I think I'll bring me some tater chips."

33

"Gee, Hetta, isn't this, uh, interesting? A theme wake," Jan mused, then took a bite of something called *crepes de chien* and chased it with Red Dog beer. She stood next to me, watching people and pets mill, snack, and bark. Elvis crooned you-know-what in the background.

Detective Martinez, a last minute drop-in, pried his pants leg from the locked jaws of Raoul's poodle, Catamite, and joined us in front of the fireplace. "Good afternoon, ladies," he said. He gingerly sampled something labeled *pâwtè*. "Nice...whatever. Hope you don't mind me being here."

"On the contrary, sir, I am very happy you're around. I had second thoughts about coming back, but RJ was important enough to make me.

And thanks for not kicking his guest, although Catamite was asking for it. See anything strange?" I asked.

Martinez rolled his eyes.

"I *meant*, anything that might help you ID Hudson's killer? That is why you wanted to come isn't it? To spy?"

"I wouldn't have put it so subtly, but, yeah, that's about it. Doesn't hurt to keep your eyes open."

"Is there something you want to share with me, Detective? We have a few minutes before Jan leads off with the first memorial toast."

"Not really. We'll talk later." It's hard to tell, but he looked more pained than usual. Maybe I'd send him some prunes.

"I'm ready," Jan said, and blew her whistle. Everyone assembled for the first, er, tail of the day: How RJ Got His Name.

"It was a little over five years ago...." she began, and my mind drifted back.

Dawg, as I called him, had been living with me for three months and we were definitely on a bonding roller coaster. At least I was. Dawg had his own agenda, doggedly escaping the confines of my newly fenced yard to attack any non-WASP he could. Which in my neighborhood was really easy.

My section of the Oakland Hills was inhabited by an eclectic tribe of which I was a triple minority: A Single White Female. Up the street, in a new upscale development, lived an assortment of doctors, lawyers and other upper income types, including those nouveau-est of the *nouveaux riches*: Oakland Raiders, Warriors, and A's. Few were single and none white. I had unwittingly inflicted a racist dog on an unsuspecting, but very muscular, pugnacious, and litigious populace. Were Dawg to survive, he'd have to mend his crappy attitude and quit dogging his well-armed fellow residents. Or get a bulletproof vest.

Hounded to seek a solution before the dogs of war were unleashed, I sought the highly recommended Dr. Craig Washington, who made house calls and was reputed to specialize in disturbed pets. I made an appointment and was looking forward to a Robert Redford double who'd whisper something magical into Dawg's ear. Or mine.

What I got was the biggest, blackest, meanest looking man I'd ever seen this side of the NFL. Or Dawg either, apparently, for ten minutes alone—I was listening from upstairs, tearing up petticoats and boiling water just in case—with the behemoth vet and Dawg found something akin to religion. Craig never revealed his trade secret, but I suspect he'd rubbed himself down with Alpo.

At any rate, the terrorism ceased and soon Dawg (still uncured of his escape tactics), instead of eating their tires, could be found cadging handouts from linebackers on the way to their Bentleys. It was enough to bring a tear. Kind of a Mean Joe Green soft drink commercial moment.

Anyhow, that story was for Craigosaurus, wearing, quite naturally, a Big Dog shirt, to tell in doggerel verse.

But first Jan finished bragging as to how she, and she alone, had saved my dog the indignity of being called plain Dawg by naming him Raymond Johnson. As in "You can call me Ray, or you can call me Jay, or you can call me Johnny, or you can call me Sonny, or you can call me RayJay, or you can call me RJ, or you can call me RJJ, or you can call me RJJ Jr., but you doesn't have to call me Johnson." Jan was a big fan of the old Redd Foxx Show.

After a couple of hours of RJ stories and some doggone good memorial toasts, I bid my former home good-bye, took RJ's picture and ashes from the mantle, and went to *Sea Cock*. God, that name! How about *Dream Catcher*? Nah, too dreamy.

34

At least I was gainfully employed again.

The Seattle debacle still rocked on with nothing settled, but I had landed a short-term contract in Southern California lucrative enough to keep me in boat parts. Barely in time, too, what with Garrison's ever increasing demands for moola to buy stuff for *Sea Cock.* I was sorely tempted to cash that buy-off check, but Allison wouldn't let me have it. I called her uppity, but it didn't help.

I had returned from a three day trip south when Jan called. "How's La land?" she asked.

"Smoggy, snarled, and smarmy. It's great to be back on the boat. Where are you?"

"At the office. Maybe I'll drop by later. I have news."

"Tell me now, you know I hate waiting for gossip."

"It's big," she teased.

"You won the lottery."

"Better. I'm moving to Florida with Lars."

"Oh, that's, uh, sudden," I said, trying to cover the disappointment in my voice. I failed.

"I knew you'd be upset. We're not leaving for a whole month. Look, I'll come over tonight and tell you all about it. I mean if you plan to be home?"

"Without doubt. After my week in La, wild horses couldn't pry me off this boat. Even with all the maintenance problems I've been having."

"More? What now?"

"Nothing money can't fix. Garrison has a list of boat chores a mile long requiring my money and his attention. Did you know there are twenty pumps on this mother? Thank the gods Garrison's been here to keep things working. You were right, he's real handy to have around."

"Hetta, I was being sarcastic and you know it. Doesn't he get in your way? I mean, you've always been a bit of a loner."

"No, when I'm here he makes himself scarce."

"Where does he go? And how? Lars says Garrison's car hasn't run in a year."

"He's using RJ's car this weekend. I don't want to go anywhere anyway," I said, then wished I hadn't. Somehow I knew she wouldn't like to hear that.

Meaningful pause, followed by, "Oh."

"What does 'oh' mean?"

"Nothing." Petulant, she sounded.

"Jan, speak."

"It's just you never wanted roommates." Was that a whine? Had she and I ever discussed being roomies in the past? If so, had I vetoed the idea? We'd always been so close, but maintained our own places.

"Jan, Garrison is not a roommate. He's only staying on the boat until I get used to it and he can find another place. Besides, now that I have to be in La so much, it's good to have someone watch the boat. What time'll you be here? I'll grill us a big ole juicy T-bone."

"On my way."

I took a shower, which blessedly delivered hot water *and* also drained, poured a glass of wine and opened the freezer. The steaks were gone.

* * *

"It's okay, Hetta, you know I love macaroni and cheese."

"Yeah, me, too, Jan. But I'd like a choice. I'll have to talk to Garrison about raiding my fridge." I poked at my salad. "Thank God he hates veggies and that I had the good sense to warn him away from my liquor cabinet before I left this week. Last time I came home, and there wasn't even a beer left."

"I can't believe you're letting him get away with this. What's come over you?"

"Fear, Jan. Abject terror. At the house, if something didn't work it was annoying. Here, if it doesn't work I could sink."

"Excellent point, but.... Never mind."

"But what?"

"Well, Lars says—"

"Lars, Lars, I'm sick of hearing that name."

Jan stared at me, obviously wounded by my waspish retort. *Merde.*

"I'm sorry. Maybe I'm jealous. Hell, I *am* jealous. After all, Lars is hauling off my best friend and I'm feeling sorry for myself. I'll miss you. I know I'm not being fair or logical, but why should I change now?" This got a small smile, so I asked, "Okay, so what does Lars say?"

"Never mind."

"Don't pout. I said I was sorry and I meant it. I was being a self-centered lout. I want you to be happy and if Lars makes it happen, so be it. Why can't you two be happy here, in California? You'll hate Florida. It's full of Yankees, you know."

"Lars *is* a Yankee, but if you'd get to know him better you'd like him anyway. Really."

"Okay, invite him to dinner here next weekend." *Maybe I can poison him.*

"That was way too easy," Jan said, a skeptical frown on her face. "What's the catch? And what kind of poison?"

Damn, the woman reads minds. "No catch. If Lars is gonna be a permanent fixture, I guess I'd better get on his good side." *If I can find it. Getting around that tub of lard could take years.*

"Why am I still worried?" she said. "Never mind, I'll ask him."

"Good. So, what did Lard, uh, Lars say?"

Jan narrowed her eyes. "About what, Hetta?"

"*Sea Cock.* God, we have to come up with a better name. I've been on this boat for a month and I'm having as much trouble with its name as I did RJ's. I've ruled out gods— Greek, Roman or otherwise—godly realms, anything with Neptune or Poseidon in it, mom's name, or anything cutesy."

"Lemme think on it. *Far Pavilions?*"

"Nope, too...stupid a plot." We laughed, and I said, "How about *High Cotton?*"

"Too Southern."

"Too bad I didn't buy a yawl. I could name her *Nice Meetin' Y'all Yawl.*"

"Now that's Southern."

"Anyhow, what did Lars say about my boat?" I asked again, somewhat reluctantly.

"He wanted to know if you'd ever seen *Gaslight?*"

"Sure. Old movie, Ingrid Bergman. Her husband, Charles Boyer? He wants her to think she's crazy, so he rigs the lamps to dim and then acts like nothing's wrong. What's it got to do with me?"

"Are you sure that Garrison is doing as many repairs as he says? You've never been afraid of squat, Hetta. Why the boat? Are you sure you're not getting gaslit?"

"I believe that would be gas *lighted*, Miz Jan."

"Whatever. Anyhow, we, or rather, Lars, had an idea."

I thought, *If I hear "Lars" once more I swear I'll scream.* But I said, "Let me guess. I should buy a condo in Ft. Lauderdale?"

"Fat chance, Hetta, I know better. He says you should hire Jenks to check out your boat. Lars..." she paused as I let out a small shriek, "says his brother knows more about boats than almost anyone on the estuary."

"Jenks hates me."

"I think 'hate' is a strong word. You two are diametrically polar."

"You've been listening to those talk shows again, haven't you?" I watch them, as well, but I try not to pick up the lingo. Diametrically polar?

"You know. You two have different interests, that's all."

"Yeah, he holds no interest at all in me and I have less in him. Also, I have my permanent teeth and I can read."

"Meaning?"

"Meaning," I said, "his interests seems to lie somewhere between a brunette from ding dong school and a dingbat aging blonde bimbo."

"Ooowee, do I detect a little green monster glint in those big brown eyes?" she asked. Since I refused to acknowledge such drivel, she answered her own question. "Oh, I think so. And for your info, you doofus, the brunette is his daughter. And the blonde? You could get rid of her in a San Francisco second."

"Why would I want to do a thing like that?" Jan must be wading in the Valium pool again.

"For one thing, we could be significant others in-law," she said with a grin. A shit eating grin, at that.

"Jan, get any idea like that right out of what's left of your brain. Jenks Jenkins is everything I hate in a man." I guess. I know I hate it when they ignore me.

"Okay, okay, but this is business. Jenks won't work cheap, but if I were you I'd hire him. He's working on his own boat right now, but I'm sure he'd take the time to come over here."

"I'll think about it. Where's his boat?" I asked.

"It's at Svensen's Boat Yard. It seems someone creamed him in a race."

"I hardly touched him!"

"Not you. Someone else hit him a couple of weeks ago. Call Jenks and hire him to do a survey. It's the same as a real estate appraisal, but for boats. Tell Garrison it's for the insurance company or some bullshit. That way you won't hurt the freeloader's feelings, if it's humanly possible to do so. And maybe you'll learn a thing or two about *Sea Cock*."

"I'll think about it."

She dug around in her purse and handed me Jenks's card.

I read aloud, " 'Robert Jenkins, Marine Specialist, Surveyor. Electronics repair and installation, diesel engine diagnostics, security systems.' Gee, does he also do windows?"

"Probably not, but at least he won't move in on you."

"Point taken. I'll keep this card, in case the world ends and Jenks and I are the last two on it."

"Hetta, you can be such a bitch. I'm gonna miss that."

35

As usual, I didn't take Jan's advice. I didn't even attempt to hire Jenks who, according to Jan herself, said I was "flighty." Whatever that means.

I did vow, however, to learn more about my own boat in my spare time. Which was suddenly scarce. I was in the big middle of the La job when I received a formal request, via Allison-at-law, to attend a settlement meeting in Seattle.

"Hetta Coffey," she said, "you are hereby requested to get your substantial ass on a plane to Washington State to meet with the parties in question." Gee, I love lawyer talk.

Allison gleefully summarized the content of the missive she received from my not-quite former client. Not only did they regret any inconvenience—inconvenience, my ass, I almost suffered a nervous breakdown—to me caused by our "misunderstanding." Misunderstanding? I think not. I understood perfectly. They'd fired me!

In a sudden change of heart, they were now willing to make the completion of my original contract worth my while. At least that was Allison's translation.

"What exactly does 'worth my while' mean, Lawyer Lady?" I wanted to know.

"It means they've found out they screwed up and are hoping you'll let them buy you off. Which of course, you will. Unless you'd prefer owning a large construction company in Seattle?"

"Let me think. Blood money sounds good."

"Actually, you really do have to think this one over. Hard. Yes, we've got 'em by their nappy, little public hairs, but if you pluck them too hard and too publicly, word gets around in the industry. On the other hand, if you don't play a little hard ball, you come off as too desperate for work to fight them. Maybe we can reach a happy medium. You know, work a miracle that makes even you look like a stone professional."

"Hey, watchit, girl."

"A stone professional with a new and exorbitant hourly rate."

"That's better. Gee, Allison, I guess that's why I pay you the big bucks."

"Hetta, you haven't paid me a red cent. Nor do you have to. Your almost-ex, now-present client is willing to reimburse you for any legal fees incurred. That's me. I am, as we speak, compiling an enormous billing for my partner to send in."

"You don't have a law partner."

"Never you mind. I have it handled."

"I love it. So, when does this gang grovel begin?"

"I'll tell them we can be there...." I could hear Allison thumbing through her Daytimer, "Say, Thursday morning? Then we can celebrate in fine style Friday and Saturday."

"We?"

"Shit yes, girl. They're payin' and I need a vacation. I'll book the flight, hotel and all. Bring your fuck-me pumps cuz we're gonna par-tay down this weekend. What's the most expensive hotel in Seattle?"

* * *

Revenge is good. It's really, really good, but much to my amazement, I actually ended up semi-defending the guy who caused the whole problem. Dale was so pitiful in his own defense I figured *someone* had to do it for him. Hell, I can be downright magnanimous when basking in the glow of victory. Also, I held my trump card, figuring if he got out of hand down the line I'd slam dunk him with it.

What trump card, you may ask? It turns out the idiot had an affair with an employee at Baxter Brothers, used her to get a slanderous letter regarding *moi,* then dumped her. Thanks to the Trob's inside info, I arranged lunch and a little chat with the dumpee. Plied with a couple of martinis, she agreed not to tell Dale's wife of his indiscretion if I agreed not to tell the brothers Baxter they harbored a file thief. The Trob was once again at the heart of my salvation.

Before Allison and I left for Seattle, I gave Fidel a call. Not only had he once again saved my ass, he had even wangled a slot for my Beemer in the Baxter building executive parking lot. When I worked for Baxter I didn't even know there *was* an indoor parking lot, much less one where they washed your car practically every day. Ah, the perks of power.

"Yo, Trob," I said, "how's your hammer hangin'?"

"Oh, hi, Hetta."

"Hey, those folks in Seattle called off the dogs and are gonna renew my contract. You are a genius. But of course, you know that."

"Yes."

It was going be a typical Trobite conversation. "Are you going to tell me how you did it?"

"No."

Sigh. "Do you mean you're not going to tell me, or do you mean you don't know how you did it?"

Silence. Two part questions not involving mathematical equations are of little interest to the Trob.

"Never mind. How's my car?" An easy question, or so I thought.

"Sold."

"Excuse me?"

"Sold," he repeated.

That's what I thought he said. Now what? "I haven't even put the ad in the paper yet, Fidel. Did you say you sold my car?"

"Yes."

"To whom?"

"Me."

Huh? "Listen to me very carefully, Wontrobski. You don't know how to drive, and I hold the papers on the car. How can you sell my car to yourself?"

"I hired a chauffeur until I can learn. I took care of all the paperwork on line. The money is in your bank account, less the small car loan you still owed."

I was astonished. Not that he had somehow managed to break several federal laws, but he had also uttered three sentences in a row. An entire paragraph! And the Trob, a borderline agoraphobic who lived in a hotel only two blocks from his office, hated riding in any conveyance except for an elevator. What on earth was he going to do with a BMW convertible?

Trying to find out was too trying, so I said, "Gee thanks, I think. Saves me putting up with the creeps who seem to crawl out of the FOR SALE section of the paper. Anyhow, what I called you about was, I have to go to Seattle to meet with those guys you somehow got straightened out. When I get back I'd like to bring you lunch. We can have a picnic in your office, then play dominoes."

"Okay."

Things were back to normal. "Bye now. I'll call you Monday or Tuesday."

"Tuna fish."

* * *

My stars, if life wasn't sprouting posies?

And it was time to learn more about that new life as a boat owner. I vowed to start the overdue education process the next week, but first Allison and I had to spend a bunch of my client's money. We had two full nights to do so.

Unfortunately, we peaked out our celebration early and decided to limp back home to recover before certain Seattle authorities could track us down.

It was mid-afternoon Friday when I hoisted myself onto a yacht club bar stool for some hair of dog.

"Paul, my man," I groaned, "I need bubbles and I need 'em fast. I'm deflating."

He quickly grabbed a split and poured for me. I downed it, hoping the icy effervescence would somehow dull the pain in my head. Kind of like an alcoholic Alka Seltzer without the plop, plop. While awaiting the hoped for fizz of relief, I gazed out the window. And blinked.

"Paul, am I hallucinating, or is my boat gone?"

Paul looked out. "Uh-huh," he said, "it's gone, all right."

"Don't just stand there, call 911! The Coast Guard. The navy. Somebody!" I jumped from the stool and regretted the jolt.

Paul looked confused. "Uh, Garrison left this morning with some other people. I think they were going fishing."

"What?" I yelped.

Misunderstanding my misunderstanding, Paul repeated, "He went fishing."

Summoning a great deal of self-control I asked, "Did he say when he'd be back, by any chance?"

"Uh, he usually gets back around four or five."

"Usually?" My words sounded foreign, detached, a clutter of verbiage perhaps suspended in a balloon over my head. Inane verbiage. This couldn't be real, so it must be a cartoon.

Paul was decidedly uncomfortable, not knowing where to turn or what to say. It is way un-cool for any yacht club bartender to get involved in the members' personal crappola. But he did say, "That's what time they got back yesterday."

"Yesterday. I see. Thanks, Paul. And Paul, please don't say anything to anyone, especially

Garrison, about this. Okay? You know, I was out of town, I did come back early, and Garrison and I don't always communicate well. I'm sure it's a very simple miscommunication on my part."

Paul looked so relieved, I was sure he wouldn't bring the matter to anyone's attention. As insurance, I asked him not to even mention I was in the club, especially to Garrison. I made a phone call, left the club and drove to Jan's apartment in a red haze. Knowing Garrison, he'd never know the car was missing.

36

Jan met me at her apartment door with two aspirins and a great deal of sympathy. "So, what are you going to do?" she asked. "I mean, right this minute?"

"I'm going to sit here a few hours and simmer down, because if I go back to the yacht club and wait for Garrison, there'll be bloodshed. And it won't be mine."

"Very smart, Hetta. Not the bloodshed part, the simmering down part. You know how you are. Now, what are you going to do about Garrison? I can hardly wait." Literally rubbing her palms together in anticipation, she looked a tad too gleeful.

"I'm glad you're enjoying yourself, Miz Jan."

"Sorry. I haven't seen you in action for far too long."

"I've lost my impetus, I guess. How long have you known me?"

"I dunno. Fifteen, sixteen years?"

"Close enough. And how many stupid, I mean really, incredibly, stupid things have you known me to do?"

She cocked her head, closed her eyes and began compiling. I was about to thump her on the noggin when she surprised me. "None. You have made a few, uh, lousy choices. Like most of us you've made a couple of less than perfect judgment calls, but in general I'd have to say you've handled your life better than most."

My eyes went all misty. Jan, I knew, wasn't simply trying to make me feel better. She meant what she was saying. So why was I *feeling* so stupid.

She patted my hand. "You know, it isn't easy being a single woman. You've always made good money and are respected in your field. Look, you managed to get an engineering degree, didn't you? Okay, so it took you a few more years than most, but you changed majors three times, which was all right. I mean, artists don't make much money and Swahili? Okay, maybe that wasn't a really great major. Anyhow, my point is this. You pay your own way and are loyal and generous to your friends."

"Yeah," I sniffed, "and I help lil' ole ladies across the street and feed stray dogs. I meant stupid about men and stuff like that."

"Hetta, we are women. Being stupid about men is our job. If we weren't stupid, we wouldn't have anything to do with them."

I giggled. "Good one. This time I'm really furious with myself. Garrison saw I was vulnerable and took advantage. Thank God I didn't sleep with him."

Jan frowned. "Hetta, Lars says Garrison says you did. Do. Whatever."

"What?"

"I'm simply telling you what Garrison told Lars and practically anyone who cared to listen."

"That son of a bitch. He lives for free on my boat, tells lies about me, and then takes my boat out fishing without my permission. What nerve."

"Oh, I think it's worse than that. Lars says he asked Jenks about the work Garrison's supposed to be doing on *Sea Cock.* Jenks thinks there's something a little, well, fishy there."

"Like he's not doing anything?"

"Maybe."

What an idiot I'd been. On a work project I was known as a maniac for maintenance records. Logs, checklists and double checks were my passion. I'd set up a logbook for Garrison, but never even looked to see if he'd made entries. What was I thinking? I made a decision.

"Jan, do you think I can get Jenks to check out *Sea Cock* tomorrow? I know for a fact that Garrison is going to Sacramento and won't be back until Sunday brunch. Garrison never misses brunch at the club because past commodores eat for free."

She picked up the phone, called Lars, and a few minutes later, Jenks called back. After I talked to him, I told her, "Everything's all set. Jenks'll meet me on *Sea Cock* tomorrow morning at ten. God, we have to do something about that name!"

"How about *Money Pit*?"

"Too true."

"So, what are you going to do about Garrison?"

"I'm not sure yet, Miz Jan, but I do know that that master-baiter has caught his last fish off *my* boat."

* * *

"You're low on oil, your batteries are almost dry and you'd best think about fueling up pretty soon," Jenks said, consulting his spiral notebook. He'd been crawling all over my boat for two hours without comment, but now he sat at the table with me, sipping coffee.

I couldn't help notice he needed a haircut, a good sign as far as I was concerned. I've learned not to trust men who are too well groomed. Real men don't get no stinkin' manicures.

"Other than that, Doctor Jenkins, how long have I got?" I asked.

He allowed me a small smile and put down his cup. "Neither alternator is working, your running lights are out and your wiring needs attention. I found wires held together with alligator clips."

He was getting my attention. "Go on."

"My guess is your injectors need cleaning, if not rebuilding, and there's a suspicious leak around your port manifold."

"Jenks, in the South a gentleman never mentions injectors in polite company," I quipped, earning a real grin. "Look, I didn't even know I had an injector, much less a manifold. I was counting on Garrison to take care of all that stuff."

"Do you have a list of his projects?"

I went to my desk, shuffled through a drawer and pulled out a notebook and a batch of receipts. Shoving them across the table to Jenks, I said, "Here's what I have. Sorry I haven't had time to sort through them. Oh, and here's the maintenance log I set up. I copied it from a powerboat magazine article. As you can see, Garrison's signed off on most items."

He carefully read the receipts, sorting them into stacks and checking them against the log. I poured more coffee and waited. Finally he sighed and looked up. "The receipts for materials and log items match."

"That's good. I was beginning to think I'd been had. And heck, I didn't even get kissed."

Jenks didn't smile this time. "Hetta, I think we should review everything together."

So we did, starting from the day I took possession of the boat. When we'd finished, Jenks blew an exasperated breath.

"Look, maybe you need to discuss all this with Garrison because, quite frankly, I'm confused. He's either fiddled the records or I'm missing something. Why don't I take care of the fluids for

268

you right now, then you can get the other stuff done later. Where's your oil?"

"Uh, in the engine room?"

"Nope."

"In the storage unit on the back deck?"

"Not in the lazarette. I checked."

"*Merde*."

"According to this," Jenks said, picking up a receipt, "you bought twelve gallons of Delo 400 a week ago."

"I know. Maybe Garrison used it?"

"Not on this boat, he didn't," Jenks said. "Tell you what, I'll make a list of what you need, put together an estimate of cost, and get back with you tomorrow. Will you be at the club for brunch?"

"Is there a cow in Texas?"

Jenks finally let out a laugh, pulled on his jacket, and pointed to a control panel by the steering console. "Oh, and Hetta, a suggestion? When you leave the boat, it's a good idea to turn off the water pump and the shower sump pump switches."

I stared at the panel, then at him. "Switches?"

"Yeah, avoids the possibility of a fire. Only turn them on when you need them."

"When I need them?"

"You can't pump water or drain your shower when they're not activated, of course, but when not in use, switch them off. Just good policy."

A little light went off in my head.

"So what you're saying is, if my shower is overflowing all I have to do is turn on a switch?" I asked, remembering my first few days aboard, when Garrison took full credit for "repairing" my shower. As badly as I hated to admit it, Jenks's brother, Lars, was right. I'd been gas lighted. Lit. Whatever.

"Yep. Flip the switch, it turns on the pump. Why?"

"Oh, nothing. I've got a little gas problem."

Jenks looked at me strangely and said, "O-kay. See you tomorrow then?" He walked to the door, then turned back. "I have to say, Hetta, you're taking all this bad news very well. Most women would have been, well, really unhappy."

"You mean to say most women would have been whining, wailing, and bitching? That, Jenks, is not my way. I don't just get mad, I also get even."

"I can believe it," he said, as he waved and left the boat.

Being hornswoggled by the likes of Garrison didn't set well at all. I went to work finding out how badly I'd been had.

According to Jenks, my fuel tanks were half empty. I had owned the boat for six weeks and had topped off the tanks, like Daddy told me to, on day one. Since then, *Sea Cock*, to my knowledge, had not left the dock. Except now I knew it had, at least twice, according to the yacht club bartender.

I pulled out the bill of sale from Morris and looked at the engine hours: nine hundred eighty on the date of sale. Moving back to the control panel

I'd paid little heed to in the past, I checked the engine hours now: one thousand ten. It didn't take a genius to figure out that *Sea Cock* had been on the move, thirty engine hour's worth of move.

I knew, from what Morris had told me, that I could use a mile per gallon as a rule of thumb. Sometime in the past six weeks, my boat had traveled around three hundred miles and burned three hundred gallons of fuel!

I was tabulating the scope of how much Garrison had pocketed in the way of un-bought goods with money I'd given him, when the phone rang. Engrossed in my calculations, I absentmindedly picked it up. Dial tone. It continued to ring. I followed the ring and found a phone in Garrison's quarters. The dirty thieving rat had had his own line installed! As I was leaving the cabin, the ringing stopped and his answering machine picked up. Needless to say, I stayed to listen.

"Oh, hi, Garrison," a female voice said to the machine. "Guess you're not home. This is Molly from Ancient Mariner Charters. I need to confirm that our charter is still on for this Wednesday. Call me back at 577-3899. Thanks."

Charter?

I dialed 577-3899.

"Hi, Molly. Garrison asked me to contact you about *Sea Cock's* Wednesday charter." Call me clairvoyant.

"Oh, yes. We're scheduled to board a foursome from Texas at Pier 39 right before noon, so we'll have to leave Jack London around ten. Oh, could you ask him to leave the Texas flag out again? The last couple from Texas was thrilled when we flew it."

"I'll bet they were. How thoughtful of Garrison," I said, my voice barely civil.

Molly continued, but sounded a little confused by my obvious sarcasm. "Uh, anyway, please tell him we should have her back by five, because these folks only want a trip under the Golden Gate, around the bay, and lunch on board. So that'll be seven hours at our usual rate. Since I know Garrison doesn't take checks, I'll leave the seven hundred in an envelope under an ice tray like I always do. We will, of course, leave the boat clean and a bottle of champagne in the fridge. It's a real pleasure doing business with Garrison. His boat is really beautiful."

"Ain't it though," I said, then hung up. Then I got really, really mad; the bastard had been getting free champagne and not sharing.

Garrison was lucky he was in Sacramento, for I'd surely have plugged him full of holes and planted him in his dust-encrusted Morgan—the one that sat in the parking lot where it had been for at least a year. The top was ripped in several places and it had two flat tires, but the vintage car was Garrison's pride and joy. His big dream was to get her fixed up and take her on one of those Tour d' Elegance things.

I spent the rest of Saturday trying to get my blood below boiling and making a few calls. With each call I felt a little better.

37

Sunday morning, bright and early, my friend Brian from London Imports, Ltd., showed up with a crew of three. By ten, Garrison's British racing green Morgan's tires were plumped and shiny. She was washed, waxed, and her top let down to expose a newly detailed interior. Parked in full view of the yacht club, she shone like a jewel in the Queen's crown.

Sunday brunch is a big day at the Jack London Yacht Club. More members show up for eggs Benedict than for monthly meetings. And this particular day, a dinghy race and barbecue slated for the afternoon promised a record turnout.

From ten until twelve, club members munched and sipped and watched while I removed everything of Garrison's from *Sea Cock* and packed it neatly into his Morgan. Several yachties made comments like, "Cleaning out the bilges, Hetta?" I only smiled my Mona Lisa best and nodded.

I was eating eggs Florentine with Jan, Lars, and Jenks when Garrison, all grins and pomp, arrived at the club. He'd obviously spotted the Morgan and figured out what was happening, for I overheard heard him tell a few folks who teased him about being evicted that, to the contrary, he had decided to seek greener pastures.

"Hi, Hetta," he gushed, pulling a chair up to our table. "Welcome back from Seattle. You must have gotten back early yesterday. Looks like you've been busy." He craned his neck for a better look at his car. "My Morgan's never looked better. And thanks for loading my stuff for me," he said loudly for the benefit of curious club members.

I had to hand it to the guy, he definitely had some balls on him. I was going to enjoy handing them to him.

Jan listened to Garrison's bluff and stared at me in dismay, raising her eyebrows in a "Are you really going to let the SOB get away with this crap?" gesture.

"It was nothing, Garrison," I cooed. "My way of thanking you for all you've done to, I mean, *for* me."

"Hetta, you are one grand old broad," Garrison said, and swaggered to the bar to order himself a drink, which he most likely put on my tab.

"Grand old broad?" Jan hissed, "Hetta, are you…"

I held her fury at bay with a "standby" finger. Picking up my cell phone, I poked in a number, whispered to Jan, "Observe and learn," then hit the SEND button.

After three rings I said, softly, into the phone, "This grand old broad says it's show time," and hung up.

Seconds later, the repeated OOOOGAHHHHH of an air horn caught the attention of everyone in the club. Those who didn't have a window seat stood for a look. Then, in a squeal of tires, a battered pickup charged across the lot, squarely rammed the Morgan's rear bumper, shoved it over the curb into the Oakland estuary. The pickup then reversed full throttle around the back of a building and disappeared. The Morgan floated for a long minute, then nosed straight down into twenty feet of murky saltwater.

Jan breathed an "Ooooh" of approval. Lars looked at me in disbelief. Jenks squeezed my hand and smiled. I noticed his eyes were really blue.

A moment of stunned silence was broken by Garrison's bellow. "My stuff! My car! Shit, did anyone get that asshole's license plate number?"

Tearing down the stairs, he began fishing for his clothes with the club's boat hook. He was clutching an armload of soggy underwear when, in a burp of bubbles, a large, silver, heart-shaped balloon surfaced and floated skyward on a gentle breeze. The message on the balloon sparkled brightly in the afternoon sun. "Have a Real Nice Day, Y'all."

* * *

"I'm innothent, I tell you, innothent. They'll never pin it on me, no thir," I lisped à la Daffy Duck. If I remember that particular cartoon correctly though, the next scene had old Daffers in stripes and chains.

Detective Martinez's dour face eked a sneering smile. "I doubt it seriously, Hetta, but what are you talking about?"

"Aren't you here because of Garrison?" I asked.

"Garrison, who?"

"Never mind. Come aboard, Detective, and take a load off."

"You're in uncommonly good spirits today, Miss Coffey. I have to assume someone has paid dearly for them."

"Why, sir, I do believe you are getting to know me all too well. I hope you aren't here to burst my spiritual balloon." Thoughts of the Mylar message floating from Garrison's sunken Morgan sent me into a fit of giggles. I caught my breath and said, "Sorry, Martinez. You had to be there."

Martinez eyed my coffee cup, sniffed the air and said, "Evidently." He looked around the boat. "You don't have an alarm on here, do you?"

"Oh, I've got all kinds of alarms. I've got low oil pressure, overflowing toilets, smoke and low fuel alarms. I got one for high water, but not Hell. However, no security system."

"Hmmm."

"Hmmm? What does that mean?" Martinez can be annoyingly cryptic.

"Nothing. It might be a good idea to get one."

"Is that why you came to see me? To see if I had an alarm system?"

"Could be. Maybe I came to see if you would finally care to share with me what your Hudson Williams was looking for. Or are you going to keep jackin' me around?"

"I hope that was an unintended segue, from security alarm to the deceased. And so you know, I think I'll just jack you around. Is it good for you? It's good for me."

"Cute, Hetta. I think I like you better in lower spirits. But remember, I can't help you if you won't help me help you."

"You think I need help?"

He looked at me under his eyebrows.

"Yeah, yeah, yeah. I know. Hudson's killer is still on the loose. Pepsi?" I asked, trying to change the subject, but to no avail. Martinez, as tenacious as a hound in chase, is not so easily diverted.

"Would it help change your mind," he said, "if I reminded you that your Hudson was listed by Interpol as a menace to society? Armed and dangerous? He was known to consort with some very nasty characters. If you didn't kill him, someone else did. And that there was a reward for information leading to his arrest?"

I was about to chide the man for calling that rat *my* Hudson when what he said sank in. "Reward? How much?"

"Twenty thou."

"Who wants him? Or rather wanted him, now that he's past tense?"

"I did."

"No Martinez, I mean who was willing to *pay* for him?"

"The feds."

"As in, F B eye?"

"As in United States Government versus one Hudson O. Williams for postal fraud, racketeering, kidnapping, and possibly murder. Amongst other things. Nice fellow, your ex-and-dead fiancé."

"Who'd he off?"

"Allegedly off. Some American guy in Singapore. Evidently the Malaysians had Williams in custody for a few months, then he escaped, turned up in Thailand, got tagged there, but slithered loose again. Slippery, your boyfriend."

"Dead and ex-boyfriend," I corrected him, mainly to buy a little thinking time. If I finally gave up the key, maybe they'd get Hudson's killer. Maybe not. Why open a can of dead worms, so to speak. Besides, maybe one day I'd hop a plane to Tokyo, drink free on Hudson if a bottle was still in the lockup, and see what else was in the Crown Royal bag. Maybe the fifteen hundred he stiffed me, no pun intended.

"I only have three questions, Detective Martinez."

"Yeah?" He looked hopeful, or as hopeful as he could look.

"Dead or alive?"

"What?"

"Was that twenty grand for Hudson dead or alive?"

"Either, I guess."

"Does it count that he was found in my hot tub? I mean, he did still owe me money."

"Somehow, I don't think the fact that he turned up in your tub qualifies you for any reward money. Next question? By the way, that was three already, but I'm easy."

"What does the O. stand for?"

Martinez broke into an honest to God belly laugh. It looked painful. "Oh, Coffey," he said when he'd almost split a gut, "you slay me. You were engaged to a guy named Othello and didn't know it?"

He had me there. I never knew Hudson's middle name. An odd middle name at that. I shrugged and said, "Maybe his mom was a fan of the bard."

"Possibly. She did some off-Broadway stuff."

"You found Hudson's mother? Where? Who is she?"

"I'll show you mine if you show me yours."

Rats.

38

Jenks was dockside early Monday morning, carting a basket full of boat parts, oil and distilled water. And probably a big fat bill, but I was so thrilled someone I could trust was finally taking control of *Sea Cock* I didn't care what he charged me. After all, I had a charter on Wednesday.

While Jenks worked, I walked over to Ancient Mariner Yacht Charters at Jack London Square to meet with Molly. She looked like her voice: confident, friendly, and a little salty. My kind of gal.

When I introduced myself and explained the situation, she was nonplussed to learn that Garrison didn't own *Sea Cock*. After apologizing profusely for the mix-up, she pulled a folder from her file cabinet and showed me what Garrison had been doing with the boat while both Morris and I owned her.

"Well, well, looks like ole Garrison-poo has been running quite a little scam for himself," I said.

Molly looked worried and I quickly added, "But not your fault, of course. How were you to know?"

"I usually check the documentation. I know Garrison from the yacht club and it never occurred to me he didn't own the boat. Speaking of, do you have a copy?"

"Of what?"

"Your documentation. You are documented, aren't you?"

"Uh, sure I am. I think. Okay, to tell you the truth, I don't have a clue. I've been relying on Garrison for everything, obviously a grandiose mistake on my part. I haven't even gotten around to changing the name of my boat."

"Oh, please let me help you get *that* done. Let me tell you, I get some raised eyebrows from potential clients. A few, all of them men, liked it, but I think a name change is definitely in order. What are you going to name her?"

"Damned if I know. Any ideas?"

"No wine."

"Wine?"

"You know, *Chardonnay*, *Chablis*, *Champagne*, stuff like that. I got a guy who'll paint the new name for you for a couple of hundred bucks. You do want to keep chartering, don't you?"

"Oh, why not? Day charters only, though. The only problem is I live and work aboard. If I'm in town, I'm on the boat. Might be a scheduling conflict, 'cause my planned trips don't always pan out."

"What do you need? For work, I mean?"

"Just a phone and my computer. I could actually do what I do anywhere. Come to think of it, I could probably work from the yacht club."

She shook her head. "Too distracting. I have an extra cubicle in back, maybe we can work something out when we need to."

"*Chic, alors!*"

Ain't it something the difference a day or two makes? Last week I was getting fleeced by Garrison, and now I had a sudden new source of income. Anyone contemplating suicide should think about those things. Not that I ever did. My job is to cause suicidal thoughts, not get 'em.

" So, bring it in and I'll help," Molly was saying when I dragged my reverie back to real time.

"Sorry Molly, I was daydreaming. What did you say?"

"I said I'd help you make sure your ducks are in a row. Bring in all your paperwork on *Sea Cock*—bill of sale, survey, whatever—and I'll look it over and tell you what you need to stay legal."

"Would you? That's great, thanks." A wash of relief ran through me and it must have showed, for Molly put her hand on my shoulder.

"You know," she said, "I admire you for taking on such a large boat without any prior experience. Men do it all the time, but few women."

I rolled my eyes. "Most women have better sense. I must have been having a hot flash."

"Real women don't have hot flashes, they have power surges." Molly, I could tell, was going be my new, next to best friend. And in the nick of time too, because Lars was stealing my old very best friend.

When I got back to *Sea Cock*, the friend stealer had joined his brother in the nether reaches of my boat. I peeked in the engine room. Both of the Jenkins men were splattered with unidentifiable stinky substances and seemed to be in hog heaven. Boys will be boys.

"Ah, the bilge brothers, I presume. What's the verdict, men? Will she sink or float?"

"Nothing wrong with this tub that money won't fix," Lars said.

"So I'm learning. Jenks, will *Sea Cock* be ready for a charter Wednesday morning? Molly Haynes needs her by ten."

"No problem. Are you still going to Los Angeles?"

"Yep, first thing tomorrow," I told him. "In fact, I have some work to do, so you two have fun down here, okay?" They waved, returned to whatever they were dissecting and I butted out. Never stop a working man.

I pulled out my laptop, but I couldn't get into work. Niggling at the back of my mind was Detective Martinez's warning about the vulnerability of my situation. Was Hudson's murderer skulking around the Bay Area, still looking for the key? I fingered the key, twirling the chain. Damn that Hudson. Even dead he could piss me off.

When Lars left an hour later, I joined Jenks in the engine room.

"Almost done here, Hetta. Let me show you a couple of things." Jenks moved expertly around the relatively cramped space. I couldn't help notice, for all his height, how limber he was. He could squat like the Marlboro man.

"It's a good thing you don't wear spurs," I quipped, striving to be glib while oofing and grunting as I crawled around the huge engines. Jenks didn't get my joke. Yankees. "What're you doing?"

"Tightening hose clamps. Now look here, see how this one is loose? You need to check these at least once a week. Certainly before you leave the dock." And so it went, my introduction to Diesel 101. After an hour I was cramping up, so we quit. Jenks washed up and joined me on deck for sun tea and tuna sandwiches.

"I got everything on the list done," he said. "Want to take her out for a quick sea trial? Never hurts to double check everything while under way."

"Out? You mean leave the dock? What a concept."

"Are you telling me you've had this boat almost two months and haven't taken her out?"

"I've been very busy," I said, a bit defensively.

"Okay, then, start her up and let's go. You do know how to start the engines, don't you?"

"Of course I do," I said, and tromped to the steering console in the main saloon.

I turned the key on the port engine. Nothing happened. I tried the starboard. Nada.

Jenks walked up behind me—real close behind me, I might add—and looked over my shoulder.

"Here's the problem," he said, turning a switch to ON. "Try again."

Both engines fired. "Your engines are on a special battery bank, and that's good. Now that they've started, turn the switch back to OFF. That way, your engine starting batteries will always be isolated from your house batteries. Now, let's get going."

I sighed and shut down the engines. Jenks cocked his head at me and waited for an explanation.

I bit my lip and stalled, until he asked, "What's the problem? Don't you want to take her out?"

It was true confessions time. "Jenks, I do, more than anything. But I don't have the slightest idea what I'm doing. Can you please teach me? I'll pay you."

"You can pay me for the work I do, but I'll throw in driving lessons for free. Now, let's start from scratch." He steered me out onto the bow and grinned. "This, my dear, is the pointy end."

39

"My, my, but you and Jenks have certainly been spending a lot of time together," Jan said, taking a slug of her beer. "Seems every time I talk to Jenks he's been with you."

"I can't say the same thing for you," I griped. Okay, I whined. I popped a cap and took a gulp of diet soda.

"Dieting again, Hetta?"

"Don't change the subject, Jan. Do I have cooties? Where have you been?"

"Packing. Sorting. And by the way, most of the stuff I'm havin' to pack is yours. Are you sure you want me to take your antiques to Florida?"

"Oh, why not. I've got no place to put anything, and I don't want my good things in a storage locker. You might as well enjoy them."

"So, word has it Jenks is a regular figure around here. What have you two been up to, Miz Hetta? Inquiring minds wanna know."

"You really want to know?" I asked.

"I really, really do."

"Then stand by to cast off, sailor." I strode to the console, started the engines and began to secure for sea.

"Er, Hetta, what are you doing?"

"Showing you what Jenks and I have been up to, as you so nosily put it." I hopped off the boat, disconnected the shore power and all lines but the spring.

Jan, hot on my heels, yawped, "Can't you, like, just *tell* me?"

"Nope. It's show and tell. Now, hold this line. When I tell you, unloose it from the cleat and yell 'clear.' Got that?"

"Oh, shit. I've got it all right, but are you sure about this?"

I ignored her, climbed to the flying bridge, and checked my instrument panel. "Okay sailor, Cast off all lines."

She, after a moment's hesitation to watch her life pass before her eyes, took a deep breath, yelled, "clear," and then mumbled something that sounded suspiciously like the Lord's Prayer. I backed slowly out of the slip, rotated *Sea Cock* on her own length, threaded her down a narrow channel between other docked boats, and entered the estuary.

By the time we cleared the marina, Jan was all smiles and had joined me on the flying bridge.

"Oh, this is sooo cool," she gushed. Then she saluted and added, "Captain Coffey, ma'am, all fenders and lines secured. Hell, I haven't been taking sailing lessons for nothing. I be good crew."

"Well done, matey. Where do you want to go?"

"Uh, gee, I dunno. How about Tahiti?"

"I think that's a bit ambitious for my first solo. Let's stay on this side of the bay for now."

"Please tell me you didn't say *first* solo."

"I saved it for you."

"Jesus. Don't do me any more favors, okay?"

"Relax. Jenks has had me doing this for weeks. Now, where to, ma'am?"

"Rusty Bucket?"

"Atta girl. Bucket, it is."

Twenty minutes later, we made a pass at the Rusty Bucket's guest dock. As Jenks taught me, I lined up parallel to the dock, but a few boat widths off, and put the boat in neutral. Within seconds I could tell the current was with me, so we made a wide circle and lined up in the other direction. The current, plus a mild breeze, made it necessary for me to walk the boat sideways, using engines and rudders. I had practiced diligently for this moment and wasn't disappointed. Not that I needed them, but by the time I maneuvered alongside, four men waited to take our lines.

Before we stepped triumphantly from *Sea Cock*, I gave Jan my best, "told you so" look and whispered. "Buy it, and they will come."

An hour later, we left the Bucket—six men helped us with the lines this time—and motored back to the yacht club to catch the end of Happy Hour.

Jan was ecstatic. "Hetta, I am so proud of you. A little miffed you kept such a huge secret from me, of course, but proud nevertheless. I'm gonna call your mama and daddy the minute I get home and tell what you've done. I know they've been a little worried."

"They have?" I think Jan called my parents more than she does her own mother. Maybe more than I do. I would have loved to hear some of those conversations.

"They're a little concerned. I guess they picked up that I didn't care too much for Garrison, but they worry about you alone on the boat, even though I'm not sure they believed you two were, like, platonic. It's that Tokyo thing, you know."

"You didn't tell them Hudson got offed at my house, did you?"

"Oh, no. No way."

"Good. If I tell you something, Jan, will you promise on a stack of Bibles, hope to die, you won't say anything to anyone? Especially the parents?"

"Needles in my eyes."

I told her about the reward for Hudson, Martinez's warning about Hudson's bad guy associates, all of it. We were approaching the yacht club by the time I finished.

"Hetta, you shit," she yelled, "give Martinez the damned key. I mean it. I swear, if you don't tell him about the key, I will. I don't care if you never speak to me again and I take back the Bible and needle thing. You are being just plain dumb."

"Okay, okay," I said. "I'll call Martinez. Soon. I promise. Meanwhile, not a word to anyone. Oh, look, Jan, men all over the dock, waiting to take our lines. What a surprise."

Knowing I had an audience, I took special pains to put *Sea Cock* alongside the dock with the flair of someone whose knees were not knocking. After securing the boat, I joined Jan at the bar where she sat with Lars and Jenks. Jenks was grinning from ear to ear.

"Well done, Hetta," he said, "I couldn't have docked her any better myself. I guess you won't be needing me any more."

"Oh, yes I will," I said quickly, and blushed.

Jan cut me a knowing look as I managed to stammer, "I mean, there was little wind and not much current, and I still have so much to learn, and—"

Jenks held up his hand. "Hey, I was joking. Don't worry, I'll be around as long as you need me."

Jan's eyebrows arched and her mouth formed a little kissy. I squared my shoulders and gave her a warning look. "Quick, I need a drink. This captain stuff is dry work."

"Yeah," Jan said, "all those men trying to buy us drinks at the Bucket and Hetta goes on the wagon."

"Booze and boats don't mix, right Jenks?" I said, quoting a Coast Guard safety slogan. "Besides, I'm on a diet, so I saved my allotted empty calories until we got back to the club."

Jenks brought me a split of champagne and for all my good intentions, bubbly continued to appear from the bar, obliging me to exceed my calorie limit. Then I decided I'd better eat something to soak up the alcohol. We ordered pizza from a delivery service and I quipped, "So much for will power. Eat, drink and be merry, for tomorrow we diet."

"No, tomorrow we learn to anchor," Jenks said, "And you don't need to diet, you're fine the way you are."

He took a bite of pizza.

I fell in love.

40

Chills. Fever. Dizziness, nausea and delirium.

Recognizing the symptoms, I hoped it was simply a reoccurrence of childhood malaria, but I suspected the dreaded love bug.

I was right. Malaria, after several days of pure horror, goes away. Love's repugnancies burrow in. Why can't I throw up and get it over with? And if falling in love is painful, falling into *unrequited* love is downright agony, although I've always found it does wonders for the waistline. The wonder is I don't have a wasp waist.

Tums helps some, as does a heavy workload. Luckily for me I had an abundance of both. I was kept really busy the next week or two, traveling on business and helping Jan finalize her move to Florida. I had little time for anchor drills with Jenks, so saved myself the embarrassment of being all mooney.

When in Jenks's presence, I became suddenly shy. Well, as shy as *I* get. I avoided being alone with him, lest I make a total fool of myself by doing something like throwing my naked, throbbing body at him. Or worse, letting him know how I felt. I really, really, really hate rejection.

It wasn't until Lars and Jan's going away shindig that I spent any time with the object of my newly formed obsession. *Obsession.* How's that for a boat name? Nah, too perfumey.

"Hetta, are you all right?" Jan asked me the night of the party. "You look flushed."

"Must be the heat."

Jan looked out at the July fog. "Oh, really? Or could it be something else? Not heat, but hots?" she teased. "Maybe something beginning with 'J'? I notice you're avoiding him like the plague."

"A pox upon you and what you notice. I don't know what you're talking about," I said loftily. And to prove her wrong, I dragged her over to Jenks's table and sat down.

"Hi, stranger," he said, "haven't seen much of you lately. Am I fired?"

"No. Of course not. I've been, uh, I think I have a touch of malaria."

He looked at me a little strangely, which he did a lot, and shrugged. "Oh, yeah. I hear that's been going around."

Jan, unable to hold her tongue, scoffed, "Yeah, in Sri Lanka."

I gave her a dirty look and turned my attention to Jenks. "Don't mind her, she's just getting uppity since she's leaving for the jungles of Florida and won't have me around to keep her straight."

He smiled. "I stopped by *Sea Cock* a couple of times. You were gone."

"You did?" I perked up.

"I wanted to check on that oil leak," he said in a "just doin' my job, ma'am" tone.

"Oh." I hope I didn't sound as disappointed as I felt. I'm such a ninny. "Maybe I should give you a key to *Sea Cock* so you can do your job when I'm not around." Did that sound snippy?

He didn't seem to notice. "Sure, if you like. Make things easier."

I dug out an extra key, slapped it petulantly into his hand, and silence befell us. Not something I tolerate well. So I filled it with something stupid. "Do you like guns?" I asked, not having any idea where that came from.

"I hunt. Do you?"

"Nope. I shoot beer cans. I feel more secure with a gun around the house. Boat."

He smiled and said, "I somehow can't imagine you feeling insecure about anything, Hetta. You seem like you take care of yourself pretty well."

Merde. Men hate women who can take care of themselves. I had an idea. "Actually Jenks, I feel a little isolated down here. Uneasy at times. When the club is closed and everyone is gone, I sometimes wish more people lived at the marina. And when I'm gone, I worry someone will break in. We are, after all, in Oakland." Was that convincingly needy? I thought so. Evidently, so did Jenks.

"I can fix that."

"One man urban renewal?" I asked.

He laughed. "I'm not that good, but I can fix you up with a security system."

"You can?" Like I didn't know that. Like I didn't know he *owned* a security business.

He nodded. "I'll come down first thing tomorrow and discuss it with you. It's....Oh, excuse me, Hetta, my date's here."

He stood, waved to the blonde I'd seen him with before, and hustled over to meet her. I rose to escape, but Jan, with a look of supreme glee, pulled me back in my chair. Jenks ferried his date over to the table, sat her in a chair next to me, introduced us, and left us to pick our noses while he went to the bar to get us a drink. I hoped hers was hemlock.

Shirley twirled a long, bleached strand of split ends with a claw painted a shade I call Bordello Red. "So, Hetta," she said, "I hear you live on a boat." Actually, Shirley *breathed* it. She must have been a Jackie O. fan. Or, meow, maybe a contemporary?

"Yeah, I got tired of working the rice paddies."

"Huh?"

"A little boat person joke. So, Shirl, you and Jenks been dating long?" I asked.

Jan, no doubt enjoying the crappy situation I found myself in, pursed her lips at the underlying bitchiness in my tone.

The object of my malevolence didn't seem to notice. She opened her very red lips to answer my less than subtle question about her relationship with Jenks, but Jan beat her to the punch. "Over a year. Right, Shirley?"

Old Shirl nodded, the little pout forming on her face threatening to crack her pancake makeup. "Over a year is right. I wish Jenks was more like his brother. I mean, look at you Jan, you've only known Lars a few months and he's taking you off to Florida. Jenks won't even take a key to my apartment, much less give me one to his."

I suddenly felt much, much, better. Maybe it was the quinine in my gin and tonic.

I actually made a little civilized small talk. Well, not exactly small. I drilled the broad for every bit of information she so willingly gave up before Jenks returned with our drinks. As soon as he did, I grabbed mine and bid them *adieu.*

"Going home so soon, Hetta?" Jenks asked.

"Oh, no, just thought I'd mingle. *Noblesse oblige,* and all that. So if I don't see you again tonight, what time will I see you tomorrow? Early, I hope. I have *so* much to do."

"Seven okay?" he asked, and I was rewarded with a Shirley pouty face.

"Perfect," I said, "I'll have the coffee ready."

I sashayed off, leaving any thoughts Shirley had of a lazy Sunday breakfast in bed with Jenks shattered in my wake. After a few steps, I turned back. "Oh, and Jenks, if I'm still out for my morning walk, use your key."

Like Mae West, when I'm bad, I'm best.

Jan caught up with me on the way to the bar. "That was quite a little show, Miz Hetta. One might think you were jealous."

"One might stick her thoughts where the sun don't shine. Hey, who's the hunk?" I asked, nodding towards the end of the bar. Okay, call me fickle.

"New member. British. Don't you think he looks like Lawrence Harvey, the actor? He's sooo elegant."

I whistled. "I'd say elegant is an understatement. Come on, let's go talk to him."

"Oh, sure. How do you plan to break through the pack of slavering WOEies surrounding him?"

"Jan, Jan, Jan. How long have you known me? Will you never learn? Follow and observe."

We went, not to the end of the bar where the new guy was holding court, but the opposite end. I finished my gin and tonic and ordered another. "And Paul, my man," I told the bartender, "be so kind as to send a drink to yon dude and put it on my tab. There's a good boy."

"Brazen hussy," Jan whispered. "I love it."

Alan, as his name turned out to be, looked up in surprise when Paul handed him a Chivas and nodded in our direction. We nodded back, lifting our drinks in a long distance toast. Five minutes later he was seated between us.

Up close, Alan was shorter than I cared for, but he had sensuous dark brown eyes, wavy pitch-black hair and a clipped accent with a hint of the haughty. Not quite the mush of British upper crust, but definitely not Liverpudlian. His clothes and manner oozed class and polish. A mite slick for my druthers, but when I caught Jenks sneaking a glance our way, I was on the Brit like flies on *merde*. So to speak.

For Jenks's benefit, I pretended to be mesmerized by everything Alan said while my crawdad vision never missed anything Jenks did. I was happy to see old Shirl seemed mightily disgruntled. She and Jenks departed, leaving me with mixed feelings of jealousy and relief.

Oh, and a randy Englishman, whom I dumped unceremoniously as soon as Jenks cleared the door. There's a name for women like me.

* * *

Jenks was on my boat at seven sharp. I'd meant to get up and doll up before he showed. I'd overslept and barely had time to wash the raccoon rings from under my eyes and make coffee. He was a little jittery and kept glancing towards my aft cabin. "Uh, if you'd like, I could come back later, Hetta."

"No, I'm awake. I'm movin' slow. Have a cup while my brain regroups. Jan and I sat up almost all night, what with it being her last night and all. She just left for Lars's place so they could hit the road to Florida. Do you feel deserted? I sure do."

Jenks looked relieved and I realized he'd thought maybe Alan was on the boat. I didn't know whether to be insulted or flattered. "They'll be back," he said. "Lars keeps forgetting how much he hates Florida."

That cheered me up. "You want some breakfast? I'm starved."

"Sure," he said. "Tell me where everything is and I'll cook." He got up, walked to my refrigerator, threw it open and a look of dismay crossed his face. I joined him in the cramped galley and peered in. Nonfat yogurt, one apple, a six-pack of beer, some Monterrey Jack and one egg peered back. Pretty dismal.

"Do you know why the French make an omelet with only one egg?" I asked. He shook his head. "Because one egg is an *oeuf*."

He didn't get it.

Through the miracle of freezer space, I pulled together two "toast it" blueberry waffles and whipped up a cheese omelet. While I cooked, Jenks asked, "You're hooked up to the Internet here, aren't you?"

"Sure am. Why?"

"I want to try something. You said you were interested in a security system and I've developed one for people who want to keep an eye on home, or their boat, from anywhere in the world. All they need is an Internet connection."

"That sounds like me. Here're your eggs and waffles."

"Looks good." He dug in and nodded his approval. "And it is. Anyhow, since I'll be working on your boat this week while you're gone, I thought, if you want, I'll install a system for you."

"What's it cost? Roughly." After Garrison, I had learned that anything that gets done (or in Garrison's case, *not* done) on a boat is big bucks.

"Oh, let's say a hundred a month?"

"That's all? No equipment?"

"I'm renting it to you."

"Deal," I said. "More coffee?"

"Don't you want to know how it works?"

"Surprise me. All I care about is that it works."

"Okay, then. I'll get started tomorrow morning early. Call me at this number," he handed me a card for his security business, "tomorrow night from wherever you are and I'll tell you what I've done and how to check it out."

He stood to leave. "Like I said, call me. I'll give you a code to type into a special Internet site. I think you'll be pleased with what I've done. And I'm giving you a big discount. I charge lots more for corporate accounts."

"Whatever. I trust you to do the right thing," I said with a dismissive wave of my hand.

"Maybe you trust people a little too much, Hetta," he said, surprising me. It was the first time he had even hinted at giving me personal advice. Maybe he'd been warned, but he wasn't scared off by my frown. "Not everyone has your best interests at heart, you know."

I felt my blood pressure rise, while struggling to keep my voice neutral. I hate advice. "You mean like Garrison?"

"Him. And maybe others."

"Who others?"

He shrugged, unwilling to elaborate. "Maybe you should think about being a little, uh, less friendly with strangers, that's all."

Jan, Martinez, and now Jenks. Could I help it if I was an extrovert? Jenks looked so sincere, I didn't behead him like I would most folks who dared to hint that my facile extroversion might lack good judgement? Coming from him, it sounded like genuine concern.

Typically, instead of seizing the moment to further our relationship, I drawled, "Why sir, I've learned to *rely* on the kindness of strangers."

He didn't get it.

41

Jan called from Tucson, El Paso, and San Antonio. By Monday night, I'd gotten a road report on a goodly portion of Interstate 10. With each call came advice. I was *not* to get involved with the British guy, Alan, or do anything to piss Jenks off. I *was* to call Martinez immediately and tell him about the Key Note Club key. During her last call to my hotel room, I told Jan I'd brushed my teeth, said my prayers, and locked my door, so she could relax.

"Sorry, Hetta. I miss you and you know how careless you are sometimes.'"

"I'm fine, quit worrying. And drive safely, okay? Say 'hi' to Lars." It was the best I could do. What I really wanted to say to Lars wasn't fit for delicate ears. I hung up and called Jenks like he'd asked me to.

"Your brother, the best-friend stealer, is in Texas already."

"Great, thanks for letting me know. Got a pencil? I have a surprise for you."

Jenks gave me a set of explicit instructions, which I jotted down carefully on the hotel notepad by my bed. After I hung up with him, I spent the next few minutes accessing the Internet. Then, on a special website he'd provided the URL for, I registered and entered my own secret set of ID numbers. Jenks had warned me not to use my birth date, social security number, or the like in my password. And, he also told me, "Don't ever, ever, tell anyone your code. Even me." I used Raymond Johnson. A return e-mail confirmed my password, and I was ready to go. I called Jenks back.

"All done, sir. Now what? What's my surprise?"

"You'll see. Get back on the Net, go to the website again, go to the section called YOU ARE SECURE, put in your e-mail address and password, then sit back and watch.

"Uh, this isn't gonna be something kinky, is it?"

He chuckled. "Nope. Just do what I told you and you'll see. Don't bother calling me back, I'm shutting down and going to bed now. Sweet dreams." Click.

Sweet dreams? I cannot remember the last time someone said that to me. Especially a man. A little quaver ran through my stomach. Well, actually a little lower.

I accessed the Website, put in my password and waited. After a brief pause, my computer screen lit up in a four-way split screen. In each quadrant was a live image of a different cabin on *Sea Cock*. "Wow."

I followed the instructions at the bottom of the screen and turned up the sound. Water lapped against my boat's hull and my ship's clock rang seven bells. Seven thirty. In the lower left quadrant I spotted something in the main saloon, zoomed on it and saw a hand lettered sign leaning against the settee. I read it out loud. " 'How's this for secure? Dinner Friday? Jenks.'"

"Double wow." That little quaver down low threatened to become an earthquake.

* * *

Dinner?

Friday?

What did it mean? For starters, it probably meant dinner, Friday.

But love, lust, or whatever you want to call it is, for me, a many splintered thing. Not unlike my thought processes when I'm in it. Every word, every gesture must be analyzed, *ad nauseam*, in search of hidden rejection. Surges of noxious anxiety emanate from what I call brain farts and travel like sewer gas to my stomach. Tums have their work cut out for them.

Most of Tuesday I spent eating calcium and obsessing over two words. Dinner. Friday. Staving off the onset of osteoporosis is small consolation when one has no one to obsess to. Who? Who? I could almost hear my father's voice saying, "Your feet don't fit no limb."

Jan was out of the question. She was sleeping in the enemy camp, probably in Florida.

Mom? Nah, no use getting her carefully pressed Hanes crinkled over a possible love match.

My sister? Too easy. Six years younger, much prettier, and the kind of gal men trip over, she'd never understand my trepidation. Besides, she was the marrying kind. Like the Gabors, she believed in one true love and intended to keep marrying until she found it.

I considered unloading on Craigosaurus, but hell, he has more insecurities than *moi*. He once had a mental meltdown when Raoul forgot how he liked his eggs cooked.

It's lonely at the bottom of the amour pond.

After I returned from La, and about two seconds after I got to the boat, I dialed up Jenks to tell him how much I liked my new security system. Sure I did. I *really* called to ferret out what he meant by Dinner Friday? He wasn't in. I left a message. He didn't call back. I sent e-mail. He didn't e-me. By Wednesday morning, I was hyperventilating. I hate love.

Poor Allison made the mistake of calling while I was breathing into a paper bag. She listened so silently to my angsty whining I wondered if she was racking up billable hours. When I finally paused for oxygen, she spoke.

"Hetta," she said, "have you lost your friggin' mind? A man has simply asked you out to D-I-N-N-E-R. It's an old American custom where one sits at a table and eats food."

"Allison, that sounds suspiciously like a date. I don't date. I hate dates. The last date I had left me with an empty bank account. And all I have to show for it is a lousy bar key and a ruby I bought myself as a consolation prize."

"Speaking of which, have you told the police about the key?"

"I will, damn it. When I get a chance. Quit changing the subject. We're talking about men here and how I screwed up with the last one."

"That was years ago," she said.

"Some things never change."

"Then say no," she said reasonably.

"You're fired," I said unreasonably.

"Good, because you don't need a lawyer, you need a nanny. Someone to give you warm milk and burp you. Calm down, get rational. A stretch for you, I know."

"I'm trying. You know how I am."

"All too well. How about some good news? Then you can fire me."

Allison outlined the final deal she'd cut with the Seattle group, one that was fair to both the client and me. She'd returned the buy-off check to the maker and I was free to go back to work ASAP.

"So Hetta, go forth and multiply, or whatever you engineers do, for our business is concluded. I cheerfully accept my sacking in this matter and that little murder thing as well. Since you no longer seem to be a suspect in the offing of old Hudson, we can both get back to our real jobs."

This bit of good news temporarily sidetracked me from my romantic dilemma. "Hallelujah! I'll go up to Seattle next week, really get down to brass tacks. Thanks, Allison. Not all lawyers are shits. "

"Gee, thanks. And speaking of lawyers, lawsuits and the like, have you heard from Garrison? He must know it was you who arranged for his Morgan to go snorkeling."

Didn't I just fire her? Lawyers, always looking for a case.

"Allison, how do you know about that, uh, unfortunate accident. Do you legal types have a So Sue Me Hotline?"

"I never reveal my sources. Boy, I wish I'd 'a been there to see the show. You never let me in on the good stuff, only your corporate crap and murder. Is Garrison still hanging around?"

"Haven't seen him. I heard he moved in with some gal from the Berkeley Yacht Club."

"Good, he was a flea."

"Does that make me the dog?"

She laughed. "No silly, you de dame. Say, when do I get to see your boat?"

"How about tonight? I'll be busy soaking myself in gasoline the rest of the week, in the event I get stood up Friday. Not that it's a date or anything."

"I'll come tonight then. I'm hydrocarbon intolerant. Can I bring someone?"

Allison never dated either, so I wondered aloud, "Any old someone, or someone *someone*?"

"Someone *someone*," she said.

"Well, day-yam. Of course. Want to give me a clue who?"

"Nope."

I hung up and felt a tug of jealousy. Our old maids club was disintegrating. All of my friends suddenly coming up with *someone*. But, I reminded myself, someone had invited me to dinner. Friday.

To my THINGS YOU CAN'T LET SLIDE LIKE YOU ALWAYS DO list, I added: Buy gasoline.

I was ensconced on a yacht club barstool late that afternoon when, to my stupefaction, my ex-Beemer, driven by Allison, screeched to halt in Garrison's ill-fated parking spot. More astounding than Allison at the wheel was her passenger: the Trob.

Fidel Wontrobski's black clad form unfolded from the car like a carpenter's rule. He rounded the car, opened Allison's door with a flourish and flapped towards the club with three long strides before he realized she wasn't next to him. Allison caught up, took his hand, and I almost dropped my drink. Her someone was the Trob? This had to be the most unlikely match in the history of the world. Several worlds. Pluto came to mind.

308

What I had originally envisioned as a girlie gripe session turned into a threesome, with me as the extra *some*. Most of the time I sat, boggled, while the lovebirds cooed.

Well, Allison cooed. Trob, even in the throes of passion, still looked like he should be sitting on top of a cactus waiting for something to die. It only proved one thing to me. The old adage, "there's someone for everyone" is true. Maybe even for me.

Which brought me back to Friday's looming dinner. It's not like I hadn't broken bread with Jenks before. We'd shared many meals, drinks and the like, but by accident, not on purpose.

Complexifying my concern was the fact that I still hadn't heard from him. By Friday morning I was considering leaving town, maybe scooting on down to Cabo for a few days. Yessiree, that would be a truly mature way to face my problem, one I'd employed successfully many times over. When in love or trouble, blow town. Before I could make airline reservations, Jan called.

"I hate Florida," she said. Actually, she whined.

"Told you so," I singsonged.

"It's full of Yankees and bugs."

"Yup."

"Nahner-nahner to you too. Thanks for your characteristic compassion."

"Sorry. So come back."

"I can't leave Lars here. I love him."

"Speaking of love, wait until I tell you…" I related the Allison and Trob story. Jan was as amazed as I was.

"Wow, that's beyond belief," she said. "She looks like a miniature fashion model and he favors a large carrion eater. Scary, Hetta, very scary. What's the attraction do you figure?"

"Damned if I know, but they are one hot item. He gave her my Beemer, for cryin' out loud. We know for sure Allison can't be bought, so it's not that. Godiva chocolates would'a sufficed from the looks of them."

"Seems love is in the air. Speaking of, I understand you're having dinner with Jenks tonight."

What? How in the hell did she know that?

"What? How in the hell do you know that?" I demanded.

"He called us from Vegas. Said he'd asked you to dinner and had gotten an e-mail 'yes' from you. Where are you going?"

"Gee, why don't you tell me? Since you know so much."

"What's wrong with you? Why are you so grouchy?"

*Why **am** I so grouchy*? "I'm not."

"Yes, you are. Oh! My! God! You really do have the hots for Jenks!"

"Do not."

"Oh, yes, you do. I know the symptoms. Does Jenks have *any* idea how much trouble he's in?"

* * *

"Am I in trouble?" Jenks asked when he called ten minutes after Jan and I talked. Was there something telegraphing through the ozone layer I didn't know about?

"What do you mean?" When in doubt, deliberate denseness always works for me.

"The system. I put more features on your security system than I originally planned, but I won't charge you full freight. I'd like to use your boat as a model. Didn't you get my note?"

Note. Note. I looked around, saw nothing. "What note?"

"On my website. I sent you more instructions. Tuesday."

"Sorry, I haven't logged onto your system since Monday night."

"That's okay, I'll show you what I did when I pick you up for dinner tonight. Unless you've changed your mind."

Was he kidding? Gosh, now I could put away the matches, and pour the gasoline into my VW's tank. "What time will you be here?"

"Five okay?"

"Sure," I said casually. I hope I sounded casual, anyway. "We can have a drink here on the boat before we go out." I tried visualizing his glass at the yacht club, but only came up with ice cubes. And something darkish. Damn, Paul wasn't on duty until six tonight, so I couldn't ask him what Jenks drank. "Uh, what do you drink, Jenks?"

"Scotch. See you at five."

He hung up and I raced to a nearby liquor store. By five, my liquor cabinet held Chivas Regal, Glenfiddich, Glenlivet, Johnnie Walker Red, Johnnie Walker Black, Cutty Sark, Haig and Haig, and several others. Luckily for my credit limit, it was a smallish liquor store. And that Jenks didn't say, "Beer."

And it would have been way too easy for me to ask Jenks something further, like, "Where are we going?" Nope, not my style.

Since he didn't ask what color my dress was so he could bring a matching corsage, I got to go through my entire wardrobe, guessing what to wear. Too dressy, too eager. Too casual, too uninterested. I settled for semi-uninterested, donning slacks, silk shirt, blazer. It didn't matter, for I could have worn a muumuu and gone unnoticed. He took me to The Willows, a gambling establishment faraway in distance, décor, and dress from Casino Royale.

Who knew that droves of Chinese are clamoring to chow down on hofbrau fare while placing thousand dollar bets at a Pai Gow table? Or that tall African Americans dressed in full tribal robes played Pan? Or housewives in hair rollers spent their milk money on poker? Or that I'd have the best five dollar corned beef ever, right in downtown Emeryville?

Jenks played Pai Gow like a pro. Not the Anglicized card game offered in Nevada casinos, but real Pai Gow, with tiles. The dealers knew Jenks, the only non-Asian at the table, by name. I demurred learning their game and since no one in the room seemed interested in playing *my* game—Dr Pepper: tens, twos, and fours wild—I watched Jenks win for an hour, then we went back to the boat for a nightcap.

No euphemism here, a nightcap is what we had.

I curled up on the settee with a brandy while Jenks folded into a director's chair with a Chivas, which he'd graciously settled on after learning I didn't stock his brand, Dewars. Ten minutes later, he left and I was left stunned. And angry. With myself. Somehow I had to learn to lower my expectations instead of raising my hopes. Most people learn this by age eighteen or so.

And what were those expectations? Had I actually planned to break a five year sexual hiatus tonight? I mean, there was a day when it was okay to hop into bed with a guy on the first date. Who was I kidding? *Instead* of a first date. But that was then, before scary sex. What had I expected from Jenks? I don't know. What I had not expected was, "I got somewhere to go. See ya."

He took off before I could slam my mouth shut, leaving me alone and frustrated at nine thirty on a Friday night. This is not good. I tromped up to the yacht club in one rotten mood.

Alan, the British hunk, spotted me at the bar nursing my second champagne in ten minutes and tore himself away from the covey of women he'd been entertaining. "Hetta, how delightful to see you again. May I join you?"

"What do you mean by *join*, " I growled.

He smiled and sat down. "I'd venture your evening, up until now, hasn't been satisfactory?"

"You'd venture right. Look, Alan, I'm not very good company right now, so maybe you'd better go back to that gaggle of silly geese and leave me to my foul mood."

"Was that a poultry joke? I can never tell with you Yanks."

I barked a laugh and relaxed. What was wrong with me? A gorgeous man was hitting on me. A gorgeous, *charming* man who probably wouldn't feed me corned beef on a first date.

"Sorry. So, Alan, what are you doing here in the States?"

"I work for Trans-Pacific Maritime and will be here at the Port of Oakland for a couple of years. I plan to buy a sailboat and thought joining a local yacht club would be a good way to meet people. I hear you live aboard yon powerboat." He lifted his perfectly chiseled chin towards *Sea Cock*. "Interesting name, that."

"I'm going to change it real soon."

"To what?"

"Don't know yet."

"Hmmm, something suitable that captures your very essence. Beautiful, yet feisty. Independent, yet vulnerable. Maybe a little naughty. Something like *Muy Salsa*. Very Saucy."

Now, I've spent a great deal of time and money perched on ginmill barstools all over the world. Yes, even in Casa Blanca. I've flirted with and chatted up men from many different countries and cultures while wearing a groove into the insteps of my shoe soles. Trust me when I tell you I can spot a world-class rotter when I meet one. And this Alan had all the makings of a candidate for president of *Roues Internationale*. My kind of guy.

There was something vaguely wicked about him, something familiar. His kind usually meant trouble. Unfortunately, my kind of trouble. With guys like this you know what to expect, namely eventual grief, preceded by a great deal of dodgy dalliance. Who needs steadfast and dependable when the Alans of the earth still skulk and charm? How could I have even *considered* falling for someone like Jenks Jenkins?

"Haven't we met before, Alan?" I slurred, then ordered more champagne. A lot more champagne.

Alan and I careened back to my boat, bouncing off the dock ramp's handrails and narrowly avoiding a midnight dip in the estuary. When I stepped onto *Sea Cock*, he started to follow and for one moment I almost let him. But warning bells clanged loud enough to penetrate my boozy brain and I sent him on his way.

I am not *always* stupid.

Nor am I always smart. Which I knew the minute I came to the next morning. I didn't wake up, I came to. A second of dread washed over me, until I felt the other side of the bed, found it empty and forced myself to sit up. Relief replaced apprehension. I was alone, fully clothed. And the phone was ringing.

"Mrffsg," I said into the mouthpiece. My tongue was glued to the roof of my mouth by something truly horrid.

"Hetta? Jenks. Can I come by and show you something I've set up for you on the security system? I didn't get a chance last night."

Hell no, you didn't get a chance last night, you were too anxious to escape.

"Umm-humm," I said.

"Good, be over in ten minutes." He hung up and I headed for the shower and Mentadent. The next boat I buy is going to have a hot tub.

Steam still rose from my body when Jenks rapped on the hull. I yelled, "Come on in," threw on an oversized tee and leggings and wrapped my hair in a towel. I didn't care if Robert Redford was waiting for me, I needed coffee and I needed it now. I trudged up the stairs to the main saloon and found, not Robert R., nor Jenks J., but Alan, Brit. *Merde.*

"My, don't you look delicious this morning, Hetta."

"Alan, what are you doing here?"

"You told me to come in."

"I wasn't expecting...."

The boat dipped slightly and I heard Jenks call out, "Ahoy, *Sea Cock.*" Jenks stopped short when he saw Alan in the cabin.

Alan took the lead and stepped forward with his hand held out. "Alan Whitcombe here. We haven't met, but I've seen you around the yacht club."

Jenks shook his hand. "Robert Jenkins. Nice to meet you. Uh, I can come back later if you like, Hetta."

"No!" I yelled.

"No?" Jenks said.

"I mean, don't leave. Alan stopped by to, uh, Alan, just why *did* you stop by?"

"Oh, to tell you how very much I enjoyed last night. Perhaps I'll call later?" Alan exited without my answer, leaving me openmouthed. I hate it when someone uses my own tactics.

Jenks grinned wryly and said, "I could have sworn you were out with me last night."

"I was. But then I went up to the club and ended up talking with Alan. He's new in town and he really did just stop by."

"Hetta, you don't have to explain what you do with your time to me. Besides, I saw him when I stopped at the club on the way down. He beat me down here. And I owe you an apology for leaving so early last night without an explanation. I'm not used to telling anyone what I do, because I usually don't give a damn what they think. In your case, I do. I went to my daughter's in San Jose. She has a nasty flu bug and I thought she needed a little chicken soup and fatherly love."

"Chicken soup?" I said dumbly.

"With stars. Her favorite. She's feeling a lot better today. Now, would you like to go get some breakfast before we go over your new system?"

I almost swooned with relief and gratitude. "Let me dry my hair. I would love some brunch."

"Breakfast, Hetta, not brunch. Real food," he said. He took me to The Hideaway, home of greasy home fries, biscuits with cream gravy, and corned beef hash. Jenks, it seems, has a thing for corned beef.

While we finished off about a gallon of coffee, Jenks told me more about the security system he'd installed for me. "If you feel uneasy with what I've done, I'll take it out. I give you my word I'll never activate the system myself, nor will any of my employees, unless you push the PANIC button."

I didn't have any idea what he was talking about. One thing I was more and more assured of, though, if Jenks Jenkins gave his word, he meant to stand by it. What a concept in a man.

We went back to the boat and he accessed his website to show me the options available for my security system. Despite ten gallons of coffee and several thousand calories worth of carbohydrates, I was still a little foggy brained from my champagne overdose the night before, but he was patient. Finally, while he was showing me how to change a camera angle, it suddenly dawned on me I didn't know where the cameras were.

"Camera number one is right there," he said, pointing to what I thought was a smoke alarm. "We call it a covert system, meaning not obvious to an intruder."

"Is it legal?"

"Sure, as long as it's in your home, being operated for your own security."

"Wait a minute, can *you* turn this system on from your office?"

"Technically, I can. That's what I was talking about earlier."

"You could turn this on when I'm here and watch me?" This was getting kinky.

"I could, but I won't. That's what I was telling you about the PANIC button. The way I've set it up, my staff can't activate the system unless you hit the PANIC button first, and then don't answer our phone call. On the other hand, I could override the system, but only me. And I won't."

"How do I know that for sure? Christ, for all I know I could be a new Internet star." Then I giggled, "But who in the hell would want to watch."

"Don't sell yourself short, Hetta."

"I guess I have to trust you and your people not to spy on me. Anything else I should know?"

"Nope. What I would like to do, if you agree, is demo your system to potential clients. I'll come aboard, hit the PANIC button and then show off for my clients, who will be watching from my office. That's the only time I will turn on the camera, and never when you're home."

"I trust you."

"So how do you like the system?"

"I love it. Not only can I see what's happening on my boat, if I need help I can punch a button. Wait a minute, who's monitoring the calls? What if you're out of town or something?"

"I have a pager and a portable satellite system. I can go on line, look at the situation and call the police or whatever. And if I'm not available, I have employees who cover for me. They work from home."

"Wow. I feel safer already. Jenks, how much does one of these things really cost? You're only billing me for service, not equipment and all. This sucker's pretty damned sophisticated. In my business, that spells big bucks."

"They ain't cheap. I'm targeting megayachts, corporate stuff. Your boat, like I said, will be my prototype, so I really shouldn't be charging you anything, but it goes against my nature. The hundred will do. If, that is, you agree."

"Oh, I agree all right. I'll be your Guinea pig, no problem. What happens when the boat leaves the dock? Is my security system dead in the water, so to speak?"

"I can rig up a cell phone that'll dial the website when the PANIC button is pushed."

"Call me impressed. In fact, call me anytime," I said, then blushed. Brazen hussy.

"I will. Oh, and there's another thing I meant to do last night, but ran out of time."

What now, my own satellite?

"What?" I asked.

"This," he said, and he kissed me.

And what they say is true, even after two thousand, one hundred and thirty-one days—but who's counting? It's like riding a bike.

In the Tour de France.

And winning.

Chic, alors!

42

What can I say? The next six weeks were magical. And no, that's not what I named the boat, it's the only word I can think of to describe my *thing* with Jenks.

I guess one could call it a budding romance, but one thankfully devoid of the hype, sleight of heart, and the general bull*merde* involved in most new *affaires d'cœur*. At least any I'd had since I was ten and my heartthrob was a horse named Wishes. As in, "If wishes were horses, beggars would ride."

Or maybe it was that Jenks and I were far from buds. One might even say a mite past full bloom. For the first time in my life, the words, mature and love, could share a sentence. Not that either of us had actually used the L-word yet.

Call it what you will—love, like, lust, or a healthy mix of all those things—we fell into a comfortable…what? Relationship: A state of connectedness between people. Okay, so that's what we had, even though I hate the word. Anyway, neither of us found it necessary to unload past baggage—another buzz word that stinks—play the hard-to-get game, or worry whether what we said to one another might constitute possible insult or injury. I never even obsessed or asked about that blowsy blonde, old Shirl. It was downright unnatural.

I was away in Seattle or Los Angeles a few days out of each week, but we frequently talked on the phone right before I went to bed. It was comforting to know someone out there besides Jan, Mama, and Daddy missed me. And told me so.

Thursday night through Sunday night we spent aboard *Sea Cock*. We left the dock on Thursday afternoon, sometimes taking what we dubbed a cocktail cruise to our destination. We'd anchor at Treasure Island's Clipper Cove, Angel Island, or some other Bay Area locale until reluctantly returning to the real world Sunday night or Monday morning. Sometimes Tuesday, if we didn't have pressing business.

We quickly fell into a natural, relaxed routine. For our weekends afloat, Jenks shopped for what he called real food, namely steaks, hamburger fixin's, pork chops. I made sure we had movies and necessities like chocolate cake, popcorn, Toll House cookies, and Merlot.

Weather permitting, Jenks schooled me on anchor drills, basic seamanship, knot tying, and diesel mechanics. If it blew or rained, we holed up on the hook and played dominoes. He always won. We'd read, he Clancy, me McMurtry. We both liked Tom Hanks movies, and while he really leaned toward action flicks, we both loved *Sleepless in Seattle*. Mostly though, we talked and enjoyed each other's company.

After being alone for so long, I sometimes found myself astonished that I could spend this much time in such a confined space with someone who still liked me when we parted. Like I said, it was downright unnatural.

But when we were apart, my neuroses surfaced. Lurking very deep in the dark labyrinth of my insecurity was a murky dread of…what? My past whispered, "Hetta, Jenks is too good to be true, and you *know* what they say about that." And if he was what he seemed, what was he doing with me? Four in the morning found me tossing and turning in my hotel room bed, trying to convince myself I wasn't dating Ted Bundy.

Thankfully I didn't carry my misgivings aboard on our weekends. Although we didn't usually go into gory details concerning our histories of loves, losses, or regrets, we did touch lightly on our pasts. Needless to say, I couldn't let the "nooner" incident go untouched. We shared a good laugh when he told me he called a nap a nooner, and I told him what I *thought* he'd meant.

One Thursday night, when entertaining Jenks with funny anecdotes of my hooker friends in Tokyo, I found myself reluctantly telling him about Hudson. After all, Jenks was in charge of my security system and we were having an intimate relationship. I thought it might be about time to tell him my last boyfriend ended up floating face down in my hot tub. Some guys could get real touchy about something like that. Evidently Jenks was made of sterner stuff.

"So," he said when I'd finished, "this guy, Hudson Williams, who disappeared in Tokyo five years ago, shows up, breaks into your house and ends up dead in your hot tub? Why do you think he surfaced," here he smiled, "after all this time?"

I didn't even hesitate. "I'll show you," I said. I went to my cabin, opened the safe, and brought back the key I no longer wore around my neck. The one from the Key Note Club in Tokyo.

"Mr. Fujitsu, my Japanese neighbor, told me these clubs keep bottles in personal boxes for up to ten years, so chances are Hudson had more in that box than a bottle of Crown Royal. That's my guess."

Jenks fingered the key. "What did that detective, Martinez, think about this?"

"Actually, I didn't tell him about the key."

"Why not?"

"Because I'm stupid. That's my defense and I'm stickin' to it. I've been thinking it was a mistake. I plan to get in touch with Martinez on Monday, give him the key and let him figure out what to do with it. I never was a serious suspect in Hudson's murder, but I can assure you Martinez is going to be really pissed when he finds out I've been holding out on him. According to Allison, he could even charge me with obstruction of justice or something. The only good news is that Hudson is no longer in the picture."

"Gee, I don't know about that," Jenks said, smiling and handing me back the key. "If he were still alive we could invite him for drinks, hit him over the head and collect the reward."

"Very funny. Although I like the hitting over the head part. Anyway, I promised Allison I'd give the key to Martinez this week for sure."

"I thought you had to leave for Seattle Monday noon. Do we have to go back to the dock on Sunday instead of Monday morning?"

"Rats! You're right. Japan Incorporated, as I call the big client, will be in Seattle. We start work early, eat late, and never have a moment in between. The good news is that after this week, I'll have some time off and can stay down here for at least a couple of weeks. I'll have to give Martinez the key after I get back."

"Want me to handle it for you? I'm not real busy and I can't really get any work done on the boat because you have a charter on Wednesday and Thursday."

"Oh, yeah, I almost forgot about those charters. I must say, they're great for the pocketbook and my champagne supply. Molly buys the good stuff."

"Who's chartering this week?"

I shrugged. "I never know. Molly takes care of everything. Whoever they are, they have bucks, 'cause I get five to seven hundred a day and Molly charges the client twice that. I think it's mostly corporate stuff and honeymooners."

I handed Jenks the key. He turned it over and looked at it. "Looks harmless enough. Give me Martinez's number and I'll get it to him so you don't have to break your promise to Allison and Jan. I'm sure, though, he'll be wanting to talk to you about it when you return."

Gratitude swept over me like a warm wave. I had been alone for so long, handling everything myself, the ability to share a responsibility with someone was a wonderment. Moisture welled in my eyes, causing Jenks to get that alarmed look men get when women cry.

"Don't worry, Jenks," I told him with a laugh, "I'm no sob sister. I'm not gonna cry. In fact, I rarely do. Nor do I throw up. If I ever do either, you'd best pay attention because we have us a serious problem. And while I'm in a true confessions mood—a rarity, you'll be glad to hear—I have to warn you I have a long-term memory like a computer. I might forget what I had for breakfast this morning, but in the end I remember almost everything anyone tells me. If two pieces of information don't add up, my motherboard screams *tilt*. So don't lie to me unless you mean it."

He grinned. "I'll remember that. So if you don't cry or throw up, does that mean you never get seasick?"

"Never have. Why?"

"I thought maybe we'd take this tub out the Gate, go down to Half Moon Bay."

"In the *ocean*?" I squawked.

Jenks chuckled and waved away my concern. "Hey, you've got to get certified sooner or later."

"As what? A lunatic?"

"Sea wench," he said.

Any other man called me a wench he'd'a died on the spot. The way Jenks said it, I smiled. Yep, I had it bad. This was a man I aimed to get— without my .38.

True to form, I didn't get seasick the next morning when we left Clipper Cove, cruised out under the Golden Gate Bridge, and plunged into fifteen-foot head seas.

"Uh, Jenks, are you sure about this?" I said as we ran up a wave, fell off it and crammed the pointy end of the boat into a wall of water before climbing the next wave. That's the way I saw it, anyway. For the properly nautical, however, we topped a swell, nosed into the trough, and buried the bow, taking on green water before climbing to the top of the next swell. Semantics aside, we were getting the crap beat out of us.

"It'll get better real soon, Hetta. We have to clear the bar, then you'll see."

"Damn. I've been in some pretty raunchy bars in my day, but this one is the roughest."

Jenks laughed. "All the weather and sea reports say we're in for a great cruise down to Pillar Point. Hang in there for an hour." He took a sip of his coffee. I'd long since given up trying to drink mine after almost taking out my front teeth.

"If you say so," I muttered, not really convinced.

In just under an hour, we were smoothly headed south, *Sea Cock* riding in the troughs or over swells, only occasionally catching an undulating wave on the beam that caused the boat to rock from side to side.

I soon adapted to the boat's rhythm and started enjoying the cruise. We changed course, picked up a following sea and rode it into Pillar Point. I whooped with delight as we surfed off the top of swells, sliding forward with dizzying speed, then almost stalling in the troughs until the next wave picked us up and pushed us forward again. It was this E-ticket ride that told me I'd found more than one new love. But, like any new relationship, mine with the sea was soon to be tested.

North of Half Moon Bay, the delightful anchorage at Pillar Point Harbor offered a peaceful respite from the waves pounding her breakwater. A flotilla of small sailboats, a group of trailerable vessels from a Sacramento sailing club, bobbed about, their crews sipping beer and swapping tales after a day of sailing on the Pacific Ocean.

Happily anchored after our own exciting day at sea, we showered, had a drink, cooked steaks on the propane grill and we went to bed at nine o'clock. Whoa, you say. Drink? As in singular? Yep, one of the most surprising aspects of spending time with Jenks was my diminished alcohol consumption. "Maybe you won't be needing those meetings after all," my Pollyanna muse chirped. My dark side, however, rasped, "Until he dumps you."

By the time we hit the sack, an unusually balmy southerly breeze gently rocked the boat. The warmish air felt good on my naked, slightly sunburned skin. A little foreplay on the foredeck during the voyage—in full view, I might add, of planes soaring out over the Pacific from SFO—had singed previously pasty white body parts to a pinkish tinge. As I fell asleep, I gave the day a ten. People spend their whole lives dreaming of a day like I'd had.

A clap of thunder brought us from dreamland to our feet in seconds. Driving rain sent us scurrying around the decks, naked as the day we were born, slamming shut doors and hatches. Lightning flashes lit building whitecaps. White horses slammed into our bow. Surf crashing on the beach astern roared the boaters' worst nightmare of ending up on the wrong side of a normally lee shore.

We started the engines.

It was, of course, pitch black outside. Where's a moon when you need one? *Sea Cock* was hobby horsing, her bowsprit scooping seawater on the dive, then throwing it over her shoulder onto the decks on the rise. Thankfully I had done the dishes and locked the refrigerator before we turned in or the galley would have been a minefield of flying food and pottery. I careened around the cabin, securing anything that threatened to move while Jenks turned on the running lights, depth sounder, VHF radio and radar.

"Hetta, can you get down to your cabin and grab us both a set of sweat pants and our shoes?" When I said yes, he added. "I'll get out the PFD's."

PFD's. PFD's. I tried to remember what they were. "PFD's? What are those?"

"Personal Flotation Devices."

"Hell, Jenks, I thought we were *on* one!"

Once we were both dressed and PFD'd, he snapped a safety line to his waist, strapped a strobe light to his arm, then one on mine. During all this time, which seemed like an hour but was more like five minutes, he was a rock of calm, doing his best to relieve my building sense of panic. However, safety lines, life jackets, and strobes are somehow not comforting. They mean shit has happened.

He gave my lifejacket ties a tug and said, "Okay, Hetta, here's the drill. Raising the anchor from down here, using the automatic switch, is too iffy under these conditions. I have to go out on the foredeck. We'll have to maneuver the boat to time the raising of the anchor between swells. Got it?"

I nodded dumbly. "Uh, yes. I think. What do you want me to do?"

"You have to drive the boat from the bridge."

"What? Are you nuts? No way. Not a chance."

"You have to, Hetta. And you have to drive from up there so you can see my signals. Remember what I've taught you. Slow is good. Follow my hand signals, just like we've practiced."

"Can't we just call the Coast Guard or something? Maybe a taxi?"

He grinned. "Nope. We can do this. *You* can do this."

"Uh, don't I need a safety line, too?"

"No, you don't have to go out on deck to get to the bridge. Hold on with both hands on the way up. Now, are you ready?"

"No."

He grinned, turned me around and gave me a gentle shove. "Sure you are. Go on up and watch for my signals." I felt the wind hit me in the back as he opened the side slider and disappeared into the storm.

I took a deep breath, cussed my way to the bucking bridge, but found when I got there I couldn't see a damned thing through the Eisenglass wind curtains. Unzipping the panels proved hazardous. First the heavy plastic tried flogging me to death. Once they were secured, rain and wind shot through the opening, soaking me to the bone and blinding me.

At last I was able to move to the console where I could see Jenks waiting patiently on the pitching foredeck. He'd fixed his safety line to a rail and turned on his armband strobe, but how he managed to keep his footing I'll never know. I looked longingly at the marina lights sparkling a half-mile away at Half Moon Bay and vowed never to anchor out again. Ever. And to replace the Eisenglass with real glass and windshield wipers.

Jenks had grabbed a flashlight before working his way to the bow and, as he fought for purchase on the deck, the beam swung wildly, as if he were doing battle with Darth Vader. I wanted Scotty to beam me up. I know, I know, mixed intergalactic metaphors.

Jenks turned the flashlight on me and, after I gave him a thumbs up, moved the beam onto the anchor chain, gauging the right time to begin raising the hook. Standing with my legs wide apart for balance and holding onto the ship's wheel for dear life, I watched wave after wave break over Jenks. I kept a death grip on the ship's wheel and freed one hand for the controls as I waited for the signal to move the boat forward.

A combination of fear and fatigue had turned my knees to jelly. I fought off panic for control of both my body and emotions. Captain Coffey, my ass! I mentally demoted myself from captain to deck ape when I glanced at the anemometer readout and I saw it peg forty knots. *Merde, alors!* How readily we are willing to hand off the reins of command when the caca hits the prop.

When I looked back to the bow, Jenks was gone.

My heart literally tripped and my already wobbly legs threatened to melt. My nose went numb. The nose thing is a big danger signal. It usually does that right before I faint. And this was no time to be coming down with the vapors, Miss Scarlet. What to do? What to do?

Thankfully, nothing. The foredeck suddenly blazed with light as the jillion candlepower spotlight over the flying bridge sprang to life. Jenks reappeared on the spotlit foredeck. He gave me a wave.

I waved back, although I knew he couldn't see me because he was blinded by all that light. That's why he'd waited to turn it on. He wanted to be sure I was ready. I began to breathe again and waited for the signal to proceed. I hoped I didn't proceed to screw up.

We had, praise the Lord, practiced so many times under more benign conditions that I began to calm down once we started the drill. Thanks to the spotlight, I was now able to clearly see Jenks's first signal to inch *Sea Cock* forward until he had enough slack to release the snubber line. I eased the boat into gear and pushed the throttle gently forward until Jenks gave me the "cut" sign. I put her into neutral.

Daring a quick look away while he coiled the line, I saw the clusterfuck happening around us. Boats doing the same drill, but with much yelling and cursing. Spreader lights and flashlights blinked to life all over the anchorage, illuminating confused crews. There were more bare butts on deck than a good Las Vegas review. If I hadn't been so damned scared, I would have enjoyed the show. The keystone cop scenario on other boats boosted my confidence in Jenks.

As he'd taught me, I followed Jenks's signals, moving the boat forward again, then into neutral, then forward again, until the anchor chain hung straight down. Now came the tricky part, raising the anchor from a pitching deck without ripping out the bow pulpit, losing the anchor to a broken chain link, or worse, losing Jenks overboard. Breaking anchor at night in a pounding sea, even with the aid of twin screws, a spotlight and an electric windlass, is downright dangerous. But not as hazardous as staying. The waves and wind were building. It was time to boogie.

Five foot whitecaps slammed the bow up and down, engulfing Jenks, but he held his footing, and soon the anchor was free and secured. I held the boat in place with the engines until Jenks could join me on the flying bridge and interpret what, to me, looked like measles on the radar screen. Every boat on our end of the harbor, it seemed, was underway, headed for the safety of either the southern anchorage or the Half Moon Bay marina.

Most were small sailboats with outboards, so I knew we could outrun them, but Jenks, overriding my hysterical suggestion to run them down like dogs in a mad dash for a dock, held us in place and let the panicked pack leave. He then found us a protected spot near the breakwater and re-anchored.

The anchor dug in and held fast. Jenks switched off the engines and I had his clothes off in about two seconds. Nothing like a little adrenaline rush to bring out the worst in me.

After a hot shower, we sat on the enclosed sundeck in the now almost empty harbor, listening to the wind howl and the lesser rabble babble on the radio. Most were still jockeying for dock space or moorings.

"Want something to drink?" I asked Jenks, hoping he didn't ask for his usual iced tea. Reformed drinking habits aside, I needed something a little more formidable than Mr. Lipton. Unless of course, it was spiked with Mr. Slivovitz.

"I think we've earned a bracer, don't you? How about a brandy?"

I poured us both a snifter, but before I could take a glug, Jenks reached over and took my brandy hand.

"First, a toast," he said, "to a full fledged, certified sea wench. Hetta, you handled yourself like a pro. I've been with seasoned sailors who didn't do as well as you did tonight."

"Gee, Jenks, I've heard tales about those navy showers, but didn't think you were the type."

He grinned. "I meant the anchor drill. You did better than most experienced sailors."

I actually blushed. "Yeah," I said, "but did they scream and cuss as good as me?"

"Not even close. I'd take you anywhere, under any conditions."

I was speechless. Never, in my career, life, whatever, was I so moved by a compliment. Nor had I ever, with the exception of my father, felt I could trust a man so implicitly as I did Jenks Jenkins.

Which is why, when he dumped me, I came close to meltdown. Or murder. Whichever came first.

43

Samurai seagulls invaded Seattle.

Every six months the big boys of Japan, Inc., my client's client, did their seagull act. They'd fly in, squawk loudly over some garbage, crap all over our plans, and fly back out. It was my job to deal with them. I excelled at Nihon-dazzle.

The Japanese clients, I knew, thrived on marathon meetings, followed by copious wining and dining. I stopped short of hustling up blondes for them, but that wasn't necessary because they always stayed in overpriced Japanese-owned hotels where such "amenities" were available. And for some unfathomable reason, not one of the men ever asked *me* to walk on his back.

Between chairing meetings and making sure our yen factories weren't insulted by our

Barbarian ways, it wasn't until Wednesday afternoon that I realized I hadn't talked to Jenks since I left the boat on Monday. We usually talked every evening, so not hearing from him was odd, but didn't ruffle my trust in him. I just figured he'd called while I was tied up with late night dinner meetings.

By Thursday, however, I was beginning to feel a *soupçon* of unease. Especially after leaving three or four calls on Jenks's machine and getting no reply.

I got a break when one of the big boys called in drunk and a meeting was postponed. Rushing back to my room, and still getting only Jenks's answering machine, I decided to log on to his website, thinking maybe he left me a message there. No message. *Merde.*

Maybe something was wrong with the boat and Molly had to cancel the charter and Jenks was working on *Sea Cock*? I logged off, called *Sea Cock* and got my own machine. Fooey.

I sat at my laptop, thrumming my fingers. Now what? I logged back on, got the security site and punched in my code. The phone rang, but nothing happened. *Sea Cock* was not at the dock. I felt a little panic attack rising but talked myself down. What to do? Then a little light went off in my skull. I had another option. My mobile security setup.

So that the system would work when the boat was away from the dock, Jenks had installed cell phone access onboard. If I was at anchor and needed help, I could activate the PANIC button by putting in a special code. He also rigged it so I could call my onboard cell phone and activate the cameras. I'd never used it before, but decided there was no time like the present.

I went back to Jenks's Internet site, brought up my system, punched in my ID and password and then clicked on the MOBILE mode. A series of dings, dongs and buzzes were followed by a delay when I feared my screen was frozen up, but the little blinking hourglass told me to just hold my horses. I went to the minibar and pulled out a diet Coke. A robotic version of "Anchors Aweigh" emanating from my speakers pulled me back to the computer. I hit another key, *et voila!* I was looking at the back of someone's head.

I felt a little voyeuristic and vaguely guilty. I had never told Molly about my covert cameras, mainly because Jenks had been so adamant in insisting that no one know about them. The key word here is security, he'd said. Telling *anyone* anything in the yacht club was like posting it on the club's bulletin board.

The head the camera was on didn't belong to Molly, but it *was* vaguely familiar. Maybe one of her staff? I squinted at the screen, mentally willing the person to turn around. When he did, a curse escaped my pursed lips. Alan Whitcombe, the smarmy Brit and royal pain in the ass, was on my boat. What the hell was *he* doing there?

Alan had taken to dropping by whenever I was alone on *Sea Cock*. It was as if he watched from the club, waiting for Jenks to leave. The Brit was always polite, but flirty in a slimy kind of way.

And now here he was, lounging on my settee like he belonged there. Why?

I sat, frustrated and angry, and watched as he got up, took a furtive look around the main saloon, and then headed for my cabin door, the one clearly marked, "Off Limits. Owner's cabin." He opened the door and went inside, shutting it behind him. Crap! Jenks hadn't installed a camera in my cabin, possibly in deference to my privacy. I'd have him fix that, but what to do now?

I used my cell to call Molly's cell. Ain't communication in this century grand? Too bad Jenks wasn't better at it.

"Ancient Mariner Charters, Molly speaking."

"Hi, Molly. It's Hetta."

"Hi, girl. I'm on *Sea Cock's* flying bridge right now. We're on our way back to your dock. What's up?"

"Uh, nothing. Just curious, who chartered the boat today?"

"Oh, I thought you knew. Your friend, Alan Whitcombe. He took some of his friends for lunch at Pier 39. Nice bunch. Mostly foreign."

"Oh. Okay. Uh, Molly, I...." *Merde.* How do I let her know Alan is where he's not supposed to be without telling her about the cameras?

"Hetta, you still there?" Molly said.

"Yes. Uh, hey would you go down to my stateroom and make sure I put my shampoo away this morning. I would hate to lose twenty bucks worth down the drain if it tipped over."

"Sure. It's been a real smooth run, though. I don't think you have to worry."

"Well, then. I guess I'll get back to work. Thanks, Molly."

"Thank *you*, Hetta. *Sea Cock* is one of my best charter vessels, even with that name you keep saying you're gonna change. Hey, how about *Sea Change*?"

"Sorry, doesn't grab me. Uh, Molly? Have you...." I wanted to ask her if she'd seen Jenks at the marina or yacht club, but my pride wouldn't let me. "Uh, have a nice cruise. See you soon."

I stared at my cabin door. Just as Molly entered the main saloon, Alan oozed out of my cabin and slid the door behind him. When he turned around and spotted Molly, a fast fury passed over his face, followed by that unctuous grin.

Over the roar of the diesels and the water sounds, I heard Molly say, "Oh, hi, Alan. Sorry, that stateroom is not part of the cruise."

"Oh, I wasn't going in. The door swung open and I was shutting it. My, Molly, don't you look glowing today. Must be the salt air. Positively glowing."

Molly looked a little uncertain, murmured something I couldn't understand and brushed past Alan to check on my shampoo. Alan looked very pleased with himself as he walked out of camera range. I cursed myself for not learning how to switch cameras faster.

After turning off my computer, I sat on the bed for a few minutes, trying to massage a faint headache away from my temples. This Alan was really starting to piss me off. I had seen him last week and there was no mention of his chartering my boat. Odd, but nothing I could really fault the man for. Besides, other than being a nosy body and probably snooping into my underwear, he was just a minor annoyance. My big problems—my missing boyfriend and a demanding client—loomed larger. I sighed, freshened up for the next round of meetings, and prepared for battle with my modern day weapons: laptop, briefcase, palm pilot, and charge card.

Almost out the door, I had a bright idea. I returned to the desk, brought up Jenks's site and turned on the video recorders on my boat cameras, a practice I planned to follow for all charters from now on. Since I had to leave for a meeting and wouldn't be back for several hours, my cell phone bill would be astronomical, but the rest of Alan's cruise would be on videotape.

* * *

I got back to Oakland Friday morning. I'd left several messages for Jenks, telling him what time I'd be home, suggesting maybe we'd have a later than usual cocktail cruise to Treasure Island so I'd have time to provision. No answers.

It wasn't until I boarded *Sea Cock* that I instantly and truly knew something was wrong. There was no bologna in the fridge. No bologna, no Jenks. The two went together like, well, bologna and Wonder Bread.

A hollow despair scourged the pit of my stomach, a feeling sickeningly reminiscent of that day in Tokyo when I returned from work to find Hudson's closet empty. Jenks didn't live with me, but he had a hanging locker where he kept a few clothes. They, too, were gone.

Almost sick with dread, I checked my telephone messages, e-mail, and faxes. Nothing from Jenks. I called his apartment and got his machine. A nasty little voice kept rasping in my ears, saying, *Yo Hetta, you've been dumped, dumped, dumped. Merde, merde, merde. Déjà vu all over again, again, again.*

I shakily poured myself a tumbler of wine. Paced. Had another wine. Paced. Tromped up to the yacht club to see if, by some wild chance, Jenks was playing liar's dice and forgot the time. Or the day? Or me? He wasn't there and no one had seen him.

I didn't stay long at the club for fear of running into that pain in the butt, Alan. In my deteriorating mood, he would be a convenient target, and I couldn't really lay him low without letting on about the cameras. Besides, the strain of trying to act normal when chatting with other club members proved too much. After fielding several, "Hey, Hetta, where's Jenks?" queries, I stormed back to the boat.

By nine I was a wreck. A worried wreck. What had become of Jenks? Please, please Lord, don't let him be dead. Unless, of course, he was dumping me, then please, please Lord, let him be dead.

I remembered the security videos. I hadn't bid *sayonara* to my charges until almost midnight the night before, so I had a good twelve hours to view. Even with fast forwarding, it would take a while to check out. I retrieved the tapes from the hidden recorder and headed for my VCR.

I hit REWIND, then PLAY and watched figures on the split screen. As Jenks had told me, the quality was shadowy and the sequences jerky. In order for the tape to last long enough, the shots were actually activated every few seconds. It all looked like an early Japanese monster flick. I watch as Alan seem to lurch to the aft deck where five more men were sitting around my Brown Jordan table. The sound quality was very bad, wiped out by the droning diesels. Three of the men appeared to be Oriental and all seemed to be having a great old time. I actually had a moment of sympathy for Alan. Perhaps he, too, had to woo a demanding client from time to time.

Molly entered the picture, said something to her guests, the timbre of the engines changed and I could tell they were docking. I fast forwarded, watching people move about like ants. Finally, everyone left except Molly and a crewmember. They washed the boat, vacuumed the carpets, gathered their catering equipment, locked the door and all was quiet. Nothing happened again until the tape ended. Certainly not what I wanted to see, which was Jenks coming aboard.

I poured more wine, retrieved some hors d'oeuvres left in the fridge by Molly, and attempted to watch TV. Actually, I was staring down the phone, ordaining it to ring, when I spotted the red PANIC button peeking from under my workstation. This was an emergency situation, wasn't it? I mean, *I* was certainly in a panic.

I hit the button.

Nothing happened.

I was getting ready to hit it again, when my phone rang.

"Jenks?" I gasped, "Where are you?"

"Miss Coffey, this is Ed Lu. Do you have an emergency?"

Ed, one of Jenks's staffers, was tall, thin, Chinese, and wore his long luxurious locks in a queue. He, like all of Jenks's employees, was hooked up at home to man the security system. This setup, while not all that lucrative for a guy with a PHD, allowed Ed time to pen his great Chinese-American novel, a existential '90's account à la *Easy Rider, but* without benefit of booze, recreational drugs, or weapons, of his journey, via motorcycle, from Brazil to New York. Dennis Hopper Lu. But sober and sensitive. The title of his novel in writing? *DWO: Driving While Oriental.*

"Ed, please call me Hetta. And no, not an emergency. Is Jenks there?"

"No ma'am, uh, Hetta. He's not."

"Do you know were he is?"

"Sorry, I don't. He left town is all I know. Now, according to company protocol, I have to ask. Do you want me to call the police?"

"No Ed, but I do want you to turn off the damned cameras." I made a face at the fake smoke alarm on the wall.

"I don't turn on the cameras unless you don't answer the phone."

"How do I know for sure?" I shot the camera the finger, just to check. Paranoia runs right strong through these veins, especially when folks keep disappearing on me.

Ed didn't react to my digital salute. "Well," he said, "I guess you have to trust us. Or, if you really feel uncomfortable, disconnect power to the system. That'll do it. But if you do, and then you have a problem, we won't be able to help you."

Fooey. I sighed into the phone. "I guess you've got me there, Ed, but let me give you a warning. I know how to access my own system on the Internet, so if I turn it on and see my large white butt on the screen, I'm going to come over there and cut off your ponytail. Got that?"

"Yes ma'am," he said with an, "Ooooh, I'm really scared" tone in his voice. I get no respect. I hung up.

I was running out of ideas. I paced and drank more. So much for reform. Here I was, right back where I started, only worse. At least before I put my trust in Jenks I was unhappy and lonely. Now I was unhappy, lonely, and furious.

I called Jan.

"Hetta, do you know what time it is here in Florida?"

I looked at my ship's clock. "Uh, one-ish?"

"Almost two-ish. What's wrong? Shouldn't you and Jenks be off on your boat, screwing your brains out?"

"If I see him I'm gonna blow his brains out."

"You've lost me. Has something happened? You two have a tiff?"

"I didn't think so, but he's disappeared."

Silence, then, "Hetta, what did you do to him?"

"Jan, nothing, I swear. We had a great weekend, then I go to Seattle, I come back, he's gone. No note. No e-mail. No Call. End of story. I didn't hear from him all week, which was really unusual, but I was so busy I didn't...." my voice wavered and trailed off. I was very close to tears.

Now Jan had reason to worry. I ain't no crybaby and she knows it. "Hetta, calm down. Hold on a minute, I'm going to wake Lars up. This doesn't sound like Jenks."

I waited and paced. Finally, a gravelly voiced Lars came on the line. "Have you checked Vegas?"

"Like the whole city?".

He ignored my acid tone. "MGM."

I was momentarily thrown off subject. Jenks, frugality personified, stays at the MGM? Back on track, I asked, "No, should I? Does he up and take off like this?"

"Sometimes. Actually, all the time. You know, whenever he can get a hop on old Uncle or one of his old navy buddies blows into town. He called a day or so ago said something about going east. Sometimes he goes back East."

Back East? Was this a euphemism for going back to see the old girlfriend? I'd never asked Jenks about her, but Jan had told me earlier, before I began seeing Jenks, that he had had a fifteen year affair with someone in Boston. I heard Jan growl at Lars and take the phone from him. But it was too late.

"Honey, I'm sure you'll hear from him real soon," she said, but without much conviction. I could hear it in her voice that she, like Lars, suspected that Jenks was most likely "back East."

My heart gave a little tug that hurt right down to my toes. With great difficulty, I leveled my voice. "Yeah, sure. Sorry to wake you up, Jan. And thanks for letting me know not to leave the light on."

"Hetta, we didn't say we knew for sure where he is."

"You didn't need to. Bye."

I hung up and then, for the first time since RJ died, I cried myself to sleep.

44

By Saturday I'd decided to get rich, because obviously the richness of love was to permanently evade me. Alone, but determined, I would throw myself into my career, working eighteen, no, twenty hours a day, seven days a week, forsaking friends, family, and food. I'd lose weight, quit drinking. Maybe take up Yoga. Or Buddhism. Better yet, maybe I'd become a Buddhist monk. Did they accept women? Would I have to shave my head? Wait, saffron yellow is a bad color on me. Perhaps a convent would be better instead. Black becomes me. And in those robes, I could nix the weight loss part.

Nope, none of the above. I'd just work hard, get filthy rich. Forget I'd ever met Mr. Robert "Jenks" Jenkins, USN Retardo.

But first, because I could, I took my boat, all by myself, to Clipper Cove. Why, I don't know. Maybe I secretly hoped Jenks would materialize? Of course, he didn't.

At anchor the first night, I sat on deck gazing at stars and a calm descended on me that was totally uncharacteristic under the circumstances. So I had, once again, been dumped by a man I trusted and this time by a *nice* guy! With not so much as a Dear Hetta letter. How annoying is that? Was I mad? Damned right. Was I sad? You bet. Did I feel betrayed? Definitely. So what?

I also knew I had changed over the past few months and could better handle my emotions. I had a new degree of self-confidence that I never had before. I reluctantly admitted it was in no small part due to Jenks. His insistence that I operate and maintain my own vessel had given me a better ability to steer the course of my own future. Probably right over the edge of the earth, of course, but steer it myself, nonetheless.

Most of my life, I'd been perceived by others as fiercely independent. A false perception, I knew, but one I didn't bother disproving. Only I knew how much I had always been at the mercy of outside influences like bad men, good booze, fattening food, hoity-toity employers, you name it. Only during the past five years, and especially recently, had I begun to realize how much I depended on props—material goods—to gauge my self-worth.

Not that I did much about it, but little by little I began to wage a mostly-losing battle for control over my own life. *Zut, alors!* I was starting to sound like Oprah fodder. Like those so-called uplifting novels and movies I hate. The ones about wimpy, but always stunningly beautiful women, who let the world use them for toilet paper and then find the strength—usually through meeting a man—to overcome adversity. Only in the movies. I needed a plan of my own.

I got out a new spiral notebook and wrote, in block letters, GOALS. I then began to list things I wanted to accomplish in what was left of my life. I figured, what with demerits for debauchery, I had at least thirty years. Next to each goal, I would make a plan, outlining the steps of how to best achieve it.

At the top of the list, since I had no business travel plans or meetings scheduled for a couple of weeks, I printed: 1. TAKE OFF TIME TO DECIDE FUTURE. Hey, it was a start, and easily accomplished. As Christopher Reeve once said, so many of our dreams at first seem impossible, then they seem improbable, and then, when we summon the will, they soon become inevitable. I'd stay at Clipper Cove on the boat, contemplate my life and make momentous mental inroads towards the inevitable.

Who was I kidding? By anchoring out, I was forcing myself to avoid the Meccas for those in pursuit of unsuitable suitors. Oases dispensing soul tonic to the disheartened athirst for companionship along with their gin. In other words, bars.

I added to the list. 2. STOP DRINKING. I hesitated a moment, crossed out STOP and changed it to CUT DOWN ON. Let's be reasonable here. I also made a note to determine whether I was an alcoholic or just a drunk. Time would tell.

First thing Sunday morning, I called the yacht club and told them I wouldn't be returning to my slip for at least a week. Let them know I was alive and well—well, alive —at Clipper Cove so no one would call the Coast Guard and report *Sea Cock* amongst the missing. I didn't bother mentioning that Jenks wasn't with me. No use setting the bar tongues to wagging already.

3. CHANGE NAME OF BOAT. *Fool's Paradise? Island Woman?*

I scratched out both names and called my parents.

"Wanted to let you know to call me on my cell this week 'cause I'm away from the dock," I said, oh, so casually.

"You and Jenks?" Mother asked.

"No," I said in a falsely cheery trill, "just me."

"Hetta, are you telling me you are all alone, at sea, on your boat?"

"No, dear, I'm at anchor in Clipper Cove by myself. You know where Clipper Cove is, right under the Bay Bridge? At Treasure Island? Right in the very heart of the City, practically. There are all kinds of boats here," I said, looking at the nearly empty anchorage and crossing my fingers. A little white prevarication to ease one's parents' minds does not necessarily earn you a one-way ticket to the devil's lair. "And," I added, "there's a Coast Guard station not a half mile away. I'm perfectly safe."

"Where is Jenks?"

Merde. "He had to go out of town." Not a lie either, exactly. I just didn't know which town. I didn't think this the time to pour out yet another sad tale of woeful romance gone south. Perhaps I'd finally grown up a little after all? Fancy that, and me only in my thirties.

"I don't like it," Mother said.

"Tell that to Jenks," I quipped.

"You know what I mean, Hetta," she said, her normally dulcet drawl hitching up an octave.

"Oh, Mama, I'm fine. You can call me anytime of day or night if you're worried. Trust me, I'll be here, because I don't even plan to lower the dinghy."

"Thank God for that. I wouldn't sleep a wink if I thought you were running around in that little bitty rubber boat in the middle of the ocean. Not a wink." She pronounced it wee-yunk.

"I promise I'll stay put. And don't forget, Jenks rigged up a smart alecky security system for me. If I have a problem, all I have to do is hit my PANIC button."

"Well," she said, somewhat mollified, "I guess that makes it a little better. Now you be careful, you hear?" She didn't add "And use sunblock," but I know she was thinking it.

I spent most of the afternoon with my cell phone hooked up to my computer, working online, contributing to the economy. Working online from *Sea Cock* at anchor would launch my phone charges into the ionosphere, but what the heck, it was a tradeoff for bar bills.

I e-mailed the Trob, Allison, Craigosaurus, Jan, and everyone I did business with, telling them I was available only by e-fax, cell phone, or e-mail for the rest of the week. My landline phone was locked in my dock box back in Oakland, along with the answering machine, so I could pick up, via remote, any message that strayed. I didn't deem it necessary to inform my clients, or anyone else for that matter, that I was under self-inflicted boat arrest due to a broken heart. Not that anyone would be overly amazed.

I was catching up on paperwork when my ship's clock rang four bells, six o'clock, and was surprised the day had gone by so quickly. And that, for about half of the day, I hadn't thought of Jenks's treachery.

I went out on deck to feed my duck, Echo. I'd named him Echo because I'd read somewhere that a duck's quack doesn't echo. My new pet was partial to Ritz quackers.

Throwing bits to my new friend, I kept a sharp eye out for wild-eyed ecofreaks who'd report me for polluting the bay. Some folks need to get a life. This from a woman who spends her evenings with a duck.

Echo downed his goodies and ignored my informing him that French ducks don't say "quack,

quack, quack," but "*coin, coin, coin.*" He perched himself on my dive platform and deposited some pollution of his own. I hooked up a hose to my saltwater washdown pump and sprayed him and his leavings off my boat.

At dusk I secured the boat, made a huge tuna fish salad, drank one glass of chilled Chardonnay, and fell asleep on the settee while watching television. Sometime in the wee hours, the tide turned the boat abeam a slight swell and, alerted by the change of movement, I got up to check my bearings. Satisfied I was safely anchored, I went to bed and slept soundly through the rest of the night. Gee, who needs Valium, hot tubs, and watered down drinks when you can have a three hundred thousand dollar yacht? I was finding it real hard to feel sorry for myself, but I'd eventually manage.

By mid-week I was really getting into this island woman stuff. I also realized that at some point, I would have to go ashore for supplies and water. After six days at anchor, I was starting to run out of things.

I'd spent time at Treasure Island when it still belonged to the navy—don't ask—but now the island had been turned over to the city of San Francisco and was destined for low income housing projects. I wasn't sure whether there was a store or even if any of the planned houses had been built. In order to check it out, I'd have to go ashore, but I'd promised my mother I wouldn't launch the dink. And if I did, she'd know. Mothers have a way, you know.

Unwilling to cruise back to the yacht club, I dug out a stack of Bay Area yachting and boating guides in search of a marina with a store. And one where I felt comfortable docking the boat alone. Pier 39, my first choice for shopping, was too daunting. I'd been there before, but the currents and winds were such that I always let Jenks handle the boat. I now regretted that.

Allison solved the dilemma when she called. "I got your e-mail, girl, but was out of town. Where are you that I can't call your landline?"

"If I tell you I'll have to kill you."

"Very funny, Hetta. I was thinking of coming to see you, but you obviously don't want company."

"Whining doesn't become you, counselor," I told her. Then I told her where I was.

"Coffey, are you out of your effin' mind? You've only had the boat a few months and got no damned bidness out there alone."

Ah ha! I smelled a contrived call. "And how, pray tell, do you know I'm alone, Miz Allie? I do not recall informing you of such."

"Uh, I talked to Jan."

"Ah."

"What, ah? It's not like we're talkin' about you behind your back, it's only that—"

"It's," I interrupted, "only that you're talking about me behind my back."

"Not really. It depends on the definition of the word *back*," she said with a laugh. Ever since the Clinton/Lewinsky debacle we'd had a running joke on word definitions. Now it broke the ice.

"You win. And I'm not upset that you two talked. So long as Jan doesn't tell anyone at the yacht club."

"What's she gonna do, call up from Florida and tell the bartender? Nope, your secret is safe. She swore me to secrecy, told me not to even tell the Trob."

"Like he knows anyone to tell. How goes the strangest romance of the century?"

"We're getting married."

"What?"

"I was getting ready to call and tell you when Jan called."

"And, you didn't want to rain on my already soggy parade. Thanks, but it's all right. Your happiness does not make me unhappy. Besides, I'm getting over it. I sure wish I knew what 'it' was."

"Jan and I talked about that. We can't figure it out either. According to her, Jenks told Lars everything was hunky dory with you two. We're all mystified. You don't suppose Jenks is some kind of secret agent man, do you?"

"Who the hell knows what he is. I don't suppose Lars has heard anything from his crappy, old brother?" I asked, hating myself for asking.

"Jan would have called you. Nope, nothing as of this morning. Sorry."

"It's okay."

"Can I do anything? Other than send you some arsenic?" she asked.

"Yeah, bring me some groceries."

"Huh?"

"I didn't know I was staying out this long, so I didn't bring much. I thought maybe, if you want to come out to Treasure Island, I'll meet you at the dock."

Silence.

"Allison?"

"Oh, I'm here. I'm making out a list of billable hours. Let's see, 'shopping for groceries for demented client,' one hour at two big ones an hour, 'travel time,' another big one, then we have...."

"Didn't I fire you?"

"Yes. But until the Hudson thing is solved, I'm still your legal counsel of record. Can you give me any really good reason why I should trot out to Treasure Island?"

"How about if I cook you dinner?"

"Oh, that's completely different. I can be there by, let's see, five-thirty? I'll take a cab because—and if you quote me on this one I'll sue you—I don't want to leave my Beemer parked so near low income housing."

"Trust me, Allison, anything I could tell the press won't do half the damage to your career as marrying the Trob will. Can you imagine him glad handing the Gov? He'd probably insist on wearing rubber gloves."

She laughed and hung up.

I e-mailed my grocery list to Allie. The first three items were hemlock, rat poison, and a personal guillotine. Then I tried to raise the marina at Treasure Island on the radio. I'd heard they were scheduled to reopen soon under new management, but even though there were a few boats in slips, no one picked up the call. I tried two more channels and got no answer. Finally, another boat responded and said the marina wasn't officially open and no one was allowed to tie up at the docks until further notice. *Merde.*

I got out the binoculars. A long dock in various stages of construction ran parallel to shore, but access from the dock to the parking lot beyond looked like it was blocked by a tall fence. Rats. Studying the situation further, I decided to go for it and figure out the details later. I started the engines.

Raising the anchor under benign conditions is easy and I soon had *Sea Cock* standing off the dock. There were several signs on the dock, NO TRESPASSING, PROPERTY OF THE CITY OF SAN FRANCISCO, ABSOLUTELY NO PRIVATE VESSELS, and my favorite, DON'T EVEN *THINK* OF PARKING HERE.

I readied lines and fenders to the middle, fore and aft boat cleats. The breast line was only a foot or so from the downstairs steering station, so all I had to do was get it around a dock cleat and I had it made. Unless I didn't, in which case, with the light northerly dead on my beam, I'd be left standing on the dock, watching my boat blow away towards the rocks on the other side of the cove. Not a reassuring picture.

I sidled up to the dock and, using my rudder and throttles, walked *Sea Cock* sideways like Jenks taught me. Even with the wind directly on the beam, blowing me off the dock, I chose the right moment, leaned over the gunwale, lassoed a dock cleat and cinched the boat in tightly. That done, I stepped onto the dock and tied off the other lines. I was hauling myself back aboard to shut down the engines when I heard applause, catcalls, and whistles. Turning around, I saw a dozen or so construction workers clapping and hooting approval. I took a bow.

* * *

Allison arrived right on time, lugging five bags of groceries and two bags of wine.

"Holy moly," I said, "all I asked for were a few frozen dinners, veggies, and some diet Coke."

"Oh, phooey, no one can live on that shit. I brought steaks, potatoes, Caesar salad fixin's, and a really great bottle of Merlot. Sorry, they were fresh out of guillotines, but I got you a garrote. I also brought my jammies and toothbrush, cuz I'm stayin' the night."

"Uh, I'm not supposed to stay at the dock overnight. I practically had to sleep with the entire construction crew to stay here until you arrived. Actually, I promised them you would."

"I wondered why they were so friendly."

"Anyhow, it looks like we have to go back out to the anchorage."

"Bull hockey. I ain't spendin' no night swinging on no flimsy piece of chain. Gimme your phone." She called the Mayor, at home, and hung up with a satisfied grin. "Hizzoner says we can stay." Noting my raised eyebrows, she shrugged and poured us each a glass of wine.

I grabbed a Brie and fruit plate, she carried the wine, and we went to the aft deck. "Hetta, I have a feeling you need a good, old fashioned, whine and jeeze party. Now, tell me everything."

God, it was good to have someone to talk to who didn't quack back.

I spent the next hour recounting, in detail, my cruise out the Gate with Jenks, the storm at Pillar Point and finished with, "Allie, I was so proud of myself. More importantly, I was pleased Jenks thought I'd done such a good job under crappy conditions. I mean, he even called me a wench."

Allison almost dropped her wine, then looked me in the eye. "Hetta," she said solemnly, "I'm your attorney. You can tell me where you left his body."

I laughed, the first time in over a week. "No silly, he meant it, and I took it, as a compliment. He said I was a certified sea wench."

"Well, shit, in that case, you'll need a whole new wardrobe. Lots of low cut blouses and dangly earrings."

We both giggled and went to the galley to ready steaks for grilling. I made a salad and slathered garlic and green peppercorns on T-bones while Allison chopped anchovies for our Ceasar. Someone rapped on the hull and we looked out to see two of San Francisco's finest standing on the dock.

"Okay, Ms. Friends in High Places, you deal with 'em," I told Allison, trying to sound cool, but my heart was thudding. Please, oh, please don't let them bring bad news about Jenks.

Allison stepped outside, talked a couple of minutes and came back in.

"Hey, how about that? De man sent those guys down to see if we were safe and sound. How cool is that?" Then she stopped dead, staring at me. "Hetta, what's wrong? Damn, girl, you look whiter than usual."

"Allie, when I saw those cops my heart almost stopped. I thought they were coming to tell me something happened to Jenks. Not logical, I know."

"Not totally *il*logical, either. Do you know anyone who would have a key to Jenks's apartment? We could have them check to see if, uh, you know, make sure he's not sick or something."

"Yes, I do know someone who might. Allison, I'm not supposed to show this to anyone, but you *are* my attorney and thereby sworn to secrecy. Watch this."

I hit the PANIC button.

Seconds later the phone rang and I spoke into the mouthpiece without waiting to hear who it was. "Good evening, Ed."

Allison cocked her head.

"Good evening, Hetta. Is there an emergency?"

"No emergency, Ed. I was testing the system."

"You know I have to ask. Do you want me to call the police?"

"No, but thanks for asking. Uh, you haven't, by any chance, heard from Mr. Jenkins have you?"

"Yep, sure have, Hetta. He called in a few minutes ago, said everything was fine."

Allison surmised Ed's answer by the furious rush of red to my cheeks. I could hardly hear Ed say good-bye, my ears were so a-thud with anger. I slammed the phone shut and exploded.

"The son of a bitch."

"What son of a bitch?"

"Jenks! He's just fine."

My bassackward fury sent Allison into gales of laughter, and despite myself, I soon joined her.

45

I renamed my duck *Eco*, Spanish for Echo.

This change was brought about by a new tack for diverting myself from thoughts of homicide and suicide by dwelling on pleasant recollections from the past and positive plans for my future. By now I was on an emotional roller coaster that dipped into depression, soared to anger, then leveled off and raced towards the brass ring. I know, mixed carnival metaphors. But the brass ring part was what made life bearable. Hmmm. How about *Brass Ring*?

One particularly beautiful evening aboard *Sea Cock*, while stargazing at those constellations the City's ambient light pollution let shine through, I was reminded of another starry night, in another body of water far to the south.

Jan and I had flown to the Mexican city of Loreto in Baja, California, rented an overpriced VW bug, and driven north to Conception Bay. We'd picked Conception Bay in hopes of recapturing some measure of the Baja peninsula's charm that once drew us to Cabo San Lucas before Cabo became a victim of her own beautiful setting and great climate. We weren't disappointed by Conception Bay.

Jan and I picked up a little local knowledge while picking up on a couple of local gringos in thatch roofed beach bars. Taking in all the info we could garner, we packed our light camping gear into rented kayaks and set out on a three day, two woman exploration of the bay.

Conception Bay, her spectacular shores sparsely inhabited by a smattering of gringo retirees and dropouts, still held a tenuous charm by virtue of her lack of amenities such as electricity and water. With the exception of those who felt it necessary to import satellite TV, run generators, and build tennis courts, most residents were hardy souls willing to rough it a little to dwell in paradise. So long as paradise remained cheap and included enough ice for their tequila, the full timers were a contented bunch of expat ex-malcontents.

Our final evening in the bay, Jan and I camped at a cove the locals called Santa Barbara. We ate cold tamales, drank the last of our wine, and lay in sleeping bags staring at stars in a moonless sky. Stars so close we felt we could touch them. The Milky Way, barely visible in much of the United States, resembled a bright white cloud against velvety black heavens. And although there was no moon, starlight alone cast shadows off the cactus and elephant trees.

Desert sounds—distant coyotes, the rustle of night creatures—were occasionally broken by the faint echo of a truck on Highway 1 using Jake brakes, or a passing fishing panga's humming outboard. The man-made noises reminded us that, as remote as we were, civilization was inexorably marching down the peninsula.

I had just quipped that our lack of knowledge regarding the heavens was astronomical when a loud splash jolted us upright. The encroachment of civilization notwithstanding, Jan and I suddenly recalled we were completely alone on an uninhabited beach and no one in the entire world knew we were there. We sat frozen, watching and listening for another sound. We both "eeked" and then laughed when a pair of dolphins leaped in unison not a fifty feet in front of us.

Aglitter with the liquid gold of bioluminescence, the dolphins frolicked, trailing fairy dust, and inviting us out to play. Without hesitation, we dragged our kayaks into water twinkling as if backlit by tiny white Christmas bulbs. Our paddles disturbed small fish, creating even more scintillating bursts of phosphorescence. We spent the next two hours in the company of the chattering, diaphanous dolphins, squealing our pleasure over a spectacle even Mr. Disney couldn't top.

Remembering that night, I came up with a plan. A plan for my future. I'd take my boat to Mexico! Then the dark shark of reality finned into my Mexican dream. And he had a calculator. If I worked really, really, really hard for five years, triple paid my boat payments and—hey, wait a minute, this was *my* dream. Screw reality!

I banished the shark and added another goal to my list. TAKE MY *RENAMED* BOAT TO MEXICO.

Then a postscript: BRUSH UP ON SPANISH.

Thus, the renaming of my duck from Echo to Eco.

He didn't give a quack, and I felt I was getting a linguistic jump on my planned Mexican cruise, even though, by realistic calculations, I was at least five years away from cutting the lines. It pays to plan ahead, especially when trying to divert oneself from murderous thoughts and depression.

Still no new word from or about that shit, Jenks. After a few more days of oscillating between rage, self-pity and worry, I leveled out to a constant state of perplexity.

One of the things that upset me the most was my inability to forget him. Even as furious and hurt as I had been with that lout Hudson, it didn't take me more than a day or two to, if not forget, then at least write him off. Maybe it was because I learned Hudson was a thief and a deceiver so quickly. Within days of Hudson's disappearance, I knew he was a married, thieving liar. That sort of thing has a way of taking the romantic edge off a relationship. Especially since one of the relations took a powder. Jenks's jury was still hung, so to speak.

Anyhow, I was waiting for the other shoe to drop this time, leaving me barefoot and emotionally free. But it wasn't happening quickly enough. I still held a modicum of hope that Jenks was kidnapped by a band of terrorists and, in his struggle to return to me, suffered a blow to the head, leaving him temporarily an amnesiac. When let free, *he'd climb the highest mountain if it reached up to the sky, to prove that he loved me he'd jump off and fly. Swim the deepest ocean from shore to shore, to prove that he loved me just a little bit more.* Wait a minute, isn't that the lyrics to an old country western song? I sang *One Woman Man* for Eco, wondering if singing to a duck constituted demented behavior.

I talked to Jan daily, if for no other reason than she actually talked back. And did not demand quackers. Lars was taking a very annoying "what, me worry?" attitude, saying he was accustomed to his brother's sudden and unannounced departures. And, after all, we *had* heard from his employee, Ed Lu, that the bastard was just fine, wherever he was.

I reminded Jan that if I killed one Jenkins brother, they couldn't hang me twice for doing in the other.

Determined to get over my latest, and absolutely last, amatory adventure, I continued adding stuff to my GOALS list. I had named this list THINGS TO DO AS AN INFINITELY UNATTACHED PERSON. The list grew daily, as did my reluctance to return to my dock at the yacht club. There was something soothing and insular about living in my own universe, self-sufficient, independent of outside resources. Well, not exactly so independent.

By conserving water (I found I could shower, wash dishes and cook with a little under ten gallons a day) I was good for some time to come. And, with reluctant thanks to Jenks, I had enough fuel to keep *Sea Cock* powered up at anchor for a year. One of the first things Jenks'd done when I turned him loose on my boat was to install two seventy-five amp solar panels on the sundeck roof, an inverter for AC power without running the generator all the time, and an extra bank of golf cart house batteries. When I'd bought *Sea Cock*, I couldn't leave the dock without the generator running, but now I only had to charge batteries a couple of times a day, depending on how much power I used.

What with solar charging plus two short generator charges per day, I could easily run my computer, printer, cell phone, TV, VHF radio and refrigerator during the entire day. Any additional required electricity, say a blender, microwave, toaster or the like, had to be carefully considered and usually called for me to turn on the generator for a few minutes. Or reconsider and make a sandwich.

The other, wonderful side of the new system, for both me *and* my fellow anchor outs, was not having to listen to the drone of a genset all day and night. I charged batteries while cooking dinner on my electric stove or in the microwave, then shut down and didn't have to fire up the generator until I charged again the next morning. My morning activities while running the generator included making coffee, taking my shower, and drying my hair. As long as all systems continued to work, I had it made.

Unless I got blown out.

Niggling at the back of my mind was the possibility of a strong westerly blowing into Clipper Cove. I remembered Jenks saying it didn't happen often, but when it did, things got ugly, pronto. That night at Pillar Point, which now seemed like another life ago, proved his point as to how quickly shit happens at sea. I didn't have any idea how I'd handle *Sea Cock* alone under the same conditions.

So, true to the old adage about leopards and spots, I'd found something new to obsess over. Local weathermen became my new saints, the National Oceanic and Atmospheric Administration, my oracle. The droning monotony of VHF radio marine weather reports were music to my ears. And to make sure all those weather gurus didn't screw up, I spent an hour each day of expensive cell time downloading Internet weatherfax data. Which, of course, I couldn't interpret, but it made me feel better to have a tangible document showing little wind arrows pointing every which way but due west. Thank God I couldn't receive cable TV, and therefore The Weather Channel, while away from the dock. I'd have been glued to the boob tube all day.

The slightest shift in the breeze had me instantly on deck, planning my getaway. The good news is that San Francisco Bay in the summer doesn't have much wind. The bad news is if it does blow, it can come from any direction. Clouds sent me into major anxiety, diving into the Oreos. Good thing I had a limited supply. Oreos, that is; anxiety for me is aeonian.

Then there were the toilets.

After the holding tank fiasco on my first weekend aboard, I had a phobia of overflowing scat. Jenks eliminated, you should pardon the pun, part of the problem by rigging each toilet for a specific purpose. Toilet #1 was for peeing and toilet #2 was for just that. Toilet #1 discharged directly overboard, while the other one was plumbed to the old dreaded holding tank. This, barring my dining on fresh salsa in Mazatlan ever again, reduced by far the number of gallons flowing into the holding tank. Okay, so one toilet was illegally plumbed, but tell that to all those construction workers, fishermen, and even Coast Guardians I've seen spraying the bay. What? My pee is toxic and theirs isn't?

I still watched the rising gauge on the holding tank ve-ry carefully. I could hardly fathom what the potty patrol boys would charge me to come out to Treasure Island.

Even with all these little problems to brood over, I was enamored with my new life as an anchor out. A floating hermit. *Hetta's Hermitage*, how's that sound? Nah, too Jacksonian.

Eventually I knew I'd have to go back to the dock and reality, but for now I was handling my life and career from afloat, thank you. I didn't even bother calling my answering machine, which was locked in my dock box back at the marina to pick up messages, because everyone I wanted to hear from already knew where I was and I was afraid I'd hear something that would force me to return.

I did call Molly the charter lady and tell her I wasn't dead or sunk, but that I was using the boat full time for now. She said she understood and she was really happy for Jenks and me. I bit my lip and mumbled something inane, but when I hung up I'd at least learned the Jack London Square scuttlebutt hadn't picked up on the demise of our romance. Or whatever we'd had.

Mail was becoming a concern until I solved it by having one of the WOEies from the yacht club drop it off on their weekend sail. To keep the barstool gossipmongers at bay, I used the "we" word when talking to yacht club members. When the WOEies dropped off my mail I let them think Jenks was taking a nap. Oh, the dreaded web.

Once in a while I'd get restless, tempted to up anchor and find a waterfront ginmill with a guest dock. Use *Sea Cock* for my original dark intentions. But somehow without Jan, my Sancho Panza, tilting at triceps had lost its appeal. Besides, even though I'd originally conjured up the concept of a yacht as a mantrap, it was my home now.

Of course, there was that Jenks thing.

Furious and hurt though I was, I couldn't quite get up any zeal to find solace in a singles bar. Besides, it had been my experience that the only thing most men in singles bars have in common is they're married. Some of them to each other.

When the urge to prowl arose, I diverted my energy into more productive activities. I tried fishing, an almost counterproductive activity since, even though foraging for extra provisions seemed like a good idea, there was no way in hell I'd eat seafood from San Francisco Bay. At least once a day I put on a Richard Simmons tape, sweated with the oldies, then did some commercial cleaning: watching television, cleaning during commercials.

I read all the books on board I'd been meaning to read forever and even began writing a few self-serving memoirs. The fictionalized version of my life was beginning to look suspiciously like a cross between Mother Teresa and Dirk Pitt, but the writing was fun and therapeutic. The more I recaptured memories of being raised by a passel of adults (I could count at least ten grownups who, like Bill Cosby's family, all had the right to wallop me) the more I realized what a rich, albeit internationally fractured, childhood I'd had.

We moved a lot, from country to country, state to state, so Daddy could build dams. But we took Texas with us. From campsite to campsite, from Haiti to Thailand, we were likely to have the same next door neighbors. Not only that, many of them were relatives. At one time, both of my grandmothers lived in camp with us. Not only did one grandmother live with us much of the time, I sometimes lived with her back in Texas, where we were surrounded by her sisters, my great aunts. Then, from time to time, I stayed with relatives on my father's side, namely a grandmother, grandfather, great grandmother, and great aunt.

I learned some very useful stuff. Not only can I speak French and a smattering of Thai, I can make lye soap and buttermilk. I'm probably the only woman of my generation in Oakland who can make her own marshmallows, shoe a mule, or skin a deer and tan the hide. I can bake or fry almost anything, even if I have to kill it first. Dad taught me to drive a car with a stick shift when I was eight and a D-8 'dozer a year later. Yessiree, I was well equipped by all those folks to face the world, right up until I reached the age of consent and my emotional maturity went into cardiac arrest.

While one faction of the greats and grands were striving to produce a proper young lady with all the basic skills of a pioneer, the others were hell-bent on toughening me up for adulthood. Of course, hardly any of their sage advice penetrated my stubborn psyche, but they even had a Texas-ism to cover that. *Good judgment comes from experience, and a lot of that comes from bad judgment.* I'd had oodles of experience and bad judgment, so when does the good judgment kick in?

I was really bummed I had so misjudged Jenks but, as they say, that's water under the keel. I had a new life to plan. I pulled out my LIST OF THINGS TO DO AS AN INFINITELY UNATTACHED PERSON and my eyes lit on TAKE MY OWN BOAT TO MEXICO. Good idea maybe, but how far was it by water? I'd always made the trip in a very large airplane. Did I have the boat for the job? A couple of hours on the Internet and I knew the possibility was solid, if no Sunday sail in a pond.

Getting further into my fantasy voyage, I continued to Net cruise, locating Ecomundo, the kayak folks Jan and I had rented from years before. They were alive and well in Conception Bay. I could tell from various other websites that the population and services available in Conception and the area were expanding, but the bay still had no electricity or running water. A good thing in my book.

While I was dreaming, I might as well go for broke. I pictured myself down to the two's. Two pairs of shorts, two tee shirts and two pairs of flip-flops in case one has a blowout. I'd spend my life waltzing to the tide and wind, but not become one of the many derelicts, mostly gringo male singlehanders, like Jan and I had met in Mexico.

The barnacle fleet, as I named them, were like their vessels, unkempt and unloved. While others reveled in the beauties of Mexican waters, these guys only viewed life through the reverse telescopic lens of the thick glass bottom of a Pacifico beer bottle. Nope, not for me. Not any more. Besides, I drink Tecate.

Sighing, I brought myself back to reality and did a little more cyber snoopery that ended up costing me some money. I ordered a copy of John Steinbeck's *Log from the Sea of Cortez*, cruising guides for the west coast of Mexico and the Sea of Cortez by Capts. John and Pat Rains, *King of the Moon*, Gene Kira's novel about a Mexican fishing village, *Into A Desert Place,* Graham Macintosh's trek down the entire Baja peninsula in the company of a donkey, and *Troubled Sea*, an adventure novel by some Schwartz dame.

When I finally got to the Baja, I'd be ready.

Then, as I was about to log off, I decided to check out something else: the Key Note Club in Tokyo. I had only typed K-E into the search engine when the browser recall popped up the words, Key Note Club. And I'd never checked it out before.

Puzzled, I stared at the screen for a minute, then clicked on the website address. Sure enough, The Key Note Club had a jazzy site listing their coming attractions. Photos of this month's stars showed a faded blonde trying to torch a mike and a natty, sixtyish black man at the ivories. The club served light meals and still maintained personal liquor lockups. So, Hudson's bottle might still be there after all these years. I wondered how many other dead people still had a drink waiting.

More importantly, who had accessed this website on my computer? And when? Only Jan, Jenks, and I used my computer and Jan had left for

Florida weeks ago. I clicked on the browser's HISTORY and was given a choice of either TODAY or previous hits. I knew about today, so I clicked on previous searches and there it was. I checked the date. It was Jenks. Right after I told him about Hudson and the key.

The key! I had given it to Jenks to give to Martinez. I logged off and dialed the PO-lice.

"Martinez here," he answered in his bored monotone.

"Hetta here," I said, mimicking him.

"Very amusing, Ms. Coffey. What can I do for you today? You shoot somebody? Body in the bilge? Boat stolen?"

"Also amusing. I need to ask you a question and you have to promise not to get all mad."

"Oh, brother. Okay, I promise."

"Has a Mr. Jenkins called you lately?"

"You mean the guy you're dating?"

"How did you know about him?"

"I keep my ears open."

I didn't know whether I was pissed off with the knowledge that Martinez was spying on me, or relieved that he cared. "And such big ears. Well, did he? Have you seen him?"

"What, you finally found a boyfriend and you've already misplaced him?"

"Sort of."

"Hetta, just tell me what you want."

"I gave him a key to give to you. Did he?" I was still worried how Martinez was going to react when he heard I'd been withholding information from him. Information relative to a murder that some still thought I had something to do with.

"No. I've been on vacation. Went down to look at retirement property in Mexico."

"Oh."

Martinez sighed. "Hetta, what key? I'm kinda busy."

I decided to tell all. And I did.

Martinez exploded. I had no idea the man had so much emotion in his being. For several minutes he raged at me, telling me how stupid it was not to level with him, especially since he had only my protection in mind. I let him give vent to all my idiocies, then, as quickly as he blew, he cooled. "Hetta, are you still there?" he asked quietly.

"Yes, but I'm several inches shorter."

"Sorry. Call Jenkins and have him get right over here with the key."

"Uh, I can't."

"What do you mean, you can't? Where are you? I know you have a phone, because we're talking on it."

"Detective Martinez, I can't call Jenks because he's sort of disappeared."

Long pause. Ragged sigh. "I'm coming over."

"Do you have a boat?"

46

Martinez did have a boat. Or rather, the San Francisco Sheriff's department did. Two hours after we talked, a blinking blue light on the horizon announced the detective's arrival. I made coffee and awaited my flogging before the mast.

And my groceries.

Martinez climbed aboard, handed up two large brown bags and groused, "This certainly gives new meaning to the term public servant. You know, I've gotten kittens from trees, taken traumatized teens home with me for a hot meal and a good night's sleep, fixed flats for little old ladies, and even given bums my clothes, but grocery shopping for a potential felon is a first."

"Thanks for the grub, kind cop. My lawyer, Allison, brought out some vittles a few days ago, but I was getting low on the fresh stuff."

"Maybe your doctor can bring a load? Then maybe your mechanic? Perhaps you can make an arrangement with the navy?"

"Cute. You know, this isn't your jurisdiction. Did you come out here to cheer me up?"

"No, I came out here to try to talk some sense into you. Probably a waste of time, since good sense somehow seems to stay out of your way. And, of course, to record your statement about the key for Interpol."

"Oh, okay. Uh, Martinez, your boat is leaving. Do you also plan to stay here indefinitely? Not that I mind, really, it's getting a little lonely."

"He'll come back if I call him," Martinez said, "but I was hoping I could talk you into returning to your slip so we can keep an eye on you."

"I feel perfectly safe out here, thank you."

"All alone?"

"I'm not alone. I have a duck. Anyhow, you, Allison and Jan are the only ones who know that I've lost my last mate. Everyone else thinks Jenks is here with me." I didn't add that that was what I *hoped* everyone still thought. Keeping a secret in the Oakland Estuary was well nigh impossible. The best way to spread gossip, other than telling *me,* was a new twist on an old sexist joke, telegraph, telephone, or tell a yachtie.

"Hetta, you have no idea where your Mr. Jenkins has gotten to?"

"Nope. Even his brother doesn't know. I understand he's prone to wild assed flights off to parts unknown via Uncle Sam airways."

"Uncle Sam?"

"Yeah, he's retired military and can fly for free all over the world. He told me once that on a flight from Denver to Florida he fell asleep on a transport aircraft and ended up in South Africa. Maybe that's where he is, Johannesburg."

"More like Tokyo."

Merde, I hadn't thought of that. "The bastard! I trusted him. He took off with the key, didn't he? I never should have told him about Hudson or that I think something valuable might be stashed in the booze box at the Key Note. Jesus, I never learn, do I?"

Martinez gave me a look that said it all. After his boat picked him up, I went into a deep blue funk. Once again I been too swift to trust, too willing to believe I had found someone I could count on. And been sold down the tubes.

In not so olden times I would have thrown myself into the seductive arms of Mr. Johnnie Walker or *Messieurs* Neiman *et* Marcus, but I girded my loins—I always wanted to say that—and threw myself into boat work instead.

I oiled all the interior teak.

Varnished the exterior teak.

Changed oil in the generator.

Hydrometered the batteries.

Cleaned the oven.

Inventoried spare parts.

Polished windows.

Shined stainless rails.

That killed the best part of two days. Then I trimmed and colored my hair, using a three day ration of water in the process, shaved my legs, and gave myself a facial. I ironed what clean underwear I had left.

Accomplishment should lead to contentment, but the truth of the matter was that I was desperately lonely. Had I been on land, I'm sure I would have headed for the dog pound. I polished RJ's urn, reminiscing of fun days with my pooch. I thumbed through a photo album, taking a dog trot down a memorable lane that, except for fond moments with my hound, was for the most part a rocky road. Taking out pictures of both Jenks and RJ, I succumbed to a deep sense of loss before dragging my emotionally and physically exhausted bod to bed at eight p.m. on a Saturday night. Which was something I'd only done on that rare occasion when a day of bacchanalia caught up with me early.

47

At oh-dark-thirty, I sat straight up in bed, straining to hear...what? Had I dreamed a noise?

I could tell the wind had picked up slightly by the rocking of the boat. Boats, even fairly new ones, creak when they sway and *Sea Cock* was no exception. But had I been awakened by something, some sound or movement, out of the ordinary?

After a full minute, which seemed like an hour, of straining to hear through pounding eardrums, I began to calm down a little. I actually took a breath. *Probably just Eco doing his little web-footed shamble on the dive platform.* The only thing between my pillow and the dive platform was the fiberglass hull, and two window hatches. Even though I kept the drapes closed, Eco must have sensed I was close, for he took up the annoying habit of nesting there. More than one night I'd had to run him off. Give a duck an inch and he'll take a mile.

It was chilly, even with the portholes closed and curtains drawn. I was reluctant to leave my nice warm bed to wash a pesky duck from his chosen roost. Pulling the comforter up to my chin, I snuggled deep under the covers. I was almost asleep again when I heard another scrape.

"Hey, Eco. Does orange sauce mean anything at all to you?" I growled, and rolled onto my knees. I parted the curtains and peered out the aft portholes, but it was too dark to see anything outside. Next to the bed was a switch for activating the lights on my dive platform, so I flipped them on and my entire body went stone-cold. Unable to move, I stared in pure terror out the porthole.

Illuminated in the eerie light reflecting off the water, a rubber dinghy was tied to my dive platform. It damned sure wasn't mine. Then I heard the unmistakable sound of feet—un-webbed feet—scrunching across fiberglass. Frightened as I was, a sudden rush of heat unfroze me as it occurred to me that I was getting really tired of this crap. But first I had to find out what crap this was. Leaping from the bed, I realized that only my anger had warmed. My legs, ice cold with fear and practically paralyzed, buckled under me when I hit the floor.

I rolled onto the carpet, crawled to where I'd dumped my sweats the night before, shimmied into them, and pushed myself up onto wobbly legs. As I was slipping on my boat shoes, I heard more scuffing topsides and cursed the day I decided not to install an extra VHF radio in my cabin. Cheap will up and bite you in the ass every time.

Reluctant to open the door, I made myself do it anyway. I crept up the dark companionway stairs to the main saloon, pausing between steps to listen. Although I was certain there was someone outside the boat, I was relatively safe inside. I knew that all outside doors and hatches were locked and bolted. Without breaking a window or smashing in a very heavy teak door or hatch, the intruder could not gain entry. And breaking in was no easy feat, for my windows and hatches were built to withstand tons of water pressure in the event of getting whapped up alongside by a wave.

Dropping to my knees, I crawled across the carpet to my desk. What to do? Call the cops? Radio a mayday call to the Coast Guard? Push the PANIC button on my security system? Or lock and load?

I opted for lock and load.

Back down the stairs I went, where I quickly unlocked the specially built gun cabinet in my cabin, pulled out Granny Stockman's shotgun, loaded 12-gauge shells into the magazine, and pumped one into the chamber.

"Right on, Detective Martinez," I whispered, thankful for his advice , which he swore he would deny giving to me should it ever come up, like in court, to stock real ammo. No bacon rind and rock salt for whatever pirate was on my ship. He or she was in for the real deal. In case the SOB was really tough, I grabbed my .38 and loaded it with hollow points. For good measure I slung a canister of pepper spray around my neck. In for a penny, in for a pound.

Bristling with firepower, and therefore confidence, I returned to the main saloon and aimed my world renowned auditory senses towards ferreting out my uninvited boarder's whereabouts. Only small wind waves slapping *Sea Cock's* hull and the whine of tires on the Bay Bridge disturbed the night air. If I hadn't seen that dinghy tied to the back of my boat, I probably would have concluded I was imagining things, but the evidence was all too clear.

Finally, something moved. I zeroed in on a scratching noise that sounded like it came from overhead, on the flying bridge. Was it a thief intent on stealing my radio and GPS unit from up there? What else had I left out for some jerk to rip off? My wine selection from the sundeck bar? I think not, I was going to be out here a while.

Another piece of Martinez's sage advice from a few months before suddenly popped into my brain. Make sure, he'd told me, that if you absolutely have to shoot someone they're already inside the house. Or boat. Maybe the detective could wait while some maniac broke down his door, but I, for one, planned to shoot *through* my door. The beautiful teak door that I'd spent half a day sanding and varnishing. On second thought, maybe I'd call for help.

I stood up and was reaching for my PANIC button when a voice called out.

"Hetta dear, open up. It's frightfully cold out here," it said.

In a British accent.

We should never have allowed them back into our country.

* * *

Alan, after apologizing for scaring the crap out of me, sat in the main saloon, sipping at a glass of Jenks's scotch. No ice, of course. Not the Brits.

Annoyed as I was, I had to grudgingly admit he made an attractive, if short, addition to any girl's living room. Casually dressed in tan from head to toe, he was GQ all the way in a cashmere sweater, chinos and boat shoes. No socks. His perpetual suntan and color coordinated ensemble set off dark brown eyes and shiny, wavy, black hair. He looked for all the world like a vertically challenged updated version of Lawrence Harvey, that debonair star of the 40's and 50's silver screen. I also wondered, as I had many times before, if I didn't detect a hint of perm and L'Oreal on those raven ringlets. When I'd lived in Tokyo, Hudson— before he so rudely took a powder and turned up dead several years later—and I attended a weekend film festival featuring Lawrence Harvey flicks. And even though the films were dated, the English actor's charm transcended the generations, still able to tickle a gal's fancy. Look alike or no, the tickle I felt now was more of an irritating twinge, one of annoyance and the slight uneasiness that I invariably felt in Alan's company.

With his uncanny knack for surfacing when Jenks wasn't around, Alan had a way of setting my teeth on edge, whether he was at the club, on my boat or around the docks. He was always friendly, always slightly flirty. Nothing overtly slimy, just charming in a smarmy sort of way. I was also still annoyed about the charter incident, especially since I didn't buy the story he'd told Molly about my cabin door popping open. I'd seen him with my own eyes as he opened the door and slimed in. If he didn't leave soon, I was pretty sure my anger would force me into confronting him, but how could I without letting him know I had spy cameras? I took a sip of wine and wondered how to get the bastard off *Sea Cock* without being too rude. Not that I mind being rude, but he was, after all, a fellow yacht club member.

"So, Alan, what brings you to Clipper Cove, and onto my boat, in the middle of the night?" I said, straining to sound civil. Why, I don't know. All that Southern upbringing, I guess.

"Shakedown cruise on my new vessel. Too dark to see her right now. Tomorrow you must come for brunch on board."

"It's already tomorrow, Alan," I said, a nasty edge on my voice.

"So it is," he said with a smile.

His insouciance finally frayed my last nerve. "And now that you have your own boat you won't have to charter mine, huh?" I said sharply, and was rewarded with a startled look.

Alan recovered quickly, though. "Oh, yes. It was a rather spur of the moment thing, that. Clients in town. You worked in the Orient, you know how it is. We enjoyed ourselves thoroughly. *Sea Cock* really has improved with a woman's touch, I might add."

"I think so. Did you like my color scheme in the master cabin?" I was through playing softball.

"Molly mentioned that, did she? My dear girl, why so huffy? I was merely looking about. I have long since given up being invited into your boudoir."

"You can take that to the bank, buster."

"Come now, Hetta, let's not get testy. I said I was sorry for frightening you. And to tell you the truth, I lied."

"About what?"

"The shakedown cruise. I came out here expressly to see you."

Merde. "Oh? How did you know Jenks and I were out here?"

"Hetta dearest, you do insist on being difficult. Jenks is nowhere near here."

How did he know that? It was time to bluff. "I guess you've got me there, Alan. You're right. He had to go to town for supplies, should be back any minute." God, that was really, really lame.

Alan rolled his eyes. "Early riser, is he? Or perhaps late on his return? Since your dinghy resides in her chocks, I have to presume Jenks swam? A sport I've sadly never quite mastered myself. Stalwart fellow that Jenks."

That did it. The gloves were off.

"Alan, what in the hell do you want? You are trying my patience more than the tad you usually do. God, I'm starting to sound like you. Let me rephrase that. You are royally pissing me off. I came out here to be alone and as you can readily see I am *not* because *you* are here. And to make matters worse, you boarded my boat without permission. If you plan to do much yachting, I suggest you learn a little boating etiquette."

"Actually, Hetta, boarding without permission could be construed as a hostile act at best, piracy at worst , and you would technically be within your rights to shoot me if we weren't in such a liberal mecca as San Francisco. You know how these California lawyers are. If I lived, I could probably sue you for even having a gun. You do still have your grandmother's gun, don't you?"

I caught myself before glancing towards the locker where I'd stashed the guns when I realized it was Alan on my deck. "If I do, it's really none....Wait a minute, how did you know about my grandmother's gun?"

"Oh, I know you much better than you think." He reached over, picked up RJ's urn from the coffee table and said, in a voice and accent meant to mimic mine, " 'RJ, my man, what are you doing? Are you being a good doggy? Yes, I miss you, too. Mommy will be home before you know it. Get off the couch'."

My mouth fell open as I recognized my own recorded message to RJ when I'd left for Seattle. And it was also the day of the Jeep-jacking. Suddenly, pieces of the puzzle fell into place and it wasn't a pretty picture. Shocked, I lost what cool I still had, and blurted, "You! It was you who let RJ out? It was you who changed my lock? Not Hudson? I don't understand."

"Goodness no, lovey, 'twasn't me. Your dear departed Hudson did those deeds. We were still friends then, he and I. Partners really."

I wish people would stop calling Hudson *my* Hudson. "More like jailbird buddies? Partners in what? International crime?"

Alan looked surprised, but recovered quickly. "Semantics. Crime is simply a point of view if you ask me. We had a little business deal. He had what my people want, or so we thought. He led us to you. And you," he pulled my Georg Jensen icepick from his pocket, "will lead me to the key."

"Erf," says I, the one seldom at a loss for words. My mind raced, trying to absorb all this information. I was finally able to say, "You bastard."

"Sticks and stones. The key, Hetta."

"What key?"

"Oh, spare me the dumb act. It makes me angry and when I'm angry I can be a very unpleasant fellow."

"Alan, you are a perpetually unpleasant fellow."

"You ain't seen nothin' yet, as you Americans say. Now, if you'll be so kind as to give me my key, I'll be off and out of your life."

Oh, shit. Now what? "Alan, I wasn't kidding, Jenks will be here any minute," I said, stalling for time, trying to think. I didn't have the damned key, but I didn't think Alan would believe me. I judged the distance to the guns. He was between me and them. Rats.

Alan wasn't buying my bluff. "Jenks, you say? Surely you can't mean the Jenks who left a note on your boat last week? A sweet little *mot* telling us—you actually—that he was going on a trip and would call when he returned? Not exactly a *billet doux.* " He pulled a piece of paper from his pocket and tossed it to me.

I unfolded the note and read, *Dear Hetta, I have something I have to do and am rushing to catch my plane. Sorry about this weekend. I'll call when I get back. I don't know how long I'll be gone. I'll really miss you. Love, Jenks.*

Despite the fact that I was fast realizing that I was stuck at anchor with a guy who was an internationally sought-after, homicidal maniac, I temporarily forgot my dire straits. I think I actually smiled as I reread the note. Jenks had signed "Love." Wow.

But reality swiftly replaced my warm and fuzzies. Maybe I'd best concentrate on how to get rid of Alan. Maybe permanently.

"Alan, uh, where did you get this note?"

"From your boudoir, of course. I was hoping to also find my little key and leave, but it was not to be. Lord knows I have searched high and low amongst your belongings. You must have hidden it well, once again. And by the by, since you've met Jenks I see you've upgraded from cotton to silk knickers. Quite an improvement."

"You touched my panties? Damn, I'll have to burn them all. And what do you mean by *once again*"?

"Plain English. I meant *once again*. I searched *Sea Cock* soon after you moved aboard, but couldn't find the key, so I decided to bide my time until I was welcome to freely roam your decks, so to speak. I wasn't counting on Jenks moving in on my territory."

"Your territory!" I spluttered, and then it dawned on me what he'd said. "How did you get onto my boat and rummage through my underwear, you pervert?"

He waved off my insult. "Your pet boat rat, Garrison, of course. The man will sell anything not belonging to him, it seems. Especially after someone drowns his car. You should have changed the locks. I'd say your past sins are all coming home to roost, Hetta. Now, the key?"

"What if I told you I gave it to the police?"

"Then I wouldn't believe you. And I'd be forced to hurt you until I learn the truth." He waggled the icepick. I was on the verge of needing a Depend.

"Now, Hetta. Get. The. Key. And be very, *very* careful as you do so. No tricks. No more stalling. I really don't want to harm you."

"Yeah, well, stand up and say that." Why was I goading him? Everyone knows short men have crappy natures. Just *my* nature, I guess.

"Tsk, tsk. Sticks and all, dearie. But then, Hudson said you always did have the ability to go straight for the jugular. Oh, now wasn't that an unfortunate choice of words," he said, fingering the pick tip and giving me a really nasty grin. "Move. I don't have all night."

"Okay, okay, I'll get the damned key."

"Atta girl."

Now what, Ollie? I stood on shaky legs, feeling like Olive Oil in those cartoons when her knees knock together like castanets. I tottered to my desk. Alan followed, but not close enough so I could mule kick him. I opened the desk drawer, leaned over, and pretended to rummage around with one hand while reaching under the desk and pushing the PANIC button with the other.

My mouth was so dry I could barely talk. I murmured, "I can't find it, Alan. I thought I put it in here, but I don't see it. I'm so damned scared that I can't think where —" The phone rang. We both stared at it.

I looked at Alan, fully expecting him to say "Don't answer it." *Hoping* he'd say "Don't answer it" so Ed Lu would turn on the cameras.

"Answer it," Alan ordered. *Merde*, doesn't he ever go to the movies? They always say "Don't answer it" don't they?

When I hesitated he repeated himself, then added, "Very, very carefully. Watch what you say."

"Hello," I said. I sounded like I was eating cotton balls.

"Hetta, Ed Lu here. Do you have an emergency?" *Oh, Ed, I love you.*

I opened my mouth to say "yes" when I felt sharp cold steel sting my neck.

"Hetta?" Ed said.

"Oh, hi, Ed. How are you? How's the book coming? You must be working so hard that you didn't realize the time difference. It's about four in the morning here," I jabbered, trying to make light conversation that didn't sound like a cry for help on my end. Ed Lu was smart, so surely he'd pick up on my inconsistencies. After all, I had hit the PANIC button. I must have woken him up, because he wasn't hitting on all cylinders yet.

"Uh, fine, thanks, Hetta. I'm rewriting it for the eighth time. And looking for an agent," he said, all chatty, but his voice was taking on a puzzled quality. Good.

"And your boss? How's he?"

"What? Oh, Jenks. Actually I expect to hear from him soon and so should you. He's due back into the country any minute now."

"Back into the country?" I said, despite the slightly increased pressure and sting of the icepick tip. I cut my eyes at Alan and he was giving me a "cut" motion across his throat with his other hand. I hoped he was only signaling for me to end my conversation. I nodded, verrry carefully.

Ed rattled on. "Yeah, if I talk to Jenks do you want me to tell him anything?"

"Oh," I said, "tell him that everything is fine except that I've been really seasick and crying my eyes out."

"O-kay," Ed said, probably wondering what in hell my problem was, "I'll tell him. You have a good evening. Morning. Whatever."

"You, too, Ed," I said, my heart sinking.

"Oh, and Hetta, you know the rules. I always have to ask. Do you want me to call the police?"

"Yes Ed, please do that. I love you," I said, and hung up. And I meant it.

"You did quite well, Hetta. And dear Ed? Does Jenks know about him?"

"You know how it is, Alan, a gal can't put all her eggs in one basket."

"Don't I know it?" he said, his voice bitter. He backed away and waved the pick in my direction. "Now, let's get back to the task at hand. The key?"

I returned to my rummaging charade. If Ed called the cops, how long would it take to get help out here? I thought Ed knew I was at Clipper Cove, but I wasn't positive. If he did know, would he call the Coast Guard? And if he didn't know my location, did Jenks have a GPS locator on my boat? *Think. Think.* A nudge in my ribs brought me up short.

"Could it be that you are stalling, Hetta? I suggest you pull that damned drawer out, dump it and find the key before I totally lose patience."

I did what he said, ever mindful of the icepick and cursing myself for cleaning all the crap from the desk drawers during my recent cleaning spree. There was clearly no key among the pens and paper clips.

"The truth is, Alan, I can't remember where I put that stupid key. I mean, I might not even have it anymore. It's been ages since I've even seen it."

Alan's eyes became very mean, indeed. "I'm warning you, do not underestimate me. I have it on good authority that you were wearing that key around your neck," he drew the icepick's tip along my neck, causing a burning sensation, "not all that long ago."

I felt a trickle of blood run into my sweat shirt collar and knew I couldn't wait for the cavalry to arrive. I had to do something on my own. Now.

"Okay, Alan. Get rid of the icepick and I'll make you a deal."

Alan laughed an ugly laugh, but stepped away. "A deal? I hardly think you're in a position to make any deals."

"No? I know where the key is and you don't. And if you kill me you'll never find it." Damn, that sounded good. Too bad my bladder didn't appreciate a good bluff.

"Oh, by the time you're dead, dear girl, I *will* know where the key is and what it's for. However, for curiosity's sake, and because I know you're such a clever bitch, what kind of deal?"

My mind whirled. Alan didn't know what the key was *for*? No wonder he was desperate to get his hands on it. Hudson kept his secret to the end and had inadvertently handed me a slight advantage. Alan, had he known about the Key Note Club, could probably have bluffed his way past the club manager, and into the box, key or no. Or he could have gone to Tokyo and simply staged a break in, searching every liquor box in the club. Risky, but doable. However, without knowing about the jazz club, he was flying blind.

"A deal you need, Alan. The way I figure it, you must need that key pretty badly to go to all this time and trouble." I paused, then dropped my bomb. "And if so, Hudson must have stashed something valuable in that Crown Royal bottle."

Alan almost dropped his icepick. "How do you know it's a Crown Royal bottle?"

"What, you think you're playing with kids here?"

"Go on."

"If I get you the key and tell you where to use it, you can retrieve whatever it is that you think Hudson owes you. Right?"

"You have a flair for the obvious."

Playing by the seat of my dampening pants, I said, "So, answer this for me. Why didn't Hudson get his own stuff? He knew where to go. And I know for a fact that if he showed up there in person, he would be given access. So why did he need the stupid key?"

Alan, for the first time, looked unsure of himself. "You tell me, Hetta, since you are so very smart."

"Smart enough to get into what that key opens, and without too much attention being paid to me, what with me being Hudson's widow and all. I produce a death certificate and a fake marriage license, *et voila*! And I know for a fact that certain police agencies have been looking for a white guy, not a white gal. I also suspect that there are some thugs even more unsavory than you looking for you or Hudson, or both. I can get the goods." I hoped Alan wasn't sharp enough to pick up on the lameness of my spiel. I didn't give him time to analyze. "That way, you don't have to take any more risks, and I get back some of what Hudson owes me. I have to assume there is something besides Crown Royal involved here."

"And, I suppose you'll trot right back and split the proceeds with me," he said, sarcasm dripping from each word.

"No, I'll meet you somewhere, say, Hong Kong. Give you the goods and you'll give me the fifteen hundred dollars Hudson stole from me, plus interest. And travel expenses."

Alan looked nonplused for a moment, then broke into laughter. "Oh, Hetta," he said when he caught his breath, "you really are a piece of work." Then his face turned dark and his voice sinister. "Cut the crap and get the key. I don't want to kill you, but I *can* make you tell me anything I want. Make it easy on yourself. Unless you'd like a new specially trained dog and a white cane."

Gulp. "It's in a galley locker. You can get it yourself." I said quickly, a little too quickly.

Alan thought so, as well. He gave me a skeptical look. "That was too easy. From what Hudson has told me about you, you've probably got the damned key rigged to a rat trap."

Now, why didn't I think of that? I tried to look guilty.

"Get it, or I swear I will hurt you very badly."

I walked woodenly towards the locker, thinking as fast as I could. Had I slipped the safety off either of the guns? Could I grab one, turn, and shoot before Alan speared me like a cocktail olive? Hell, could I get to the closet without leaving a wet trail behind me?

Alan followed close on my heels, keeping his free hand on my right shoulder, his lethal hand somewhere behind me. Probably poised over some vital organ.

I opened the cabinet, reached high to divert his eyes upwards, away from the shotgun propped on the floor. In one swift movement, I ducked, grabbed the gun and swept the buttstock behind me, into his shin. *Much* lower than I'd planned, dammit. However, the stock connected with a satisfying crack of bone, and Alan howled in pain. I whirled, coming face to face with his hate-filled eyes. I gave him a shove, using the gun as a ram. I'd hoped to push him onto his butt. Instead, he tottered and then righted himself. Not only did the short little shit have good balance, he still had a firm grip on the pick. He took two involuntary steps backwards, allowing me room to aim the gun at his middle. We were in a Mexican standoff, five feet apart. We both panted with exhaustion and fear, me with the gun, he with the pick.

"Gee, Alan, ain't it just like a damned Limey to bring an icepick to a gun fight? Now, drop it. And get off my boat." I tried my best to sound like Harrison Ford.

Incredibly, Alan smiled. Or rather, something between a smile and a snarl. "You won't shoot me."

"Wanna stake your life on it? I am, after all, a member of the DAR, you know. Not only am I willing to shoot you, I *want* to, you Redcoat."

His smile wavered, but he stood his ground for a full minute, considering his options, before dropping the pick to the carpet. "You win," he said, and turned to go.

I followed.

Too closely.

In a flash he dropped, turned, swooped up his weapon, and lunged at me. Caught off guard, I was knocked to the floor. I deflected his arm with the gun barrel, but it slid forward and I felt the icepick plunge into my neck. A quick, sharp jab, then it was out and I lay stunned. Instinctively, I grabbed my neck as Alan wrenched the gun from me.

He had my gun and I was going to die. Now that he thought the key was actually in the closet, he had no reason to keep me alive. Sometimes I'm way too clever for my own good.

"Hetta," Alan crooned, "you have really, really pissed me off. Say good-bye now."

"Alan," a voice boomed, "drop the gun."

"Huh?" he said, whirling and looking around.

I peeked up from the floor, also looking for Jenks. That was his voice we heard, right?

Jenks's disembodied voice repeated, "Drop the gun, Alan, the boat is surrounded by United States Coast Guard personnel. Every move you've made in the past fifteen minutes has been video taped. Surrender your weapon."

I was as puzzled as Alan, but he figured things out and reacted faster than I did. He shot an obscene gesture at a hidden speaker mounted behind a fake smoke detector and snarled, "Then you can record me blowing her fucking head off. On second thought, get up, Hetta. I believe I've found a use for you after all."

All those hostage scenes on television flashed through my mind. Let's see, was I supposed to do as told? Scream? Faint? What? Alan nudged me with the gun barrel, and I meekly stood up. No Kinsey Millhone, here.

Prodded along by my own shotgun, I led as we exited the cabin—away from those lovely cameras and Jenks's voice—back to the aft deck. As we prepared to descend the swim ladder to the dive platform I looked around, hoping to see the promised armada of gunboats. I wasn't the only one trying to pull off a bluff. Not a blinking red or blue light or a circling copter in sight. Crap, there's never a warship around when you need one. I'd have to write my congressman.

I turned to go down the ladder, but Alan jerked me back by my tee shirt collar. It hurt. And I noticed his hand, when he let go, was bloody. I had a feeling the blood wasn't his.

"Hold it," he said, wiping his hand on his sweater.

"You know, Alan, you'll never get that stain out," I said, giggling. What the hell was wrong with me? I'd only had one sip of my drink.

"Aren't you the cool one. I fail to see the humor in our situation. Especially *your* situation. Now listen carefully, Hetta. I'm going down the ladder first. I don't want you to get any smart idea about jumping."

"Look, you don't even need me. You can see for yourself that Jenks was bluffing."

"Maybe, maybe not. The Coast Guard isn't here yet, but I'll wager they're on the way, so I'll need you for a bit longer. You stand very, very still, because if you so much as blink an eyelash I'll blow you into tiny pieces."

I nodded numbly as he began down the ladder one rung at a time, the gun trained on my forehead. I was losing hope. We'd be long gone before the Coast Guard showed up. After Ed called, he'd obviously turned on the cameras and been listening and watching, but had Alan or I mentioned that he had a dinghy and a sailboat nearby? I didn't think so. We could be in Alan's boat and out of the cove before anyone showed up. They wouldn't know to look for his boat. Drat.

Alan, standing on the last rung of the ladder, never took his eyes from me as he stepped onto the dive platform. And smack onto Eco.

My duck protested with a loud, gravely squawk that sounded a great deal like "AFLAC" and began pecking wildly at Alan's fashionably bare ankles.

Alan, startled, fell backwards, but not before he pulled the trigger. I shut my eyes and dodged as the shotgun roared. I was a beat too slow. Hot buckshot parted my hair in several places, one pellet plowing a stinging trench down the center of my scalp and knocking me backward onto the sundeck. Prone and dazed, I heard Alan flailing in the cold bay water and Eco quacking to beat the band.

Pushing myself to seated, I was almost forced flat again by my whirling head. Bracing on one arm, I could hear the persistent thumping noise of Alan trying to get purchase on the slimy, duck-fertilized dive platform. I crawled to the rail and looked over the side.

The shotgun was gone, no doubt twenty-five feet or so under the boat. Alan, who by his own admission was a non-swimmer, gave up on the slick platform and dog paddled towards his dinghy. If he got into the inflatable, he was only a short step away from boarding *Sea Cock,* and it would be over my dead body. Which, by the way, was what I was sure I would be if he managed to board. Blood ran into my eyes and my head spun. With one last burst of adrenalin-fueled will, I pulled myself to my feet, staggered down the stairs to the galley locker and grabbed my .38. Seconds later, I was back on the sundeck. Lights shown from many boats in the anchorage, their crews no doubt juddered awake by a gunshot vibrating the tranquil early morning. Finally, I heard a siren and saw, racing towards the anchorage, several flashing blue lights. The cavalry.

Fussy quacking and a splashing noise drew my attention back aft, where Alan, much to the displeasure of Eco, had one foot in his dinghy and another on my dive platform.

"Oh, Alan," I called sweetly.

He looked up and I trained the Smith and Wesson to a spot between his eyebrows. The dark eyes that one time sought to mesmerize and seduce now were wide with alarm. And rightly so, because I was extremely pissed off.

Looking me square in the eyes, Alan, despite his obvious fear, defiantly shifted his weight forward, preparing to step from the dinghy onto the dive platform.

I put the first round into a section of his inflatable's flotation chamber, not six inches from his foot. It popped like a balloon and he fell back on his ass, cringing and stunned. As he huddled in the center of the dink, I took aim at one of the remaining air chambers.

"This," I pulled the trigger, "is for stealing my mail." *Kapow*! The bullet hit with a satisfying smack and whoosh of escaping air. The dinghy listed to port.

"And for shooting at me and sticking me in the neck with my own Georg Jensen silver." *Kablooie!*

"This is for stepping on my duck." *Kablam!*

I was really starting to enjoy this. *POW! POW! POW!* One by one the remaining chambers blew and the dingy began to take on more and more water.

Satisfied I had sunk the bastard, I started to put down the gun, then changed my mind. I reloaded. "And for invading New Orleans, you Redcoat!" I let his dinghy have three more rounds.

As the smoke cleared, I was rewarded with a whimper from Alan and the satisfying hiss of escaping air. I *think* it was from the dinghy.

"In case you didn't count, you lowlife son of a bitch, I saved three special bullets for your gas tank. I can't miss in three. Try putting one foot on my boat and I'll turn you into extra crispy shark bait. Here, let me get that line for you."

He watched with dull eyes as I untied his dinghy painter and threw it in the water. A stiffening breeze immediately started blowing what was left of his dinghy away from *Sea Cock*.

Alan sat, dazed and adrift in a sinking dink, foisted by my own *canard*.

48

"Help me, Hetta! Hetta, please. I'm sinking. I can't swim."

Who could ignore such a pitiful plea?

I could. I yelled back, "I can't swim either, Alan. Looks like this ain't your day. Night. Whatever." Even if I could swim, I couldn't and wouldn't jump in that old cold bay. I was so overwhelmingly exhausted that there was no way I could save the rat bastard if I'd wanted to. Which I didn't.

I crumpled to *Sea Cock's* deck, cradling the still warm .38 in my lap. I was shaking badly and nauseated by the sight of my own blood running down my arms from wounds in my neck and scalp. Wounds, I might add, inflicted by the very man now pleading for me to save his sorry ass. I wondered if the words "divine justice" meant anything at all to him.

Evidently not. He continued to whine lies.

"Hetta, I'm truly sorry. I really mean it. I wouldn't have killed you. I was desperate for that key. I'll do anything. Don't let me drown. Please, as a friend."

A friend in need is a pest.

I struggled to my feet, worked my way to the flying bridge and flipped on the spotlight. After a couple of sweeps, I saw Alan. A one-foot chop slapped at his rapidly deflating dinghy. Yep, he was sinking, all right.

Alan shook his fist at me, which caused what was left of the dinghy to slip out from under him. He went under as well, but came back up spluttering. He glared in my direction and yelled. "Hetta, you fat bitch. May you rot in hell."

I always *was* a sucker for sweet talk.

I sighed and began releasing the clips on my dinghy chocks. I would lower it and let the wind carry it in Alan's direction. If he hadn't drowned by then, he could crawl in. Before I was able to launch the inflatable with my electric davit, I had to first start the generator. Alan would just have to, appropriately, dog paddle. The anchorage was getting choppier by the minute, whipped up by, wouldn't you know it, a west wind. Friggin' dandy.

I made my wobbly way to the main cabin, but by the time I reached the control panel to turn on the genset, I could barely stand. I didn't understand why. Sure, I was bleeding pretty good and feeling featherbrained after the struggle with Alan, but surely I could handle—

"Hetta. Hetta, can you hear me?" I heard a disembodied voice say. My first thought was that Alan had somehow regained access to the boat and was here to finish me off. Then I realized the voice belonged to Jenks.

"I hear you, you...deserter." I wanted to say more, a lot more, but I was too tired.

"Sweetheart, we can talk about that later."

Sweetheart? *I'd like to carve his sweet heart out and stuff...*. Jenks was still talking. His voice was all wavy, coming in and out. And the lights in the cabin were dimming. The batteries must have been lower than I thought. Must be the spotlight drawing them down.

"Hetta, listen to me. Put your fingers over that neck wound and push really hard. Someone will be there to help you in a few minutes. Hang in there, honey."

"No problemo, *honey*," I said, and giggled.

I tried to lift my hand to do as he said, but it was soooo heavy. I sat heavily into my desk chair and, by leaning onto my elbow, was able to cradle my neck and apply pressure. Blood ran down my arm, pooled on the desk and then dripped onto the rug. Well, that would have to go. Never can get bloodstains out of wool, you know. *Merde*, a gal just can't seem to keep a carpet these days.

I suddenly felt very, very cold and then the lights went out.

* * *

"...and just look at what this boating has done to your hands. These nails!" I felt mother's hand holding mine, heard her soothing voice and then an emery board began smoothing ragged edges from my fingernails.

"Mama? What are you doing on the boat?" I said. Evidently she didn't hear me, because she kept filing and talking, filing and talking. I forced my eyes open so I could see her, but when I focused, it was Daddy holding my hand.

"Thanks for the manicure," I said, startling him. He grinned, I went back to sleep and when I next opened my eyes Mama, Daddy, Jan, Detective Martinez, and Jenks were all staring at me. Was I dead? Oh, *merde*.

I then realized I couldn't possibly have croaked, because RJ wasn't there and I know for absolute damned certain that when I do die I'll see that dog again. So I figured, if I'm not dead, I must still be at Clipper Cove. How did these folks all get on *Sea Cock*? I never even got the dinghy lowered for Alan. Alan? I struggled to get up, get away from him, but Jenks pulled me to his chest and I went back to sleep. But not before wondering who in the hell redecorated my boat. In white, for pity's sake!

Zut alors! That blue had started to grow on me.

49

I was released from Berkeley's Alta Bates Hospital two days later, still a little weak and with a few stitches in my neck and a couple of new parts in my hair. Other than that, I was fine, if you can call losing three days and several pints of blood "fine."

Alan, it seemed, had managed to barely nick my carotid artery with my designer icepick, but because it was a quick in-and-out puncture, the muscle layers constricted, closing off the wound. It was only when we struggled again on the back deck that the puncture wound suddenly opened and put me in serious jeopardy. If Alan had jabbed a little slower, or if medical help had not already been on the way, I'da been residing in an urn next to RJ.

Jenks drove me from the hospital to the boat, helped me settle in and then dropped Mama and Daddy at their hotel at Jack London Square. I was still too tired to give him a ration of shit for his disappearing act. Besides, he was being way too nice to me and, on top of that, he had my parents totally charmed. I'd extract my pound of flesh later, when the parental defense league returned to Texas.

I took a little nap after Jenks left and when I woke up, I could hear someone rattling pots and pans in my galley. Pulling on a robe, I worked my way up the stairs towards the racket. Jenks was frying something that smelled wonderful.

"I hope you don't think feeding me, treating me so well in the hospital, and buttering up my parents is going to get you off the hook, Jenks Jenkins."

"Why would I think that? You already told me, in no uncertain terms, how you felt. Back at Alta Bates."

"I did?"

"You sure did. Let's see if I can remember...."

"Uh, never mind." I didn't remember, that's for sure, but taking into consideration my frame of mind before Alan attacked me, I could only imagine what I'd laid on Jenks. "It was the drugs talking, I'm sure."

"Those drugs have some vocabulary, Hetta. I don't think I've ever heard so many ways to call a man a bastard, and I was in the navy for twenty years. The nursing staff started taking notes at one point." Jenks grinned and turned over the bacon. "How do you want your eggs?"

"Over easy, with a little crow on the side, I guess," I said meekly.

Jenks nodded and started breaking eggs. "Martinez said he'd stop by later and fill you in on Alan, or whatever his real name is. My money's on sharks, though."

"Huh?" I vaguely remembered Martinez standing at my bedside at the hospital, but I couldn't remember what he'd said. "Sharks?"

"Alan. The guy you tried to kill? Threw off your boat into a stormy sea?"

"I know who Alan is," I growled, "I don't remember what Martinez said. Quit treating me like a two-year-old."

Jenks ignored me and flipped my eggs over, easy. "Toast?"

"Are you gonna tell me, or am I going to have to nail you with that frying pan?"

"Now, that's more like it. My little Hetta, back at last."

"Your little Hetta? Listen buster, I haven't decided yet whether to kiss you or kill you, so don't push your luck."

"I'll settle for the kiss."

Our eggs got cold.

* * *

Fresh out of a hot shower, I was munching on reheated bacon when Martinez knocked on the hull and came aboard. He handed me a bunch of daisies. "You sure look a lot better, Hetta. I got to admit, though, I sort of liked you comatose."

"I've always liked you comatose, Detective."

"She's baaaaack," Jenks quipped from the galley. "Want some coffee?"

Martinez shook his head. "No coffee, thanks. Trying to quit. So, Annie Oakley, I guess you want to know about your Alan."

"He is not *my* Alan. And Jenks tells me you can't find him, so what's to know?"

Martinez looked at Jenks, who shrugged.

"You don't know about the rubies?" Martinez asked.

"What rubies? Oh, let me guess. In the locker at the Key Note Club. Rubies?"

"You got it. Lots of 'em. Jenks had to turn them over to the Japanese police, but …"

"Jenks? So you *were* in Tokyo. Why didn't you call me? Let me know what you were doing? You, you…."

Martinez intervened. "Uh, Hetta, save it for later. I didn't come here to referee a love spat."

"Then why *are* you here, Detective? Sorry, that sounded really rude and I didn't mean it to. I get cranky when people try to kill me and others don't tell me why."

"No offense taken."

"Good, then I can continue to be cranky? I mean, you don't have Alan and you don't know where he is, so do you think that maniac is still alive? Why am I not getting a warm and fuzzy feeling here?"

"He could possibly still be alive, but he would have no reason to mess with you now. If he is alive, he must know the rubies have been found. It's in all the papers." He dug a newspaper clipping out of his shirt pocket and handed it to me. "Extra, extra, read all about it. I've always wanted to say that."

I took the clipping and Jenks handed me my reading glass. For his kindness I gave him a dirty look, then read the article. "Holy shit!"

The *Examiner* article claimed a cache of rubies recovered in Tokyo by an unidentified Bay Area man had an estimated value in the millions. The bag of flawless Burmese Mogok rubies, not one of them less than six carats, could be valued at up to fifteen thousand dollars a carat because they are becoming so rare.

"So, unidentified Bay Area man, how many stones were in the bottle?" I asked Jenks.

He grinned. "A bunch. The bartender and I counted at least twenty before the Japanese police showed up to take them into custody."

"I'm surprised they didn't take *you* into custody."

"They did. And didn't allow phone calls."

"You've been in a Japanese jail?"

"For several days. Nice jail, but the food! Lower sea life forms and noodles. I would have killed for a Big Mac. But, I've been in worse brigs."

"How'd you get out?"

"Commander let me out. They were short on pilots."

I gave Jenks the look he deserved. "How did you get out of the *Japanese* jail?"

He nodded at the detective. "Martinez, here. I was finally allowed a call to the American Embassy and they called the OPD for me."

"Wait a minute! When was that? The last time you were on my boat, Martinez, you didn't know anything about the key until I told you. Why didn't you call me when the Japanese called you? You knew I was worried."

"You were already out cold by the time I could tell you."

"I was? Then how did Jenks...Aha! You used the security system from Japan? You were in Japan when Alan was on my boat? Oh, boy, am I glad I didn't know that. I thought you were coming to my rescue."

"Nope, I was out of jail, waiting for a hop home. Once I realized what was happening on *Sea Cock*, I talked my way onto a general's jet headed for Hawaii and from there I got another fast hop. You were in the hospital by the time I finally got here."

Martinez was nodding and grinning. "Brinkmanship, Coffey, brinkmanship."

He had a point. Once again I had narrowly skirted the brink.

"Okay, okay, I get your not so subtle message, Martinez." I said. He only continued giving me that idiotic, lopsided grin, so I waved the newspaper clipping in the air. "Now, you two, let's talk about something really important. Rubies. I want to hear more about these here rubies." My mental calculator whirred. "Twenty stones, six carats each, fifteen grand a carat. Almost two million bucks, give or take a hundred thou or two. Wow! No wonder Hudson and Alan were so desperate to get those rocks. And to think, I had the key all the while. *Zut, alors!* I coulda been a contender."

Martinez shook his head. "And you could have been dead. Hudson and Alan were lightweights compared to their cohorts. One of the reasons Hudson waited so long to try to find you was that those stones evidently belonged to a bunch of very nasty Southeast Asian hoods he ripped off. He couldn't show his face anywhere in the Pacific Rim without losing it. I figure he hooked up with Alan, thinking if he could get the key maybe Alan could retrieve the stones, but Alan had other plans. No honor amongst thieves and all that. Not too swift, your Hudson."

I let the *your* slide. "No shit."

"Interpol wasn't the only one looking for Hudson. My guess is Alan sold Hudson out to the bad guys, waited for him to get the key, then offed him. Problem was, Hudson didn't have the key. You did. In Texas."

Jenks nodded. "And when Alan realized he'd messed up, he followed you to your new boat, joined the yacht club, and now his face is plastered over every newspaper in the world. Jewels, dope, and the like make for great copy."

"So, who owns the rubies?" I was trying to stick to the important stuff.

Martinez shrugged. "Eventually, I guess the Burmese or whatever they call their country these days."

"Myanmar," Jenks said, impressing me.

"Yeah, that's it. Anyhow, they claim the stones belong to them, part of some heist or something. It'll be in litigation for years."

"Well, rats. Hudson owed me a ruby, among other things. Too bad I didn't get a chance to shoot him before Alan whacked him. Oh, dear, granny's gun!"

"Got it. Sent down a diver after hearing you rave in the hospital."

"I am woman, it's my job. Thanks."

"No problem. Besides, we needed to check that shotgun to see how many times it was fired. What with a missing perp, he could have gone to the bottom with a load of shot in his ass, you know."

"They think I killed Alan?"

"Not with *that* gun, they don't. They're still counting bullet holes in the dinghy, and spent cartridges from .38. Anyway, when the San Francisco Sheriff gets through with the guns, they are all yours. Glad to see you in such good shape. Keep in touch." Martinez rose to leave, but I grabbed his hand.

"Uh, Martinez."

"You can call me Marty."

"Marty Martinez? I like it. Anyhow, Marty, how about coming over for drinks and dinner next week? Bring the wife."

Marty smiled. I mean he really smiled. "I'd like that and I know my wife would love to meet you. You've kept her entertained for months now."

"Glad to be of service."

Martinez left and I glared at Jenks, the holdout. If he was going to hang around me he'd have to be trained in the fine art of information trading. He was grinning from ear to ear.

"What?" I demanded.

"Oh, just wondering if you're still mad at me."

"Sort of. Actually, not really. However, don't ever run off like that again without letting me know where you are. And never, ever, withhold gossip. It's un-American, you know. Okay?"

"I promise," Jenks said, "if you promise to stay out of trouble."

"Where's the fun in that? Why should I?"

"Maybe a reward? All good girls deserve a reward."

"What kind of reward? I can be a very, very good girl," I cooed, giving him an eye bat and pulling him toward me by his belt loops.

"Stick your hand in my pocket."

"Is this gonna be a Groucho Marx kinda moment?"

"Lower."

"How about if I take them off you?"

"How about if you reach way down into that pocket?" Jenks said gruffly.

So I did.

There was something hard in there.

And very big.

"Now, pull it out, Hetta."

So I did.

The biggest damned ruby I ever saw.

Holy shades of *Romancing the Stone*! Joan Wilder, eat your heart out.

Epilogue

We said a final farewell to RJ on one of those rare, but magical, Indian summer days that bless San Francisco Bay in the fall.

Brilliant sunlight and ninety degree temperatures favored the anchorage at Clipper Cove, just as I'd hoped when I scheduled the end of September event. There was no fog, but the tinge of coolness on a light breeze promised

Mother Nature's air conditioning would, to paraphrase Carl Sandberg, dogtrot in on little puppy feet later in the afternoon.

Seagulls circled the boat quizzically, hoping for a handout, but Eco, not one to duck his own importance, kept them at bay. In addition to the bits of canapé he cadged from the guests, I'd brought him popcorn and Ritz crackers to keep him at the back of the boat, away from RJ's ashes when they were scattered. Can't have your duck dining on the deceased *n'est-ce pas*?

With me to bid adieu to my fine hound were Jenks, Dr. Craig, Raoul and his dog, Catamite, Allison Wontrobski and her new hubby, the Trob, Detective and Mrs. Martinez, the Fujitsus, and Pancho-san. At the last minute Jan and Lars showed up at the dock with a surprise: my mother and father.

Mama was helping me arrange the canapés on a platter when the boat wallowed slightly on a swell. She sat down quickly on the settee. "What was that?"

"Oh, probably a whale wake."

"Very funny. I don't know how you can live on something that moves all the time. Where does Jenks live?" she asked, a tad too casually.

"When he's not in prison, he rents a cold water flat in the ghetto."

Mother looked aghast until Jan snorted a laugh and said, "Mama Coffey, Hetta's giving you a hard time. Jenks is a perfectly respectable guy with a nice apartment, a job and on top of that, he's really nice. Obviously *much* too good for Hetta."

"You two should make yourselves useful and mind your own bidness. As it so happens, Jenks and I have a great relationship." *Merde*, I used the "R" word. I hate being on the defensive. It makes me so...defensive.

"That's good, honey. He does seem to like you. And your father likes him."

"Mama, get those wedding bells out of your head. Jenks and I both like being single, but we also like being single together."

"I'll settle for that," Mother said with a sly grin. "For now."

"What'll you settle for?" Jenks said, entering the galley area.

"You, Jenks. Mother thinks you're wonderful and Jan thinks you're too good for me. What do you think?"

Jenks looked at the three of us and backed towards the door. "I think I'll have a drink."

"Wise choice." I gave my tormentors a smug look and spooned capers onto smoked salmon.

Mama had to have the last word. "I hope your Jenks isn't easily run off, if you know what I mean. I won't waste my breath trying to tell you not to scare him away."

Why does everyone in the whole world keep referring to my male acquaintances as *your* men? *Your* Hudson, *your* Alan, and now, *your* Jenks. Well, the *your* Jenks thing sounded just fine and dandy with me. "Uh-huh," I said, noncommittally. "Mama, could you pass around the deviled eggs?"

"Of course, dear. Did you make these yourself? They look very...interesting. What are these little spots?"

"Caviar."

"Oh. I'll warn your father."

She wandered off with the tray. Actually she didn't wander at all, but made a beeline for Jenks at the bar, where he was dispensing fountains of champagne.

I busied myself arranging more trays of goodies and when I checked, Jenks and mother were on the sofa in deep conversation. Dad had been relegated to bartender.

"Looks like we could use your mom on the OPD," Martinez said as he plucked a tiny bagel laden with lox and cream cheese from a tray. "She's giving your Jenks quite a grilling."

"Yeah. Think I should rescue him?"

"Nah, he's doin' okay. How about you? All healed up?"

"Sure am. Any word at all on Alan, or whatever he calls himself these days?"

"Nothing. A rumor. Street talk." He grabbed a stuffed shrimp and gazed out over the bay.

"Are you gonna tell me or shall I stuff that shrimp in a new and indelicate place," I groused.

"Now I *know* you're back to yourself," he grinned. "Scuttlebutt has it the boys who once owned those rubies found him and took him on a one-way fishing trip where he was featured as bait."

"Fooey, I thought I turned him into bait. Oh, well, can't win 'em all."

"No, you can't. Too bad about those rubies, though. I was hoping maybe Jenks would get some kind of reward. Not even a thank you, the cheap bastards. And speaking of rubies, Hetta, that's quite a rock you're sporting 'round your neck."

"This old thing?" I said, fingering the ruby. "A garnet, actually. Family heirloom. Had it for years. Say, could you gather everyone on the foredeck? It's almost time."

"Only if you'll tell me what's under that drape over the transom."

"You'll find out when everyone else does. Did you put your hard earned bucks in the name pool?"

"Yep. Put my money on *Coffee Break*. Was I right?"

"Gee, you're the detective, why don't you tell me?"

"Smart ass," he said, and left to round everyone up.

I took RJ's urn from the coffee table and worked my way forward. I was glad the breeze had dropped to nil so RJ would scatter over the water, not my decks. Convention called for throwing ashes from the transom, but I didn't want to confuse my duck. RJ, I'm sure, would understand. Food, or the promise of food, is nothing to muck about with. Jan scattered an entire bowl of popcorn aft to distract Eco before she joined us on the bow.

Craigosaurus did the honors, first with a toast to a grand mutt, then he began reading a little ceremonial speech that sounded suspiciously like the one used at my grandmother's funeral. "Those of us who loved RJ knew what a great contribution he made to society," he began, but then he grinned, put down the book and adlibbed a glowing tribute. When he finished, we all had tears in our eyes. Even the poodle looked a little misty, but I think that was because Raoul wouldn't let him go after Eco.

The talking done, there was nothing left but for me to open the urn and dump the ashes. Which I did. Only, at the very moment I upended the urn, a strong gust blew all the ashes right back at us, covering the entire party in a fine dusting of RJ. After a stunned silence, we all began to laugh and I could swear I got a whiff of dog fart.

After a light lunch it was time for my unveiling.

For this, we moved to the dock and offloaded our guests. Eco refused to leave the dive platform, stubbornly maintaining his position in case a couple of hors d'oeuvres escaped a tray.

I stood on the aft deck and loosened the strings holding the tarp covering the transom. Hoisting a glass of bubbly on high, I doused the duck, let go the tarp and announced, "I christen this ship the motor vessel *Raymond Johnson*."

I *know* I smelled a dog fart.

*We lose sight of what we really need and want—someone to love and a good boat that will stick with us through our lives—*Ferenc Máté

Chic, alors!—Hetta Coffey

The end

Raised in the jungles of Haiti and Thailand, with returns to Texas in-between, Jinx followed her father's steel-toed footsteps into the Construction and Engineering industry in hopes of building dams. Finding all the good rivers taken, she traveled the world defacing other landscapes with mega-projects in Alaska, Japan, New Zealand, Puerto Rico and Mexico.

Like the protagonist in her mystery series, Hetta Coffey, Jinx was a woman with a yacht—and she's not afraid to use it—when she met her husband, Mad Dog Schwartz. They opted to become cash-poor cruisers rather than continue chasing the rat, sailed under the Golden Gate Bridge, turned left, and headed for Mexico. They now divide their time between Arizona and Mexico's Sea of Cortez.

Jinx's seventh book in her award-winning series, *Just Deserts*: Book Four of the Hetta Coffey mystery series, was recently released.

Her other books include a YA fictography of her childhood in Haiti (*Land of Mountains*), an adventure in the Sea of Cortez (*Troubled Sea*) and an epic novel of the thirty years leading to the fall of the Alamo (*The Texicans*).

For more on Jinx and her books go to: www.jinxschwartz.com

16465335R00241

Made in the USA
Middletown, DE
16 December 2014